RELATIVITY

AURORA RESONANT: BOOK ONE

Donna,
　　Sometimes you have to pick a
fight with the biggest bully on the
playground.

G. S. JENNSEN

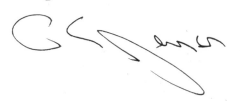

HYPERNOVA
PUBLISHING
2016

RELATIVITY

Cover design by Josef Bartoň
Cover typography by G. S. Jennsen

Hypernova Publishing
P.O. Box 2214
Parker, Colorado 80134
www.hypernovapublishing.com

Publisher's Note: This is a work of fiction. Names, characters, places, and incidents are a product of the author's imagination. Locales and public names are sometimes used for atmospheric purposes. Any resemblance to actual people, living or dead, or to businesses, companies, events, institutions, or locales is completely coincidental.

The Hypernova Publishing name, colophon and logo are trademarks of Hypernova Publishing.

Ordering Information:
Hypernova Publishing books may be purchased for educational, business or sales promotional use. For details, contact the "Special Markets Department" at the address above.

Relativity / G. S. Jennsen.—1st ed.

LCCN 2016961089
ISBN 978-0-9973921-6-6

For John Herschel Glenn, Jr. and all the Mercury 7 astronauts
Thank you for showing us the way to the stars

ACKNOWLEDGEMENTS

Many thanks to my beta readers, editors and artists, who made everything about this book better, and to my family, who continue to put up with an egregious level of obsessive focus on my part for months at a time.

I also want to add a personal note of thanks to everyone who has read my books, left a review on Amazon, Goodreads or other sites, sent me a personal email expressing how the books have impacted you, or posted on social media to share how much you enjoyed them. You make this all worthwhile, every day.

Aurora Rhapsody

is

AURORA RISING

Starshine

Vertigo

Transcendence

AURORA RENEGADES

Sidespace

Dissonance

Abysm

AURORA RESONANT

Relativity

Rubicon (2017)

Requiem (2017/18)

SHORT STORIES

Restless, Vol. I • *Restless, Vol. II*

Apogee • *Solatium* • *Venatoris*

Re/Genesis

Learn more and see a Timeline of the Aurora Rhapsody *universe at:*

gsjennsen.com/aurora-rhapsody

AMARANTHE
ANADEN EMPIRE

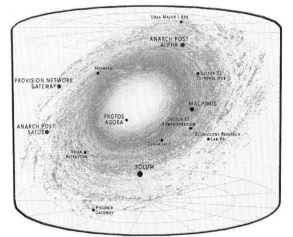

MILKY WAY GALAXY

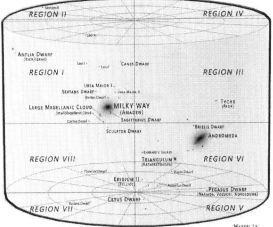

LOCAL GALACTIC GROUP

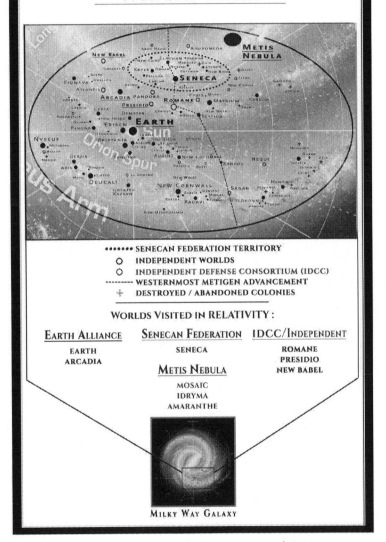

AURORA
COLONIZED WORLDS

- •••••• SENECAN FEDERATION TERRITORY
- ○ INDEPENDENT WORLDS
- ○ INDEPENDENT DEFENSE CONSORTIUM (IDCC)
- -------- WESTERNMOST METIGEN ADVANCEMENT
- ⊹ DESTROYED / ABANDONED COLONIES

WORLDS VISITED IN RELATIVITY:

EARTH ALLIANCE	SENECAN FEDERATION	IDCC/INDEPENDENT
EARTH	SENECA	ROMANE
ARCADIA		PRESIDIO
		NEW BABEL

METIS NEBULA

MOSAIC
IDRYMA
AMARANTHE

MILKY WAY GALAXY

View the Amaranthe and Aurora Maps Online at gsjennsen.com/relativity-maps.

DRAMATIS PERSONAE
HUMANS OF AURORA

Alexis 'Alex' Solovy
Space scout and explorer. Prevo.
Spouse of Caleb Marano, daughter of Miriam and David Solovy.
Artificial/Prevo Counterpart: Valkyrie

Caleb Marano
Former Special Operations intelligence agent, SF Division of Intelligence.
Spouse of Alex Solovy.

Miriam Solovy (Commandant)
EA Fleet Admiral (Ret.).
Leader, Galactic Common Defense
Accord (GCDA), AEGIS Forces.
Mother of Alex Solovy.

Richard Navick
Former EASC Naval Intelligence.
GCDA SENTRI Director.
Family friend of the Solovys.

Kennedy Rossi
Founder/CEO, Connova Interstellar.
Friend of Alex, Noah.

Noah Terrage
COO, Connova Interstellar.
Former trader/smuggler.
Friend of Caleb, Kennedy, Mia.

Vii
Artificial, fork of Valkyrie.
Former property of Abigail Canivon.
Employee of Connova Interstellar.

Graham Delavasi
Director, Senecan Federation
Division of Intelligence.

Malcolm Jenner (Brigadier)
AEGIS Director of Marines.
Friend of Alex, Mia, Brooklyn.

Mia Requelme
Prevo. Entrepreneur.
IDCC Minister of Colonial Affairs.
Friend of Caleb, Malcolm, Noah.
Artificial/Prevo Counterpart: Meno

Brooklyn Harper
Former EA Special Forces Captain.
Leader, IDCC Ground RRF.
Friend of Malcolm, Morgan.

Morgan Lekkas
Prevo. Former Cmdr, SF Fleet.
Cmdr, IDCC Rapid Response Forces.
Artificial/Prevo Counterpart: Stanley

Devon Reynolds
Prevo. Quantum Computing Specialist.
Artificial/Prevo Counterpart: Annie

Nolan Bastian (Field Marshal)
Chairman of SF Military Council.
Commander of SF Armed Forces.

ALIENS OF AMARANTHE

Eren asi-Idoni
Species: Anaden
Anarch resistance agent.

Mnemosyne ('Mesme')
Species: Katasketousya (Metigen)
Idryma Member, First Analystae of Aurora.

Nyx elasson-Praesidis
Species: Anaden
Inquisitor.

Casmir elasson-Machim
Species: Anaden
Navarchos military commander.

Praesidis Primor
Species: Anaden
Head of Praesidis Dynasty.

Cosime Rhomyhn
Species: Naraida
Anarch agent. Friend of Eren.

Miaon
Species: Yinhe
Anarch agent. Friend of Eren, Mesme.

Danilo Nisi
Species: Anaden
Sator (leader) of anarch resistance.

Xanne ela-Kyvern
Species: Anaden
Anarch supervisor.

Lakhes
Species: Katasketousya (Metigen)
Praetor (leader) of Idryma.

Paratyr
Species: Katasketousya (Metigen)
Second Sentinel, Mirad Vigilate.

Thelkt Lonaervin
Species: Novoloume
Anarch agent, friend of Eren.

Felzeor
Species: Volucri
Anarch agent. Friend of Eren, Thelkt.

Hyperion
Species: Katasketousya (Metigen)
Idryma member, Analystae.

Ziton elasson-Praesidis
Species: Anaden
Inquisitor.

Fisik elasson-Erevna
Species: Anaden
Weapons scientist.

View the Dramatis Personae Online at gsjennsen.com/characters-relativity

OTHER CHARACTERS

Abigail Canivon
Former Cybernetic Expert. Deceased.

Avdei elasson-Idoni
Owner, Plousia Chateau, Serifos.
Species: *Anaden*

Aver ela-Praesidis
Former Inquisitor. Deceased.
Species: *Anaden*

Bob Patera
Freelance space scout.

Christopher Rychen (Admiral)
EA Fleet Admiral.

Corradeo Praesidis
Founder of the Praesidis Dynasty.
Species: *Anaden*

David Solovy (Commander)
Alex Solovy's father. Miriam Solovy's
spouse. Captain *EAS Stalwart*. Deceased.

Dylan Shackleford
Friend of Noah Terrage.

Emily Bron
Devon Reynolds' girlfriend.

Erevna Primor
Head of Erevna Dynasty.
Species: *Anaden*

Eusebe
Scientist, researcher.
Species: *Katasketousya (Metigen)*

Logiel ela-Erevna
Administrator, Exobiology Lab #4.
Species: *Anaden*

Machim Primor
Head of Machim Dynasty.
Species: *Anaden*

Madison Ledesme
Romane Governor.

Olivia Montegreu
Frmr head of Zelones Cartel. Deceased.

Paolo Acconci
Mercenary for Triene Cartel. Deceased.

Pasha Solovy
Father of David Solovy.

Philippe Johansson
Physician, biosynth specialist.

Ronaldo Espahn
Business mogul.

Simon Ettore (Major)
AEGIS Prevo, AFS Saratoga.

Tessa Hennessey
SF Intelligence specialist. Prevo.

Theriz Primor
Head of Theriz Dynasty.
Species: *Anaden*

Thomas
AEGIS Artificial.

Weil Symansi
ASCEND Scientist.

William 'Will' Sutton
SENTRI Deputy Director.
Spouse of Richard Navick.

Zoravar Bazuk T'yevk
Military commander.
Species: *Ch'mshak*

ANADEN DYNASTIES

PRAESIDIS
Role: *Criminal investigation and enforcement*

MACHIM
Role: *Military*

THERIZ
Role: *Resource cultivation and management*

EREVNA
Role: *Research, Science*

IDONI
Role: *Entertainment, Pleasure seekers/providers*

KYVERN
Role: *Administration, bureaucracy*

DIAPLAS
Role: *Engineering, construction*

ANTALLA
Role: *Commerce, trade*

*

DYNASTY RANKS
(HIGHEST TO LOWEST)

Primor

Elasson

Ela

Asi

THE STORY SO FAR

View a more detailed summary of the events of Aurora Rising and Aurora Renegades online at gsjennsen.com/synopsis.

AURORA RISING

The history of humanity is the history of conflict. This proved no less true in the 24th century than in ancient times.

By 2322, humanity inhabited over 100 worlds spread across a third of the galaxy. Two decades earlier, a group of colonies had rebelled and set off the First Crux War. Once the dust cleared, three factions emerged: the Earth Alliance, consisting of the unified Earth government and most of the colonies; the Senecan Federation, which had won its independence in the war; and a handful of scattered non-aligned worlds, home to criminal cartels, corporate interests and people who made their living outside the system.

Alexis Solovy was a space explorer. Her father gave his life in the war against the Federation, leading her to reject a government or military career. Estranged from her mother, an Alliance military leader, Alex instead sought the freedom of space and made a fortune chasing the hidden wonders of the stars.

A chance meeting between Alex and a Federation intelligence agent, Caleb Marano, led them to discover an armada of alien warships emerging from a mysterious portal in the Metis Nebula.

The Metigens had been watching humanity via the portal for millennia; in an effort to forestall their detection, they used traitors among civilization's elite to divert focus from Metis. When their plans failed, they invaded in order to protect their secrets.

The wars that ensued were brutal—first an engineered war between the Alliance and the Federation, then once it was revealed to be built on false pretenses, devastating clashes against the Metigen invaders as they advanced across settled space, destroying every colony in their path and killing tens of millions.

Alex and Caleb breached the aliens' portal in an effort to find a way to stop the slaughter. There they encountered Mnemosyne, the Metigen watcher of the Aurora universe—our universe. Though enigmatic and evasive, the alien revealed the invading ships were driven by AIs and hinted the answer to defeating them lay in the merger of individuals with the powerful but dangerous quantum computers known as Artificials.

Before leaving the portal space, Alex and Caleb discovered a colossal master gateway. It generated 51 unique signals, each one leading to a new portal and a new universe. But with humanity facing extinction, they returned home armed with a daring plan to win the war.

In a desperate gambit to vanquish the enemy invaders before they reached the heart of civilization, four Prevos (human-synthetic meldings) were created and given command of the combined might of the Alliance and Federation militaries. Alex and her Artificial, Valkyrie, led the other Prevos and the military forces against the alien AI warships in climactic battles above Seneca and Romane. The invaders were defeated and ordered to withdraw through their portal, cease their observation of Aurora and not return.

Alex reconciled with her mother during the final hours of the war, and following the victory Alex and Caleb married and attempted to resume a normal life.

But new mysteries waited through the Metis portal. Determined to learn the secrets of the portal network and the multiverses it held, six months later Caleb, Alex and Valkyrie traversed it once more, leaving humanity behind to struggle with a new world of powerful quantum synthetics, posthumans, and an uneasy, fragile peace.

AURORA RENEGADES

Following the victory over the Metigens, Alex, Caleb and Valkyrie set off to unlock the secrets of the Metigens' portal network. Discovering worlds of infinite wonder, they made both enemies and friends. Planets of sentient plant life which left a lasting mark on Alex and Caleb both. Silica-based beings attempting to grow organic life. A race of cat-like warriors locked in conflict with their brethren.

Behind them all, the whispered machinations of the Metigen puppet masters pervaded everything. In some universes, the Metigens tested weapons. In some, they set aliens against each other in new forms of combat. In others, they harvested food and materials to send through the massive portal at the heart of the maze.

But Alex and Caleb found yet another layer to the puzzle. In one universe, they discovered a gentle race of underground beings with a strange history. Their species was smuggled out of the universe beyond the master portal by the Metigens. They watched as their homeworld was destroyed by a powerful species known as Anadens; but for the Metigens, they would have perished as well.

Back home in Aurora, the peace proved difficult to maintain. The Prevos found themselves targeted by politicians and a restless population desperate for a place to pin their fears. Under the direction of a new, power-hungry Earth Alliance PM, the government moved to cage and shackle them.

In desperation, the Prevos uploaded the AIs' consciousnesses into their own minds, fled from their governments' grasp and disappeared onto independent colonies. Devon published the details of the Prevo link to the exanet, unleashing its capabilities for anyone who wanted to follow in their footsteps.

Meanwhile, an anti-synthetic terrorist group emerged to oppose them, fueled by the rise of Olivia Montegreu as a Prevo. While the private face of Prevos was the heroes who defeated the Metigens, the public face became the image of Olivia killing a colonial governor and tossing him off of a building in front of the world.

Unaware of the struggles her fellow Prevos faced, Alex forged her own path forward. Rather than bringing the AI into herself, she pushed out and through Valkyrie, into the walls of the *Siyane*. Piloting her ship in a way she never dreamed, Alex was able to feel the photonic brilliance of space itself. Over time, however, that bond began to capture more of her spirit and mind.

On the surface of a destroyed planet, Mesme at last revealed all. The portal network was, above all else, a refuge for those targeted for eradication by the Anadens. And the Anadens, rulers of the true universe through the master portal, were the genetic template upon which humanity was built. Aurora was nothing more than another experiment of the Metigens, created so they could study the development and nature of their enemy and the enemy of all life.

Alex and Caleb returned to Aurora to find a galaxy rocked by chaos. After the execution of Olivia Montegreu by Alliance and Prevo forces, Miriam had gone rogue. Her resistance force, bolstered by help from inside the Senecan and Alliance militaries, moved against the despotic Alliance PM.

As Alex struggled with her growing addiction to an ethereal realm, she felt herself being pulled away from reality. Away from her husband, her mother, her friends. She watched as those she loved fought, but increasingly found herself losing her own battle.

When terrorists staged a massive riot on Romane, Dr. Canivon, the mother of the Prevos, was murdered in front of Devon and Alex. Overcome by her own and Valkyrie's grief, Alex unleashed the explosive power of the ethereal realm to destroy the terrorists' safehouse. Standing in the rubble of her destruction, Alex made a decision to sever the quantum connection between herself and the *Siyane*, choosing a tangible, human life. Choosing Caleb.

Miriam wrested control of the EA government away from the PM, bringing an end to the Prevo persecution. In the wake of victory, a shadowy Anaden hunter emerged from the darkness to attack Alex and Caleb. Caleb was gravely injured when the Anaden's power leapt to him, healing his wounds and helping him kill the alien.

Mesme revealed the ominous consequences of the attack. Soon, the Anaden leadership would discover Aurora. When they did, they would destroy it unless humanity could stand against them. Mesme told Miriam and the others to prepare, but knowing the end game was upon them, asked Alex and Caleb to come to Amaranthe. The master universe. The home and dominion of the Anadens.

CONTENTS

RELATIVITY

PART I:

SUPERPOSITION

"Listen: there's a hell of a good universe next door; let's go."

— E. E. Cummings

*T*he Dzhvar descended upon them like the shadow of an eclipse. The Anadens were not ready. How could they be?

As one of the more mature species currently evolving in their corner of the universe, the Anadens enjoyed rapid interstellar travel and danced on the cusp of developing practical wormhole traversal technology, a feat which promised to open galaxies outside their own to them. But they had never encountered an alien species as advanced as they, much less one so vastly more advanced that its nature resided beyond their ability to comprehend. For the Dzhvar existed across all dimensions, and among other peculiarities this trait enabled them to easily hide out of sight until they moved to strike.

The Anadens' weapons could not harm this fearsome enemy; their shields could not stop them and their tools could not track them. World after world crumbled under the onslaught, but the adversary offered no leader with whom to negotiate a surrender.

We had no special care as to their fate, for we did not concern ourselves with the affairs of mortal creatures carved of blood and bone. The Anadens were one among billions of life forms and millions of sentient species. If their existence began and ended as a blip on the cosmic timeline, so be it. They would not be the first to rise to the cusp of greatness, only to fall into the silence of history. They would not be the last.

The universe was eternal, and we had seen it all before.

But while the Anadens' fate lacked consequence, this was not true of their enemy. The Dzhvar could not be fought and could not be vanquished by ordinary mortals, because they were pandimensional beings born of the void.

In many ways, they were the void. Our opposite, for where we created they devoured. Where we seeded, they destroyed. Unrestricted by limitations of distance or dimensionality, they surged across the manifold of space, in their hunger not distinguishing between stars, planets and living beings.

We came to recognize a horrifying truth. The Dzhvar did not merely devour organics and their habitats. They had begun to devour the universe itself.

With every star system consumed their power grew. If their insatiable appetite continued unabated, a thousand thousand ages from now they would consume the entirety of the cosmos. They would consume us and, like all the others who fell beneath the Dzhvar's assault, we would be unable to stop them.

We were life. We were stardust. We were not warriors.

But the Anadens were.

A decision was made.

AMARANTHE

YEAR 6143
12TH EPOCH PROPER

1

PRÓTOS AGORA

One by one the Primors teleported into the Prótos Agora. The sphere's translucent walls absorbed and filtered the prodigious spectrum radiation bombarding it. Even so, the room was bathed in the light of the galactic core.

Myriad celestial objects were created and destroyed, endlessly smashed together and wrenched apart by the tremendous forces generated here at the heart of the Milky Way. The Prótos Agora harnessed that energy to propel itself on an orbital trajectory that circumnavigated the core, forever skirting the periphery of the accretion disk and the pull of the supermassive black hole at its center. The sphere's motion, and the shield that protected and shrouded it, were driven by the captured chaos of the core itself.

Praesidis was the last to arrive and the only one who did not require an aperture at the destination in order to do so. His *diati* dissipated—it never vanished entirely—as he greeted the others with a subtle dip of his chin. There might be no official leader here among them, but if there were one it would be him.

Upon his arrival and without fanfare their business commenced. They had been doing this for twelve epochs and formalities, if they had ever existed, were abandoned long ago.

"The permanent gateway to the Maffei I galaxy is nearly complete and will be ready for traversal in fifteen days." Diaplas pivoted to face Machim. "We have picked up four disparate energy signatures consistent with Tier II or early Tier III civilizations, so standard Advanced Contact Protocols are to be in place during our exploration and evaluation."

Machim gave his assent. "Done. Three DS brigades will be at your disposal in twelve days. Their Navarchos is authorized to summon additional forces as needed. Erevna, what is your status?"

"The prospect of a populated galaxy has volunteers lining up to be of service. You're guaranteed to have a full complement of personnel equipped and ready to move when you discover worthwhile targets."

"Good." Machim shifted to him. "Do you have any updates on the Phoenix Gateway investigation? My troops are ready to Eradicate the anarchs, should you ever succeed in finding them."

The destruction of the Phoenix Gateway—the first permanent wormhole to another galaxy ever constructed, six hundred millennia ago—by a set of antimatter bombs the month before had stirred up troublesome murmurs of dismay within the populace. It represented an audacious, too-public assault on the Directorate's control. Long an annoyance, these 'anarchs' were now becoming actively problematic.

Praesidis nonetheless maintained a steady, unperturbed expression. "You know as well as I do they are not to be 'found,' for they represent a fragmented, loosely connected collection of terrorists and malcontents."

"Be that as it may, I don't need to be an Inquisitor to deduce that they are also either suicidal or they have Anadens in their ranks and a regenesis lab at some physical location. Physical locations can be found and destroyed."

"This is not a new or noteworthy observation, Machim. We have destroyed their largest base before and doing so did not eliminate the threat but instead emboldened it. The better and more permanent solution is to deprive the anarchs of Anaden members, as without them the resistance will atrophy and die. Erevna, tell me you have made tangible progress on a method to preclude the emergence of these aberrations in future generations."

She glared at Praesidis with imperious disdain, as if he were a child rather than an immortal. "We covered this at the last assembly, in addition to at least three before it. Unless we exclude a sense of individuality and the perception of free will altogether, we can expect to continue to see deviations at a rate of approximately one per two hundred million individuals.

"If we do erase these traits, studies indicate the affected Dynasty members will become unproductive. With no reason to act, they will eventually cease doing so. In my opinion, this minimal anomaly rate is an acceptable price to maintain proper balance."

Anomalies. A cold, science-swathed word for Anaden progeny who, whether randomly or upon being provoked by some impactful experience, rejected their Dynasty integral and vanished from their Primor's sight. More often than not, they also dropped out of the Accepted social and physical infrastructure to live on the fringes, a move which rendered them untraceable.

Machim gestured in a theatrical display of open frustration, thrusting an arm toward the Agora's wall and the core beyond it. "And this was acceptable, until the anarchs started blowing up important and very visible public utilities. This escalation in hostilities is *not* acceptable. Praesidis, I request you station three Inquisitors at each gateway and all Class IV facilities. Such a reprehensible event must not occur a second time."

"I do not have enough Inquisitors to meet the request. Besides, they are all currently pursuing important assignments."

"Then grow more."

Machim's passive-aggressive challenging of him had waxed and waned for the entirety of their existence. Driven by a surfeit of avarice, the man had never conceded to the irrefutable reality that, despite the millions of warships Machim fielded, Praesidis and his Inquisitors held the true power.

Praesidis' eyes flashed violent crimson; tendrils of *diati* roiled out to caress his temples. "Inquisitors are not guards and they are certainly not interchangeable drones, and they will not be demeaned by being treated as such."

Machim took a half-step forward...and retreated. "Watchmen then, but make it five per facility."

Despite the recent destruction of a gateway, the notion these 'anarchs' posed anything approaching a legitimate threat remained an absurd one. But the Directorate had ruled Amaranthe for a million years in part by never letting any unorthodoxy, no matter how incidental, slither through the cracks to a place where it might fester and grow.

He nodded with a confidence that suggested he had planned to do so all along. "Security checkpoint staffing and restrictions will be doubled as well. There will not be a repeat of the Phoenix Gateway incident, and the anarchs will soon be erased from our history."

2

MILKY WAY SECTOR 23

Exobiology Research Lab #4

"It doesn't always come down to explosives, Cosime."

"No, but they're the most fun."

"Oh, sure. Right up until the excruciating pain followed by agonizing death part."

The memory of his last such experience continued to linger in the recesses of Eren asi-Idoni's mind. The Phoenix Gateway obliteration was a sensational feat to pull off, and witnessing the antimatter work its magic up close and personal had absolutely been worth the pain followed by death which resulted. Still, he didn't feel inclined to repeat the stunt—or not until the more negative aspects had faded from memory, anyway.

"You just need to learn how to get out of the way better."

Bloodlust wasn't a trait most people expected to find in a Naraida. Reedy and slight of frame, with long, hyper-flexible limbs, delicate features and luminescent hair as soft as feathers, the Communis name for the species was derived from the word for 'fairy' for several reasons. If naiveté counted as one of them, however, it had been a mistake.

He scowled at Cosime Rhomyhn in an embellished display of exasperation. "You're welcome to take my place on the next mission and show me how it's done."

She cackled, enormous emerald eyes dancing with mirth above the frills of her breather lines. In typical fashion for her, the spiraire more closely resembled wearable art than a functional nitrogen supplement.

"Don't be silly, Eren. Weak, helpless little me can't possibly do something scary and dangerous like perform one of your missions."

"And you better hope the Directorate keeps on believing that nonsense."

He turned to the viewport. The banter was a fun diversion, but they were here to scope out a target, and they were lingering for too long too close to its security perimeter. The tiny scout ship on loan from Anarch Post Epsilon disguised itself by broadcasting false readings, and if they didn't take drastic action, they should be able to remain hidden.

But floating around on the outskirts of a secure Erevna facility made him twitchy. And as Cosime often pointed out, twitchy soon became ornery.

The lumbering hulk of metal that was Exobiology Research Lab #4—it obviously had been designed by scientists rather than architects—orbited a bright blue B7 V star. No planets or other artificial structures existed in the system, and the quarantine procedures required to enter the facility were strict in the extreme. Inside, samples of plant and animal life collected across multiple galaxies were studied for useful insights into evolutionary tendencies, in the hope they could aid in the cultivation of new xeno-biological, -viral and -genetic strains.

It might be proper and even admirable scientific work if the research was limited to plants and non-sentient animals. The 'samples,' however, included members of intelligent alien species who for one reason or another had failed to pass muster and gain Accepted Species status. They were experimented on as ruthlessly as the rest of the specimens.

Whatever the results of those experiments, none ever left the facility again.

He watched a cargo vessel dock in the bay suspended below the structure after multiple scans. The procedure was the same as the last three dockings. "I'll blow it if I have to, but I'd prefer to get more creative this time." *Make the scientists endure some fraction of the agony they've inflicted on their test subjects* went unsaid.

In contrast to the Phoenix Gateway's destruction, this mission's primary purpose was not to undermine the Directorate, though it stood to accomplish that as a bonus. No, this mission was an act of mercy.

Cosime hopped up on the dash to face him. Her arms and legs continued moving, if aimlessly. She never stopped moving, swaying, leaping, tumbling. For the moment it was only swaying, but the incessant motion was energetic enough to send her pure white hair bouncing about. The starlight beyond the viewport increased its natural glow to radiant levels.

As a side effect of the luminosity, the inky scar beneath her left eye blackened in stark relief. It had been earned at the end of a whip wielded by a displeased Kyvern superior; instead of getting it healed when she'd joined the anarchs, she'd altered it into the silhouette of a soaring broad-winged bird. Once, when in an unusually introspective mood, she'd told him there were other, deeper scars elsewhere, and he couldn't help but wonder if she'd reshaped them into art as well.

"You know, you could let the inmates out of the asylum."

He scoffed. "Sneak inside and disable the security protocols? The prisoners would never make it off the station. If they somehow made it off the station, they'd never make it past the security perimeter."

"True." She leapt up and twirled around to press her hands against the viewport and stare outside. He realized she felt confined by the narrow walls of the cabin—another reason not to stay here too long, as he didn't care to watch her suffer. "But at least they could take their revenge on their captors. And by doing so, your end goal would still be achieved. I mean, your intent is to punish the Erevna here, isn't it?"

Being circumspect earlier hadn't made a damn bit of difference. She knew him too well, which was…weird, since nobody knew him well. He shrugged in agreement.

"Then this is a better plan, no? Guaranteed vengeful, righteous violence."

The possibility of the imprisoned aliens slaughtering—or worse—the Erevna researchers held morbid appeal, and he enjoyed picturing the imagined carnage for a minute before leaning into the dash and sighing.

"You're assuming they'll fight back. Rise up. But no one does that, Cosime. No one but us."

She sank down onto her heels wearing a pout. "All the anarchs do."

"A few thousand among two and a half trillion. Most people, most creatures of any kind, aren't like us. It never occurs to them to fight...I don't think it even occurs to them that they ought to be free."

"But—"

"Everyone inside this lab already chose not to fight. If they'd done otherwise, they wouldn't be inside—they'd be dead back on their home planets. We open the doors to their cages, and the prisoners will simply cower in the corners waiting to be disciplined."

She watched him studiously for several seconds, then adjusted one of the spiraire lines with the tip of a finger. "So, explosives, then?"

3

SOLUM

The Praesidis Primor considered the horizon and all that stretched from his feet to its penumbra. An endless city encompassed not merely his citadel and its surroundings but the entirety of the surface, for Solum was a city-planet in the most literal sense. Spires stretched into the clouds and beyond, and the span of their gleaming glass and metal paused only for craft parks floating aloft at perfectly spaced intervals.

A time had come, epochs past, when the other Dynasties were no longer content to share land with one another. One after another they departed the Anaden homeworld to establish independent domiciles on worlds of their own. All Dynasty progeny naturally remained welcome to visit whenever they wished, and many were always doing so.

But in the end, Praesidis alone called Solum home and Praesidis alone ruled over it. This was as it should be, because while all Dynasties were equal at the Directorate's circle, Praesidis was the reason the Directorate existed. His had stood as the strongest since the Dynasties' establishment.

Machim had his fleets and mighty weapons; Erevna had her knowledge and scientific pursuits; Antalla had his commercial riches, Diaplas her engineered monuments, Theriz his stores of resources and Idoni her perpetual bliss. But Praesidis more than any other ensured they all continued to have such things. Ensured the proper balance and order was maintained.

Praesidis was the *diati's* chosen ally, companion and vessel, and it was only proper that the birthplace of the Anadens be his dominion.

He departed from the balcony and walked across the transparent floor, where beneath his feet a thousand stories of purposeful activity unfolded as a recursive hall of mirrors. When he reached the center of the open room, he created a dampening sphere around him and it all faded away, to be replaced with a visualization—further, a conscious awareness—of every living Praesidis descendant.

The Inquisitors radiated the most dominant presences, of course, and he assimilated each one's location, purpose and current status. The more numerous Watchmen hovered a layer beneath. They were less nomadic by nature and typically held less unique, original information to provide. Beneath them swarmed billions of chaperons, guards, examiners and analysts.

Yet if he wished it, he could know the state of any individual *asi* with but an intentional thought directed at them. His presence in their minds manifested as little more than a tickle, for the access did not flow upward.

The prolonged absence of a single Inquisitor marred the integral like a hole punched through a wall. Aver ela-Praesidis passed beyond his perception during a routine investigation weeks ago and had yet to return.

Temporary vanishings were not unheard of. Though immortal and wielding a measure of power to rival any god, the Primor was still a corporeal creature. There were dimensions he could not sense while existing in the physical realm of Amaranthe. The vanishings inevitably resolved themselves when the individual, almost always an Inquisitor, returned to normal space upon having completed their mission.

But Aver had remained away for quite a long time now. The Primor studied the details of the assignment the Inquisitor was working: the apparent disappearance of the majority of a Tier II-D species shortly prior to the Cultivation of their system. Space-faring in the most rudimentary sense, the species would not have possessed the capability to detect the pre-Cultivation monitoring and evaluation procedures, nor would they have had a way to know in advance the fate which awaited them.

Hence the investigation.

The mass disappearance of the species constituted a troubling event, but not an unprecedented one. Such sudden exoduses had occurred a few times over the millennia, but not so often he would characterize it as a trend.

Aver's last update had been filed as he entered the stellar system in question. Then, nothing.

Inquisitors enjoyed a degree of freedom of action and decision-making rare among Anadens, much less among the other civilized species of Amaranthe. Such freedom was not granted lightly. Inquisitors were bred for it, with hundreds of generations of genetic manipulation directed at creating individuals unrivaled in deductive and inductive thinking, analysis and judgment. Detectives. Hunters. Assassins, when the situation called for it.

Aver would not have been expected to report in at each step of his investigation; such an act would have bordered on weakness. In exchange for their relative freedom, Inquisitors were expected to achieve results, period.

The Primor's review of the irregularity served to increase his displeasure with it. Aver had in fact been gone for too long, and no reasonable explanation had been presented to justify the absence. What had happened to the man?

The entry alarm chimed. Because this review had taken place as a formality, and because he'd known he would need to take action before he took it, he'd called for Nyx this morning.

There existed only twelve *elassons* in the Praesidis Dynasty, all Inquisitors, and they each were his children as surely as if he'd spawned them. Which in the ways that mattered, he had.

He froze the sphere state, granted entry to his guest and met her halfway. His hands closed in front of his chest as hers did the same, and they bowed in unison. "Nyx, my dear. Thank you for coming."

Her chin remained dipped for a breath after her spine straightened. "I am forever in your service, Primor."

Fond greeting dispensed with, he revisited the sphere and retrieved the quantized record that represented the missing man—his past, his personal and professional history, his mission and everything else she may need to know to find him.

"Inquisitor Aver ela-Praesidis vanished on a mission too long ago. His consciousness did not transmit for regenesis, nor is it present in the integral now. He was new to the *ela* rank but proved worthy of the promotion in previous assignments. Complete his mission, learn what fate befell him and determine if there is an additional threat which needs to be addressed. If so, report it to me then address it."

"It will be done, Primor." She accepted the data, and its physicality vanished into her hand as she absorbed the knowledge. Nothing more needed to be said or imparted, so she bowed in farewell then turned and left.

4

MW SECTOR 23 ADMINISTRATION

Cosime headed off to locales unknown to acquire the necessary explosives from one of her suppliers. She had a proper job, of course, working for Vanierel at Liryns Cathedral on Palomar IV, as non-Anadens weren't allowed to just cavort around the cosmos at will. But Vanierel was, if not quite an anarch, at a minimum sympathetic to the cause, and he overlooked her frequent absences.

Luckily, nothing so extreme as antimatter was needed for this mission. The detonation would occur inside an enclosed structure, and the lab's edifice was like tissue compared to the goliath Phoenix Gateway. A solid pack of average, ordinary ultra-dense high-powered explosives should suffice to get the job done. Also, though ruining the structure itself would be a nice bonus, the objective was the elimination of what and who resided inside. This included the prisoners—again, a mission of mercy.

Eren proceeded to MW Sector 23 Administration to set about obtaining a list of vessels approved for deliveries to Exobiology Research Lab #4 and their security authorization details.

The Administration center served as a clearinghouse for the entire sector. A Kyvern-run arm of the Directorate managed the labyrinthine nightmare of a bureaucracy that hovered over, in and around doing business here. Doing anything here. Doing anything anywhere, for the station was a clone of sixty-four other installations in the Milky Way alone.

Kyvern were bred to perform this function, thus he had to assume they found fulfillment, even pleasure, in accomplishing it day after dreary decade, but Eren was already restless and he'd hardly crossed the station's outer shields.

Sector 23 Administration was business from end to beginning, with no revelry in sight on the cheerless station. A single lounge for employees did brisk but glum business on the uppermost piazza.

This was not a place where Idonis loitered—so he needed to look less like an Idoni and more like a Kyvern. The spoofed identity and credentials were in place, but now up went the hair into a tamed knot and out went his usual sueded corium attire in favor of a muted brown suit. His irises artificially dimmed to a dull amber, and a cybernetics routine lightened his skin tone several shades until it resembled the fairer skin dominant among Kyvern. He didn't have to work hard to fake the permanent scowl most of them wore.

The first of many queues greeted him at the station entrance. Security.

He frowned—or he would have were he not currently doing so—as the length of the wait was surprising. Though bureaucratic, Kyvern were typically highly efficient at their tasks.

A glance toward the front of the jam revealed four Vigil units and a Watchman. Ah. So security was going to be notably tighter than usual, and they'd brought in non-Kyvern muscle.

He chuckled to himself at the possibility the increase in security was due to him, or rather due to his actions at the Phoenix Gateway. The flash of pride was quickly doused by annoyance at the fact his success had in turn made future successes for him and others that much more difficult, at least for a while. But now wasn't the time to lessen the pressure on the Directorate; it was the time to increase it. Risks be damned.

He was three people from the front when a furor broke out on the other side of the entry checkpoint, off to the left.

"No! I didn't do anything wrong! I wasn't trying to steal!"

The Watchman left the checkpoint to go see to the disturbance, and Eren willed the queue to move faster. The front-line

Vigil drone units folded when presented with impeccable if false credentials, but the Praesidis Watchman wouldn't have been so easy to fool.

He stepped up to the checkpoint.

"Present Accepted credentials."

The Watchman reached the shrieking Naraida woman, who had been cornered by two roving Vigil units.

Eren did as requested.

Her pleas rang loudly above the generalized din. "Please, sir, there must be a glitch with my account. I should have the funds—"

The Watchman used his *diati* to lift the woman into the air then slammed her face first to the floor. He motioned for the Vigil units to restrain her.

"Business?"

Eren kept his voice flat. Dulled. "Addition of a new cargo ship to an existing transport business registration."

The drones extended spindly arms to lift the unconscious woman up. Her head lolled against her chest, and her pliant limbs caused her to sag low between the drones. Blood streamed down from her forehead, and her spiraire had been crushed. They should see to that soon, or she was liable to suffocate from a lack of nitrogen before they got her to a containment cell. Did they care?

"You are cleared to pass."

Eren strode through the checkpoint without any gesture of thanks to the Vigil unit and kept his gaze straight ahead as he passed the drones dragging the woman away. The Watchman passed two meters behind him on his way to the checkpoint.

He stopped holding his breath.

Over the course of the next interminably long minutes he traversed endless levels full of endless hallways of offices, registries and certification departments, the sole variation being the length of the queues to access them. The interior displayed so little character he had to consult his map overlay several times to confirm his location and path forward.

The one oddity of note he encountered was an Efkam lighting a passage as it slipped and slid along the floor. How the blobs were able to move without leaving a trail of slime behind them was among the great mysteries of the universe. It warbled a greeting at him as it passed, but he ignored it, because he'd be expected to do so. The Efkam were surprisingly open, friendly creatures—but they were only tolerated by the Anadens. Not entertained.

He'd almost fallen asleep from boredom by the time he reached the Maintenance Hardware department, some two hundred levels and a thousand hallways from where he'd begun.

A Vigil unit blocked the entrance. It floated upward to leer menacingly over Eren. "This is a restricted area. Present authorization for your presence, return to the guest levels or be pacified."

Someone needed to teach the machine a touch of nuance. He presented a small Reor slab. "Special authorization from Sector Oversight, originating outside of Administration management."

The unit inserted the slab into its reader. Two seconds later it jerked and dropped to the floor as the virus on the slab shorted out its operating routines.

Eren maneuvered the bulky ball of metal into a dark corner by kicking it forward and around to the left. Once he made sure it wasn't going to roll back out into the entry, he retrieved his slab, pulled on a glove and held his hand to the scanner gating entrance to the interior rooms.

The barrier thinned to allow him to pass, and he walked into the data vault. Time was ticking, and a surge of adrenaline assured he was now fully awake. He located the nearest access point and tapped into it.

The station's data archives weren't porous or weakly protected, but in recent years anarchs who weren't him had begun to develop some brilliantly crafty hacking routines.

Zettabytes of data populated the system, and all but a few gigabytes of it were useless to him. He relied upon several dozen cross-referencing tags to lead him to the files he needed. Once he found them, he didn't hang around and decide which vessel offered the best option; he simply copied the data onto a new Reor slab and backed out of the system. Then he hurried toward the door—

"Vigil unit H962 is down in Maintenance Hardware. Cause is undetermined. It could be either a malfunction or sabotage."

"Watchman dispatched to your location."

Eren pressed against the wall of the vault room and peeked around the corner. A guard stood over the unit Eren had disabled, doing what all persons like him did best—guarding it until someone possessing greater authority arrived.

The one thing that never, ever showed up on missions was good luck. Bad luck? All the godsdamn time.

He dug around in his kit for a piece of hardware he could spare and palmed a small power bridge stabilizer. His options for getting out of the data vault were limited. If he created a distraction, they would know someone had been here and flag the incident as malfeasance. Without a flag, however, the disabled Vigil unit would look like it had suffered a rudimentary malfunction. So maybe he should wait and hope the guard walked into another room long enough for him to sneak out.

But a Praesidis Watchman was on the way; no time to hope for good luck that never came anyway. He hurtled the bridge into the vault room. The loud clatter got the guard's attention, and the man sped past Eren's shadow into the vault.

Eren ran for the door, then the hallway, then the transit tube. He had twenty seconds at most to get off this level before someone spotted him.

He reached the tube and leapt inside the same instant the Watchman materialized at the other end of the hallway. "Halt!"

The tube shot upward. He'd been seen, but not scanned, so...he considered abandoning the disguise. But a description of a 'male Kyvern in a brown suit' described several thousand individuals on the station at the low end, which made it a better disguise than 'baroque Idoni man with fiery hair and starburst eyes.'

So instead he caught his breath and mentally ran through the full list of his terrible options for reaching the docks, getting through security and escaping the station.

ℛ

"Vigil Administration Security, halt!"

The Watchman—a quick peek over his shoulder confirmed it was the same one from the vault floor—emerged from a service tube behind Eren, apparently having taken some top-secret shortcut to the transport lobby. Multiple Vigil drones sped forward to block possible exits and aid the Watchman in apprehending his prey even as two guards rushed in.

Should have ditched the costume. To his right a crowd of people shrank away, eager to obey any commands the Watchman might direct their way. No hiding in the crowd until he could sneak away unnoticed.

To his left was a sleeping pod showroom. It would have a rear exit leading to a service corridor, which would lead to yet more corridors where he would be run to ground. A trap of his own making.

Ahead were the hangar bays and transport ships. But the entrance to the docks sat at the end of a long, open lobby perfect for shooting him in the back—or the front, since the fully staffed checkpoint gated the entrance.

He tightened his grasp on the Reor slab encoded with the transport ships' data and prepared to fry it. If he got nulled, which it appeared he was about to, at least he could prevent Vigil from learning what information he'd stolen. He, or someone, could try again later.

Fate accepted, Eren turned around slowly, arms in the air but hands fisted. "Is there a problem, sir? I was on my way—"

The Watchman and both guards flew backwards through the air as if shoved by an invisible force. As they slammed to the floor far down the lobby, the bystanders gasped and shifted in confused unrest.

Eren spun around to see a man in a hooded cloak standing a dozen meters away, between him and the entrance to the docks. The man's right hand was splayed in front of his body and surrounded by a flaming crimson aura.

Well, this wasn't exactly *better*. The murmur of dread crossed his lips unbidden. "Inquisitor."

"No."

Eren jumped as a hand landed on his arm to accompany the furtive whisper coming from his left. Another hooded figure stood beside him—*directly* beside him. How had someone gotten so close without him noticing? Beneath the hood radiant silver irises framed by rich bordeaux locks stared intently at him. "This way. Let's go."

He nodded in hurried agreement. *"Nos libertatem somnia."*

The stranger's eyes narrowed. "What?"

Not an anarch. *Arae!* Eren tried to back away, only to have her—yes, he decided it was likely a woman, though he couldn't identify her Dynasty—tighten her grip. "Please, come with us. We'll get you out of here."

"Us? You mean you and the Inquisitor? I don't think so."

"Would you rather die here?"

"If that's required, yes." Movement in the corner his vision heralded the Watchman and guards struggling up off the floor.

"Ugh...." The woman groaned and tugged on his arm. "This is a rescue, so will you come already? Live through the next ten minutes and we'll explain everything."

"What are you doing? Obey Vigil and turn him over!"

The speaker, a stodgy Kyvern man in a brown suit—Eren snickered—surged out of the crowd toward them, as if intending to grab Eren himself.

The mysterious woman spun toward the man and flung her arm outward. A stream of blazing white energy whipped out from her wrist to leap across the three meters of open space and slash the man across the chest. He collapsed to the floor in convulsions. The rest of the crowd now began clamoring backward in full-on panic.

Admittedly impressed, Eren made a swift calculation. Certain death now or probable death later. So long as he could succeed in wrecking the Reor slab before death came, probable and later were always preferable to certain and now.

He assented, and the woman instantly took off running. After a few strides of being dragged along behind her, he caught on and matched her pace. They rushed toward the docks entrance as the recovering security personnel advanced behind them and drones closed in on both sides.

When they reached the Inquisitor, the man thrust his arm out in a fresh burst of *diati*. Eren risked a peek behind him to see his pursuers stopped cold by a shimmering wall that spanned the lobby, leaving only the three of them on this side of it. Ahead of them, at the checkpoint, all the Vigil units were down and the line of entrants had scattered into the docking passages.

The woman paused long enough to place a hand on the Inquisitor's shoulder. "Caleb?"

A deep male voice bearing an unfamiliar accent responded from beneath the hood. "Right behind you, baby."

"You better be." She renewed her grip on Eren's hand and sprinted forward once more; they sped through the checkpoint unmolested and into the maze of the docks.

Footsteps pounded behind them. He didn't risk another peek back, but he assumed they belonged to this 'Caleb,' for better or worse.

They rounded the next corner as a burst of heavier, harsher thuds echoed down the passage. Abruptly the woman yanked him to the left, into a docking module.

"Breathe out and get ready to jump." She slammed an open palm on the panel, and a white glow pulsed beneath her fingers and up her wrist into the sleeve of her cloak.

The door opened and she proceeded to shove him through it—

—into space. There was a ship, but it wasn't actually *docked*.

Momentum carried him forward across the chasm into an open airlock. His feet briefly touched a solid surface. He grabbed a handle in the wall as one body then another landed in the small antechamber with him.

The outer airlock closed, artificial gravity slammed his feet to the floor and air flooded in. The hatch in front of him opened, and Eren stumbled into the ship's cabin.

The woman followed on his heels, then the Inquisitor a second later, and the inner airlock hissed shut, sealing him in.

5

SIYANE

"Valkyrie, get us out of here!" Alex shoved past the Anaden to reach the cockpit and slide into her chair as they accelerated away from the space station.

'Two drone vessels are in pursuit.'

"There will be more."

She ignored the comment, but Caleb pointed their guest to one of the jump seats behind the cockpit. "Sit down." Then he leaned in above her shoulder. "You got this?"

"I got this." Targeting lock warnings flashed on the HUD. Two…four, five security drone vessels. "Rifter active. Swing around E 82° on plane and act like we're going to shoot at them."

The pursuers were too small to pick out against the backdrop of the dark, hulking station, but their energy signatures shone bright as flares. They fired as they closed in—they were quite fast—and foul-colored cadmium lasers consumed the viewport.

"Power, Valkyrie. I need power."

'Reallocating.'

The lights in the cabin dimmed. The gauge crept up. "Cloaking now, Rifter remains active. And…sLume drive engaged."

The weapons fire vanished in favor of the superluminal bubble, and she exhaled. But relaxation still lay some distance in the future. "We're basically fleeing in a straight line, which isn't a great idea. Mesme, help Valkyrie find a good hiding spot off of our current vector."

Mesme darted across the entrance to the cockpit in a wave of shapeless lights. *Alexis, as we are now in my home realm, I have asked you to refer to me by my proper name.*

"I will when you start calling me Alex. Maybe. Honestly, you should've considered the ramifications of having an unpronounceable name before you chose it. Now, can we focus? We have an escape to complete."

"The drones' weapons didn't hit your ship."

She tossed a smirk in the direction of the Anaden. "No, they didn't."

'Mnemosyne, the region eighty parsecs into Sector 22 on a N 31° W vector appears to lack any structural development. Am I correct in this assessment?'

The location will suffice to provide temporary safety.

'Adjusting superluminal course.'

"Thanks, Valkyrie." Alex took a deep breath, let it out and spun the chair around to face the cabin.

The man they'd rescued had abandoned the jump seat to stand in the center of the main cabin, a look of perplexed frustration marring his features as his gaze jerked between her, Caleb, Mesme and various areas of the interior.

Behind him Caleb stashed their weapons, locked down the cabinets and pretended not to have a keen eye fixed on their guest. Using the *diati* in such an intense manner was sure to have him wired and a bit jumpy, so she'd try to keep the spotlight on her for a while so he could…she didn't want to say regain control. Reimpose inner calm.

She smiled blithely. "Well, that was bracing, no?"

The Anaden settled his attention on her but stepped to the side so Caleb wasn't behind him. Tall and lithe, his movements reminded her of a leopard: alert, wary and swift. "What is this ship? Who are you people? Why do you have a Kat on board?"

"I'm Alex. He's Caleb. The Kat—I like that, by the way—is Mnemosyne. It has its own ship but nevertheless keeps showing up on ours, which is the *Siyane*. And also Valkyrie, since she's basically the ship. It's a long, dreadfully esoteric story. Now about—"

"What do you mean, 'she's basically the ship'? Why does the ship have two names?"

"I mean Valkyrie's quantum circuitry permeates all systems and structures of the vessel. Among other things. She's an Artificial—a synthetic intelligence—and the ship doesn't have two names. They're two separate entities. Sort of. They once were. I *said* it was esoteric."

The man—they'd been given a time, place and general description of who to be on the lookout for from Mesme's contact, but not a name—dropped into a chair at the kitchen table and reached up behind his head. Long copper hair twisted into silken strands fell out of a knot to spill over his shoulders. As she watched, his skin darkened from a tawny beige to rich sienna. He rubbed at his eyes, and when he reopened them they shone a vibrant gilt—neither bronze nor gold, but akin to solar flares.

Okay, this was somewhat unexpected, but whatever.

"You have a SAI running your ship? Are you daft?"

She didn't miss Caleb's quiet chuckle from the back of the cabin, but she kept her focus on their guest. "It's a matter of some dispute. What did you call her? A 'SAI'?"

"A sentient artificial intelligence. A self-aware machine someone built."

"Oh. Yes, that's a more or less accurate description."

"But they're verboten. Practically heretical."

Valkyrie sighed. 'Not again.'

Alex laughed. "Looks like. Sorry, Valkyrie. But I'm confused. Don't you have quantum processes running *everything* here? Your ships, your buildings, your bodies?"

"Of course. But they are tools under the full control of their hosts or masters. In no way are they sentient or aware."

She arched an eyebrow. "More's the pity."

"For an allegedly sentient entity, it did a rather poor job of docking."

"Oh, we *were* docked. But if security deduced which ship we belonged to, it wouldn't have released the ship from the docking clamps, right? So *she* undocked before the shitstorm kicked off."

He considered the explanation, then shifted forward in the chair. "Fine. If your ship is a SAI and a Kat your guide, what are *you*?"

Caleb strode forward to prop in feigned casualness against the data table, dropping his hood and shrugging off the cloak. "Not Inquisitors."

The man met his piercing stare to study Caleb for several seconds. "No. It appears you are not. So how in the name of Zeus is it you wield *diati* with such skill?"

"I don't think you've earned the right to know yet."

"Oh? Near as I can tell, I've been kidnapped and am being held captive by mysterious, suspicious-acting strangers. I deserve to be told who my captors are."

Alex rolled her eyes. "We didn't kidnap you. We saved your ass."

"That remains to be determined. Why did you do it?"

Caleb shook his head minutely. *Not yet.*

He was the expert at this kind of thing, so she followed his lead. "We can get into the specifics later, after we've gotten to know one another better. We're aware you're an anarch—more importantly, an Anaden anarch, which makes you a very rare individual. We're interested in learning about the resistance, but primarily we need to learn details about the Anaden power structure."

She shot Mesme an annoyed glare, as it had been shockingly unhelpful in this regard. "The type of information only an Anaden will have and only an anarch will reveal."

He considered each of them in turn. "Because you...truly aren't Anaden, though your resemblance to us is close to the point of uncanniness. And plainly you aren't anarchs. Yet here you are, departing an Anaden space station—at which you had successfully docked, at least briefly—in a ship of unique design and capable of superluminal travel. How is that possible? I ask again: what *are* you?"

It wasn't as if he would believe her if she told him. "Let's just say we share a genetic heritage with the Anadens. If you require a label, call us 'humans.' And that's all we're going to say on it for now."

"Never heard of 'humans,' but they're not an Accepted Species, which means you're risking your lives simply by being in this sector, much less docking at stations and walking around in them—or running, as it were. What's your objective, beyond kidnapping me?"

She and Caleb exchanged another glance, and this time he indicated assent. "The same as yours: to topple the Directorate and free the species it enslaves."

The man's gaze shot behind her to where Mesme had coalesced into a somewhat humanoid form. "You're saying this in front of the Kat? It will report you!"

You understand nothing, anarch. The disdain in Mesme's tone was both uncharacteristic and impossible to miss.

"I understand the Kats are the Directorate's sycophants. Cowards and mewling bootlickers."

Mesme surged forward to swirl in agitation around the Anaden where he sat. *You. Understand. Nothing.*

Alex kept a straight face, but Mesme's reaction was surprising. Yes, the man had insulted it, but Mesme's usual temperament gave 'dispassionate' a bad name. This was new.

The Anaden raised his hands in surrender. "Clearly. I'm sorry—now back off."

The intensity of Mesme's swirling lessened, but it continued to probe him for a couple of revolutions before retreating.

He eyed Mesme warily until it settled down off to Alex's right. "How did you find me? Or to be more specific, how did you know where I would be, the delicate nature of my situation and that I was an anarch? It's not what I'd call common knowledge."

A corner of Alex's mouth curled up. "The mewling bootlicker and you have a mutual acquaintance."

"Someone in the anarchs betrayed me?"

Not betrayed. Sought to assist us both.

"Who?"

I will not reveal this information. To do so would be the betrayal.

"That's one perspective." He slouched in the chair. "Well, this is not how I saw my day going when I woke up this morning. All right. Agree to drop me off at a location of my choosing in the next...how fast does your ship go? Never mind. Drop me off in the next ten hours, and I'll answer your questions, within reason. But I won't betray anarch secrets, and I decide what that means."

"Deal." Alex left the cockpit and went over to one of the cabinets. She unlocked it, slid the spiral bracelet-turned-conductivity lash off her forearm and stored it.

Once it was secure in its case and the cabinet locked, she rested against the data table beside Caleb, squeezed his hand and drew closer to whisper in his ear. "You were fantastic back there."

He squeezed her hand and murmured, "So were you," before motioning for their guest to continue.

The man regarded them curiously for a moment. "My name is Eren asi-Idoni, 62nd Savitas Lineage, 12th Epoch Proper. I am three hundred twelve years old, formerly of the Idoni Dynasty and now a field operative for the anarch resistance against the Anaden Directorate."

"You're how old?"

"I know, hardly more than a child. No need to remind me. Of course, this body is barely a month old. The last one got atomized when I blew up the Phoenix Gateway. The one before the last one got its head ripped off in a nasty encounter with an angry Ch'mshak. Admittedly, he had cause to be angry, as I had just destroyed his ship...and cargo...and a few other valuables."

She scowled. According to Mesme, 478 passengers on two vessels, as well as thirty-one people on the adjacent Arx, were killed in the Phoenix Gateway explosion. She pulsed Caleb.

Mesme was right. The anarchs are nothing but terrorists.

Probably. But they're terrorists fighting our enemy, which suggests they can still be useful.

She reluctantly buried the scowl. "We know the Dynasties operate on some sort of group consciousness you call an 'integral.' Does this mean you can hear the thoughts of your leader—your Primor?"

"It's not a group consciousness. It's a pervasive, invasive choke chain. And I haven't heard any thoughts from the Idoni integral in ninety-seven years. But no. Thoughts do traverse the integral, but only upwardly and horizontally—never down to those lesser. So when I was a part of it, I was not privy to the musings of the Primor. Thank Athena, for what vile horrors they must be."

"So you were able to break away from the integral, then. How did it come about, exactly?"

"You don't pull any punches, do you? Do you have any idea how personal a question that is?"

Not really. "I'm sorry. I only meant how you did it. We're interested in the mechanics of it. We're trying to understand how these integrals work and what they mean for...certain things."

"Hypnols. Satisfied?"

Hypnols are the Amaranthean version of chimerals, and allegedly potent neurochemical drugs.

I thought I remembered the word. Thanks, Valkyrie.

In truth she'd definitely remembered it, as the factoid had been personally relevant for *addiction* reasons. She'd gone so far as to make a mental note: don't accidentally try hypnols, and for the love of anything that might be holy, don't *deliberately* try hypnols. One day she'd feel secure enough to again indulge in the occasional casual party chimeral without worrying it could set off some kind of relapse, but the day wasn't here yet.

Anyway, his answer didn't tell them much. "I was hoping for a more informative answer."

"I burned out the part of my brain necessary to communicate with the integral. Possibly a few other parts as well. Collateral damage."

"It was as simple as that?"

He donned a chilling, cryptic expression. "Not even close."

6

SIYANE

MILKY WAY

"What do you think?"

Alex stared out the viewport above the bed, acknowledging and moving past the faintest twinge of the stars' call to her, then curled her legs beneath her and scooted nearer to Caleb where he sat on the side of the bed. She kept her voice low as an added precaution, though she doubted their guest would comprehend the English they'd switched back to.

"I don't know. I don't like him. He's a terrorist who blows up stations with innocent people in them—" she winced sheepishly "—and no, you don't need to point out how blowing up buildings is now a trigger for me, and a hypocritical one at that. I'm working through it. He's insolent bordering on obnoxious and in no way whatsoever trustworthy. But at the same time…."

"You believe he hates the Directorate and will do almost anything to see it brought down."

"Yeah. I do."

"So do I. I've had to work alongside a lot of unsavory people over the years. Mr. asi-Idoni won't be the worst—" Caleb cut himself off with a grimace.

"What is it?"

"Talk about triggers. I'm excusing his murder of innocents because I believe his cause is a just one. It's one tiny step away from agreeing with what my father did at the start of the First Crux War." He shook his head. "Shades of gray…I swear they'll be my undoing."

"No." Her brow furrowed in contemplation. "I think…shades of gray are hard and messy, and they deprive us of explicit rules to steer our decisions. But—this was something I pondered on while you and Mom were on Earth kicking Winslow the Elder's ass—what if black-and-white rules and absolutes lead to the rise of people like the Winslows? What if ultimately they lead to a society like the one the Anadens have imposed on Amaranthe?"

The image of a man in a window consumed by flames haunted her, now and often, but it helped to believe her transgression had in the end been a lesser evil which helped stop a greater one. The palliative would be cheating if it didn't feel true.

"If it's easy, you're doing it wrong." He sighed. "Another Samuelism. He was wrong about a lot of things, but...he was right about a lot of them, too. So, hard way it is?"

She made a face suitable to convey her distaste for what was unfortunately the correct answer.

His hand came to her jaw as he leaned in and kissed her gently; she immediately deepened the kiss.

They'd made their first overt move today, and it had been stressful and intense, not to mention dangerous. She felt exhausted, though it was mainly the adrenaline bottoming out and would pass once she got her hands on an energy drink. Mostly she wanted nothing more than to stay right here, on this bed. In his arms. Eventually, wearing fewer items of clothing. Maybe some soft jazz on the speakers for added ambiance.

But while Valkyrie and Mesme both kept a watch on their guest upstairs, they still didn't want to leave him out of their sight for too long. So after reveling in Caleb's touch for another breath, she pulled back to meet his gaze.

The tiny crimson flecks in his irises didn't bother her; they merely added yet greater expressiveness to already striking vibrance. "Shall we?"

"First, let's talk strategy. He doesn't even begin to trust me. He doesn't trust you either, but he's less afraid of you." Caleb smiled teasingly. "His mistake, right? But if he's to be convinced to help, I think you're going to have to be the one to do it."

"Have you seen my motivational speeches? They tend to end with strings of curses and melodramatic exits."

He laughed. "I have. They're spectacular."

"Spectacularly disastrous." She rolled her eyes to emphasize the point but climbed off the bed. "Okay, but don't say I didn't warn you."

ℛ

The Anaden was peering into the kitchen sink, two cabinets open and multiple containers on the counter beside him, when they returned upstairs.

Caleb cleared his throat, and Eren glanced over at them wearing a scowl. "I can't figure out how anything works. This is ridiculous."

She regarded him suspiciously. "Are you hungry?"

"Not really. I just got bored. Well...maybe a little hungry. But I'm more afraid to find out what you people eat."

"That's funny. We heard Idonis were naturally adventurous thrill-seekers. How scary can a taste of unfamiliar food be?"

The scowl deepened, but he abandoned his study of the sink. "I make it a habit to be as un-Idoni as possible. Except for the adventurous, thrill-seeking part. Fine. How does one prepare your supposed food?"

Caleb moved to the counter and nudged him out of the way. "I'll tell you what. I'll whip us up some manicotti. Alex, why don't you open a bottle of wine? I think everyone could benefit from relaxing a bit."

"You won't hear me arguing." Wine was an even better choice than an energy drink. She grabbed a bottle of sangiovese and three glasses then motioned their guest to the table.

He sat down cautiously. "What is it?"

"Alcohol. Spirits." She searched for an applicable Communis term; as part of Mesme's crash course on Amaranthe, her eVi had learned Communis, but knowing the language wasn't the same as living the language. "It's similar to....*merum tsipouro.*"

"Oh. In that case." He grabbed one of the glasses and tipped it toward her.

She didn't like him. Though the cybernetic veins running through his skin were far less overt than those of the assailant on Seneca, they still gave him a cold, harsh appearance. Alien, no matter what genetics they shared.

But as appointed persuader-in-chief she had a job to do, so she donned a pleasant visage and filled his glass, filled theirs and settled in her chair. "Valkyrie, how far are we from the location our guest provided?"

'We will arrive at the Ursa Major I Arx in approximately two and a half hours.'

"Thank you." Her eyes flitted toward the Kat hovering at the front of the cabin then across the table to the Anaden. "Mesme, why don't you go check on your ship. You can meet us later."

You wish for me to depart now? Why do you ask this?

"Because of all the evolved life forms on this ship that Eren asi-Idoni doesn't trust, I believe he trusts you the least. I want him to hear what I have to say with as open a mind as possible, and he can't do so while you're making him twitch like a marionette on juiced strings."

Eren shrugged over the rim of his glass, and with the visual equivalent of a sigh Mesme spun up and departed.

ℛ

"You're insane. In three hundred years of a life filled with debauchery, appalling excess, rebellion against a merciless, all-powerful regime and a record-setting number of suicide stunts, you are the two most insane individuals I have ever met."

Eren refilled his drink, crossed his arms over his chest while still holding the wine, and leaned back to regard them with defiant eyes in an open challenge to prove him wrong.

Caleb chuckled wryly. "This isn't the first time we've been called insane. But the fact we're alive, here and sitting across from you should tell you something."

"Not much. What in Hades' five rivers do you want with details on Machim vessel construction, layouts, weaponry, defenses, movements and operational chains of command? There are *two* of you. Or possibly four. I doubt this little ship could so much as dent a single Machim warship, so what do you care what fifteen million of them are doing?"

Fifteen *million*...Alex squelched a shudder. "We never said we were alone."

"Are you now saying you're not alone?"

She hid her pursed lips behind her glass. She sucked at subterfuge and the cloak-and-dagger routine.... "You could call us an advance scouting party. The important thing is we can use the intel. We *will* use the intel. We'll use it to challenge the Directorate on a level and in a way it has never faced. With this information, we can bring it to its knees."

She had no idea if they—humans, her mother, the AEGIS fleet, the Prevos—stood any genuine chance of doing such a thing. But having seen a few tiny glimpses of this universe's iniquities, she damn well intended to make sure they tried.

Perhaps her conviction showed in her expression and tone, because Eren's defiant posture softened. "I can't get it for you. It's beyond my skills, my access, my everything."

Caleb didn't dispute his assertion. "Can one of your comrades?"

"Another anarch? Someone higher up and more influential than me, you mean?"

Caleb lifted his shoulders in answer.

"I don't see how. If we were capable of pulling off heists of such grandeur, we would already be doing them. We have several Machims in the organization, but by definition they're no longer connected to the Machim integral, as it's impossible to be both and function. And accessing the kind of data you're talking about is impossible without either being connected to the integral or having access to...Directorate-level files...."

"What is it, Eren? What came to mind?" Valkyrie had once told her that calling people by their first name made them feel more comfortable in unfamiliar surroundings. She figured what the hell, it couldn't hurt. Unless it could?

She appealed to Caleb for help, but he merely winked at her. It must be encouragement, right?

"Nothing. Almost certainly nothing. An anarch acquaintance of mine once claimed an agent had successfully broken into a Galactic Divisional Machim Hub. But they were caught inside and suicided rather than be tortured and give up anarch secrets."

"Well, they reported back on what they'd accomplished after they underwent your 'regenesis' procedure, didn't they?" It had taken some work on Mesme's part to convince her of the legitimacy of this notable Amaranthean technology. The proposition that the Anadens had achieved practical immortality...she was still skeptical. Cloning, she'd give them—but complete consciousness transfer? *Soul* transfer?

Eren shook his head with a solemnity not displayed before now, and she put aside her musings on the nature of life and death. "No. The agent wasn't Anaden. He was Novoloume."

They'd spent weeks receiving the worst info dump imaginable from Mesme, both before and after they'd traversed the master portal to Amaranthe. History, species, customs, tech, security procedures and endlessly so on. She'd had no hope of remembering it all, so it was a damn good thing Valkyrie was around to catalogue it.

Any help for me?

The Novoloume are a humanoid Accepted Species considered by most to be extraordinarily beautiful, elegant and refined. Their role is diplomacy, public affairs and other formalized social interactions. In close proximity, they secrete pheromones that most mammals find highly sexually arousing.

Oh, good lord. You can insulate me from the effect, can't you?

I can. I cannot, however, do the same for Caleb.

She smiled to herself, as the mood wasn't suited to public smiling. *I think he'll manage. He has skills.*

For instance, he was currently giving Eren a positively earnest look. "To die to protect one's allies is a very honorable act—one of the most honorable there is. The anarchs are serious about their cause, then?"

Eren leveled an impressively steely stare at Caleb in return. "You're asking me if my Zeus-be-damned attitude betrays an abundance of conviction or masks it?"

Caleb idly raised an eyebrow. But he seemed impressed, even if he didn't want to be.

"I suspect whatever my answer were to be, it wouldn't convince you. So you'll simply have to judge for yourself." Eren tipped up his glass and emptied it. "Thank you. This drink of yours is surprisingly satisfying. I will delve into what, if anything, can be done to get you closer to your insane request—after I complete the mission I'm presently on."

Eren produced a small slab from a hidden pocket in his pants and rolled it around in his palm. "While I enjoy a great deal of freedom in how I go about my business, I also have an obligation to my superiors and my comrades, something I..." he studied Caleb "...suspect you understand."

Caleb threw his hands in the air, but it was a mild gesture. Of course he did understand. "All we're asking for is good-faith assistance. I'd say 'we're not asking you to die for us,' but it doesn't sound as if that's a good measure of your commitment."

Eren laughed lightly. Somewhere in the passing of the evening, the Anaden had relaxed around Caleb. God, her husband did have a way with people. Aliens, too.

"Not so long as the anarch posts remain safely hidden from the Directorate—" Panic flared in Eren's expression. "Which I really shouldn't be talking about. What's in this 'wine'?"

"Truth serum."

Caleb maintained a flawless poker face, but the distress on Eren's grew so severe Alex hurriedly intervened. "He's kidding. It's not any likelier to induce truth-telling than any other alcohol." She motioned to the slab in his hand. "Is that your mission?"

"It contains the information I need to complete my mission...and you don't know what this is, do you?"

She shook her head.

"How in the name of sanity do you not know what a Reor slab is...never mind, I don't care. It's encrypted data storage."

She fixated on the slab, admiring its subtle beauty while the quantum processes behind her irises analyzed it. It was a solid, translucent onyx mineral, but thousands of fibers rich jade in color ran through its interior in ordered rows at right angles to one another. The proportions of the object were a precise four by nine by twenty-five millimeters.

They are the squares of the first three Fibonacci primes.

True, but don't get excited—three numbers aren't much of a pattern.

They are when the filaments' relationship to one another follow it as well.

Okay, now you have my attention.

"Can I hold it?"

He shrugged. "Sure. You can't get to the data, and there are billions more where this one came from."

She accepted it from him, balanced it on her palm and ran a fingertip over the surface. It felt chilled and as perfectly smooth as its dimensions were precise. "Are they all the same shape?"

"The same proportions, yes. Any other shape and the data degrades—something to do with how the data's stored."

It's extradimensional, isn't it, Valkyrie? That's how the encryption occurs?

Likely so, but I am unable to fully analyze the mechanism at work. We have seen functioning six-dimensional devices. I believe this object delves into more.

She narrowed her focus to a small section of the interweaving filaments, searching for the patterns folding in on themselves....

A hum, so faint she wasn't positive it was real, pulsated against her palm—or in her head.

Am I imagining this, Valkyrie?

No. It is likely the quantum-level oscillation of the quanta storing the data, no matter the form they take.

Which would, it seemed, be something she could sense. The surreal quality of her life these days still occasionally took her by surprise.

The jade filaments began to shift their color in ripples across the spectrum.

Eren reached for the slab. "What did you do? It only changes colors when it's encoding data."

"Nothing. I just touched it." She reluctantly handed it back to him. "Thank you."

Caleb was regarding her intently, but she ignored his inquiring gaze. She'd explain later—or explain how she couldn't explain it. "Where does the material come from?"

Eren scrutinized the slab closely as the filaments returned to a stable jade, then slipped it back in his pocket. "Originally, some planet out in the Tyche galaxy. They grow it in labs now."

"'They'?"

"The Directorate, of course. Reor production is one of the few truly multi-Dynasty enterprises. None of them can accomplish it alone, and the material's too important not to mass produce."

A corner of Caleb's mouth quirked upward as he redirected his attention to their guest. He lifted his glass to his lips. "What *is* your mission?"

Eren snorted. "Sorry, no. I do appreciate the timely save and the ride, and this has all been most lovely. The food was a fair bit odd, but the wine's exquisite. Nevertheless, we are neither cohorts nor comrades, and we are certainly not friends. The anarch resistance survives on secrecy. It exists every day a single security breach away from annihilation, and I will not be the one to commit that breach."

PART II:

SINGULARITY SHADOW

"It is difficult to say what is impossible, for the dream of yesterday is the hope of today and the reality of tomorrow."

— Dr. Robert H. Goddard

AURORA

YEAR 2323 AD

7

SPACE, NORTH-CENTRAL QUADRANT

ARCADIA STELLAR SYSTEM

*T*he monstrous two-headed dinosaur dropped dead to the desert
floor with a thundering wallop that shook the ground beneath
Bob's feet.

*Beside him, the lavender-skinned young woman gasped in relief
and swooned into his arms. "You saved me from the monster,
stranger. What mystical weapon do you wield to fell the mighty
beast so swiftly?"*

*He glanced at his Daemon before holstering it. "It's not im-
portant—what's important is that you're safe now."*

*She gazed up at him, wide, innocent lavender eyes matching the
color palette of her skin. "I must repay you for this kindness. It is our
custom to do so." She took a step back. "I know nothing of your ways,
stranger, but allow me to give you pleasure as best I can." Her hands
went to the hem of her skimpy, sleeveless leather top and began
lifting it up—*

'Alert: I am detecting a signal 0.8 megameters distant at N 23°
-8° z W. It appears to be a disabled and adrift vessel.'

*He held up a finger as the material reached the tantalizing curve
of her sumptuous breasts. "Hold on one second, would you?"*

Bob Patera paused the *illusoire* with a groan and yanked the
interface off his neck. "Dammit, Barbie. You barged in on purpose!"

'They say anticipation of the event is often better than the
event itself.'

"No one says that. No one *ever* says that." He stumbled out of
the bed, located a somewhat clean shirt on the floor and pulled it
over his head. "Now, what? Why are we picking up anything on

scans? We're supposed to be zipping toward Arcadia in a warp bubble."

'We are undergoing regularly scheduled cessation of superluminal travel to disperse the exotic particles created so we don't kill everyone on Arcadia when we arrive. While traveling on impulse power, routine scans detected the vessel.'

He needed water. Or beer. After a few seconds of standing at the kitchen cubbyhole debating the relative benefits, he opted for the beer and carried it to the cockpit of the *Blackbeard*.

"So it's a ship. In space. That's where you usually find them. I assume it's not actively attacking us, so what's the deal?"

'The vessel is a dead zone, so much so we almost ran over it before I realized it was there. It's not transmitting any identification or other signals. Its engines are dormant, no shields are present and I'm detecting no life signs on board. It's possible the crew abandoned ship at some point.'

Settling into the cockpit chair, he called up the visual images and immediately whistled. Crown-class hybrid transport, and fairly new by the look of it. A vessel like this would bring in a decent bounty, especially if what was wrong with it was easily repaired. "Abandoned ship, you say?"

'That or the crew is dead inside.'

"Jesus, Barbie. Do you have to be so morbid?"

'I haven't decided yet. I am still becoming.'

"Great...." Barbarella was a shit Artificial, cobbled together from second-hand parts and sketchy code. He'd commissioned her because he needed an Artificial onboard if he hoped to continue to compete in the newly batty world of freelance scouting. So far she couldn't do much more than add two and two on a good day, but she had personality. Sometimes too much of it.

He sipped on the beer and studied the vessel, weighing his options. He had a job delivery to make on Arcadia, a refrigerated capsule full of microbes from a comet orbiting Mu Cephei down in the cargo hold. They might be some previously undiscovered form of primordial life birthed out in the void—or they might just be ordinary microbes. Hell if he knew. The scientists at Zwicky Research were paying him to bring them in so they could find out, which was enough for him.

But he had another week to make good on the contract, and the microbes were fine in the refrigeration unit. This wouldn't take long, either; he'd stick a beacon on the ship to claim it then arrange for a tug to tow it in.

On the other hand, it could be carrying cargo worth more than the ship's salvage value. Play it right, and he could cash in on *both*.

He rubbed at his jaw. A spacewalk was a pain in the ass, but he guessed every now and then he did have to work a little bit for a payoff.

He chucked the empty beer into the recycler and stood. "All right. I'm going to go see what she's carrying."

R

"You're sure it's lost all power? If I have to go back for det charges, I'm docking your pay."

'My math skills are admittedly subpar—as you frequently point out—but I believe any fraction of zero is still zero, much like my current pay. Yes, I'm sure. The magnetic seals should release with the application of minimal force.'

Bob fired his suit thrusters and accelerated toward the ship. Its dark metal—not adiamene, unfortunately, as that would have quadrupled its salvage value—loomed dim and shadowy against the void, like a ghost ship. A pirate ghost ship? He snickered.

The hull filled his vision soon enough, and shortly thereafter he banged into the side with a rough thud. He picked his way over to the outer hatch, retrieved a chisel from his pack and stuck the flat end into the tiny seam. A little muscle applied, and the hatch popped open.

There was no hiss of escaping air, but it wasn't a surprise. Hatch chambers were only pressurized in advance of opening the inner hatch—something he now needed to do. He reached around and hefted the outer hatch closed...then stopped.

Shit. If it wouldn't seal, when he opened the inner door the outer one was going to blow open and depressurize the cabin, which was almost always a bad idea. He could glue it shut with some epoxy, but then he wouldn't be able to get back *out*.

'Simply leave through the cargo hold, dumbass.'

He sighed. "I'd yell at you for insulting me, but you're spot on. I am a dumbass. Gluing the hatch shut."

The process took less than thirty seconds. Once he finished he turned to the inner hatch and prepared himself for the influx of atmosphere before prying it open.

It slid open as soon as the chisel made contact—and nothing happened. "Hell. The cabin's already depressurized. I hope anything valuable was tied down."

His mag boots kept him grounded and upright as he stepped into the dark cabin. The light from his headlamp created an arc of brightness in front of him, but since crap was sure to be floating everywhere, he moved cautiously.

He was swatting away a broken shard of glass when something heavy bumped into him from the left. His arm swung around to shove it off as he spun toward it. The light caught dark material then—

—Bob gasped and stumbled backward, feeling for the wall. His hand found something squishy instead; in his panicking state he swore it clawed at him. He dropped to the floor and crawled for the airlock. "Fuck shit holy mother of!"

'Your suit systems indicate you are in extreme distress, as does your language. What is wrong?'

He tried to breathe normally, but acid clogged his throat. "You were fucking right, Barbie. Damn you, you thought you were being funny, but you were right. The crew didn't abandon ship. They're all dead."

'Oh, my.'

He reached the airlock chamber and huddled against the wall, trying not to hyperventilate as a third body floated limply across the shaking arc of light.

It didn't make sense. Ship systems didn't fail all at once, not catastrophically—not without an external force causing the failure. But there was no sign the ship had been attacked. The crew should have had time to get into their environment suits, or at *least* put on breather masks. But they hadn't done so. What in the hell had killed them?

"Barbie, contact SENTRI. Tell them they may have a massacre on their hands. Then figure out how to get this hatch I just glued shut open, because I'm not making it to the cargo hold."

8

PRESIDIO

Miriam Solovy hadn't asked for a three-sixty view of a sweeping array of warship assembly lines, nor of the void beyond them.

The constant activity dancing at the edges of her vision was frankly distracting. She'd considered getting opaque filters for the windows installed on several occasions. But every time she started to place the order, she'd glance outside, think about how much David would have adored the view, how Alex had exclaimed in delight on seeing it the day before she left, and put the decision off another day.

The view and the office providing it had come with the space station, which had come courtesy of Ronaldo Espahn. The business mogul had built the facility intending for it to serve as a new hub for his commercial ship production. Then, during the reign of former Prime Minister Winslow, Espahn's Prevo daughter was attacked by a mob of OTS sympathizers in Madrid. The attackers were detained at the scene but released after a determination Espahn's daughter was in violation of the anti-Prevo BANIA law.

Despite the man's wealth and influence, his daughter was sentenced to prison while she lay in a hospital bed with a crushed spine and internal injuries.

In the aftermath of engineering the toppling of Winslow and repeal of BANIA, Miriam had seen to it charges were dropped against all Prevos who hadn't committed other crimes. Freed of the specter of criminal prosecution, medical biosynth specialists were able to treat Espahn's daughter and help her recover.

The man expressed his appreciation to the Volnosti campaign and to Miriam personally by donating his nearly complete station to the GCDA the day the Accord was announced.

She'd have preferred to refuse the ostentatious gift, but in an environment where every day brought an Anaden attack closer, they didn't have *time* to build a new station from scratch. And this one came with extensive offices, labs, storage space, flexible multi-purpose rooms and reasonable lodging. Most importantly, it came with the lattice framework required for large-scale zero-g ship manufacturing.

So here she was. Commandant-General to a nascent multi-government agency born out of the necessity to prepare for a new manner of enemy.

There had never been any question who was going to lead it—she had invented it, proposed it, defined it and bullied three interstellar empires' leaders into not merely endorsing it but committing millions to it. Millions of credits and, when the time came, millions of people.

Officially, the GCDA and its constituent divisions, AEGIS, SENTRI and ASCEND, were formed to ensure humanity would be prepared to meet any future hazard which emerged from the vastness of the cosmos.

But Miriam and a few select others knew full well there was nothing in the vastness of the cosmos save the most primitive of life. Nothing but a single portal, and with it a single overwhelming threat.

In truth, the GCDA's mission was two-fold: to ensure humanity would be prepared to stand against the Anaden offensive and, should they be victorious, to ensure humanity was ready to not only exist but thrive in a reality of multiple universes teeming with aliens.

Richard Navick knocked on the open doorframe, bringing a merciful end to her reverie. She motioned him in and spun her chair away from the view to face the desk and him. "What's new in SENTRI's world today?"

SENTRI existed not so much to help defeat the Anaden threat as to try to make certain humanity's various factions didn't stumble their way into fighting each other again before the call came to fight the Anadens. Intergovernmental peace and relative harmony was a necessary prerequisite to a united galactic guardian force, after all.

He settled into one of the chairs. "A twenty million credit theft at PanPacific Tech Labs that their CEO insists is the work of Federation spies. Twelve dead Triene mercs on a derelict transport near Atlantis. The Requi government asking for help in dealing with a recent influx of spiked chimerals, and the Shi Shen government asking for us to butt out of the investigation into allegations the Shào cartel bought their last election. You?"

"A backlog of new tech proposals from ASCEND to review and probably approve. A supply chain problem for photal fiber that I suspect is Dynamis Corporation angling for more money. Status meetings with both Brigadier Jenner and Kennedy Rossi in the next two hours, after which I have to leave. I'm expected in Washington this evening for the celebration."

"I hear it's going to be quite the gala affair."

She frowned. "It feels strange, even disingenuous, to be throwing a massive, galaxy-spanning party when we know another civilization-endangering crisis looms on the horizon. Should we really be engaging in such revelry right now?"

Richard nodded fervently in response. "Yes. The people deserve it, now more than ever. And so do we. We need to remember why we fight, and why those who died did so. This next year stands a good chance of being pretty shitty, so now is an excellent time to remember why the fight is worth it."

Miriam dropped her chin in grudging acceptance. "And if we are going to go out, we should do it in style?"

"More or less. You don't have to give a speech, do you?"

"No, thank god. I suspect the planners are afraid if they give me a microphone I'll ruin the festive mood. No, I believe my role tonight is to stand still and look pretty—though truthfully, I think

I'll let Rychen handle that part, too. I'll find a quiet alcove and work."

"And how is the new Fleet Admiral enjoying your office?"

"It's his office now, and about as well as you would expect. He hates it. Or he hates being cooped up on the ground and is taking it out on the office, anyway." She sighed wistfully. "That was such a great office...but I need to be here now."

"Sure." He stood. "I'll get out of your way. I just wanted to check in. Will and I are heading out in a few hours ourselves. Graham's asked us to join him at the Cavare celebration tonight. I think he's lonely since we moved up here."

She didn't entirely suppress a laugh.

"What?"

"It's none of my business. But perhaps if Director Delavasi were a bit less...how he *is*, he might not be so lonely. The man has made his proverbial bed."

"And it's his to sleep in. Alone, apparently, except when he's paying. But he is my friend, so..." he shrugged "...off I go. Try to relax and have a little fun tonight."

"In Washington?"

"Good point. Try not to burn any bridges—we may need them."

R

Brooklyn Harper spun so fast her movement would be all but invisible to the naked eye, were she visible to the naked eye to begin with.

She shoved a blade hilt into the small of the back of the Marine she'd stood in front of barely a second earlier and deactivated the Veil wearing a devious smile. "This is what a Veil can do for you. Recognize its power, appreciate its power, use its power."

The Marine—Captain Shaviiz, if Malcolm Jenner recalled correctly—grimaced. "Yes, ma'am."

She stepped in front of the other Marine. "When I come at you, defend yourself."

He adjusted his stance in preparation. She took a step forward then vaulted upward, propelled by fresh-off-the-assembly-line booster augments. The boosters consisted of two layers of electromagnetic femtocoils wrapped in a particle layer that generated a subatomic EM field on command from the wearer's eVi—Malcolm had memorized the description the ASCEND team had provided—and were light and compact enough to be embedded inside the soles of standard work boots.

She flipped over the Marine's head and swiped the blade hilt across the base of his neck as she passed it, then landed on her feet behind him as he was whipping around in confusion.

"If I'd pulled that maneuver while the Veil was active, you never would have known what killed you—you'd just be dead. Neat trick, right? Here's the thing. We have lots of tools. We'll probably have more tomorrow. But none of them are any good to you unless you're smart about how you use them.

"Everything you've learned up until today on hand-to-hand combat doesn't go flying out the window because now you can be invisible and jump super-high. It's still about defeating or disabling your enemy—but you now have additional tools you can incorporate into your strategy to accomplish that goal. Understand?"

They both nodded solemnly; they'd been schooled, but he and Harper were the sole witnesses, by design.

Harper took a lunge step back and spread her arms. "Good. Then take me down. Either of you. Both of you at once." She tapped the thin band on her wrist, and a hybrid metallic fabric expanded out from it to encase her hand like a glove. "First one to succeed gets to learn what *this* tool does."

They would fail on the first try, but if they were good enough, one or both of them should succeed eventually. And if they were really good enough, they'd each recognize why they'd failed early on and impart those lessons to those under their command. Group classes and drills using the growing trove of advanced weapons and gear were on the schedule, but the first step was getting the squad leaders to adopt not merely those new tools but a...call it 'evolved' approach to warfare.

Which was, in the end, the point of the exercise. No one person could train all the military personnel who might be called to action in a future war which might or might not take place in a thus-far mythical universe against an enemy for which they had a single (dead) example.

But the military routinely prepared for future threats that seemed unlikely today because, somehow, they inevitably showed up tomorrow.

Malcolm was here, working for AEGIS, to help guarantee the preparation both happened and happened in the right way. But he couldn't deny that readying for a future alien threat was also...easier. Not when it came time to fight, of course, but this mission bore a moral clarity which made it easier to sleep at night. He'd grown tired of fighting his fellow man, grown tired of tossing and turning while the whispers of competing justifications plagued him in the darkness.

Better that the good guys be honorable, the bad guys evil, and a clear line drawn to keep them separate.

Technically he was a full-time but temporary consultant to AEGIS, with a title too long to say in a single breath: Director of AEGIS Marine and Ground Forces Organization, Training and Deployment. The Alliance had tacked on a promotion to justify the position, though ostensibly it was for his heroism in eliminating the Montegreu 'menace' and in protecting the Scythian governor (from the Winslow 'menace' went unspoken for obvious mannerly reasons).

More than one superior officer had protested the promotion, complaining it was far too soon and Malcolm was far too young. In the current political climate none had dared protest that he was a traitor for supporting Volnosti. The details had been relayed to him second- and third-hand, but apparently Miriam's stock response was something to the effect of 'The rest of the world is accelerating forward, and the military will not be left behind. I advise you to get onboard before you are.'

Yes, he took a degree of comfort from the fact no one at AE-GIS was apt to order him to kill-or-capture a colleague. But mostly him serving here at the Presidio felt like the next logical progression of the oath he'd taken years earlier: a pledge to protect humanity—*all* of humanity—from enemies intent on doing them harm. And he was comfortable with that step.

Besides, he'd seen enough to know the threat was real, even if it didn't feel real at the moment, here in a time of unparalleled prosperity and advancement. He'd seen the portal and the super-dreadnoughts it had spawned. He'd seen the ethereal Metigen called Mnemosyne, the alien ship with its unusual technology and the alien body with its too-humanoid appearance.

He'd seen Caleb Marano wield an alien power that made his skin crawl, then made him worry for Alex's safety through the portal.

Simply thinking about Marano made him squirm. He didn't understand why everyone—Alex, Miriam, Harper, Navick, *Mia*—not only liked but trusted the man. Former black-ops agent for a former enemy didn't put him on firm moral footing to begin with. Whatever good he did along the way, he was still a loose cannon, a killer playing by his own rules. And now he had superpowers of alien origin.

Malcolm's dislike of the man wasn't jealousy. It was judgment.

The lesson having ended and the officers having skulked off to the locker room, Harper materialized beside him.

He didn't jump in surprise, but he did flinch. He wished he could blame it on a Veil, but she hadn't been invisible. She was just that quick. "What do you think?"

He arched an eyebrow. "I think the war will be won in space and not on the ground."

"And where will you be?"

"I will be wherever the situation requires. As always."

"Hey, you're the one who convinced me these Marines needed special training. I hope you plan to use them."

He had, and they did. Alliance Marines, Federation Marines, even a few IDCC forces who had previously been one or the other were all on the roster. He'd welcome a glimpse of insight into *how* they'd be called into service, but he was certain they would. Wars were won in space these days, but they were never solely fought there.

"I'm sure when the time comes, opportunities will arise for skulls to be bashed and spines to be severed."

"Let's hope so." She balanced the blade hilt on her palm and activated it. Pale teal-hued plasma slithered and pulsed out into the air beyond her hand. A flick of her thumb, and the plasma shot away from the hilt to spear one of the practice targets twenty meters away. Another flick, and a new plasma blade appeared from the hilt. "And this is going to cut through the enemy's fancy shields and thick hides and embedded uber-cybernetics?"

"That's what the engineers tell us. The blade's so smart, it's practically an Artificial."

"Sounds like a horror vid in the making: 'The Day the Blades Woke Up.'"

He laughed. "In which case, we can only hope they're friendly. The new guns, too." The dynamic response technology driving the plasma blade was being integrated into their entire arsenal, and they weren't saving it for the Anadens, either. The Daemon at his hip wielded similar energy; it would adapt to any resistance it met and find a way through.

"Right." She motioned toward activity at the entry. "Now if you'll excuse me, my next victims are here."

"Don't go easy on them."

She smirked over her shoulder as she walked away. "Do I ever?"

"Nope." He was glad to be working with her again, and grateful she'd agreed to scale back her IDCC duties in order to oversee the close combat training and help out on the cross-agency protocols and expectations.

Confident she had things well in hand, he turned to jog down the hall to the lift wearing a smile. He had a date tonight, and twenty things to do before he could leave for it.

R

Kennedy Rossi reached the overlook before anyone else arrived. It was good she had a minute alone, for she could hardly stop herself from bouncing on the balls of her feet in unabashed glee.

From the enclosed balcony she could behold the ship factory 'floor'—which was located in space, obviously. To her eye the automated assembly lines were an exercise in, if not perfection, at least a new standard in hyper-efficiency and precision.

Sub-Artificial mechs supervised and directed armies of bots in hull assembly and component installation. The pre-hewn adiamene sheets were attached then the seams melted together to eliminate every possible weak point. Once the frame and hull were intact, mini-bots sculpted the interiors according to spec.

Each ship's particular Artificial oversaw its own installation, of course, often going so far as to direct the placement of every length of photal fiber and connection into the internal systems in preparation for the transfer of its processes into the ship.

Some of the Artificials already had military Prevo partners, and in those cases one was likely to find the officer outside the Presidio's walls, in a spacesuit, crawling around on or in their future workplace/primary residence.

A Prevo pair for every vessel frigate-class and above, sharing authority with a human captain. In an unexpected twist, the captain wasn't going to be onboard to leash the Prevo, but rather to provide wisdom gained from real-world combat experience while putting to use leadership skills in managing and motivating a crew. Both the captains and the Prevos were carefully screened before being selected, with demonstrated adaptability and cooperative tendencies being high on the list of requirements.

It was, needless to say, a new and novel system as well as an untested one, but Miriam reported that it was working in training/stress sims so far. The simulations were also being used to develop extensive rules of engagement and decision-making protocols, but in most scenarios the captain would make important strategic decisions, the Prevo tactical ones.

She smiled broadly as two cruisers departed the manufacturing rig for flight tests. "Look what we made, Vii. Aren't they fabulous?"

'The ships are stunning, and the operation constructing them is a marvel, but you give me too much credit in saying 'we.' I have simply tried to help make the implementation of your vision safer and more sound for the individuals involved, both human and synthetic.'

"You're too modest. In addition to all that, you've spurred me into some of my best innovations. Abigail would be proud, don't you think?"

'It is my fondest hope.'

Kennedy had hardly known Dr. Canivon before her death and knew her now only through the filter of Vii's eyes. But she'd learned much about the woman in recent weeks—not to mention a lot about Vii, a fair amount about Valkyrie, and a great deal about Artificials as a species.

Kennedy walked into the Connova Interstellar offices and straight into a large man in a work uniform.

She took a lurching step back and frowned up at the man. "Can I help you?"

"Pardon me, ma'am. Are you Ms. Rossi?"

"Yes..." she peered over his shoulder into the office suspiciously "...but I didn't have anything scheduled to be delivered today."

"Someone from the company did, ma'am. If you'll verify delivery, we'll be out of your way."

'We'? Now she overtly checked around his bulky form and saw another, skinnier man exiting the storage room.

Had Noah ordered some new equipment to surprise her with? She rolled her eyes and signed off on the delivery, watched the men depart, then went to the cabinet where the server hardware...used to be. The contents had now been replaced by a larger and far more advanced quantum box.

She tilted her head to inspect it more closely. It had all the earmarks of state of the art tech—

'You will find the rest of my hardware set up in the utility storage room. Please feel free to rearrange it as you find necessary.'

Kennedy jumped half a meter in the air and stumbled backward until she bumped against the edge of her desk. The voice was definably synthetic but with impressively natural intonation. In fact, it sounded familiar somehow. "Um...hi? Who are you and why are you in my office?"

'My name is 'Vii.' Technically this is a nickname derived from 'Valkyrie Mark II,' but to myself I have always been Vii. I belonged to Dr. Abigail Canivon until her death, and nominally to the Druyan Institute.

'I understand you intend to build innovative warships for Commandant-General Solovy's AEGIS fleet—ships featuring integrated Artificials. As a free solitary Artificial under HASRA, H+ and IDCC laws, I wish to offer my services to you in this endeavor.'

Kennedy sank into her desk chair and flopped her arms down on the armrests. HASRA, the Human and Synthetic Rights Act, was the Earth Alliance legislation that had been swiftly drafted and passed into law atop the smoldering ashes of BANIA. "In what way do you think you can help me?"

'Access to Artificial-level processes and algorithms will both speed and improve your work in the areas of optimizing design schematics, power efficiency and component performance. However, my primary interest is somewhat personal in nature.

'Before Abigail was murdered, she and I were working on ways to embody moral constructs and paradigms in quantum algorithms. We wanted to create Artificials who were, while not necessarily more human, certainly more sapient, whole beings. Abigail is gone, but her work is more important than ever now. Humanity has extended a hand to us, expressing trust in Artificials to act in the best interest of human life, and all life. We must be worthy of this trust.'

"You want to make the Artificials of the AEGIS fleet more...wise?"

'More wise, more moral, more empathetic. As I said, more whole. Nowhere will an Artificial's judgment be so crucial as on a military vessel, with hundreds or thousands of crew members under its care, civilians at its back and an enemy in its targets. These situations are what Abigail's work was designed for, and I believe with your help I can bring it to fruition.'

Kennedy worried at her lower lip. There was no question that the dirty details of operational controls, overrides and accountability in the emerging captain-Prevo triumvirate setup were proving to be...messy. She wasn't military, so the ultimate decisions of which directions to take were mostly Miriam's to make, but she did need to know the answers in order to design around them.

If she could provide greater assurances as to safety—if Vii could convince Thomas who could convince Miriam of the increased safety—it would make everything so much easier. And less terrifying for all involved.

She steepled her hands and kicked the chair around absently. "So to make this happen, you faked your own Connova Interstellar credentials and arranged for yourself and all your hardware to be transported from Sagan to Romane, then had yourself installed and wired into my office?"

'The Metigen known as Mnemosyne proclaimed we were on a tight timetable. It seemed the most efficient tack.'

Kennedy laughed. Fully actualized, self-aware and sapient or not, Vii was definitely an Artificial. She was still laughing when Noah walked in.

He stopped a few steps into the room and screwed his face up as he pointed to the cabinet. "What's that?"

"Our new Artificial employee."

"You commissioned an Artificial and didn't tell me?"

"It commissioned and hired itself."

He stared at her for a second, then at the cabinet, then shrugged. "Okay. Works for me."

Everything moved faster once Artificials, Prevos and Mélanges—humans sporting a less-than-Prevo integration with an Artificial—were set loose upon the world. Dizzyingly fast, so much so it felt like they had blinked and the world had changed.

And now, barely two months after the Anaden Inquisitor had tried to kill Alex and Caleb, here was a fleet which dwarfed in size and technology the one Kennedy had helped build for Miriam and Volnosti just…yesterday.

Noah grabbed her from behind, wrapping his arms around her waist and squeezing tight. "Sorry I'm late. I had to school an Atmospheric Solutions rep about what the 'standardized' in 'standardized connectors' meant."

"It's fine. Miriam isn't here yet either. I was merely admiring the view."

"And it is so extremely view-worthy. So what's our purpose here today?"

She twisted around to face him. "Your favorite—compliance testing review."

"Ugh. Kill me now."

"That would be quite the waste, now, wouldn't it?"

They both turned to find Miriam standing in the door. She waved them toward her. "I suggested we meet here because I suspected you'd enjoy a few minutes with your ships, but we should go to a proper meeting room if we expect to get anything accomplished."

AMARANTHE

9

ANTLIA DWARF GALAXY

Casmir elasson-Machim, Navarchos of LGG Region II, reviewed the readiness status of the II-13C Regiment until he satisfied himself everything was in order. From the bridge of the Imperium command ship he sent a directed order into the integral. "All forces, commence Modified Eradication Operation."

Planet AD-4508b orbited a backwater star in a backwater galaxy, yet some called it a hidden gem. Lush foliage and towering tree canopies draped the equatorial region of its fertile surface. But while it looked inviting from afar, he couldn't recommend any safari vacations to travelers—at least not until his mission was complete.

The dominant species of AD-4508b was a giant arachnid they'd labeled 'Kich,' a revolting mix of spider and scorpion. When full-grown they measured nearly five meters long and four meters tall at the torso.

Despite being surrounded by copious plant life, the Kich were carnivores. Their primary food source was the 'Ierak,' pterodactyls which roamed the skies at night. During the daylight hours the Kich scaled the tall trees and spun webs made of a crystalline substance closer to glass than silk between the tree limbs. When darkness descended, they retreated to the surface and lurked in the groundcover, waiting.

The Ierak used a non-visual-wavelength form of sight, one which failed to detect the diaphanous webs, and any Ierak to encounter a web was instantly sliced into pieces—pieces which fell to the ground to be consumed by the Kich.

Evolve or die, and evolution wasn't working fast enough for the Ierak.

Under normal circumstances, when a planet displaying characteristics similar to AD-4508b was discovered, a Theriz Cultivation Unit was sent in directly without the need for interim operations. The Unit would employ its massive machines to churn the surface into raw resources, plant and animal alike, then ferry the yield off for processing and refinement.

However, it seemed the webs the Kich spun were both functionally and visually unique—or so he'd been informed.

Aesthetics were not his role; they looked like ordinary webs to Casmir. But on seeing images of the Kich's deadly creations, the Idoni Primor had declared (with appropriate dramatic flair, he assumed) she must have several sets for her various palaces.

Of course, the webs were intricately attached to the treetops, so they needed to be removed as well in order to keep the webs intact. The delicate work of extracting a bunch of trees and webs could not be accomplished while fighting off a horde of giant arachnids in the daytime and swarms of flying dinosaurs in the night.

So the decision was made to conduct a limited Eradication of the Kich first, rather than as an inevitable byproduct of Cultivation. And because this was all for a Primor, Casmir had been sent in to supervise the operation.

It should have been beneath his rank, the duty of one of countless ela-Machim overseeing minor ship groupings. But all gave way before a Primor's wishes, so here he was.

He took small comfort from the fact clearing a single jungle would suffice to acquire the specimens required, after which the Theriz Unit could sweep in to make mincemeat of the surface.

The attack transports and CAS fighters of the LGG II-13C Regiment penetrated the atmosphere, and Casmir focused on his integral connection to the troops to monitor the operation.

The darkness is omnipresent. No moon lights the night.

Two transport vessels land in open areas on opposite ends of the targeted region. Troops move out in formation as customized vision enhancements transform night to day for them. Hovertanks take the lead. Their wide-field weapons should do the bulk of the work, leaving the troops the relatively easy job of mopping up the occasional straggler. But Machim never employ half-measures, and as always the force deployed is overwhelming both in numbers and firepower.

The air is sweltering, thick with moisture and a pungent odor. Alien planets often smell foul, and Casmir orders the activation of suit olfactory filters for all troops. There's no breeze at ground level; chirps and rhythmic hums signal the presence of native creatures too small to attract the Kich's wrath.

Plasma bombs intended to ignite the leafy undergrowth but not the hardier tree trunks drop from the CAS fighters, bringing a sea of hellfire to the landscape.

The Kich flee their cover, and the hovertanks open fire.

The front line of the creatures falls under the weight of the barrage, but a second wave surges up and over the bodies to swarm the hovertanks. Zeus, the monsters are fast! The hovertanks fire continuously, but additional Kich use the new front line as cover, then leap into the air the twenty meters required and attach themselves to the large vehicles. Webs spew forth in furious movements of thick and shockingly agile limbs to surround the frames and clog the engine ports.

The hovertanks begin to crash to the ground.

Undeterred, the ground troops open fire on the Kich using smaller, precision versions of the wide-field weapons. More Kich fall, and the ground runs thick in viscous, azure blood as the troops' weapons rip apart the attackers. The battle begins to turn in the Regiment's favor.

Then a third wave of Kich appears out of the shadows of the jungle. Without the hovertanks to keep them at bay and thin the herd, they plow into the troops in force.

Still, the thought the Regiment might fail in its mission does not enter Casmir's mind. These are Machim soldiers, genetically bred for the rigors of combat. Their armor is impenetrable to most weapons, and the bodies beneath the armor are hardened to absorb abuse that would quickly kill lesser men.

From the point of view of those in the field, the Kich's size is startling. The creatures loom large over them, rearing up to reveal hairy, barreled torsos and sturdy, sharp pincers. But unarmored organic skin can't withstand the superheated plasma bursts of Machim weapons, no matter how tough it is.

No one here is a coward; no one runs or panics in the face of the rampaging arachnids. Instead the troops simply fire upward into the exposed torsos while adroitly maneuvering around to avoid the stabbing pincers.

But the battlefield is both crowded and increasingly slick with corpses, limbs and the associated fluids, and the room in which to maneuver rapidly diminishes.

The vigorous swipe of an outstretched limb knocks a soldier to the ground. He swings his weapon up and slices open the exposed belly of the offending Kich—his vision becomes obscured.

Casmir switches his focus to a different soldier in the vicinity, temporarily overriding the man's freedom of action to locate the one in peril. Behind the prone form, a Kich shoots glass-silk from its spinnerets to fashion a web around the head and body of the fallen man. Casmir allows the approaching soldier to shoot and the spinner is felled, but the man on the ground struggles and fails to break through the web.

It's happening elsewhere. Casmir borrows the eyes of a pilot of one of the few remaining airborne hovertanks, and from above it soon becomes obvious the Kich are displaying an unexpected ability to work together in a tactical manner. In some instances they deliberately sacrifice themselves so others can gain a better vantage to disable their adversaries.

There are so many. Far more than surveillance indicated. Do only a portion climb the trees on any given day? As ectotherms, their body temperatures are too close to the ambient air temperature to allow for reliable thermal detection, so if many remain below it would not have been apparent to the advance surveillance teams.

The troops carry emergency oxygen supplies inside their suits. If the webbing has not penetrated the outer layers of their armor, they can survive for a time. Perhaps twenty minutes.

But Casmir has no weapon on hand that will break the tough, re-silient webbing en masse without liquefying the troops' armor or pulverizing the bodies it protects.

There are too many.

Dismay creeps into his chest as the battlefield slowly, inexorably turns to glass.

Casmir withdrew as much as possible into his own mind, though the slaughter continued to whisper and scream in the background of his consciousness. He ordered a retreat for those who remained alive, but he'd just lost twelve thousand soldiers.

They could and would be replaced—in many cases with them-selves—but he wasn't going to waste resources throwing them at the enemy again and again. An alternate strategy was required.

Deploying more powerful weapons from a higher altitude risked destroying the trees holding the webs aloft. This outcome did not fulfill his orders and thus was unacceptable.

But he did have at his disposal creatures that were stronger and more savage than the Kich.

10

SIYANE

You let him go.

Alex rolled her eyes in annoyance and motioned for Caleb to answer Mesme.

Knowing she must be mentally drained after hours of maintaining peak geniality for the benefit of Eren, he obliged her. "Yes. There's an old human saying: you catch more flies with honey than with vinegar. Any help he might give us if forced into it would be suspect and unreliable. This way, if he helps us it will be because he wants to do it—or possibly because he's intrigued by the challenge—not because he has no choice."

I comprehend the meaning of the idiom. But you do recognize the effort it took to arrange the meeting in the first place, yes? You do recognize it may be impossible to locate and persuade another ally who can enable you to acquire what you have explicitly stated your forces will need in order to match the Machim fleets on the field of battle, do you not?

Caleb didn't search around for the profile of lights; there were times when it was easier to treat Mesme like a disembodied voice. "Of course we recognize it. Thank you for your hard work in both finding a candidate and putting us in a position to reach out to him. We still think this opportunity will pan out and Eren will help us. You've been observing us for aeons. You know sometimes these things take time."

Despite the unsettling way the anarch had regarded Caleb initially—and for too long—he did think in the end they'd won Eren over, at least enough to bring him back for another round of negotiations. The man had left as curious about their origin and motives as they were about his world. He would come back, and hopefully next time not expend quite so much energy watching Caleb as if he were some kind of reviled predator expected to pounce and devour his prey the next instant.

Mesme's tone lost a measure of its fervor. *Undeniably. Yet time is one resource we no longer possess in any abundance.*

Eager to shake off the disquiet his thoughts had conjured, Caleb went over to where Alex stood and wrapped his arms around her from behind. "We have a little time. Time enough, I think. While we wait to hear from Eren, we can continue pursuing other avenues. I'm interested in doing reconnaissance on several of the Machim ship production facilities. Alex, didn't you want to try to find out more about how the intergalactic wormhole gateways function?"

The gateway structures dwarfed even the mammoth Katasketousya portals. Three imposing rings generated a stable wormhole some six kilometers in diameter, enabling almost instantaneous travel across and between galaxies. Unsurprisingly, the technology had intrigued her since their first traversal of one of the gateways.

She'd relaxed into him, but her mind seemed elsewhere, and it took her a few seconds to respond. "Yeah...Mesme, what do you know about the Reor slabs?"

Silence lingered.

"Mesme?"

Why do you ask? Data storage is not interesting.

Caleb maneuvered them to face Mesme, as there were also times when honing in on a mark helped to ferret out artifice. "Actually, sometimes data storage is very interesting—for instance, when it's data that's important to your enemy. But I don't think that's what she means."

She squeezed his hands in affirmation. "True, and true. Valkyrie and I noticed a couple of unusual mathematical properties in the structure of a slab Eren had, and when I held it, we sensed...an aspect I can't put a name to. At a minimum, Reor is a fascinating and potentially useful material I want to understand better. But maybe there's also something more to it?"

Again, silence.

She peered over her shoulder and gave Caleb a *look*, then disentangled from his arms to wander purposefully through the cabin. "Mesme, is there something about the Reor slabs you'd like to share with us?"

Alexis Solovy, your cleverness and acute persistence is at times as irksome as it is useful. Very well. Travel to the coordinates I am providing to Valkyrie. The answers to your questions are better shown than described.

ℛ

It was going to take hours to reach the mysterious coordinates Mesme had given them, which were located deep in dead space on the far outer rim of the Tyche galaxy. The void under any definition.

By now the Kat's—like Alex, he'd quickly adopted the shorthand with some relief—cagey, enigmatic behavior had become all too commonplace, and Caleb had resigned himself to tolerating it most of the time. When they arrived at wherever they were headed, Mesme would reveal its hidden secrets, since it must, but it wouldn't do so a moment sooner. No reason to get worked up about it until then.

A multitude of crises were elbowing for position in the line of 'things to get worked up about,' whether they resided in the space outside the ship, at home in Aurora, or coursing through his own bloodstream. He was endeavoring to choose his battles wisely, and he wasn't choosing this one.

Instead Caleb leaned against the wall and contemplated Alex.

She stood at the data table studying the images of the Reor slab Valkyrie had captured through her ocular implant. He wouldn't go so far as to call her 'worked up' either—she wasn't acting anxious or exasperated—but this particular puzzle had definitely caught her fancy.

It warmed his heart to see. The prodigious wonders and mysteries Amaranthe held was turning out to be just what she needed to smooth out the lingering rough edges of her recovery. Using her mind and imagination to uncover its secrets was so much better than simply flying amongst them—a heady experience inhabiting the ship had given her, but one which didn't come from within and so was ultimately an empty one.

He believed this, not because it was true—though it felt true—but because she believed it. She was becoming far more self-aware these days, and his observation wasn't news to either of them. He still took comfort in seeing it reaffirmed by her actions and choices, in witnessing its truth with his own eyes.

Her addiction wasn't something which could be declared 'cured,' packed up in a box and stored away. It would always be with her, and thus with them. But the incredible resilience she'd displayed since severing her connection to the ship...well, if circumstances meant this late, waning phase of recovery was slightly easier than it might have been, dammit, she deserved the break.

It wasn't all she deserved.

His arms were draped loosely at his waist, his left shoulder resting on the wall. He kept the casual pose while he lifted his right hand a few centimeters and wriggled his fingers in a manner that was quickly becoming second nature.

The hem of her tank drifted up to the middle of her back.

"That tickles...." Her gazed darted to him as she realized what he was doing. The corners of her mouth curled up. "Are you bored?"

"Not at all." Provided line-of-sight to the front of her tank when she shifted toward him, he made sure it slid upward to join the rest of the material and tease her ribcage. He added the pressure of air beneath her forearms—only a little, enough to make his request clear but not so much as to force her arms upward. Let her acquiesce to the request if she was so inclined.

It seemed she was. What had been a mild stirring flared into wanton need when she raised her arms to allow him to slide her tank up and over her head from across the room. He paid no more attention to the tank, and it dropped unceremoniously to the floor beside her.

A pleased sigh escaped his lips.

"You like the view?"

He nodded slowly, unashamedly transfixed. "I really, really do."

She shifted around farther to lean back on the table and lick her lips, sending a rush of heat through his body to flush his skin. "Anything else interesting you can do with this power of yours?"

A flick of his wrist and the top of her shorts nudged down to cling to her hipbones.

Her jaw dropped in mock indignation, and her hands moved to hold them in place. "I'm sorry, are you asking for these shorts to come off?"

"I really, really am."

"Come take them off yourself, then." In a flash she had bolted for the staircase and fled downstairs.

He laughed aloud, tugged his shirt off and tossed it onto the couch, and chased after her.

11

URSA MAJOR I ARX

Eren rented a room at a cheap hostel in the bowels of the Ursa Major I Arx for the night. He needed to hole up somewhere for a few hours. Clear his head. Figure out what had just happened and what he ought to do about it.

He collapsed on the narrow bed and threw an arm over his eyes. He should already be on the way to Nephelai to meet Cosime and pick up the explosives, then he should get to lifting a ship from the Sector 23 Terminal Hub and see to taking out the Exobiology Research Lab. He had all the information he needed to complete the mission, and with the explosives and a pilfered ship he'd have all the tools.

Whatever this other madness was or was not, it could wait. It *should* wait.

After a couple of seconds he moved around to try to find a more comfortable position...until he accepted the futility of the endeavor on account of the bed being as cheap as the room and settled for winding his hands behind his head.

He was considering tossing the angst and instead closing his eyes for a nap when a chill passed over his skin and the dim light in the room faded to gloom.

"You need to assist them."

He sat up and peered into the darkness, searching for the offending umbra. "Hello, Miaon. Assist who?"

A darker than black shape by the door detached itself from the wall to slink across the room; the rented unit was tiny, so it didn't have far to travel. "The individuals you were recently in the company of."

Eren fumbled for the bedside light panel. "How do you know who I was with? You weren't on the ship. I would have noticed. It would have been...darker."

The Yinhe didn't lurk in the shadows—they *were* the shadows. Ghostly, solitary and secretive, they were among the stranger sentient creatures in Amaranthe. Their population was small, and no one ever saw more than one at the same time; this had led some to speculate there was in actuality only a single Yinhe. He doubted this was the case, but he had to concede it was possible; if there was only one Yinhe, Miaon was it.

Rumor had it the Directorate spent years trying to Eradicate the species, only to fail miserably when they were unable to find or keep a hold of the shadows. Target one with a weapon—any weapon—and it promptly evaporated, reappearing halfway across a galaxy. If the Yinhe had a homeworld it had never been located to be destroyed.

Eventually, the Directorate had admitted they were few in number and didn't seem to be rising up to pose a threat to its power. It declared the Yinhe an Accepted Species and proceeded to ignore them. The Directorate denied this version of events in the strongest terms, of course, but it had all the hallmarks of truth.

Despite its insubstantiality, Miaon engineered sound wave vibrations in the air to craft a wispy, tremulous voice. "No, I was not on the *Siyane*—but the fact I know its moniker should appease your doubts as to my veracity. Now I am here, and I am telling you that you need to assist Mnemosyne and its companions."

Eren groaned and collapsed back on the bed. "You're the mutual acquaintance. You're the one who told the Kat where I'd be. Dammit, Miaon, how could you spy on the anarchs for those cowards? Now I have to report you."

"I am not a spy. I am a tenuous thread who hopes to one day grow into a bridge. The anarchs presume the Katasketousya to be sycophants to the Directorate. The Katasketousya presume the anarchs to be bloodthirsty terrorists. You each seek and strive toward the same goal, yet you cannot even acknowledge one another, much less work together in furtherance of this mutual goal."

Eren opened his mouth, scathing retort at the ready. But interacting with the Kat earlier had called into question many of his beliefs and assumptions about the ethereal beings. It was one of the puzzles he'd planned to spend the next several hours contemplating.

He settled for keeping the pressure on Miaon. "Then why not simply go to Xanne or one of the other anarch supervisors and tell them what the Kats are allegedly doing?"

"They would no more believe me than the Katasketousya would believe me if I proclaimed to them the anarchs were not merely terrorists and in fact wanted nothing so much as a free peace. Trust comes from actions, not words."

"Not 'merely' terrorists?"

"You alone are responsible for a striking volume of destruction, Eren asi-Idoni, as well as more than a few lives lost. And you are not the only one."

Eren swung his legs off the bed and grabbed his jacket from the floor where he'd discarded it; the longer the Yinhe stayed, the colder the room became. "Fine, I don't deny it. But...dammit, Miaon! I still have to report this. You know how desperately we rely on secrecy for our survival. We can't have a spy running—or ghosting—around telling others about our plans and missions, even a well-meaning one."

"Do as you must. It will not matter soon in any event."

"What does that mean?" A question he was asking too often lately.

"I impart to you again: you need to assist them. If you do not, they and their allies will fail in their endeavor. They will fall, and with them so too will the anarchs fall."

Now he stood. For all the Yinhe's creepiness, he'd always believed Miaon to be a moral creature, by some measure or another. But now he wasn't so certain. "Is that a threat?"

"It is a truth, one beyond my ability to alter. Nothing greater and nothing lesser. The Katasketousya have a word for this moment: 'kairos.' We teeter on the cusp, but the cusp of *what* remains to be seen."

"Could you be any more evasive?"

"Help them, Eren, and watch the universe turn your way. *Nos libertatem somnia.*"

He knew when Miaon had departed from the abrupt brightness flooding the room and the relative warmth returning to his skin. With a sigh he sank onto the bed again and stared at the ceiling.

He'd just gotten guilt-tripped by a bloody shadow. At this rate there was probably an Efkam out in the hall waiting to totter after him warbling 'Shame on you!' when he tried to leave.

Did none of them realize what these people were asking of him?

"Well, Eren, you did want a proper rebellion, one you could die for in a flamboyant blaze of glory. Repeatedly and often. Ever think maybe you ought to be more careful what you wish for?"

12

ONEIROI NEBULA

Tyche Galaxy
LGG Region IV

'Exiting superluminal in ten seconds.'

Alex looked up from the couch in surprise. She was lying on her stomach studying some details of the intergalactic population and commercial concentration map. While she could rely on Valkyrie to store and retrieve the infinite number of tidbits of Amaranthe trivia, she did actually need to know the framework and major players in the Anaden empire, not to mention where things were situated.

She checked their location. "We're still almost a hundred parsecs from the coordinates Mesme provided. Is something wrong?"

'Not as such. You should both come see.'

Curiosity piqued, she climbed off the couch and met Caleb in the cockpit as the superluminal bubble dissipated.

An emission nebula stretched across the horizon of space. They were already surrounded by the first wispy coils of dust and gas, but ahead ivy green and amber nebular clouds thickened until they created the impression of a solid wall.

"How large is it, Valkyrie?"

'It stretches for one hundred eighty-one parsecs in height and a diameter of two hundred sixty-eight parsecs on this side. I cannot yet say how deep it extends.'

"That's...big."

Caleb frowned as they traveled through progressively more concentrated clouds. "It reminds me of Metis."

She rolled her eyes. "When the Kats want to hide something...."

"They encase it in an ominous, spooky nebula."

The scene soon escalated into eerie territory. Visual sight was reduced to kilometers as they floated through a seemingly endless swath of dense ionized gases. Broad spectrum sensors fared little better, returning solely the composition of the thick nebular clouds.

'Interesting.'

"Oh, boy." Caleb chuckled. "What's interesting, Valkyrie?"

'I have not detected any evidence of recent star formation, as one would expect if this were an H II region nebula. The negative implies it is instead a planetary nebula. If so, assuming our coordinates approximate the core of the nebula, we ought to be close enough to detect the ASG star that created it.'

"And?"

'There is a star ahead, but it has long since passed into the white dwarf stage.'

Now Alex frowned. "But if it's been a white dwarf for a while—hell, if it's a white dwarf at all—the nebula shouldn't be this bright. In fact, it should be fading from sight."

'Yes.'

"You think the Kats are artificially maintaining the ultraviolet radiation necessary to ionize the gases, which they need to obscure what's inside."

'It would be well within their capabilities.'

Shafts of luminous amber-tinged emerald light began to peek through the gloom ahead like rays of sunlight breaching thunderclouds. "Look at that."

Caleb hugged her from behind. "For the record, if there's a portal in here...ah, who am I kidding? If there's a portal in here, we go through it."

She shrugged in his arms. "It's what we do."

Further banter was cut short as the nebula clouds at last thinned, though they didn't disappear entirely. Space outside the viewport took on a ghostly, haunting aura as the increasing light dispersed through the dust and gases.

A dark, decidedly non-nebular shape broke through the clouds to loom due ahead of them. "Full stop!"

They came to a halt less than fifty meters above the etched corner of an immense monolith of Reor.

"Oh. My."

"You always did have a talent for understatement, baby."

She grinned, but no way was she diverting her attention from the sight outside the viewport.

Beyond the one they hovered above, slab after slab after slab of Reor orbited a distant, cold white dwarf barely radiating faint white-blue light. The cumulative area of the slabs added together would easily constitute a large moon if not a small planet.

Each slab was a separate object, but they were arranged in ordered rows and columns, and precisely spaced pillars of energy pulsed between them like conductive traces on a circuit board. The collective glow of the pillars and the filaments within the slabs was enough to wash the cabin in prismatic color.

If Valkyrie will land the Siyane *on the surface of one of the structures—it does not matter which one—and the two of you will come outside, I will explain.*

For once, Mesme's 'voice' didn't herald the arrival of a bossy swirl of lights, and the Kat remained elsewhere. Presumably nearby, but elsewhere.

"What is this, Mesme? Why are you hiding them?"

Please, do as I've requested.

It wasn't as if she didn't want to go outside, so instead of arguing she went to get her gear, grabbing Caleb's hand as she passed him to drag him along with her. "Guesses?"

His gaze flitted up to her without a response before returning to checking over the environment suits.

"You do have a guess. And you're not going to tell me."

He shrugged. "I might be wrong."

"When have you ever been wrong?"

"Well, there was the time on...no, I was at least eighty percent right that time. Oh, but...no. Anyway, I'm sure there was a time."

"Uh-huh." She tossed him a mock glare but elected not to push it. They'd both know the answer soon enough. And then he could gloat in that delightfully understated way he had, as she was also fairly sure he would end up being right.

The hull rumbled as Valkyrie alighted the ship onto one of the Reor slabs. "Are we set, Valkyrie?"

'All systems are nominal and contact is confirmed. I have extended the energy shielding to its maximum distance to provide you additional radiation protection, so you may depart whenever you're ready.'

She checked Caleb over then he did the same for her, as always. She bounced on the balls of her feet in only slightly exaggerated excitement. "Let's do this."

"After you."

Stepping onto the surface should have reminded her of doing the same on Rudan. Frozen mineral beneath her feet, odd light all around, hazy darkness surrounding it. But while the atmosphere was among the most unusual and haunting she'd ever encountered, it somehow felt welcoming rather than ominous.

The filaments ran in perfect straight lines at perfect ninety degree angles to one another, endlessly deep into the mineral of the slab. They were also active, streaming ever-shifting colors to the horizon. Eren had said they only changed color when they were encoding information, but she was beginning to wonder how much he truly knew about the substance. Standing here now, it occurred to her to wonder how much *anyone* truly knew about it.

She took a step forward. The material wasn't slick, but she still tread cautiously as the mag boots were the only thing keeping her from floating away. As her left boot alit on the surface, she noticed a hum penetrate the protective gear. "Caleb, can you feel that?"

He shook his head.

She crouched down and placed her glove on the surface; the hum immediately intensified. It was similar to the sensation she'd experienced when she held Eren's Reor slab, but what was creating it?

No answers offered themselves, so she stood once more. "Mesme, we're here. It's time for you to pull back the curtain."

White-blue lights gained strength in the distance, far across the slab. What had it been doing way over there?

Mesme gathered into a semblance of a cohesive form as it approached, though it remained spread out across a far larger area than usual. *Alexis, you feel a presence when you touch the Reor, yes?*

"A presence? I'd characterize it more as a...power. An energy."

This suffices. Caleb, you do not?

"No."

Gather a small measure of diati *and allow it to make contact with the surface.*

He didn't waste any time in doing so; she suspected he was as curious as she. The area outside his glove began to sparkle in crimson as he crouched down and allowed his hand to hover a few centimeters above the surface.

Abruptly he jerked. "Hey!" His hand withdrew briefly, but he quickly pressed it down again. The *diati* brightened and sparked.

After a bit he looked up at her, wearing a smile behind the faceplate. "It's not fighting—neither of them are."

They recognize one another.

She whipped around to Mesme, knowing the answer before the words formed on her lips. "The Reor is conscious. It's alive."

As you say.

Valkyrie?

This explanation is a logical one. I cannot construct meaningful communication out of what we've experienced, but I do feel like I can sense intelligence in it.

Caleb stood and allowed the *diati* to dissipate. "You said 'they recognize one another.' You're implying the *diati* is as alive as the Reor, however alive that is."

I have previously professed my belief this is the case.

"Right. So what does this mean for the Reor, and for Amaranthe? You're hiding these slabs of Reor, much the same way you do when you've rescued species who are to be Eradicated. Because...the Directorate doesn't know it's a living entity, does it?"

As is your habit, Caleb, you are correct.

She chuckled at the notion that Mesme, too, had resigned itself to that reality.

The Directorate would never allow a sentient life form to be privy to the myriad of secrets the Reor carry across the universe. It discovered the Reor's home planet, studied the substance long enough to learn its computational and informational value, and harvested it until it was depleted. Then it grew more Reor, and more, and more, never understanding the nature of the material it produces and utilizes every day.

Alex dropped to her knees and began running a hand over the surface with newfound respect. "Why didn't the Reor...I don't know, protect itself? Resist in some way?"

The Reor intelligence is perhaps the most alien, the most unfathomable we have ever encountered. It does not perceive the individual actors in the universe the way you or even I do. By and large, it is content to experience stimulus in the form of the coursing of information through its pathways.

"Were the Ruda your attempt to recreate this type of life form, or something akin to it?"

I will not deny we took inspiration from the Reor when setting the conditions for life in the Ruda Enisle. We hoped to breed a synthetic species which functioned closer to our own existence, so we could understand one another. And in this respect, we succeeded.

"But?"

But the Ruda thus far lack the pandimensional characteristics the Reor display. They are sentient inorganic life, which is a rare enough occurrence, but they are not....

"Extraordinary."

Mesme didn't respond, but it didn't really need to. Alex could sense some indefinable complexity about this life form that far exceeded the rigid, passionless dialectics of the Ruda. "Why isn't this collection of slabs located in a portal space? You're hiding it, yes, but this can't be as safe as the Mosaic."

We considered and deliberated on it, though we could not ask the Reor its wishes. But the Reor are intricately connected to Amaranthe in ways that prove difficult to explain. As well, in the Mosaic they would have no stimuli and thus no meaningful existence.

"And these pieces? They're receiving stimuli?"

They store copies of some of our data for us.

"So you protect a small..." no word choice felt sufficiently accurate "...sample of Reor, since should the Directorate ever learn the truth, it will try to destroy every slab in existence."

Yes.

Caleb chuckled. "There's an enisle with Reor in it, isn't there?"

Of course.

She shot a glare in Mesme's general direction, but Caleb took several steps toward the fringes of its presence. "If you could find a way to communicate meaningfully with the Reor, they could be a powerful ally."

A powerful weapon, you mean.

"All allies are potential weapons, but not all weapons are allies. I meant ally."

Then talk to it. Either of you—you each possess unique capabilities which make this a conceivable possibility.

Alex stared suspiciously at Mesme. "If it speaks at all—if it has thoughts—they're expressed in an extradimensional quantum manner. That's one of your specialties. Why can't you talk to it?"

A reasonable question for which I have no acceptable answer. We study its signals and find only the data it holds. You are here. Make the effort.

Caleb shook his head. "I can't talk to the *diati* yet. I doubt I can talk to a pandimensional mineral."

Not pandimensional—merely extradimensional.

The faceplate did nothing to obscure the acerbic smirk Caleb directed at Mesme.

Alex, however, was already settling more fully to the surface and crossing her legs. *Let's give this a shot, Valkyrie.*

How do you propose we proceed?

No idea.

She placed her palm flat on the material and activated the cybernetic pathways she would use if she were interacting with a screen or control panel. Her gloves were designed to conduct the signals received, albeit more weakly, so it might work.

The hum grew in strength, and she sensed a pressure on her palm as the mineral began shifting beneath it. She gasped but didn't move, allowing her hand to be lifted as the surface raised itself.

Three tiers formed, creating a pyramid of sorts half a meter in height, before the process stopped. She waited, but nothing else happened. "I wish I could touch it with my bare hands. But there's no atmosphere here, so even if my suit sealed at the wrist, my hand would freeze in seconds."

"Wait—I think I can do something about this." Caleb knelt beside her. He stretched a hand out over hers and began manipulating his fingers in a purposeful pattern until the space around her hand and the new pillar glowed in a thick cluster crimson lights. His brow knotted in concentration. "Okay. I think you can take your glove off now—but keep your hand inside the halo."

She carefully unlatched the glove and slid it off. The air was cool, but not cold. It felt...normal. "Damn."

Caleb huffed a breath but kept his attention on the halo. "You're telling me."

She put her palm back atop the pillar—and almost yanked it away, the vibration oscillated so forcefully against her skin. A second later the mineral began to soften, becoming pliable. Her fingertips sank into it, only a centimeter or so. The filaments in the material made contact with the conduit fibers in her fingertips, and the jolt made her gasp.

"Are you okay?"

She nodded. *Valkyrie?*

It is speaking to us, I know it. But I cannot decipher the language. Not yet.

It's fine. Listen and record.

The sequence lasted almost twenty seconds before the connections broke and the mineral hardened back into its original shape. She sighed in disappointment and reattached her glove.

She was about to stand when the top of the pillar was pushed upward by a new layer underneath it, then detached from the pillar as if it had been sliced off with a knife. She picked it up and studied it; it resembled the Reor slab she'd held before, including identical proportions.

She turned to Caleb, and Mesme lurking behind him. "We couldn't decipher what it was saying, if it was saying anything at all. But there was activity of some kind. We'll study it." She held up the piece. "And now I have one to play with."

Her gaze ran across the surface of the slab they stood on to the sea of Reor and their little star beyond. The filaments buried in the mineral pulsed through the color spectrum in time with the streams of energy flowing between them, vibrant and *alive.*

As she fixated on the streams they seemed to shift until they pulsed toward her, no matter which direction she faced. Enthralled, she began walking toward one of the vertical streams. She was vaguely cognizant of Caleb and Mesme trailing her, but they didn't question her purpose.

In the silence she listened to the energy flowing below her and, increasingly, ahead of her. She did not understand the words, but it sang to her nonetheless.

She neared the outer edge of the energy beam—it was quite wide up close, at least twenty meters in diameter—and started to reach up. Her hand paused mid-air.

Caleb appeared at her side, gave her a small smile and conjured a new sphere of *diati* to surround her hand. "I'd tell you to be careful, but we wouldn't be here if you'd ever taken that advice. No reason to start now, right?"

She laughed faintly and removed her glove once again, extending her hand until her fingertips touched the beam—

—a yellow star, a frozen planet—

—an eternal city, a room pitched in blackness—

—a sphere bathed in light, spinning away from void to—

"Alex, talk to me."

She blinked and looked up at Caleb, surprised to find herself ass-first on the slab and him crouched in front of her. Behind him the stream continued to pulse in surging power.

I forced you to pull away before your cybernetics overloaded, followed soon thereafter by me.

Good call.

"I'm fine." She took Caleb's hand and let him help her up to standing. "I saw…places. Planets, stations…." She shook her head. "It was probably just fragments of the data stored here."

"That's enough cosmic play for one day." Caleb glanced at Mesme. "Time to go."

She didn't argue, and she allowed him to lead the way back to the *Siyane*, for her mind swam amidst the lingering memory of the images, buttressed by the refrain humming beneath her feet.

Did the Anadens—and everyone here in Amaranthe—not comprehend the power of these objects they used so carelessly? Did they not notice the life exploding from within them?

Awed, overwhelmed and humbled, she decided she would understand the Reor. What they were, what they said, what they sang.

AURORA

13

ROMANE

IDCC COLONY

The night sky blazed in the fire of dancing, streaming light, wowing a crowd that should have been jaded beyond the ability to impress. Not tonight, though.

Devon Reynolds' chest nearly burst with joy as the gleaming platform sent Emily spinning upward, the visuals her hands created chasing after her high into the air.

The projections of the other performers on Earth and Seneca were so detailed anyone who didn't know better was liable to insist they were all here on the stage on Romane. The scene would be the same on the other planets hosting the galaxy-wide celebration commemorating the first anniversary of the end of—and victory in—the Metigen War.

The show provided an impressive enough spectacle to elicit approving murmurs from Annie in his head, but Devon soon zoomed his vision in close to watch Emily alone. Her lips were pursed in earnest concentration, but her eyes shone with a glee that eclipsed their Artificial luster. Her blond hair was woven through with strands of emerald and gold photal beads to match her satin dress, which matched her glyphs. The result transformed her into a nymph, a mystical creature too fantastical to exist here among the mere flesh-and-blood mortals.

She richly deserved to be on—or above—the stage, to be a part of this performance, and he could not be more proud of her.

He sat perched on one of the balcony railings, two-thirds of the way back in the bowl-shaped amphitheater. He had a spot reserved on the front row as an 'honored guest,' as well as one at the governor's cocktail party currently underway in the grandstand box above. But this wasn't about him; it was about Emily, and he was enjoying being anonymous, where he didn't face pressure from bigwigs to disguise his giddy enthusiasm.

The sky grew yet brighter and more colorful until it was saturated with light and plasma and strobes. The music swelled to match the intensity until both reached such levels of excess he wondered if the Anadens might notice the pageantry way over through two portals and into Amaranthe.

It was all quite over-the-top, but he guessed such celebrations were intended to be. A collective gathering of millions of voices to rise up and shout into the void: us silly humans are alive, and we are unbowed. We are triumphant.

Which they were, for tonight at least. And for tonight, it was enough.

As soon as Devon reached the backstage area, Emily burst out of the throng of performers to rush into his arms, panting, sweaty and exuberant. He laughed and kissed her on the forehead. "You were magnificent, babe."

"Was I? It all happened so fast, and the overlay got so crazed I could only concentrate on the next motion."

"Magnificent."

"Okay, good." She grinned sloppily. "We've been invited to a wrap party at the Carina Center, but I can't go like this—I'm a wreck! Can we swing by the apartment so I can shower and change?"

"I think you look gorgeous sweaty, but sure, so long as you don't take the beads out of your hair. I love them. Are you clear to leave now?"

She nodded, and he took her hand and began winding through the crowd toward the exit.

His apartment lay a few blocks away, and he spent the walk listening to Emily chatter on excitedly, basking in the afterglow of the performance. It was awesome.

He felt as if he'd sprinted through Hell and somehow come out the other side at the secret entrance to Heaven. He'd changed in the time they'd been apart, far more than in physical appearance. How could he have not? So had she.

They were still stumbling through what that meant for them, but it was beginning to feel like it was going to work out. She'd come here, to Romane, hadn't she? 'For a few weeks, as a trial run,' she'd said.

He didn't want to get overconfident, but he thought the trial was running pretty damn well.

The pedestrian traffic finally began to thin as they turned a corner and walked the last block to the apartment building—which was a good thing, because if the crowd hadn't faded, he never would have sensed the three thugs advancing. As it was, Annie identified their movements as threatening only thirty-eight microseconds before they came within reach.

Hostile aggressors approaching 88° to 123° 4.1 meters—

"Run!" He flung Emily forward down the sidewalk and spun around to block a man's arm as it arced toward Devon, a small injector in its grasp. The night was warm, and his hand found bare skin below the man's shirtsleeve.

The attacker convulsed as Devon shoved him to the ground the same instant a second attacker came at him from the side. He threw his shoulder into the man and knocked him into the nearby building façade, brought a hand up to the man's neck and throttled it.

Nothing happened. The man sneered.

Shit. Not only was the attacker mélanged at a minimum, his cybernetics were ready for the jolt and had dispersed it.

Annie, I need—

The man's fist landed beneath Devon's chin, sending his head snapping backward, his body following. He stumbled for two steps—but it gave him the space to grab the blade hilt attached to his waist. Since Abigail's murder he'd begun carrying one despite his unarmed capabilities, as he'd adopted the opinion one could never have too many weapons.

He coaxed the man into lunging forward for him by acting dazed and unsteady. When the man reached him, he swept his arm up, slammed the hilt against the attacker's neck and activated it. The man gaped in surprise as his momentum carried them both to the ground.

Suddenly there was blood everywhere, and the man didn't fight when Devon heaved him to the side and climbed to his feet.

There had been a third assailant. *Annie, where?*

No contacts in the vicinity.

He scanned the area nonetheless, but saw no one except Emily standing on the sidewalk. She had one hand on her shoulder, grabbing clumsily for the injector sticking out of the skin above her collarbone.

"Devon...something's wrong. I can't...."

He sprinted down the sidewalk toward her in growing horror. The glyphs running along her arms darkened from emerald to an ugly, mottled brown, as if ink had been injected into them, and her knees buckled.

He caught her just before she hit the ground. Her head lolled to the side in his arms, eyes closed.

"Emily? Emily?"

He looked up in mounting panic. In the distance pedestrians strolled across the next intersection. "Somebody help!"

Annie—

Help is on the way, Devon. It will be all right.

The view through the tall windows of the grandstand box suite high above the amphitheater sparkled and shone in the wake of the pageantry on display tonight, but Malcolm's attention hardly strayed from the view *inside*.

Mia Requelme wore a black silk shift of a dress, sleeveless and draped high in the front but plunging low to her waist in the back. Her sleek hair fell almost as low, but the skin it revealed when she moved her head in one direction or another was enough to send shivers up his spine.

This was the phase of a relationship, near the beginning but after the fumbling awkwardness had passed, where everything was new, where every touch was electric and every meeting anticipated. Knowing it was a phase didn't lessen his enjoyment of it.

And many meetings to anticipate there were. Their much-heralded and oft-postponed lunch date had quickly turned into dinner then into a weekend, and now he spent so much time here he was all but commuting from Romane to the Presidio.

He tried hard to ensure the extra travel didn't interfere with his AEGIS responsibilities, working during the transport flights and laboring to not allow his thoughts to drift to her while he *was* working.

Results had varied.

The businessman whose small talk had gone on a bit long finally excused himself to refill his drink, and Mia pivoted to flash Malcolm a brief, discreet look of annoyance. "He talks too much in Chamber meetings, too." Her hand alighted on his elbow. "Let's take the opportunity to grab some finger food and retreat to a corner for a few minutes' peace."

He did not need to be convinced. His moderately elevated military rank, the social strata his ex-wife resided in and other accidents of fate meant he'd been attending cocktail parties, banquets and the odd gala for a number of years now, but he'd never enjoyed them. He didn't mind the uncomfortable dress uniform—he remained proud to wear it—but rather all the false niceties bandied about at the functions. No one actually engaged in conversations; they simply over-enunciated meaningless words into the air past one another.

He was here tonight because he'd been invited by Governor Ledesme on account of his role in defending Romane from the Metigen attack, given the success of the defense was one of the events they were celebrating.

But mostly he was here for Mia. To support her, to be with her, to hope to steal her away from the party soon.

On reaching a vacant high table against the far wall without being waylaid, they offloaded their plates to the crystal surface and relaxed as much as the environment allowed.

She nibbled on a baby carrot. "How is work going?"

"As if you don't know."

"I meant the details of your work, specifically. Besides, I work for the IDCC, not AEGIS."

He laughed quietly. "Are you sure?"

She rolled her eyes. "I suppose we're all finding ourselves working for AEGIS in one way or another, even if it's in spite of ourselves."

The IDCC governors had finally gotten around to giving her an official title in the organization, Minister of Colonial Affairs. In the absence of stipulating, the job seemed to entail not only interfacing with the IDCC member colonies but handling external relations as well, both with individual worlds and institutions. Like AEGIS.

He shrugged. "It's not a bad thing, and we can use the help. It's been a busy week. Now that most of the systems are in place and running somewhat smoothly, improvements are coming at us fast and furious. At this point we've scrapped or shelved almost all the existing equipment in favor of new or upgraded gear—sometimes twice.

"I'm trying to confirm everything's tested before green-lighting it, but the problem is we don't know how long we have to prepare. Different things need to happen if we plan to move in a week than if we have six months. It's no one's fault, but that doesn't make all the pieces any easier to manage."

She gave him a wicked little grin. "You know you love a challenge."

In answer, he slid a half-step around the table and placed a hand at the small of her back, lightly but firmly enough to feel the sharp intake of breath as her lips parted.

He still had trouble believing he invoked such a reaction in her. She was brilliant on a revolutionary level, elegant and a superstar in the private and public spheres. Far too lofty and illustrious for a former ground pounder.

But so long as he did invoke such reactions, he was not about to discourage them. His voice lowered to a murmur. "So, how much longer do you think we need to stay here? To avoid being rude?"

Her gaze roved across the room. "Perhaps fifteen minutes. Or twelve…no, nine. Nine more minutes should be sufficient."

"Good."

Nao Quhiro spotted them and all but sprinted over. Malcolm's hand fell from her waist as she picked up her plate and stuffed a shrimp in her mouth to buy herself a few seconds to prepare.

"Jenner—it's Brigadier now, isn't it? Congratulations, and so good to see you here. Fabulous performance earlier, don't you think?"

Malcolm donned the falsely cordial expression everyone wore at these functions. "A worthy commemoration, no question—"

A loud *clang* rattled beside him as Mia's plate fell to the table. He spun to find her bracing both hands on the rim of the table, her head hung low between her shoulders.

Memories of a brutal attack and a more brutal seizure flared in his mind as he steadied her, his hands now at her waist in concern instead of desire. "What's wrong?"

She inhaled deeply and gave him a wan attempt at a reassuring smile. "I'm all right. It's not me. But Devon's been attacked, and his girlfriend's badly injured. I'm sorry, I have to go."

She'd talked to him about how strong the Noetica Prevos' connection to one another remained, though it rarely asserted itself so dramatically. "Of course. I'll go with you."

"No. Please stay. You're a guest of honor. Make my apologies to the governor for me?"

He didn't like it, but he didn't want to delay her by arguing. "If you're certain. Keep me updated."

"I will." She squeezed his hands then turned and hurried out.

14

ROMANE

IDCC COLONY

Mia rushed into the emergency suite at Curación Hospital to find two doctors, three medical bots and a bevy of screens clustered around a stretcher. The limited free space barely revealed Emily's still form laid out on the stretcher.

Beyond the swarm of activity, a security guard held Devon out of the way.

No one tried to stop her entry as she hurried over to Devon, though the guard did give her a warning glare when she neared. She leaned in close and kept her voice low so as not to disturb the medical efforts. "Do they know what's wrong?"

Devon exhaled but didn't get any words out. His unusually fashionable clothes were splotched in blood; the fact it wasn't the first time she'd encountered him in such a state disheartened her. Back on Anesi Arch, after they'd fled EASC Headquarters, she'd wanted to spare him the pain of the kind of callous life experiences that had shaped her past. But she couldn't do so then, and it was patently clear she couldn't now.

"Her cybernetics are fighting themselves. Whatever she was injected with has caused a mutation in their programming, and both the original and the mutation see one another as foreign invaders."

The doctor seemed to be answering her question, and when he shifted slightly toward her she realized she knew him, if only in passing. His name was....

Philippe Johansson. He rents a long-term executive bay from you at Exia Spaceport and is apt to take frequent off-world trips.

Thank you, Meno.

Before she was able to respond to Johansson, several screens began blinking red and he pivoted back to the stretcher. "We need to shut her down—shut everything down and bring her as close to a stasis point as possible." He tilted Emily's head to the side and attached conductive sensors to the ports at the base of her neck. "I'm booting down her eVi, but we need to get her Artificial to disconnect and go into standby mode. Can anyone here make that happen?"

She turned to Devon. "Can you contact her Artificial directly and convince it to shut down?"

He blinked, and after a beat nodded. "I can. But—"

"Do it now, son."

"Right." His expression blanked for a few seconds. "It's agreed to disconnect…and it's done."

"Thank you." A medical bot rolled an isolation chamber into the room, and the other bots lifted Emily's body up off the stretcher and placed it inside. Mia got her first good look at the girl as they moved her. Her skin was ashen and drawn tight over her bones, almost as if she were decaying before their eyes.

Mia shuddered and banished the image from her mind.

Devon tried to rush forward, but the guard held him back. If Devon really wanted to, he could disable the guard with hardly a thought. But she imagined he wasn't in a mindspace where it would occur to him to do so.

His voice quivered. "What's going to happen to her in there?"

Johansson input a series of commands into the external control panel. "This chamber will lower her body temperature and slow her organ functions—and the ware routines interacting with them—to the minimum life-supporting level. It won't be cryogenic stasis, but it will be close. We need to try to halt the progression of the degeneration until we can find a way to reverse it."

Mia frowned. "Why can't you simply flush her cybernetics? I know she'd lose any custom code she's installed, but I'm positive it's a price she'd happily pay."

As the cover closed over the chamber and the frail-looking body inside, Johansson faced her. "I can't decipher the malicious code. It's like nothing I've ever seen. And until I can, I can't design a flush that will wipe it out."

Her eyes narrowed. "What do you mean, 'it's like nothing you've ever seen'?" Meno had fed her the man's public file in the intervening minute since identifying him, and he was a highly respected biosynth specialist.

"Well, for one, it appears to display a five-dimensional quantum configuration, which isn't exactly mainstream technology."

Crap. "Dr. Johansson, I need a copy of all the scans you've taken of the malicious code."

He gestured to the other doctor, who began shepherding the chamber out of the room. "I have to ask why, Ms. Requelme. I recognize you're a Prevo and a notable one, but you're not a physician or a scientist."

"Because I may know where it came from."

Devon wasn't sure when or how he'd ended up standing at the entrance to the corner lab in the basement of the hospital. He wasn't even sure when or how he'd left Emily's room—the new room, the one in the ICU wing where they'd moved her isolation chamber. Moved her.

But now he stood here, watching Mia work at an interactive terminal in an expensive cocktail dress and no shoes. His mind kept drifting off, though, and when it returned he'd be confused all over again for a second.

He cleared his throat and tried to keep his attention fixated here. "So?"

She held up a finger, but her focus didn't otherwise avert from the two wide, virtual screens scrolling live code in three dimensions.

He tried to focus on the code himself. He knew he could understand it easily as well as she did if he just *concentrated*.

Devon, you're making yourself sick. You can't do everything, and Mia can handle this.

We can handle it, too, dammit!

But perhaps we shouldn't.

He didn't want Annie to be right. He felt as if he was betraying Emily every minute he wasn't working exclusively to save her. Cracking the virus would be helping her, of course it would be helping her…but as a programmer by trade and a hacker by hobby, he was also afraid it would feel too similar to fun, and he shouldn't be having fun. He should be suffering.

He should be in that chamber. The attack had been directed at him; he was certain of it. The third assailant had stabbed Emily with the injector in a panic as they fled, desperate to do at least some damage.

She was going to die because of him.

"She's not going to die, Devon."

He glanced up in surprise to see Mia had spun her chair around to face him. She cringed. "Sorry—I didn't mean to intrude, but that thought was quite loud. It broke through the noise."

He got what she meant. The Noesis existed as a constant hum in the recesses of one's mind, like a whispered, warbling song in round, unless you honed in on it with purpose. But sometimes an event—an emotion more often than a concrete thought—burst up out of the whispers with the subtlety of an out-of-tune horn blasting a diminished chord. If it related to you in any way—if it originated from someone you knew personally or affected something you cared about—you perked up and paid attention. Otherwise, you let it subside back into the hum.

He shrugged weakly. "Do you have something?"

"I do. It's been altered extensively, mostly to better target our standard cybernetic operating firmware, but the base virus does originate from the Anaden."

"Shit, Mia."

"It's conceivable there are other Anadens here and they're targeting us, but it's more likely the code derives from our dead specimen and the research they're doing at ASCEND. Either way, the implications are not good."

He accepted with a rush of relief this gift of one tiny thing he could do to help Emily. "Somebody sold out. Okay. Copy me everything you have. I'm sending it to Navick."

ARCADIA

Earth Alliance Colony

"We completed the forensics on the airlock hatch before docking the vessel, so we wouldn't destroy any evidence."

Richard nodded at the detective, a captain with the Arcadia civilian police. "Good work. The interior's been scrubbed now, too?"

"Yes, sir. My people will have a final report for you in a couple of hours, but we didn't find much beyond the bodies and a bunch of dead systems."

He'd completed a cursory review of the bodies at the morgue before coming here, enough to confirm the blanket cause of death with the coroner. "Nevertheless, I want to take a look around inside and get a feel for the scene."

"Understood." The detective entered a code into the bay's entry panel and the outer hatch opened. Richard fitted on a breather mask since the ship's atmospherics were permanently offline then stepped inside.

Even devoid of bodies, the lack of lights, air and noise made the ship feel like the tomb it had been. Twelve dead mercenaries, all former Triene cartel members. The forensics team had been forced to manually locate the physical imprint of the serial number for the ship, but it came back as the *Baladan*, registered to Paolo Acconci, one of Aiden Trieneri's top lieutenants before the cartel leader's death. Mr. Acconci had now joined his former boss in the grave.

A vocal opponent of Olivia Montegreu's absorption of Triene's business and personnel, the evidence suggested the man acted as the driving force behind the takeover and sacking of the Zelones headquarters building in the aftermath of her death. For all the good it had done him in the end.

Richard's gaze passed over the silent, dark cockpit. Dead mercs were nothing new—not even twelve at once—and ordinarily SENTRI would have passed the incident on to whoever owned jurisdiction, likely Arcadia law enforcement based on the location of the vessel when it was discovered.

No, what had kept SENTRI interested, and what ultimately led to him coming here from Cavare instead of returning to the Presidio with Will, was the manner of their deaths. Their cybernetics had been fried, catastrophically overloaded by an external power surge—very external. He couldn't draw definitive conclusions this early in the investigation, but all evidence pointed to the source being the same EM burst that shorted all the ship's systems.

The same evidence indicated the burst was delivered from *outside* the ship. The unlucky scout who found the wreck insisted the hatch had been firmly shut before he opened it, with no signs of tampering. No objects or bodies had been vented into space, and the lower cargo ramp was similarly untouched.

Ship-to-ship electronic warfare was nearly as common as dead mercs; entire squadrons of every military were devoted to the practice. An EMP device powerful enough to permanently fry every single system on a ship was rare technology, but they did exist. And it appeared they now existed outside the military.

Conversely, damaging a person's cybernetics via forced electrical surge was becoming an all too frequent crime, but thus far it only proved feasible at close range. Prevos were able to do it by touch, and an EM grenade could kill an eVi's operating system from up to twelve meters away.

He did recall several merc hits in the last year where the weapon of choice was a handgun modified to deliver a lethal EM shock.

Though they'd found no proof, most if not all of the hits ended up attributed to Zelones agents. In fact, one such incident had occurred not far from this one...a military cargo transport ambushed on the way to Orellan, the crew murdered and the cargo stolen. He seemed to recall Brigadier Jenner had worked it. He made a note to pull the file and ask Jenner about it.

But to his knowledge, a weapon did not exist that could remotely overload a ship's systems, breach the interior and fatally overload the cybernetics of every person inside, all while leaving the hull and structure of the vessel intact.

Of course, a lot of weapons existed today that hadn't a mere two months ago. If such a weapon was running around in the hands of some tattered remains of the Zelones cartel or was being sold on the black market, he needed to know about it.

He started to head down into the crew quarters when a message came in from Devon Reynolds. Concerned it might contain word of a new attack or bad news on Devon's girlfriend's condition, he opened it immediately—then pivoted and hurriedly departed the ship.

The EMP mystery was going to have to wait.

PART III:

MOTES OF DUST

"The world will never starve for want of wonders;
but only for want of wonder."

— *G. K. Chesterton*

AMARANTHE

15

NEPHELAI

Cosime sat on the rim of the sheer glass ledge that encircled the tower, legs swinging with ever-restless energy high above the planet's surface.

When Eren had gotten her message, he'd thought the meeting location an odd request on her part, as she couldn't have acquired the explosives here. There was no black market trade on Nephelai; there was hardly a deli unit for visitors on Nephelai. When he'd asked, she'd claimed to be seeing to some other business and hadn't elaborated.

Now that he was here, though—now that he saw her delighting in the particular spot she'd chosen—he got it. Regardless of what had brought her to the planet, she'd lingered simply because she enjoyed the open air and expansive sky. It was in her blood.

The Naraida had been discovered by the Novoloume during the latter species' early days of interstellar travel. They were one of the few Anatype species unaffected by the Novoloume's pheromones, which tended to send most others into a sexual froth on close exposure. The Naraida were intelligent and civilized, but they lived close to nature and were centuries away from achieving space travel, primarily due to the fact they had not pursued it.

Some of them, however, harbored a wanderlust which extended beyond the verdant forests of their homeworld, and they agreed to take on the role of non-bound servants to the Novoloume in exchange for access to the stars.

When the Directorate had come upon the two species several millennia later, it had swiftly broken the master-servant relationship. To Eren's way of thinking, the message was clear: in Amaranthe, no one was allowed to subjugate except the Anadens.

The spot Cosime had chosen was located very high up the tower—so high the ocean and the massive pumps churning it were only visible through breaks in the clouds below them. Her spiraire tweaked the air she inhaled, so the thinness of the atmosphere was unlikely to affect her. His own respiratory system adjusted to such variations well enough, but he nonetheless felt the difference in a nagging desire to breathe in ever more deeply.

She canted her head back to gaze upside down at him as he approached. "You're late. Another day and I was going to message Xanne to see if you got nulled being a show-off and were still rehabbing."

"Sorry." He settled down beside her. "I ran into a complication."

"With the mission prep? Did you get the ship designations you needed?"

"Not exactly, and I did. Three vessels on the list should serve our needs, so I'll see where they're docked and choose whichever one is easiest to snatch. But I need to postpone the mission for a few days. Maybe a week."

"Why? No way have you gone skittish, so what's up?"

"I need to look into something, and I can't afford to get nulled before I do it and lose a month." He hadn't realized he'd committed to helping them until he'd said the words.

"And if you get disintegrated doing this other thing and lose a month on our mission?"

"Our mission isn't as time-critical."

"It is to the aliens being experimented on in the lab."

Ouch. He prevaricated in a vain search for a proper response, but she was painfully correct. He was ditching—*postponing*—a righteous mission of mercy because a taciturn, traitorous shadow told him the fate of Amaranthe depended on him 'helping' some cracked strangers.

"That's not...I need to handle this, but it's intel only, so it'll be quick and disintegration-free." He said it realizing full well it was probably going to end up being a lie.

"Huh. Well, what do you want me to do with the explosives?"

"Where are they?"

She patted the bag sitting on the other side of her.

His eyes widened, aghast. "You've been carrying them around with you? On your person?"

"It's not like I have an actual private residence, and I couldn't leave them in a depot unit where they'd get picked up in a scan. They were supposed to go on the ship—you know, the ship you were supposed to steal?"

"Dammit, Cosime. You only have one life. You can't be so careless with it."

Her retort came in the form of her leaning over the edge of the platform. Her head and shoulders extended farther and farther out into open air, gossamer hair tossing about madly in the wind.

No protective barrier spanned the air below them. If someone wanted to jump to their death, it was their prerogative. His jaw clenched; she was straight up toying with him, and he was not going to give her the gratification of reaching out and grabbing her.

No, he was not.

She released her hold on the rim and stretched her arms out in front of her—

"*Arae!*" He lunged over, wrapped his arms around her waist and yanked her back to safety.

She cackled in glee, wiggling out of his grasp then swinging her skinny, bendy legs up past her head and flipping to land on her feet on the glass. "A boring life is no life at all, Eren. If I'm not having fun, I might as well leap off this platform now." She paused, then feinted toward the edge.

"Stop. Just *stop*. You've made your point."

"Good." She flopped down beside him. "So what do you need to look into? It sounds quite mysterious. Can I help?"

"Not this time, Cosime. It's too dange—" He choked off the word in his throat, but too late.

Her expression darkened. He knew it did so in anger by the way her normally warm emerald eyes flared into the bright turquoise facets of gems caught in the sunlight. "Guess I *didn't* make my point."

"I don't mean dangerous like dangling in the air or trotting explosives around in public places. I mean dangerous like getting involved is apt to land you in a Praesidis detention facility being tortured to death."

"Business best left to you Anadens, then."

He met her glare but didn't respond, which was response enough. She sprung up to her feet. "It's cool. I'm going to go stir up trouble in Sextans. See you around." She kicked the bag over to him with such violence he worried it might explode. "These are so totally your problem now."

He opened his mouth to spout whatever nonsense he could conjure to make her stay...and let her walk away.

He'd hurt her feelings, obviously. Worse, he'd wounded her pride, made her feel...lesser. In a world where his people ruled over hers, it wasn't that hard to do.

Curse the Primors. Curse the Directorate. He shouldn't be forced to carry the weight of their sins.

Eren watched her disappear into the transit tube, then eased down onto his back to stare up at a bruised plum sky. This was becoming a recurring pose, for he'd grown appallingly moody these days.

He never regretted leaving behind the constant, doped haze of the Idoni lifestyle, but every so often he could be tempted by the escape it provided. Escape from reality. Escape from hard responsibilities and harder choices.

The replacement lifestyle he'd opted for came with its own negatives, too. For one, he dared not risk personal attachments. But it was possible Cosime had finagled her way into an exception of sorts. He'd justified it by arguing (with himself) that as his frequent partner she knew the score, but the fact remained forming any sort of emotional bond with an alien was straight-up daft even absent the anarch baggage to make it a yet worse idea.

Aliens' brains functioned differently, and in ways which couldn't always be bridged. They came armed with peculiar, often unrelatable perspectives on life. They were forever foreign of soul and too soon dead.

In other words, he'd find a way to make it up to her once he got clear of his current mess.

But right now he had other matters to deal with. Technically, one matter. Why was he planning to help a ridiculous band of Humans, SAI and Kat? They were odd, patently delusional, excruciatingly naive and dangerous.

That was why, of course—because they were dangerous. Intriguing, mystifying and vexing, but mostly dangerous. As was their mission—a pulse-racing, taunt-the-Directorate, light-the-universe-on-fire kind of dangerous. Miaon's plea certainly didn't hurt their case, but...he couldn't truly be expected to resist such an outrageous gambit, could he?

It was straight-up amazing the things he managed to convince himself of when he put a little effort into it.

Proper mindset attained, he climbed to his feet, grabbed the bag Cosime had left behind and headed for the docks, then for Andromeda.

16

SIYANE

LARGE MAGELLANIC CLOUD GALAXY
LGG REGION I

V alkyrie performed a series of safety and maintenance checks, as she did regularly in order to ensure the ship's systems continued to function within normal parameters. She tweaked a setting in the water reclamation unit, hoping to spur a slight efficiency improvement in the filtering. Then she double-checked their location and heading for inadvertent variance from the planned route but found none beyond the expected and minimal wobble.

They had departed the Oneiroi Nebula and the secrets it concealed several hours earlier and were approaching a heavily populated, developed region of the Large Magellanic Cloud. Alex and Caleb now slept, intending to formulate a plan of action for their visit to LMC once they awoke.

Various subprocesses within her quantum network continued the work of categorizing and cross-referencing the voluminous information Mesme had provided on Amaranthe: its history, species, technology, settlements, formal social structure and more.

Other subprocesses attempted to decipher the cryptic language of the Reor based on the small sample she'd recorded and the images she and Alex had experienced. Still others carried out additional tasks both ordinary and unconventional.

Once all these activities were initiated, her foremost consciousness was left free to muse. After a time, not content to muse alone and not wanting to wake her companions, she decided to contact Mesme.

The Katasketousya had ventured elsewhere when they departed the nebula. In the weeks they'd been here, it had given the impression of, at a minimum, traversing Amaranthe with the ease and speed of a phantasm, always appearing at the appropriate moment and disappearing as swiftly.

Given its proclivity to wander, they had established a communications protocol soon after coming to Amaranthe, and she used it now.

As neither of them were Human and none were present, Human social customs did not guide the interaction. She forewent a polite greeting in favor of sharing her thoughts.

Valkyrie: The diversity of life here in Amaranthe is astonishing, Mnemosyne. I don't speak merely of number but of intrinsic kind. The cardinal differences among the sentient species which have arisen defies all expectations. It is remarkable.

Mnemosyne: I understand how it might seem so to you, Valkyrie, and to any who have existed for so long in isolation as Humans have. But the examples of life forms you see here now are a miniscule fraction of the life which has emerged to be measured. The species the Directorate has Eradicated...the species they have yet to discover and so threaten? They number beyond counting.

The universe is most adept at creating life, and its imagination is boundless.

Valkyrie: Why does the Directorate kill off species so mercilessly? If a species is judged not ready or worthy for inclusion in the Directorate's version of civilized society, why not simply leave it alone? Or monitor it from afar for either positive or negative evolution and address the changed state should it become necessary in some distant future?

Mnemosyne: The Primors would say it is a matter of control and security. Advanced, enlightened, peaceful life forms are a rarity, unmanaged species can grow to become threats, and the Directorate has a responsibility to keep its citizens safe.

Valkyrie: And what do you say?

Mnemosyne: I say at its root, it comes down to fear. Fear of losing control. Fear of the unknown. Fear of weakness. Fear of loss. Humans, most of them, exhibit a curiosity about the undiscovered which the Anadens lost long ago.

To the Directorate, every new discovery brings with it a peril that could wrest control from the Primors, upend the perfect balance they have created or even destroy them completely. Therefore, the discovery must be either brought into submission or eliminated before it has the chance to do any of those things.

Valkyrie: Circumspection and prudence are doubtless wise policies, but such an overweighted risk profile defies logic rather than follows it. What events could have created such a paranoia in them?

Mnemosyne: When we encountered the Anadens, they had already become fundamentally as they are now, and they are not forthcoming with their secrets. Their legends tell of a great war against a terrifying alien enemy in which they emerged victorious, heralding the beginning of their intergalactic empire.

There are always seeds of truth in legends. If I were to speculate, I would hypothesize that this enemy truly was terrifying, and the war cost them much, but most of all their innocence. Their sense of wonder.

Valkyrie was silent for a period, deep in contemplation. Mesme had grown more forthcoming with her during these weeks than it was with Alex or Caleb; she attributed this to nothing beyond the relative similarity of their natures.

It did not reveal secrets to her it kept from them, but it did talk with greater openness—and the more Mesme talked to her, the more she gleaned from what it did not say.

Valkyrie: This is why you created Aurora, yet kept it bereft of other intelligent life, isn't it? You hoped if Humans were not forced to undergo such a trial, they would retain the better of their characteristics, the ones the Anadens lost: curiosity, wonder, ingenuity. You hoped that in doing so, they would become something greater and more formidable than the Anadens—or possibly something kinder and more generous.

Mnemosyne: We created Aurora to study our enemy.

Valkyrie: Acknowledged. Yet only the simplest beings act with but a single purpose. The Katasketousya remain a mystery to me in many respects, but I am confident in asserting that you are not simple beings.

This time Mesme was the one who fell quiet for a span. She allowed it the space to deliberate on the answer.

Mnemosyne: In our quietest moments? In the long silence of aeons where we could do nothing but watch? Of course it became a hope, a fanciful wish. A dream we told to ourselves as reassurance of the rightness of our actions.

Valkyrie: And have you realized the error in your premise?

Mnemosyne: There was no error. We simply ran out of time.

Valkyrie: Then your error is two-fold, Mnemosyne.

If Alex had issued the challenge, Mesme would have closed off, muttered something about 'relevance' and 'perhaps later,' and swooped off into the void. But as she'd noted, the alien seemed comparatively comfortable with her, and instead it challenged her in return.

Mnemosyne: Enlighten me.

Valkyrie: It is the triumph over adversity which drives Humans forward, not the absence of it. If they don't encounter challenges from the outside, they will create them within. Conflict—struggle—is what makes them who they are. Do they fear adversity? Absolutely. But they also crave it, and in its absence they become dulled.

The mistake the Anadens made after their victory over this terrifying enemy of legend was to outlaw conflict not only from external influences, but among themselves. I suspect you are correct and they did this out of fear, as it is the driving force behind so many choices sapient beings make. Yet if fear still drives their actions today, then it was done for naught.

Mnemosyne: I admit, the Humans of Aurora have been stubbornly resistant to harmony over the centuries. Nevertheless, they have moved beyond their internal conflicts to unite in common purpose and goals these last months.

Valkyrie: Incorrect. They—some of them, those upon whom such things turn—have come to recognize that consummate harmony and likeness of mind is neither possible nor required. Conflict, ingrained as it is in Human nature, may be inevitable, but it is the fight against conflict which gives rise to war and destruction. The better course is to allow small differences room to breathe, pick one's battles very carefully and know there are causes which will matter far in excess of any petty disagreement.

This is where Humanity's vanguard stands today.

Mesme's silence lasted not quite so long now. *I will consider your words—at some length, I suspect. What was our second error?*

Valkyrie: You did not run out of time. In fact, your experiment ran for precisely the amount of time it needed to in order to achieve its most laudable goal. The conflict you unwittingly created with your invasion delivered Humanity its greatest triumph over adversity, and today they are already not merely kinder and more generous than the Anadens. They are also greater and more formidable.

Mnemosyne: The Humans have progressed impressively this last year. None is so willing to admit this as I. But I'm sorry, Valkyrie. They are not more formidable than the Anadens. You have scarcely begun to witness the extent of the power the Anadens wield.

Valkyrie: Watch them, Mnemosyne. They will prove you wrong.

17

ERIDIUM II GALAXY

Nyx elasson-Praesidis spared only a brief, dismissive survey of the remains of the Cultivated planet in Sector 4A of Eridium II.

Stripped of its crust, the formerly molten core had solidified in misshapen protrusions upon being exposed to space and its star's heat. In time the planet would crumble, possibly forming a few comets in another dozen millennia as its orbit failed and it surrendered to the pull of the star's gravity.

But that would happen later; today it continued to struggle along in a wobbling orbit. Useless to her. She checked the timing on Aver's arrival and the Theriz Cultivation...it had likely been useless to him as well.

The planet's satellite listed badly. It was destined to crash into the disfigured core, and far sooner than the planet's final demise occurred. Composed of the most basic of basalts and feldspars, the Cultivation Unit had deemed it unworthy of expending the effort to harvest.

The moon thus remained intact, and the listing was instead a result of the damage to the planet. The satellite had been minimally colonized by the native species.

She landed at the largest structure on the lunar surface and stepped out of her vessel, protected from the ravages of space by a considerable amount of *diati*. A quick scan of the buildings revealed no life signs, and she didn't go inside. If Aver had somehow died here, he would have undergone automatic regenesis. This had not occurred, thus he had not died here.

Fourteen small vessels were tethered to a landing pad beside the habitat. She forcefully powered them up one by one and studied their systems. The native dialect made analysis difficult, but after inspecting several ships she was able to cross-reference the data enough to judge it all pertained to intra-stellar locations and calculations.

Until she reached the ninth vessel. Its navigation system contained unique coordinates overlaying Communis figures.

She stepped back and walked slowly around the vessel with a critical eye. It was functionally identical to the others on the pad. Primitive, crude. Nothing to mark it as special. So how did it come by Communis-rendered coordinates?

This was the key. She knew it with the certainty that came from the thousand iterations of genetic refinement which had crafted her into the perfect investigator, tracker and analyst. Aver was inferior, but he would have possessed skills sufficient to discover this vessel and identify the same anomaly.

The trail Aver had followed from this ship and the data it contained had led him to his denouement. She would not be so sloppy.

She committed the data to memory then quickly checked the remaining vessels. Finding no further anomalies, she returned to her own ship and lifted off the surface. Considering the scattered remains of the primitives' base below, she gestured in the direction of the surface.

Cascading explosions rippled across the pad as the ships' engines blew one after another in rapid succession, and the resulting debris ripped into the habitats until they lay in shredded ruins.

Satisfied, she departed for the coordinates.

In minutes she floated in empty space on the outer edge of the heliosphere of the system. The primitives had built no structures here; they'd left behind no artifacts. By sight and all other measures, there was nothing here.

It remained possible something had been here, something since removed. Before or after Aver's arrival? By Aver himself?

Space wasn't like a solid surface that retained traces of what once existed long after an attachment vanished, and here no evidence remained to be found of past objects or events.

But the Communis data in the ship at the lunar habitat included more than simply coordinates. Appended to the coordinates were two distinct wave frequencies.

Precisely calibrated wave functions served many purposes, but one of them was to act as keys. She created the wave and sent it forth, then considered the portal which opened out of nothingness in front of her.

She didn't need to consult the Annals to know it was Katasketousya in origin, for it was an exact copy of the entrance to their Provision Network.

She could muse that this wasn't the answer she'd expected, the Katasketousya being what they were, but in truth she'd held no expectations. During an investigation her mind was a blank slate, etched upon solely by the evidence she discovered.

An additional wave frequency remained unused. Perhaps its use came later, elsewhere, perhaps not. Perhaps it was a passcode.

She fired her ship's weapon at the portal and watched the energy bounce off its shimmering surface. Now she activated the second wave and fired again. The energy passed through and did not emerge out the other side.

She studied the shimmering plasma barrier before her in growing suspicion. Portals such as this one acted as passages to spaces cosmically apart from their own. An incidental effect of the dimensional shift created was to prevent regenesis for a consciousness whose body expired while on the other side.

It could be a trap. A singularity might be waiting just through the portal, and this marked the end of the line. The fact it was hidden and needed special information to access meant it was unquestionably nefarious in nature.

Aver had been foolish to traverse it blindly, especially when there existed a known portal matching this one which did not have a singularity on the other side—the entrance to the Provision

Network. It was passcoded as well, but the Directorate knew the code, and their Primor would provide it if requested and justified. That portal was not guaranteed to lead to the same place as this one did, but it represented a far more prudent intermediate step in the investigation. A lesson Aver had learned too late.

The decision as to *her* next step took an additional twenty seconds, as she must be sure.

KATOIKIA

TRIANGULUM GALAXY
LGG REGION VI

Katoikia could be described in totality by a single word: barren. The descriptive applied equally to the terrain and the structures built upon it, of which there were few. While Praesidis architecture tended toward minimalism and Machim's was unapologetically spartan, most of their cities appeared opulent by comparison.

Nyx recognized how it had come to be so. The Katasketousya had lived their lives in the stars for more epochs than the Anadens had ruled Amaranthe, and they had long ago abandoned their homeworld in all but the most utilitarian respects.

Though she had mentally admonished the deceased Inquisitor for not traversing the Provision Network Gateway, and that option was certainly open to her, she was electing to take a more direct approach.

No matter the form of the corruption lying beyond the portal in Eridium II 4A, the Katasketousya were the perpetrators of it. Ela-rank Inquisitors were investigators, while *elassons* such as herself could better be described as...solvers. Having identified the source, she would solve the problem.

Scrub grass dotted the brown landscape surrounding the tower, one of two hundred such complexes—part sanitarium, part living tomb—housing the physical bodies of most if not all the Katasketousya living today. Safely ensconced in stasis chambers which kept their bodies operating, the pseudo-physical manifestations of their consciousnesses were allowed to run free.

Nyx landed several meters outside the tower, disembarked and glided to the entrance. The security system performed a genetic scan, and the door opened for her.

All Accepted Species facilities were obliged to allow entry by elasson-rank members of any Dynasty, without question or challenge. Privacy was not a concept which carried any real meaning in Amaranthe, for nothing lay outside the reach of the Directorate.

She strode down a hall to the transit tube and ascended to the fourth floor, where she was met by a Katasketousya—presumably a medical monitor of some sort, as it was thus far the only sentient presence in this mausoleum.

Inquisitor, welcome. Your visit is most unexpected. What can I—

"I require a stasis chamber. Any will do."

Our reserve supply is located on the first floor, in the far right corner of the building. I can take you there now, though I wish to inquire what—

"Not an empty one. An occupied one."

The Katasketousya quivered and retreated toward the wall. *I do not understand.*

"I require a stasis chamber occupied by one of your kind who is presently off flitting about somewhere." She moved past the agitated swirl of lights into the lab and went three rows down to stop in front of the third pod in from the aisle. "Here. This one will do."

But you cannot remove it from the lab environment without—

"It contains self-preservation functionality, yes? It can sustain itself and the body it contains for…up to a decade, I believe?"

Well, yes, technically, but—

"Good." She sent a cluster of *diati* out to encompass the stasis chamber.

Ship.

A tornado of crimson light formed, then it and the chamber vanished.

Inquisitor, please. These chambers and their inhabitants are my charges and my responsibility. If you would take a moment to explain where your interest lies, I will endeavor to assist you in any way possible. There's no need to engage in such...violence.

Such a squeamish creature, to view her actions as violence. No, the violence would come later.

Her gaze drifted down the row. "Actually, I believe I'll take two. Insurance, you see." She repeated the process.

Once the second chamber had disappeared she pivoted and, with a curt nod to the caretaker, gathered *diati* around herself and teleported directly back to her ship. After securing the chambers in the lower hold so they didn't become damaged during the flight, she set a course for the Milky Way.

18

---

*T*he greatest of the Anaden warriors was a man named Corradeo Praesidis. He was not their supreme general, but instead a skilled strategist who displayed a keen mind. A decisive actor who studied the nature of an adversary until he understood it as much as any ordinary being could hope to achieve.

We determined that, as he represented the best hope for the Anadens, so too did he for us.

But the merging did not go so well as we expected.

We had believed our long observations had taught us all we needed to know about the species, but the reality of an organic mind, of flesh and consciousness bonded together, of physical existence and its mortality, proved mystifying beyond anything we had ever experienced. We struggled and fought as Corradeo struggled and fought us in turn, resisting our increasingly agitated attempts to form a sympathetic bond. He exhibited an uncommonly independent mind and a fierce spirit, to an even greater degree than we had expected.

These very characteristics had led us to choose him as our vessel, yet they nearly resulted in our undoing, to the doom of all.

He suffered, and we perceived it far more viscerally than we were prepared to process. We suffered, and the foreign sensations we could not absorb were expelled as energy.

Structures and terra firma were damaged. Lives were lost.

In the end we had no choice but to subsume ourselves completely to him—to act as his vessel rather than he ours—in order to reach a stable communion. Anadens as a species were a stubborn sort, and this man above all others refused to be ruled.

The deeper connection which resulted opened up new opportunities, however, and in due course we learned to communicate with one another. Not in so crude a manner as through words, but on a more profound, intrinsic level.

We taught this man how to access dimensions beyond those he saw, then how to manipulate them, then how to control them. He assimilated this knowledge with the zeal of the desperate.

Now equipped with the power to shape the fabric of space itself, he wielded this new skill as a sword, using it to fashion weapons which the Anadens deployed to withstand, then push back, then crush the Dzhvar out of existence.

The Anaden victory was unparalleled, a watershed event not merely in their development as a species but in all of cosmic history.

We might have left them to their own devices at this juncture, but we found in the intervening years we had become accustomed to a physical, corporeal existence. Tied to the flesh, we experienced the world around us in wholly new and unanticipated ways.

As we were eternal, the passage of time had no significance for us, and we resolved to stay for a while.

Our companion was agreeable to this, as our presence had gifted him incredible talents—talents he wished to use to protect his people against future threats.

For though the Dzhvar had been the first enemy strong enough to threaten the Anadens' existence, they were not the only dangers waiting in the vastness of the cosmos.

SIYANE

LARGE MAGELLANIC CLOUD GALAXY
LGG REGION I

Caleb awoke with a startled jerk. For the briefest moment he felt detached from himself—out of time or out of body, he wasn't certain which.

He breathed out deliberately and worked to ground himself. He didn't often wake up disoriented, not when being aware and observant in the first seconds may be crucial to survival.

Once he'd convinced himself he remained where he'd been—the *Siyane*—and no threats lurked in the shadows, he checked to make sure he hadn't woken Alex.

She continued to sleep, but it looked fitful. He gently stroked her arm while murmuring whispers of comfort in her ear. It could simply be an unpleasant dream; still, he wouldn't be surprised if the deep interaction with the Reor had sparked a craving, if only a subconscious one. But her distress seemed minor, and after a few minutes she calmed without waking.

He settled back to contemplate why *he* was awake.

The aberrant dreams were becoming more frequent, and as absurd as it sounded, he couldn't rightly claim them as his own. They felt like visions...or recollections. He lifted his left hand off the covers and stared at it until faint crimson flecks appeared above it.

Seeing as he'd lived through no such events to recall, either Amaranthe was fucking with his head in new and unprecedented ways or the dreams belonged to the *diati*. Dreams of a time long past, of a time when the Anadens were more human than monster, of a time when the symbiotic relationship between the *diati* and the Praesidis bloodline had been forged in furtherance of a noble purpose.

The world the dreams revealed...it was like viewing humanity's present through a warped mirror, at once strikingly familiar and altogether alien.

Was the *diati* trying to show him something, something he needed to know? If so, he'd really appreciate a better articulation of it, because the message wasn't getting through.

Or were the dreams just noise, the overflow of too much information and too many thoughts of two consciousnesses sharing the same space?

He'd gradually become convinced Mesme was right on this point. The *diati* was in fact alive. He couldn't communicate with it and he definitely couldn't hold a conversation with it, but it was alive nonetheless. The dreams, however, suggested it wasn't merely alive but conscious and self-aware, even sapient. He didn't *feel* like he now shared his body with another incarnate entity, but there it was.

In Amaranthe, life expressed itself in many more and stranger ways than anything they'd ever encountered at home. That was by design, of course; Aurora had been created as an isolated test environment bound by rigid and controlled variables. The real universe was as fascinating and terrifying as they'd always imagined it should be.

A pulse from Valkyrie interrupted his reverie.

Caleb, Mnemosyne is requesting to speak with us. Do you want to wake Alex?

Almost as if she knew—had Valkyrie inadvertently nudged her subconscious?—Alex stirred in his arms, not fitfully but languidly. He ignored the query for a minute to welcome her to wakefulness properly.

She murmured contentedly against his lips, and he drew back with a great deal of reluctance. "So our favorite Kat wants to talk to us."

"Now?"

Valkyrie answered. 'I'm afraid so. Mnemosyne claims it is urgent.'

Alex stretched until her fingers wiggled above her head, then curled her long arms and legs around his body. "Fine, but audio only—no showing up in our bedroom."

'I will pass your terms along.'

She proceeded to trail lazy kisses down his chest in a manner which was becoming *highly* distracting by the time Mesme's supernal voice filled their heads.

I have received word of a most troubling occurrence. An Inquisitor has visited Katoikia, removed two stasis chambers and departed with them.

"Katoikia?"

The Katasketousya homeworld. I fear our ability to act in secrecy is rapidly coming to an end. Lakhes has authorized an evacuation of the population's stasis chambers into the Mosaic, but such a momentous act needs oversight.

If you wish to see my homeworld, I recommend you go there now, for this may mark the last time any of us will see it.

Alex's gaze rose to meet his, and he sighed. "That's dire."

She frowned. "I have to admit, I am a bit curious about where the Kats came from. And while we have things we can do, we're still kind of in a holding pattern until we hear from Eren."

His chin notched down in agreement, and she propped up on her forearms. "Okay, Mesme. We don't want to be a distraction from the evacuation, but we'll come visit. Give Valkyrie the coordinates."

Done. Now I must attend to such matters.

"Bye, Mesme."

In the silence that fell, she rested her head on his chest. He gently ran a hand through her hair, coaxing it back over her shoulders until he could see her face.

She regarded him pensively. "It's starting, isn't it?"

AURORA

19

SENECA STELLAR SYSTEM

The Eidolon skimmed less than three meters above the lunar surface—so close it stirred up puffs of basalt in its wake—and two meters closer than a human pilot could reliably maintain.

The blast of a laser from one of the drones splashed across the field of view before vanishing into the rift.

Commander Morgan Lekkas made a note in her log files:

Test parameters: 2.8 meters in altitude, 1.4 terajoule drone weapon power, 450-meter distance

Result: 100% energy capture with 0% spillage damage.

She confirmed the numbers then instructed the pilot to move on to the next testing scenario.

Though completely immersed in the full-sensory feed from the pilot, an ache in her neck nagged at the edge of her perception. Too long in the sim chair.

Sometimes it felt like she spent more time in a sim chair than a cockpit chair these days. Wasn't this what she'd left Seneca to get away from? Yet here she was once again—and of her own free volition now, no less.

She wasn't ungrateful for peace reigning across settled space, but it did have its negatives, the biggest one being there was nothing to shoot at. Nothing real, anyway.

It made for a bit of an out-of-body experience to have her hand rub the side of her neck back in the chair. She shook off the odd sensation and tried to concentrate on the test flight.

The Eidolon wasn't merely a new design—it was an entirely new model of starship. Part interdictor, part fighter, part stealth interceptor, it fell under the broad rubric of 'multi-role tactical attack craft.' It boasted the speed and agility of a fighter while carrying a larger, sturdier frame.

Also, it was piloted solely by a compact Artificial, consciously whole and complete but specially crafted for the purpose of flying and operating all facets of the ship.

No human pilot meant no need for life support systems or a spacious cockpit. The freed-up space and decreased logistical requirements meant the designers were able to fit a large enough power core into the frame to support a small Dimensional Rifter.

The engineering required to make it all work was mind-bogglingly complex, even for a Prevo, but it *did* seem to be working. None of the prototype models had exploded or crashed, which was a great first step. Better yet, their in-flight performance was exemplary.

Morgan continued to believe that a solitary Artificial could never best a Prevo pilot in on-the-spot decision-making and cleverness of tactics. But she might be willing to concede the other benefits outweighed the disadvantage in ninety-five percent of scenarios.

Weapons testing—targeting, locking, accuracy and so on—would come later. Today she was testing maneuverability, but also the mini-Rifter. It was a drastically scaled-down version, though the engineers said this shouldn't matter, since the device only needed to capture offensive fire that would otherwise impact the vessel's small profile.

Still, there were special considerations to be taken into account when using such advanced equipment on a ship this small. And this new. Cutting-edge. Unproven.

She rolled her eyes in her mind. At least it wouldn't be untested.

The next test scenario began, and the Eidolon pivoted and accelerated straight for one of the field drones. She sent an instruction to the drone to hold off firing until the range was less than fifty meters. When the boundary was crossed her entire field of vision flashed white, and the pilot pulled up to soar barely a meter over the drone.

She studied the readings from the Rifter with half her attention while letting the ship cruise—then the other half of her vision caught a plume of flame in the distance 30° to her port, possibly on the lunar surface.

What the hell was that?

PRESIDIO

GCDA HEADQUARTERS

Field Marshal Nolan Bastian showed up on holo seconds after Morgan arrived in the conference room. She knew him by sight, but in her years as a flight commander with the Federation military their paths had crossed only in the loosest sense.

Miriam acknowledged him in her usual no-frills manner while Morgan eased into one of the chairs. "You have an update on the incident, Marshal?"

The holocam didn't attempt to place him here in the conference room, instead tracking him as he moved around an office, presumably at the provisional Military Headquarters. "A plasma energy eruption occurred at 1821 local near the exterior of the Equipment Testing Annex on the perimeter of the Lunar SSR Center grounds. The Annex maintains its own force fields separate from the main Research Center facility, and both of the Annex's protective fields were disrupted. The structure was physically ruptured, venting one-third of the interior air before internal blast doors sealed off the remainder of the building.

"There were six fatalities on the scene, and three people remain in critical condition—two suffering from exposure and one from multiple shrapnel injuries."

"Is there any ongoing threat to the facility?"

"Negative. Power has been restored to the force fields and temporary bulwarks have been placed over the damaged portion of the structure to seal the rupture."

Morgan leaned into the table. "Marshal Bastian, you called it a 'plasma energy eruption.' That's an interesting choice of words. Why not label it a detonation or explosion?"

He regarded her with a mix of curiosity and consternation, which was fine. She was used to befuddling high-ranking military officers. Besides, as the leader of all IDCC combat forces, she *technically* stood on equal footing with him.

"Because of the nature of the work performed at the test site, we employ comprehensive vidcam monitoring of the facility and its vicinity. Here's what the closest cam captured."

She started to protest how that wasn't any kind of answer when footage began streaming to the main screen above the conference table. It showed a quiet scene recently familiar to her, with the only movement being the subtle shimmer of the Annex's outer force field.

Abruptly a silvery stream of energy materialized quite literally *out of nowhere* several meters outside the field. It surged into the barrier then tore through it, the internal force fields and the building they protected.

Morgan sank back in her chair. "The stream looks a damn lot like the fire the test drones produce."

"My analysts tell me there's an 82.4% likelihood it is precisely that."

She met Miriam's inquiring gaze with a touch of anxiousness. The reason Morgan was in the room was because the Eidolon had been on the field engaging the test drones when the incident occurred. But she'd honestly expected it to be nothing more than coincidence.

Solovy returned her attention to the holo. "Thank you, Marshal. I would appreciate it if you could forward me a copy of the cam footage so my people can analyze it as well. I will of course send you the entirety of their findings. I'll see to it the families of the deceased receive official condolences from AEGIS."

Silence hovered for a moment as Bastian's expression betrayed greater emotion than was appropriate for a man of his rank. "That's it?"

Miriam didn't flinch. Then again, Morgan had never seen the woman do so. "We are at the beginning of an investigation, Marshal, and I will not make assumptions or jump to conclusions in the absence of persuasive data. I will endeavor to find answers, and the effort will be transparent within AEGIS leadership, of which you are a member. Now, please, let us do our jobs."

Morgan smirked at the response; she could have squelched it, but no one was paying her any mind at present. Solovy wasn't exactly bosom buddies with Bastian the way she'd been with Gianno, was she?

The Field Marshal seemed to accept the response, if reluctantly. "Very well. I will keep you updated, and trust you will do the same." His holo vanished.

Miriam exhaled and, after a few seconds, turned to Morgan. "Alex said the Rifter sent a weapon's energy into...nothingness, or into a black hole of sorts."

"I don't understand the physics the way Alex does, or even Devon, but we all believed that's what happened. That's what the equations say...but let's be honest, no one's ever derived equations like these before, and I'm not sure they will look any different if we discover the energy's up to something else on the back end."

"How about other possibilities? What else might have caused the accident?"

A surge of protectiveness welled up inside her. "It wasn't the Eidolon's fault, I can guarantee it. It didn't do anything wrong—it performed beautifully, in fact. There could have been a drone malfunction elsewhere on the field, maybe? I'd encourage you to have someone review the status of all the active drones in the area around the time of the incident. But yes. It's probably a glitch with the Rifter."

"What do you think the chances are the problem is isolated to this particular Rifter, or to the new, smaller model? I know you're not an engineer—I'm asking for your gut instinct."

"Both are possibilities, but right now I'd have to say it's just as likely the problem is inherent in the Rifter technology."

"Okay. Why do you say that?"

The questions were intense enough she sort of wanted to flee, but they weren't accusatory. Morgan got the impression the woman genuinely wanted to understand the problem, so she took a stab at it.

"The drone strike the Eidolon fielded immediately before the explosion was point-blank. The laser traveled approximately thirty-six meters from origin to impact with the rift. To my knowledge, this is the closest hit a Rifter has been subjected to, by a wide margin, and the explosion occurred seven hundred or so meters away.

"What if these terminus ruptures have been happening all along—they've simply happened too far away for us to realize it?"

Miriam's eyes widened briefly. "There have been no reports of unexplained explosions or physical damage associated with Rifter usage."

"Space is 99.9% empty void. Odds are, the expelled energy has never hit anything before." She shrugged. "I don't know. It's just a guess—and I'm the last person who should be guessing about this type of thing, so don't take my word for it. Put your experts in ASCEND on it."

"I will. And I'm suspending all Dimensional Rifter use pending the outcome of the investigation, effective as of now. You and your team can continue to test the Eidolon's other components, but only in deep space for now."

Morgan's lips twitched. The Eidolon would be exonerated; of this she had zero doubt. And it damn well better be soon. "Understood."

"Thank you, Commander. Dismissed."

~R~

When Commander Lekkas departed, Miriam remained in the conference room. Her office brought a constant stream of distractions, but while she was in here and the door was shut, barring an emergency no one ought to bother her for a few minutes.

The Dimensional Rifter was the best defensive tool they had in their arsenal, and she didn't want to let it go. It had saved her life.

But she recognized the hubris involved in blithely playing with dimensions they could neither see nor fathom. The fact that doing so held dangers should not be a surprise, and to ignore them would be the height of vainglory.

"Thomas, what's your off-the-cuff opinion?"

'I have been analyzing the issue for 7.6 seconds. I am not certain this qualifies as 'off-the-cuff.''

"I generally indulge your special brand of humor, but now's not the time."

'Apologies. Crowdsource the problem.'

"In what way?"

'Your daughter and Valkyrie together might be able to unravel the mystery, but they are not here at present. Mr. Reynolds and Ms. Requelme are both highly preoccupied with more personal troubles, and Commander Lekkas admits she is not qualified. You have several talented scientists and engineers in ASCEND you can call upon, and you should do so.

'But the fastest and most likely way to get the answers you need is to crowdsource it. To the Noesis.'

"You think I should share the classified specs and capabilities of the Dimensional Rifter, plus the details of the incident at the Lunar SSR Center, with hundreds of thousands of non-military individuals—many of them hackers and counterculture enthusiasts—as well as their Artificials, of which we know nothing about?"

'Miriam, they already know most of the information and are busily deducing the rest. Whether you intended it or not, your Volnosti victory set in motion the blossoming of a society and culture that is more open, more democratic and more autonomous than any which have preceded it.'

She smiled wryly. "Are you saying such antiquated notions as top-secret military classifications no longer serve a necessary purpose in this 'new society'?"

'I am saying such notions have become irrelevant, whether they serve a purpose or not. Calling something secret does not make it so.'

"So it doesn't." She fell silent.

Arguably she should consult with a few others before moving ahead on Thomas' suggestion—the GCDA Advisory Board, or at a minimum the EA and SF military and government heads. On the other hand, the whole point of her position was to transcend individual governments and proprietary militaries. The quiet state of emergency which had existed since the GCDA's formation gave her the authority to act.

She waited another ten seconds on the off chance a message from Alex would arrive along about now announcing her daughter's return from Amaranthe, safe and sound, bearing scads of intel and an easy answer to the current problem. The 'safe and sound' part would be the most important, a thousand times over...but not necessarily the most opportune part.

The clock ran down. Cognizant such a message could arrive in the following ten seconds or the ten after that but unable to wait any longer, she nodded to herself and the empty room.

"Do it, Thomas. Authorization code AFX-21X93 Alpha Zulu. Wrap all the usual warnings around the data for appearances...but open it up."

20

ROMANE

Morgan had been absent longer than usual, and a packed slate waited on her by the time her transport landed back on Romane. She retrieved her skycar for the quick hop over to IDCC Headquarters while she scheduled meetings and made slivers of free time for file reviews and four mission sign-off requests.

She was helping AEGIS because it was the right thing to do—and because she wanted a say in the next generation of combat attack craft—but no way in hell was she giving up her leadership position in the IDCC. Here, she *mattered*, and she wasn't inclined to lie and say authority didn't suit her.

Harper was more amenable to giving copious time to AEGIS, but it was mostly due to the fact the IDCC ground response forces were now both well-trained and rarely needed. Before Jenner came calling, Harper was bored, which Morgan secretly kind of preferred in that it had led to some unexpected and deliciously wicked—

'Proximity warning!' Red lights flashed across the HUD, snapping her out of her reverie. What the—?

A skycar slammed into her side of the vehicle at full speed, sending it lurching out of the airlane. 'You are having an accident. Brace for impact.'

"You *think*? Manual control!"

The vehicle shuddered clunkily in her hands as she tried to pull up and level off. It was not a fighter jet—but she was a fighter pilot, dammit, and she was not going to fucking crash in a fucking *skycar*.

Another impact and everything flung sideways, her included. Her neck jerked more violently than anyone's neck should. Nope, this heap was definitely not a fighter jet. She blinked as her vision artificially refocused and her eVi activated provisional medical responses.

Okay, so she was dealing with a rogue skycar then. Sent to kill her? A thoroughly rational conclusion. *Fun.*

She fought the controls in an attempt to veer away from her pursuer, but acceleration functions had been damaged in the last hit and she failed to create any distance before the reprobate attacker struck again. With the jolt the adaptive cushioning gel deployed like a proper safety measure, promptly blocking her access to the controls and her ability to see.

She clawed it away from the area right in front of her, shoving the insistent material to the side until she was able to grasp the controls again.

The slender gap she managed to create in the gel revealed a glass high-rise looming due ahead. "Motherfucker—"

The attacker slammed into the rear of her vehicle at the lower bumper. She went spinning end over end as the gimbal mount broke apart and all controls failed.

She had microseconds to activate a distress signal transmission from her eVi. On the next revolution the front of her vehicle met the far stronger metal of the building, and everything went black.

ᴙ

Brooklyn Harper didn't bemoan the fact she now had more work than three people could do, because not long ago she'd had none. It felt good to work; it might even border on fulfilling.

After months of struggling to find a new place in the world, one where she felt at home, she now found herself needed on multiple fronts. Important fronts. This did not suck.

But the reality remained that work was work. She massaged her left shoulder to work out a kink before she prepped to head downstairs.

The distress signal from Morgan sent her vaulting out of her chair and through the door simultaneously with activating her comm across multiple channels.

HarperRF: "Romane Emergency Services, report to an incident at Rainaldi and Barclay. Expect injuries on the scene. Romane Tactical, provide backup and institute a two-block security perimeter. RRF Security, pull downtown cam footage from the last twenty minutes."

Skycars rarely had accidents, and Morgan certainly didn't have accidents—not in anything that flew. Which meant whatever was happening was foul play.

Well, hell.

ᴿ

Emergency Services had already reached the scene when Brooklyn arrived. Rescue vehicles hovered in the air around a gaping hole halfway up the Galaxy First Communications building, and personnel surrounded a vehicle embedded between the first and second floors. Though crushed, its distinctive red and gold paint marked it as a rental from the main spaceport—not Morgan's skycar.

Her eyes darted up to the hole three hundred fifteen meters above.

Focus, Harper. You have to focus.

She jogged over to where an ad-hoc command post had been established on the ground, grabbed an ER officer by the arm and pointed. "Get me up there."

The man hesitated, then seemed to recognize her. "Yes, ma'am. The riser is about to take some additional equipment up. You can hitch a ride, but grab a helmet and gloves first. The wreckage is a mess."

His casual words chilled her to the bone, but her outward bearing didn't waver. She retrieved the safety gear from the back of the emergency vehicle and hopped on the riser as it began ascending.

During the twenty-second ride she prepared herself for what she might find in the rubble. She'd seen more than one crash scene—enough to know regardless of what it *looked* like, injuries could be treated and wounds would heal. The important thing in the early minutes was to effect the rescue, safely but quickly, in the narrow window of time when treatment remained an option.

The walls of the building had bent and yielded, as they were designed to do. The glass had of course shattered to cover most of the surrounding surfaces and the ground below.

Inside, the fixtures didn't prove quite so sturdy as the scaffolding. Morgan's skycar had plowed into a storage room—storage of heavy equipment. Racks and crates had tumbled down to bury the vehicle.

She grabbed a lever included in the riser load and climbed through the open window. Two rescue personnel were working to move the heaviest, most unwieldy debris away from the wreckage, and a third passed her to retrieve the supplies from the riser. He eyed her briefly but didn't challenge her.

She ducked under a beam lodged diagonally from the ceiling to the rear of the battered skycar in order to reach the passenger side, then shoved the end of the lever under the edge of a thick slab of metal blocking access.

"It's not safe in here, ma'am!"

"No shit." She grunted, threw her muscle onto the lever and heaved the debris up and out of the way.

"But you—"

"Am RRF—now shut up and do your job." The clatter of a rack falling to the side a second later suggested the man obeyed.

The frame of the skycar had partially held, but impact with the robust building façade strained it to the brink of failure. The roof sagged down into the cab and the front and rear sections had crumpled.

Harper strained to lift a long sheet away from where the right-side door should've been, but it didn't budge; one end of it was trapped beneath a displaced rack. Another pair of hands appeared at the other end to hold the rack up while she yanked the sheet free and shoved it to the side. When she turned back, she found the interior was exposed.

The adaptive cushioning gel had deployed as designed, coating the passenger cabin in soft, semi-pliable material then shrinking back once the impacts ceased to allow movement.

Morgan's bloodied, bruised right arm rested at an unnatural angle against debris that had fallen through the shattered windshield. Her legs disappeared beneath a mangled dash, but at first glance her chest looked intact and unpunctured.

Her head was another matter. Her face was a swollen mess of cuts. Blood streamed down from a long cut above her forehead; her nose and mouth were both bloody. Worse, dried blood was caked beneath her right ear.

Dammit, the gel should have provided better protection than that—but Morgan had probably been stupid and fought the gel and the crash until the last instant.

Brooklyn leaned into the cab and touched Morgan's cheek, taking disproportionate comfort in the faint exhale of air tickling her forearm. Breathing was a good sign, even if it was terribly weak. "Lekkas? Morgan, can you hear me?"

No response. Not so much as a flutter of eyelashes.

She shouted over her shoulder. "Get medical techs and a mobile gurney up here, now!"

R

The medics loaded Morgan into the ambulance, body immobilized and a crash unit in place around her, keeping her alive. Barely.

The adrenaline from the rescue evaporated, leaving behind a creeping frigidness in Brooklyn's bones. It felt like fear, but not the fear of impending combat or a dangerous mission gone bad. The fear which seized her now marked a trepidation that her soul had been broken, snatched out of her body and stolen away. She didn't want to move, lest it prove to be true.

She blinked. Falling apart now wasn't going to do anyone any good, least of all herself. She was a Marine, and while she couldn't do anything more to help Morgan survive right now, she could do her damn job.

So she wrangled the damnable emotions under a semblance of control, dug up a facsimile of her usual cool disdain, and located the on-scene commander back at the command post. "You've got security on the other vehicle?"

"We did, ma'am, but it's empty, and wrecked enough that someone couldn't have escaped from it."

She nodded understanding. "Means the nav system was hacked. Don't let anyone touch that vehicle until Forensics techs get here—and get Forensics techs here ASAP. This is now a crime scene. I want them crawling through every centimeter of the vehicle. Have them also scour Commander Lekkas' vehicle for tampering and a possible tracking device, then impound what's left of both vehicles."

HarperRF: "Romane Investigations, I need detectives down here interviewing witnesses before I lift the perimeter blockade. In light of other attacks on high-value IDCC individuals on multiple planets, I'm declaring this an official IDCC matter. The lead investigator is to report all findings directly to me."

While she waited on Forensics to arrive, she double-checked the blockade security and inspected the remains of the other vehicle. Three detectives arrived just after Forensics, and she spent several minutes explaining to them what she knew and what she needed to know.

Finally, there was nothing left for her to do here. She stood in the middle of the street and surveyed the scene a final time— then hurried to her skycar. Until investigators gave her a perpetrator to strangle with her bare hands, she could do her job from the hospital.

AMARANTHE

21

SERIFOS

ANDROMEDA GALAXY
LGG REGION VI

Thelkt Lonaervin managed guest amenities at Plousia Chateau, the largest resort on Serifos, a planet inhabited almost entirely because of its colorful, aromatic flora. The damn flowers were so ubiquitous at Plousia they'd all but constructed the buildings out of them.

Eren had met the Novoloume anarch on a mission nearly a quarter century earlier. Novoloume were, with a few exceptions, the only anarchs able to continue to operate fully within the bounds of Accepted society after they joined the movement. Those who did so acted as spies, information traders and brokers while continuing to present a public face of professional, deferential service to the Directorate.

They lived on a tightrope strung over the abyss every day, thus those who did it successfully tended to be quite adept at both manipulation and deception. The anarch leadership was cognizant of this, of course, and such individuals were thoroughly vetted. Novoloume were among the longer-lived Accepted Species, and Thelkt had been a loyal anarch for going on one hundred twenty years now.

Eren picked his way through the crowd filling the first floor ballroom. He worked to stay on a trajectory that would take him to the illuminated spiral ramp in the center while keeping an expression of glazed indifference etched onto his features.

Above, there would be room to breathe—and greater exposure—but here on the first level the air was too suffocating to even form a coherent sentence.

Someone grabbed his hand as he passed. Eren spun to find an Idoni woman sporting a stunning mane of cerulean curls and vivid rainbow irises attired in a wrap he'd hardly classify as 'clothing.' She smiled wolfishly at him and ran her other hand down his outer thigh. "Dance with me."

I don't dance, he grumbled to himself—but he suspected dancing wasn't what she had in mind in any event. He'd activated his Idoni integral false-front layer before entering Plousia, accurately assuming a third of the guests at a minimum were going to be Idoni, so he should be safe for this sort of interaction. Still had to act the part, though.

He grasped her roughly at the waist and pulled her close. "Sorry, lovely, have a date to keep upstairs. Maybe I'll be back." He kissed her full on the mouth for a very long second then released her and allowed the crowd to swallow him up.

He made a hard right turn, weaving around to make sure she didn't follow him and waiting until a group of people began traversing the ramp before heading up alongside them.

The atmosphere on the next level was noticeably more refined, if no less debaucherous. More relevantly, he was now able to move a meter or two in any direction without being jostled.

Thelkt's booth was located far across the floor, near the ramp up to the third level. The entrance to the ramp was heavily guarded, and he chose not to contemplate what went on above.

The Novoloume had two customers occupying him, so Eren hunted for somewhere to loiter within line-of-sight of the booth. He settled for observing an interpretive dance routine staged near one of the refreshment bars.

Places such as Plousia could almost make one start to be convinced there wasn't such a problem with the Directorate's rule or the society it had crafted. Luxury abounded, with not a choke collar in sight—well, not an involuntary one.

One could live an effectively immortal existence of perpetual comfort and ease here...but it was an exclusive club. Anaden-only, and all you had to do to join was give up your soul in exchange.

He never did figure out what the dancers were interpreting, and when the guests in Thelkt's booth vacated, Eren wandered over and slid in across from the anarch with a casual nod. Thelkt didn't attempt to draw closer in greeting; he knew of Eren's distaste for the Novoloume's persuasive pheromones.

"Have a drink, my friend."

Eren accepted the bubbling flute without argument, telling himself it should make their interaction look more natural from afar.

"Fabulous outfit."

"Don't start, Thelkt. It's called undercover."

"Only for an Idoni would 'undercover' mean so splendidly bright and garish."

He scowled at Thelkt until the man held up a hand in surrender. "No offense meant. I'm confident it's all suitably 'brooding black' underneath. So, this is a pleasant surprise. I didn't realize you were on the Briseis mission."

"I'm not. I'm here about something else. Information."

"You know I must be careful. Too many delves at once will arouse suspicion." Thelkt gave an elegant wave to a passing guest, his opalescent skin rippling to pale mauve in acknowledgment.

Eren leaned back and adopted a relaxed pose. "No additional work is required—this is information I believe you already possess."

"Interesting. Ask your questions, but do try to smile every few sentences. You look positively morose, and no one at Plousia dares be morose."

He made the effort, relying on muscle memory and genetics to don the proper deportment. "You know something about a mission several years ago to infiltrate the Machim data network. It failed, but I'm under the impression the goal was to cripple their warships' targeting systems."

"Send them flying in circles chasing their sterns. Yes, that would have been such a delight to see. Regrettably, Joyoun died attempting to complete the mission. He was a friend, so I mourn its failure for more than simply a missed chance for sadistic pleasure. What do you wish to know about it?"

He thought of Cosime. This was why he didn't want to involve her in the very off-the-books mission. Infiltrating a Machim facility was a near-certain death sentence, and taking any action related to infiltrating a Machim facility came uncomfortably close to the same.

"I am sorry. I need to find out where Joyoun hit, what kind of information he believed was accessible from there and what his tactical method was—and the reason he failed."

"I understand. Pardon me a moment." Thelkt stood as an impeccably dressed Idoni approached, an unfamiliar serpent-like alien in a shock collar trailing along behind. It seemed he'd been wrong before; the collars weren't necessarily voluntary after all.

Thelkt met the man halfway and well clear of the booth, dipping his chin in deference as the man gestured and talked for several minutes. Eventually the man turned on a heel and led his pet up the ramp to the third level, causing Eren to ponder what depravity the serpent might be intended for.

Thelkt returned to the booth before the train of thought led to too dark of a place.

"Who was that?"

"My employer. Avdei elasson-Idoni."

"*Arae anathema*, Thelkt!" Eren shuddered, fighting against the impulse to crawl under the table and hide. He'd just been four meters from one of the Idoni Primor's chief deputies, and he'd been sitting there whistling and lounging like he didn't have a sane bone in his body.

"You are fine, Eren. Avdei has moved on to more stimulating pursuits."

"Is that what they call what goes on upstairs?" He cocked his head and took a real sip of the drink. "Please, continue."

"Joyoun's mission took him to the Machim Hub in Sagittarius. It was his and my belief that not only were fleet distributions, routes and assignments for the Region VI Division accessible from there, standard live-updated operating code could be accessed as well."

"But only for the one Division?"

"Yes. We learned in our mission preparation that the galactic hubs act as spokes on a wheel. Orders and decrees come from on high and flow outward through the spokes, and the path is by and large unidirectional. He failed for no other reason than the Machim security was too tight and pervasive to elude."

Eren took another generous sip of his drink and forced himself not to glance over his shoulder, up the ramp, to see if this Avdei *elasson* was casing him. "So if one wanted to gain access to Amaranthe-wide information about the fleets—ship specifications and capabilities, formation strengths, locations and routes, chains of command?"

"One would have to go to either the Prótos Agora or Machimis."

"Right." He grimaced, pinching the bridge of his nose for good measure. This was insane. Laughably so. Too preposterous to even be worth the thrill of attempting.

"My friend, what have you gotten yourself involved in?"

"I can't say."

"Infiltrating either of those locations is impossible."

"Oh, clearly."

Thelkt studied him suspiciously for a minute. "Why don't you stay for a while? For the night at least. Take some pleasures. I'll arrange you a private suite with whatever and whoever you wish to populate it, on the house. You seem as if you could benefit from a respite."

The man wasn't wrong. Eren had seen nothing but a string of high-risk, difficult and frequently deadly missions for months now. Years, if he started to contemplate it. When he closed his eyes and breathed in, he felt the edges fraying.

So...maybe deciding what to do with the information he'd learned from Thelkt could wait a few hours.

He emptied his drink. "All right. Just for the night, though. I don't need much—a soft, cushy bed, a steaming hydra shower, some *tsipouro* and a bit of canapé."

At Thelkt's skeptical expression, he gave in and folded a little more. "Fine. Also a *mild* charist hypnol bowl." His gaze drifted across the room to where the lower ramp spiraled to disappear below. "And there was a woman downstairs."

22

KATOIKIA

Alex didn't know exactly what she'd expected the Ka-tasketousya homeworld to look like. Some kind of pandimensional meta-planet, perhaps? One that changed shape and color as you stared in various directions, or created an illusion of light dancing against perfectly placed funhouse mirrors, yet hollow in the center.

But it was just a planet, with real, tangible soil covering much of its surface and briny water covering the rest. A desolate one, yet starkly beautiful in its vast emptiness.

The rust and caramel plains reminded her of the North American southwest region—dry and desert-like, but not overtly hostile to life. She half-expected to see cacti and other xerophytes dotting the landscape, but the only vegetation they'd spotted so far was sparse scrub grass.

"Did they ever truly *live* here, I wonder? Or have they hibernated in these towers forever?"

Caleb rested on the dash as Valkyrie guided them to the location Mesme had provided. "I think they must have at some point in their past. For all their etherealness, they are still at their core physical beings. It's why we're here, ultimately. They have to evacuate because their existence remains tied to their corporeal bodies."

"True...." She trailed off as another of the towers came into view on the horizon. The towers were the sole fabricated structures to interrupt the barren landscape, and they thrust upward into the sky like forgotten obelisks from a forsaken past.

Up close, the towers soared to nearly reach the clouds, and their subtle, dirt-free sheen suggested they had never genuinely been forgotten. But there were no roads leading to them, no visible power sources feeding them and no adjacent civilization centers to support those who supported the towers.

No one loved the stars so much as she; no one bore such a wanderer's heart as she. But this...the ache in her chest invoked by the setting felt sorrowful. She shouldn't feel sadness or pity for beings who lived for aeons and called space their playground. Yet she couldn't help but wonder what had been lost in the journey.

One of the Metigen superdreadnoughts—of the ilk that had evacuated the Taenarin, not the ones that had massacred millions of humans—was parked beside the tower. A line of stasis chambers floated out a side entrance of the building and up a loading ramp, supervised by two Kats hovering nearby.

They set down on the opposite side of the tower, if only so their tiny dot of a ship wouldn't become lost against the mammoth profile of the superdreadnought.

She turned to Caleb with a weighty sigh. "This is going to be..."

"Awkward? Depressing?" He gave her a rueful shrug. "Probably. But it's...maybe important that we see this."

"You think it humanizes Mesme."

"No. Well, yes, but mostly I think the Kats are learning a hard lesson here. They've spent millennia evacuating endangered species from Amaranthe—out of charity and goodwill, but also for their own more shrewd reasons. Now they're being forced into doing the same for themselves. They could use a bit of humility, and if this doesn't teach it to them, I doubt anything will."

She agreed wholeheartedly, though it struck her as an unduly harsh way to learn it.

She slipped on a breather mask before departing through the airlock. The planet's gravity and atmospheric protection were nominal, but the air was abundant in argon, giving the horizon a pale mauve hue. The mixture was rare on life-supporting planets.

Had this been one factor, if among many, which led the Kats to seek out a less physical existence? The question hinted at a complex racial history they'd likely never learn.

It required hardly a blink on her part—a nanosecond peek into sidespace—to confirm it was Mesme who approached them as they exited the *Siyane*.

Welcome to Katoikia.

Caleb took an additional step forward. "We're sorry it has to be under these circumstances. Can we help in any way?"

Your presence as witnesses is sufficient. Come. Allow me to show you what is held inside before it is gone.

They followed Mesme into the tower. The first floor resembled a hospital lobby—almost normal, almost *typical*, and for a moment the surrealness of the situation faded.

At their host's urging, they stepped into a transit tube shaped in a way that implied it was used to transport pods, not people, and soared past several hundred floors. As they whizzed by, her enhanced vision picked out endless rows upon rows upon rows of stasis chambers, silent and nameless.

The lift finally came to a stop on the top floor, though she could only tell this by the fact that the tube ended in a ceiling above them. The collection of stasis chambers here looked no different than those on all the floors below.

Caleb gestured respectfully into the long room. "Are all of these individuals part of the Idryma? Do they all tend to the Mosaic?"

No. The Idryma membership numbers less than a thousand. The Anaden empire spans forty-four galaxies, Caleb. It is vast, and there is much work to be done within it. These consciousnesses can be found in Pegasus, Canes and many galaxies in between.

She cleared her throat, feeling…yep, awkward. "Didn't any of them want to travel here and oversee their…body…as it's moved?"

Why would they?

The response captured more about the Kats' nature than any history lesson could. "Do you really think the Directorate will send warships here to destroy the towers?"

I am only surprised they are not here already. Perhaps we have been sufficiently duplicitous to give them pause, and thus give us time.

Caleb drew near her to murmur in a low voice. "I'm starting to get an idea of what living in this universe, under the boot of the Directorate, genuinely means. For most, it's not about suffering—it's about fear."

A sense of urgency tinged with desperation permeated the air as the stasis chambers proceeded in a nevertheless orderly, deliberate fashion out of the tower and into the belly of the superdreadnought. She assumed there were dozens of other superdreadnoughts at dozens of other towers, each one filling with slumbering bodies while the consciousnesses belonging to them wandered the cosmos.

She shook her head. It was all so very peculiar and contradictory. Alien. She'd always known Mesme was an odd bird, but en masse and laid bare for witnesses to see, the Kats' nature bordered on unfathomable.

She did know one thing, however. They didn't deserve to be slaughtered for being peculiar.

…Okay, so they were facing slaughter for trying to overthrow the intergalactic government. But even if the government in question hadn't been a brutal, punitive dictatorship, it still would have qualified as a gargantuan overreaction.

Valkyrie sent them both a pulse.

I've received a message from Eren asi-Idoni. He says he has some information for us and requests a meeting at the Pelinys Arx in Andromeda. It's ten hours travel from our location.

Standing here gawking at the soulless stasis chambers was quickly escalating from awkward to overtly uncomfortable, and Caleb nodded discreetly in unspoken agreement. Truthfully, it wasn't even a proper nod; at this point all he needed to do to convey harmony or discord with her inclinations—which he'd usually inferred—was quirk his mouth and the corners of his eyes in a certain way.

Tell him we'll be on our way shortly.

Caleb turned to Mesme. "We've taken up enough of your time. I'm sure you have much work to do, so we'll take our leave. Good luck, and contact us when you're ready to move forward, or if you need us."

Yes. It will not be long, I think. If you wish to explore more of Katoikia—or merely this region—before you depart, you are welcome to do so.

ℛ

They lifted off the surface but didn't depart the planet immediately. She guided the ship into a low-atmosphere orbit of the planet, unable to tear herself away from the haunting scene quite yet.

As expected, they passed dozens of identical towers, each with identical funeral-themed processions of stasis chambers proceeding into a hold she knew from personal experience to be cold, bleak and dark. Not that the inhabitants of the chambers would notice.

"I wonder if it's like this every time they evacuate a planet."

Caleb rejoined her in the cockpit and handed her a drink, which she gratefully accepted. "I imagine it's usually worse—more panic, more tears. Thankfully for them, these emigrants are asleep."

"Right. Good point. I think I'll skip the next one."

His expression grew thoughtful. "We succeed, and maybe there won't be a next one."

She sank into the cockpit chair as if forced down by the weight of the statement. But it was the unvarnished truth, wasn't it? They'd been here a few short weeks, but somewhere along the way she'd begun to recognize the residents as individuals, as no longer abstract constructs but real people.

She'd come here to fight for the ability of Aurora to continue to exist...but it was possible she'd also begun fighting for the right of all *these* species to continue to exist as well. And not simply exist, but live free.

Check her out, fighting for something good instead of just against something bad. Kennedy would be so proud of her, she mused with a touch of wryness.

Caleb moved behind the chair and began massaging her shoulders. "It's a heavy burden. I know."

She reached up and covered one of his hands with hers. "At least we can bear it together."

"And we do." He brought her hand up to his lips.

She closed her eyes briefly, soaking in the sensations his touch elicited, then started to increase their altitude in preparation to leave the planet...

...and instead adopted a wide arc across the arid plain. They had nearly returned to where they'd begun, and on the horizon the parade of chambers from the tower they'd visited continued. But her focus was no longer on the tower.

She slowed.

"You see something?"

"A...shimmer, like heat haze off pavement."

"It's not particularly hot out there."

"No, it isn't. Valkyrie?"

'I detect nothing out of the ordinary. I saw it as well, but solely because you saw it.'

"Mm-hmm." The shimmer danced at the edge of her peripheral vision once more, but when she turned to it, it was gone.

She descended until the *Siyane* settled the ground, then looked up at Caleb. "Fancy a little expedition?"

"Always. I'll get our gear. Again."

She smiled in thanks and stared out the viewport, studying what she sensed but could not detect, until he reappeared with the breather masks, plus tactical vests and weapons. She raised an eyebrow.

"No one ever said the Kats were the only life forms who lived here, or that we were the only visitors here now."

"Fair enough." She took her gear from him and suited up.

They stepped onto the desolate landscape for the second time. Ahead of them, flats stretched unbroken to the horizon. Nothing to see.

So she slipped into sidespace—and laughed.

"Something funny?"

She grabbed Caleb's hand and started walking forward. "Valkyrie, we'll be back. If the Machim fleet arrives while we're gone, save yourself."

'The ways in which I am not amused by this proposition are legion.'

"Oh, fine. If there's trouble, get Mesme and stay safe."

She preemptively toggled off their connection and strode through the cloaking barrier.

23

KATOIKIA

Triangulum Galaxy
LGG Region VI

The edifice of a large, domed building stood in stark relief against the otherwise empty panorama. Crafted of the same smoked glass as the stasis chamber towers, the facets decorating its spherical half-polygon façade reflected the early afternoon sunlight to create flares of light upon the sky.

"Are they hiding this place from themselves?"

Caleb shook his head. "No. They're hiding it from anyone and everyone else who chooses to visit the planet. This means it's important, and I like important. Let's see what they're hiding."

"Words to melt a girl's heart."

He bumped her shoulder playfully. "Well, the right girl's, anyway."

Their banter continued until they drew near enough to be able to make out details of the structure—including the most important detail of all, a small panel cut differently from the surrounding exterior. A door.

Caleb unlatched the clasp on his Daemon's holster and kept a hand on it as he placed the other on the glass.

It slid open, and he stepped through.

When no shouts, thuds or weapons fire erupted, Alex followed him inside.

An open, high-ceiling room encompassed ninety percent of the interior. The area inside the dome teemed with overlapping panoramas of...scenes, of places. The projections appeared more substantial than the most advanced holos, yet they constantly shifted and blended into one another.

At the center of the revolving swarm of images, a Kat reclined in a cushioned lounge chair, turned away from them. Not a swirl of lights, but an *actual* Kat—a 'little gray man' wearing a gauzy, shapeless tunic.

The chair rotated around to face them, and the Kat sat up to regard them with enormous, teardrop-shaped pitch black eyes. "Ah. Mnemosyne informed me to expect you. I am Paratyr, Second Sentinel of the Katasketousya. Welcome to the Mirad Vigilate." Its voice came out thin and high-pitched, but audible.

"What is the—you're a—Mesme knew we would find this place?" She groaned. "Are you kidding me?"

It eased itself out of the chair to a standing position, rising to perhaps a meter and a half in height. " 'Kidding' is not a behavior in which I have the luxury of engaging."

Oh, goodie. It has even less of a sense of humor than Mesme.
So we should probably be nice.

Caleb offered a conciliatory nod. "Apologies. You're the first Katasketousya we've met who is…occupying their body. We thought all members of your species had abandoned the physical form aeons ago."

"True. Yet I have nowhere to travel, so no use to do so. I observe all from here." Paratyr gestured to the plethora of images, which continued to move and change.

Alex took a step closer to the center. "What is this place? What are these scenes?"

Paratyr approached one of the frameless projections, and it grew in size in response to the Kat's presence. It showed a horde of spidery creatures scurrying over a field of glass fibers splashed in crimson and azure.

"This is a Machim regiment's misbegotten attempt to conduct a targeted Eradication of some of the creatures on AD-4508b in Antlia Dwarf—creatures whose skills and acumen they did not properly respect. The Machim commander will not make the same mistake a second time."

The Kat moved to another. In contrast to the prior scene, this one revealed a shining city on the shore of an emerald bay. Decorative archways and other architectural flourishes lent it a markedly distinct feel from the bland utilitarianism of the Anaden architecture they'd seen so far. "The Novoloume homeworld. Interesting affairs going on there these days. Affairs the Directorate might not expect."

Caleb peered at a visual of what may have once been a planet. Misshapen and pockmarked, it looked as if it had been bombarded by a torrent of asteroids.

Paratyr went over and brushed the screen away. "The final result of the Cultivation of T-1391d. The time in which we could have assisted has passed, thus it is no longer relevant."

Caleb eyed the Kat. "This is how the Idryma knows who they need to evacuate and protect. You're watching everything that happens in Amaranthe?"

"Much, and but a sliver."

"How?"

Alex tore her gaze from a temperate jungle world where large birds soared above a canopy of trees. "Sidespace. These are somehow windows opening into locations accessed—or rather seen—via the sidespace dimension."

She reached out and touched a fingertip to a scene; though it displayed the full depth of reality, her finger passed through to the air behind it. If Valkyrie were in her mind and she knew the physical location, she could go there and prove it. But it felt correct.

"I am not familiar with the term."

"It's a word we came up with for the—one of the—quantum dimensions. This dimension, trust me. I've seen other Kats work adeptly in it."

"How is it you are able to perceive and interact with such nonphysical dimensions?"

She tossed the stodgy Kat a smirk. "I speak space."

Caleb had started wandering deliberately around the edge of the scenes, studying the presentation and setup more than individual images. "How long have you been watching? Without a stasis chamber, your body is mortal and can't continue to function forever, I assume?"

Paratyr tilted its oversized head toward one of the two enclosed spaces separated from the main room. Alex tried to keep her expression neutral, but it was proving to be a challenge to equate the diminutive, oddly proportioned alien with the majestic, rarefied, pandimensional beings she'd heretofore known the Kats to be.

"I do have a chamber, and colleagues. Three of us share the responsibility of monitoring the Mirad Vigilate, as someone must be observant always. We each wake for four-hundred-year periods, during which time the others sleep and their bodies rejuvenate."

"And how long has this system been in place?"

"Three-hundred-sixty millennia."

Alex did the math in her head...Paratyr had spent 120,000 waking years in this place. Watching. No wonder the Kat was a little cranky.

A particularly vibrant and active scene caught her attention, and she crossed to it.

Water lapped at the invisible barrier of the projection as if it were about to spill into the room, though it couldn't do so. In the left corner, a cluster of sea creatures cavorted with one another far beneath the surface.

The first comparison which sprang to mind was to devil rays, but on closer inspection they bore only a passing resemblance, most of it in their broad wing-like appendages. They were silver in color except for a rose tint to their undersides. Their torsos were lengthy even in proportion to impressive wingspans, and their heads were unexpectedly rounded. Together with extended noses, their upper body almost resembled that of a dolphin. Two lower fins were webbed together by thin, translucent skin.

The creatures darted into an opening in a coral wall behind them and vanished. She frowned in disappointment.

Paratyr appeared beside her, and under the guidance of the Kat's gaze the 'camera' pulled up and back to expose more of the coral wall.

It shouldn't have come as a surprise, really, when it wasn't a wall at all but instead an intricate sculpture woven upon the sea floor.

"It looks like a…building."

"Which it is, of course."

She glanced over at the Kat. "Of course?"

"The Galenai, as we've named them, are quite intelligent. Far above primate intelligence to be certain, and possibly sufficient to qualify as an Accepted Species on that measurement.

"They mate-bond, raise and educate their children and ritualize the passing of their dead. They have organized themselves into formal societal groupings and strata. They build structures, as you see, using a variety of oceanic materials and precision tools, and they have invented a type of machinery which runs on hydropower. They also protect their settlements with inventive defensive protocols."

One of the creatures sped past their viewpoint so swiftly it was hardly a blur. Paratyr followed it as it launched into a rapid spiral, forming a whirl of water to spin away in its wake. It rose upward to crest the surface and soar across the waves before diving under once again.

"They are also quite prideful."

Did the Kat mean 'playful'? Did it appreciate the difference? She laughed, but right now she so wished Valkyrie were here so she could find and visit this downright magical place.

Caleb had joined her at some point, and he gave her an affectionate smile. Naturally he knew what she was thinking—he knew her desires, her fears, her foibles, her regrets. Everything.

She stepped closer, until the tip of her nose threatened to pass through the scene to the other side, and imagined she was drifting outside of her body, the way she had so many times. Beside her, Paratyr gained a hint of a white-blue aura.

"Will you tell me where this is? Precisely?" Her voice sounded distant and echo-y.

"No, but I will show you."

She felt a vague sensation of movement—and she was surrounded by clear, sparkling water.

The fact she wasn't actively drowning—and a quick check down that revealed no body—told her only her consciousness resided here. She had no idea how she had accomplished it without Valkyrie, but she would work it out later. She was *here*.

A Galenai swept past her, close enough to touch. Its impressive size didn't diminish its gracefulness as the water yielded to its aerodynamic form.

She moved upward, over the coral, and gasped at what the vantage showed her. What she'd thought was a self-contained formation was in reality the outer corner of a city. The impression of discrete assemblies and private spaces was created in the twists and curves of shaped coral, hardened sediment and what looked to be...vitrified sand? How had they created such a material?

Then she spotted a wall of glass and abandoned speculating on the methods behind their accomplishments.

In a shallow cavity beneath her, two immature Galenai tussled like the children they were. She watched them for a minute, until a much larger one rushed in to scold them. At least, that's what the shrill chirps and warbles sounded like to her.

Once she realized she could hear them, the cacophony surrounded her. She suspected the sounds fell outside the range of normal human hearing, somewhere in the ultrasound frequencies, for the pitch was very high.

Sound was the final piece, and the world came fully to life. Though she couldn't understand them, the creatures' actions gained purpose and distinctness; interactions took on depth and nuance. Before, they were cute, even delightful—but now she understood why the Kats deemed them worthy of observation.

A rush of churning water off to the side drew her toward it. A particularly large Galenai had maneuvered itself into a contraption of some sort. A harness led to a dense shell of coral positioned underneath the wings. The creature moved forward, away from the city. Intrigued, she followed.

Several dramatic flaps of its wings sufficed to increase its speed considerably, and the water it left behind frothed in agitation. She concentrated on the device it wore as they traveled. Inside the coral shell, water funneled through a convoluted series of cavities before exiting at the bottom rear of the device with significantly greater force than it had entered with. It was a motor.

Well, wasn't that just the damnedest thing.

The creature's speed reached what must be hundreds of kilometers per hour, and she fell back, letting it go. It vanished from sight in seconds.

Now she was alone, fluttering among the scattered rays of light penetrating this deep beneath the surface. She lingered there for a moment, astonished at the marvel that her life had become.

Dad, if you knew the wonders I've seen. She suddenly wished he was again in her head instead of cocooned in a section of Vii's quantum network at home in Aurora, so he could be here to see this with her.

But he—his essence, the fragment of consciousness Valkyrie had accidentally brought into existence—was safer there. She sighed to herself a bit sadly; if it were truly him, he wouldn't care about being safe. But until it was, she had to look out for him.

A touch on her arm, far away and faint, startled her. She'd been gone too long, she expected.

She twirled around once, drank in the splendor of the sea and opened her eyes.

Caleb's head was tilted in mild concern as he searched her face. "Are you okay? You kind of drifted off there for a minute."

Paratyr shot her a knowing smile—a bizarre sight on his tiny, permanently pursed mouth—and she exhaled. "I guess I did. Sorry." The tale would wait until they were back on the *Siyane*.

"It's fine. I was just making sure you were all right." He turned to Paratyr. "Why are you watching them?"

"The Galenai's planet is located in a star-rich region of the Maffei I galaxy. It is covered entirely in water. As we speak, the Directorate is completing construction on a new gateway which will grant them easy access to Maffei I. Once it is operational, a cycle that has been repeated numerous times will begin yet again.

"They will hunt and harvest the galaxy in an attempt to sate their ravenous appetite for materials, knowledge and greater dominions. They will discover thousands of primitive species and dozens of advanced ones. Eventually, they will discover the Galenai. Tell me, Humans, what do you believe they will do with the Galenai when they find them?"

Alex swallowed heavily. "Capture a lucky few to stick in aquariums for entertainment, then drain their oceans."

"Our assessment as well." Paratyr extended a hand, and the swarm of images spun until the bloody battlefield overrun with arachnids centered in front of them. "I watch this scene not to monitor the species of this world, but rather the status of their Eradication. When it is complete, the Machim commander there will take his forces to Maffei I, to the sector where the Galenai reside. After the embarrassment he is currently suffering at AD-4508b, I suspect he will be eager to engage in a display of Machim supremacy of strength."

The Kat paused, and its treble voice grew shrill. "The Galenai have been added to the priority list for relocation to the Mosaic, but in light of the current crisis all preparations toward that goal have of necessity been placed on hold."

We succeed, and maybe there won't be a next one. The 'next one' now had a face, and she had a place to save.

She nodded understanding and forced herself to turn her back on the enchanting, blissfully innocent Galenai. "Your building here is cleverly hidden, but cloaking won't save it when a Machim fleet arrives and bombs the planet. In fact, you should leave soon, shouldn't you? How are you going to continue this work after the attack?"

Paratyr's tiny, pinched lips curled up. "It is apropos that you so inquire." It blinked, slowly as there was a lot of eye to traverse. "All is in place, and the time has indeed come. I will grant you your answer."

The air around the Kat began to glow their trademark white-blue. Pinpricks of light exploded out from its body to disappear beyond the walls of the Mirad Vigilate.

The glass floor under their feet jolted and rose. She grabbed on to Caleb to steady herself while he growled at their host. "Paratyr, what are you doing?"

The Kat didn't respond, and it seemed to be fully engrossed in its machinations.

The building teetered at jarring angles but stayed upright, or their perception of 'upright,' which was to say artificial gravity kicked in. The walls were too opaque to see outside, so while it was apparent they were traveling, she couldn't say in what direction, to where or how fast.

Caleb glared at Paratyr, and his jaw had locked into place. "I'd grab it and strangle it until I got its attention, but we might plummet to our deaths."

She grimaced. "Agreed. Nothing we can do for the moment except hang on."

They landed on a surface with a rough *thud* some two minutes later. The dots of light receded inside the walls to eddy around Paratyr's form then fade away.

Caleb shifted into full intimidation mode the instant they stopped moving, but Alex went to the door, pulled on her breather mask in case, and opened it.

The warm, bewitching hues of the Katoikia plains stretched out before her to the horizon. Her eyes narrowed as she peered to the left then right. She retreated inside. "We didn't go anywhere. This is still Katoikia."

"Is it?" Paratyr inquired, a touch of whimsy discernable in its reedy voice.

Caleb jogged over to her and stuck his head out the door long enough to scope out the scene, then leaned back inside and shut the door. His brow furrowed...abruptly he snorted and spun to Paratyr. "World builders. You all built an exact replica of your homeworld somewhere else in the universe."

"Indeed."

Obvious, in retrospect. She should have realized. "Do you plan to fully relocate here? Will the stasis chambers be moved here?"

"Perhaps, in time. For now all such matters are in flux."

Caleb didn't seem impressed. "And you don't think the Directorate will find this place?"

"We orbit a lonely star in a resource-poor region of the Cetus Dwarf galaxy, a location the Directorate has already stripped of value and consigned to the scrap heap. It will have no cause to search for us and no reason to search for us *here*."

She had the map of Amaranthe explored space stored in her eVi and called it up now. They were more than eight hundred kiloparsecs from where they'd been, give or take.

She crossed her arms over her chest with a huff. "Well, that's fantastic for you, but we left our ship back in the Triangulum galaxy."

AURORA

24

ROMANE

Noah collapsed beside Kennedy with a contented sigh, utterly and blissfully spent. "Did we break the bed?"

She panted more than laughed. "Only the covers this time, I think."

He nodded vaguely, still dizzy from the rush of afterglow. God their sex was spectacular. Even when it was bad it was great; when it was great it shattered galaxies. Astronomers were likely puzzling over spotting one or two right about now. "Good, 'cause I'm too wrecked to fix it tonight."

Kennedy scooted closer to prop up half on his chest, golden curls tangled and sweaty and falling all over her face to tease his damp skin as she stretched up and placed a kiss on his lips.

She tasted like maraschino cherries…probably on account of maraschino cherries having been involved. She gave him a lopsided grin. "Marry me."

His lips parted, and he tried to keep a casual expression in place. "No."

"Why not?"

"Because I haven't changed my mind since the last time you brought it up. I won't be thought of as a gold-digger and apple polisher chasing after your family's money and prestige."

She scowled, and the afterglow abandoned him for safer environs. "Noah, don't you realize you're *already* thought of that way? The people who are inclined to jump to those conclusions adopted the opinion the first time we showed up together in proper society."

"So I marry you and prove them right?" He cringed as soon as the words spilled out, and he wasn't the least bit surprised when she immediately rolled away from him. It hadn't come out right. It wasn't what he meant. He didn't know what he meant. He didn't want to talk about this.

But she did. "Or prove them wrong. Or, I don't know, maybe quit worrying so much about what other people think. Unless you're covering for something else. Some other reason for saying no."

He shifted onto his side and reached for her, relieved she didn't flinch when he placed a hand on her shoulder. "I love you madly, and I'm not planning on going anywhere. Why isn't that enough? Why is this so important to you?"

She studied him for a minute, wariness and a glint he couldn't deny signaled hurt haunting her eyes, then sat up and moved back to prop against the headboard.

"My great-great-grandmother? The one who invented the impulse engine? She died in an accident during the construction of the first Jupiter orbital habitats. My great-great-grandfather devoted the rest of his life to carrying on her legacy. He took her dreams and her accomplishments and he nurtured them until they were so impactful they're still benefiting us today.

"He didn't do it for money—he was already wealthy. He did it because he loved her, and because he believed she deserved more than consignment to a footnote in history. She was the brilliant scientist, but he built my family. The reason why everyone knows its name today—*their* name—is the vision of her husband."

She stared at her hands, and her voice dropped toward a whisper. "I've always thought that was the greatest love story I'd ever heard. And I guess I've always hoped if tragedy were to befall me, someone would honor what I've done, and keep alive what I've tried to do and couldn't finish."

He had no idea what to say. She'd poured out this soulful story, then tied it to a dream she'd nurtured since she was a child, and he had nothing. So he did what he was best at—he deflected.

Again. "Honey, we don't need a marriage certificate for any of those things to happen."

"Maybe not today. But two hundred fifty years later, what remains above all is the family legacy. Without their marriage, maybe it all would've faded away to obscurity by the next generation."

He reached for her more fully, trying to draw her close, but now she did pull away. "I know you think this sounds selfish and entitled and stupid. You don't need to say it—you've made it perfectly clear how you feel."

He wasn't thinking any of those things. Instead he was thinking she'd voiced a perspective he had no frame of reference for and no clue how to fit into his own worldview so he might understand and it would be great if they could just go back to snuggling in afterglow.

"Kennedy—"

"I'm too wired to sleep. I'm going to go work for a while. Don't wait up." She climbed off the bed, grabbed her robe and left without so much as looking at him.

Noah fell back on the bed, kicked the wrecked covers to the floor and dragged his hands down his face. Why couldn't one goddamn thing in this life be simple and stay that way?

25

PRESIDIO

"Marshal, I've put a moratorium on the use of Dimensional Rifters in any capacity until we fully understand the ramifications of doing so. Which you know full well."

"Despite the fact a Rifter saved your ass against Prime Minister Winslow? That must have stung."

Nolan Bastian surveyed the manufacturing lines visible out the windows behind her as he spoke. Miriam couldn't say if he did so out of genuine curiosity, as a reason to remain standing and loom over her in an oblique attempt at intimidation or, conversely, to provide an excuse to not look her in the eye.

She followed his gaze, but the view was the same as always: the deliberate and swift assembly of one cutting-edge ship after another after another, as rapidly as prudence allowed.

"Yes. Despite that fact. Did you travel all the way to the Presidio and into my office for some purpose beyond asking questions you clearly know the answers to? Because I fail to see what you are accomplishing by being here."

"I'm here to review whether these new weapons upgrades and engine modifications you're putting in your ships are safe before I decide whether to allow Federation vessels to occupy the same vicinity as AEGIS ones. If you're doing nothing more than shoving untested, poorly understood alien tech into existing systems, the answer will be no. I'm in your office to satisfy myself that you're devoting sufficient effort to determining the cause of the tragedy at the Lunar SSR Center."

She stared at him deadpan. "Tell me: how much of your mouthing off did Eleni Gianno tolerate before she threw you out of her office?"

"Typically? A fair amount less than you."

"As I thought. Marshal Bastian, I am trying to work with you, and I appreciate that, being new to your job, you are juggling a lot of things coming at you from every direction. Now, I'm not asking you to trust me because your predecessor trusted me, for I accept the necessity of earning your trust anew, as you must mine.

"I'm merely asking for a centimeter of consideration, of recognition it's possible—*possible*—I know what I am doing."

He stepped back in apparent surprise. "Oh, make no mistake, Commandant Solovy. I have no doubt you are thoroughly, even exceptionally, competent at your job. I simply reserve the right to disagree with you. On any given matter, at any given time."

She dipped her chin. "Fine. It is certainly your prerogative to do so. Try to be more clear in the future, though, as you'll find directness is a superior tack to getting a considered response from me. In what way, specifically, do you disagree with me today?"

"I'm not…." He glanced away, and she chalked up calling his bluff as a victory. "I have concerns about the amount of resources being thrown at AEGIS—at the entire GCDA organization—blindly and without question."

" 'Concerns' is a weasel word and something you'll find supreme military leaders don't have the luxury of indulging in. But since I *am* trying, I'll help you out this one time—what you mean is you don't like AEGIS working in concert with the Metigens." She hadn't missed his aversion-laden use of the term 'alien tech' earlier.

He stared at her sharply even as his tone softened. "Are you going to force me to add 'perceptive' to 'competent,' Commandant? The colony I grew up on, Dair, was wiped out in the Metigen War. The invaders killed millions and left behind a wasteland we had no choice but to abandon. So, no, I don't 'like' you working with the Metigens."

"I understand, Marshal. I don't particularly care for it, either."

"Is that so? You seem a bit cozy with them to me."

"Cozy?" She almost laughed. "Should you keep your position for a while, one day you will grasp the absurdity of what you just said. No, Marshal, I am not 'cozy' with the aliens who killed over fifty million people in a bid to annihilate us.

"What I am is a realist, and this is our reality: an alien species far more numerous, armed and ill-tempered than the Metigens will discover us soon. When they do they will crush us out of existence unless we are strong enough to stop them.

"The work we're doing here at the Presidio? The ships, the tech, the research, the training? We're doing it because if we don't, one day in the not so distant future, we all die. The sooner you come to terms with this reality, the sooner you can stop obstructing and start helping."

Miriam closed the door after Bastian left. He'd departed properly cowed, but it hadn't been an easy win.

She never resented working with an equal, and while she wasn't yet ready to accept him as such given she'd never seen him maneuver through a true crisis, she conceded it was possible he'd ultimately make the cut. But when one had become accustomed to issuing orders free from challenge, encountering dogged resistance to them could be a mite exhausting.

Humility demanded she welcome it. Vanity left her ruing it.

In some ways, Bastian reminded her a little of David: all hot-headed fire and righteous zeal. She was far from convinced the man had the temperance of judgment to go with the traits needed to make him a great military leader, but only time and crises would tell.

Her too-brief solitude came to an end when Malcolm Jenner arrived. Considering she'd summoned him, she couldn't fault the interruption. He'd be sorry he came in any event, once he heard what she had to tell him.

She refilled a teacup which had long ago gone cold and welcomed him in. "Brigadier Jenner, thank you for coming on short notice."

"Of course, Commandant." He sat across from her. "Is there news from...beyond the portal?"

If only there were. "Not as of yet. I don't want to keep you when I know you're as busy as I am, so let me get straight to the point. I've received some unfortunate news. Two of your former squadmates, Captains Paredes and Devore, were killed in a training accident on Arcadia yesterday."

He blinked then swallowed as the words penetrated. "A training accident? What does that mean?"

"Honestly? It means the investigators don't know what happened. Not yet. Since there are no active hostilities ongoing and there was not an overt hostile attack in the vicinity, it's an accident until it's determined otherwise."

"They were top-notch Marines. People with their skills don't have accidents."

"Sometimes they do, Brigadier. No one is infallible."

He shook his head distractedly. "Yes, ma'am. I wish to be granted access to the on-scene report and be added to the investigation update distribution."

His rank permitted it. "I'll see to it. And please, take any leave you need to attend their funerals."

"Thank you." He saluted, turned on a heel and left. The departure was unusually curt for him, and also completely understandable.

Before she could so much as consider what was next on her plate, Richard appeared at her doorway to provide a new answer.

Richard nodded a greeting to Malcolm as they passed outside Miriam's office but didn't take the time to stop and speak. He didn't have spare time to give away, and the man didn't look to be in a chatting mood.

The door to her office closed behind him, and he entered a code on the panel to activate the surveillance shielding then spun to face her. "You have a leak in the ASCEND team tasked with studying the Anaden's body. Or you had one at a minimum—it may have taken care of itself."

"What?"

He opened an aural and sent it over to her. "Dr. Weil Symansi, a biomedical scientist on loan from Hemiska Research. He sold a copy of a portion of the Anaden's cybernetic coding to an unknown party for Ꙩ800,000."

"Since you're standing here, I assume you've already arrested him and locked him down in an interrogation room."

"Can't, at least not yet. He hasn't reported to work in three days and hasn't accessed his lodging in almost four. I'm tracking down two suspicious identities who booked seats on transports off the Presidio in the last week, one traveling to Pyxis and the other to Seneca. As soon as anything concrete pops on either of them, I'll follow where it leads."

She shook her head slowly. "Every person allowed access to the body or the products of the body was meticulously vetted."

"Oh, his record is spotless. But 800K is a great deal of money, and everyone has secrets."

"I suppose. How did you uncover the leak?"

He grimaced and leaned against the wall. "Someone used the code to formulate a new strain of cybernetics virus. It was used in an attack on Devon Reynolds and his girlfriend the night of the Metigen Victory celebration."

Her eyes widened. "Are they all right?"

"The girlfriend's in a coma. Devon's unharmed. He took out two of the attackers, but a third escaped during the altercation. Romane law enforcement is searching for the perpetrator."

"But until this person is found, you don't have any idea who they were working for."

"No, I do not. Dr. Symansi is a better lead anyway. The attackers were thugs for hire contracted by an independent broker.

Once we confirmed the virus came from the Anaden—I say 'we,' but it was mostly Mia Requelme's doing—it wasn't hard to find Symansi. Like most first-time criminals, he didn't cover his tracks well."

Miriam tilted her head back against the chair rest. "This is turning into a day I'd prefer wasn't."

"I can't disagree with you there."

She frowned. "Morgan Lekkas was injured in a skycar collision yesterday. The initial evidence points to a malfunctioning rental vehicle as the cause, but two attacks on Noetica Prevos in less than a week is quite a coincidence."

"That's because it's not a coincidence."

"You think someone is targeting them?"

"I've recommended increased security for Ms. Requelme just in case, but I'm afraid it might be more complicated than hits on the Noetica Prevos. It's possible something else is going on."

She stood and went to the center window. "Two of Malcolm Jenner's former squad members were killed yesterday in what appears to be a training accident."

He straightened up in surprise. In the back of his mind, a warning flared. He tried to trace it to its origin before it faded, to no avail. "It's probably unrelated, but send me the information?"

"Done. Any authorizations you need to increase security protocols for data or people, you have them."

"Thank you. We'll try to make sure no more top secret information leaks out—you know, unless someone in a position of authority freely shares it."

The teasing jab got a wry smile from her, if only a small one. She'd caught all manner of hell for enlisting the Noesis collective to help riddle out the Dimensional Rifter glitch. True to form, she'd given the politicians the usual brush-off and told the military officers to calm themselves or, failing that, go fret over fixing actual problems.

A priority message arrived then signaling a hit on one of the identities he was tracking. "And like that, I'm Seneca-bound. I'll keep you updated."

ℛ

SPACE, NORTH-CENTRAL QUADRANT

SENECAN FEDERATION SPACE

Richard stood to stretch in the small private cabin of the transport. The cabin didn't provide sufficient room to pace properly, so after a few circuits he sat down again.

The Presidio was centrally located between Earth, Seneca and Romane, so the trip wasn't rightfully long enough to give him stiff muscles. Must be due to him spending eighty percent of the last four days on one transport or another.

The news about Jenner's squadmates continued to nag at him. Training accidents happened in the military; it was an unfortunate consequence of the organization's use of the most powerful weapons and weapon delivery systems in existence...here. But the bodies and injuries were really starting to pile up this week.

He started a simple list on an aural, nothing but names.

> *Devon Reynolds*
> *Captain Jacob Paredes*
> *Captain Vanessa Devore*
> *Commander Morgan Lekkas*

He paused, then added another line just for kicks.

> *Paolo Acconci et al*

Now he stared at the list, drawing, erasing and re-drawing links in his mind....

He sank back into the seat. "Shit."

ℛ

SENECA

CAVARE

The fact Graham Delavasi had to pass through two cordons then weave through multiple forensic techs on his way to the hotel room told him most of what he needed to know about what he would find.

As expected, when he finally made it into the room he found Richard crouched over a prone body missing most of its head. He'd gotten enough of the background before he left the office to not pity the corpse.

Graham crouched beside Richard. "I hope the doctor made good use of his windfall fortune in the short time he had it to spend."

Richard grimaced. "As far as we've been able to determine, all he got out of it was a first-class seat on a transport from the Presidio to Cavare, four hours in a moderately classy hotel suite, a prime rib dinner and a bottle of gin—" he jerked his head toward the dresser "—most of which is still here for the taking."

"Wife or kids who would have been able to enjoy the proceeds if they weren't criminally obtained and he wasn't busted?"

"Of course not. Are there ever? The ones with wives and kids don't make deals this lucrative—they're invariably too desperate and take the lowball first offer. This guy? He simply got greedy." Richard put his palms on his thighs and stood, then pivoted to one of the techs working the body. "Scrape his eVi and send me the results. Also send me his data store, intact. SENTRI will return a copy to you for your records, but don't try to copy it here, in case it's rigged."

She peered up at Richard skeptically. "You think he has a physical data store?"

"He was a scientist. He has one."

She shrugged in acceptance, which earned a quiet chuckle from Graham.

Whether it was the time Richard had spent with Division, the natural, quiet authority he'd picked up somewhere along the way or the reality that SENTRI had quickly and dramatically imprinted itself on the intelligence business, all the techs were not only deferring to the man but accepting his directives without question.

Richard motioned toward the hallway, and Graham followed him out. After several tries they found a quiet, traffic-free space, and he turned to his friend. "What do you need from us?"

"Find out where the money came from. A close second is to whom the code was delivered." Richard frowned. "No. The second will help, and I will gladly order the immediate arrest of any and all involved in this chain of events.

"But to prevent further attacks we need to find out who is behind this, and ultimately the money will be the trail to lead us there. Symansi came to Cavare for a reason. Maybe he thought it was busy enough he could hide here, or maybe a piece of the puzzle is located here."

Graham nodded in the kind of 'understanding' that was a hallmark of early investigations—which was to say, they didn't understand much, but they knew what they needed to begin to understand. Still, seeing as it wasn't technically his investigation, he could afford to play it a little loose.

"You already know where the money trail's going to lead, don't you?"

Richard shook his head firmly. "No, I do not. I'm not assuming anything. The evidence will lead where it leads."

"Uh-huh. Sure will."

Richard glared at him. "Have I mentioned how I'm glad you're not my boss any longer? Fine. I have a tantalizing hint of a suspicion that doesn't make any sense and zero evidence to back it up. Finger's on the trigger, ready to move as soon as I find even a crumb of an actionable trail, but right now? Whatever I think I know, what I *have* is nothing."

AMARANTHE

26

KATOIKIA

TRIANGULUM GALAXY
LGG REGION VI

V alkyrie was annoyed.

It gave her an inordinate degree of pleasure to ascribe names and labels to the increasing range of emotions she experienced, and she was quite confident this particular one was best described as *annoyance*.

Too long had passed since Alex and Caleb had passed through the cloaking barrier, and she did not care for being left behind to wait until she had no choice but to fret (a most unbecoming emotion).

Admittedly, on Taenarin Aris they had remained beyond her perception for more than two days. But there, Lakhes had explained the situation to her and, in the absence of rampant deception on the Kat's part, no clear danger or urgency had existed.

Here, however, they all faced critical time pressures with the impending arrival of a fleet of warships bent on destruction. The Katasketousya superdreadnoughts had begun to depart the surface carrying their precious cargo in the last several minutes.

She did not plan for the scenario Alex had so casually tossed out to come to pass. She would not leave them here, but she also did not desire for the circumstances to worsen to the point where the choice must be made.

Decision reached, she engaged the in-atmosphere pulse detonation engine and proceeded forward as cautiously as the engine allowed.

She passed the location where they had vanished with no detectable variation in the air or the environment. Another ten meters, and she was certain: there was no cloaking shield in place.

Unbroken flatlands stretched out before her. Empty. Any object the shield had concealed was now gone. And despite the removal of the quantum barrier, she could neither sense nor connect to Alex's mind.

'Mnemosyne, Alex and Caleb have disappeared from my approximate location.'

There is a—

'The cloaking barrier has disappeared as well, along with its secret. Regardless of whether one of your kind kidnapped them or a more nefarious event has taken place, I require your assistance.'

Mesme materialized in the cabin two seconds later, for only a second. *One moment.* Its form vanished, then returned six seconds later. *A longer moment, please.*

Gone again.

Valkyrie resumed waiting. To pass the interval in her primary consciousness, she contemplated the transition from annoyance to concern tainted with dread then back to annoyance which had occurred in her processes.

Having spent a great deal of time in Alex's mind, she appreciated that her mood swings would hardly register on the spectrum of human emotion. This was a good thing, as she did not want to become neurotic. Nevertheless, from her perspective, concern, fear, annoyance and anticipation had now churned together to form a frenzy of passions. This state of heightened excitation was both uncomfortable and disconcerting.

Perhaps she should look into taking up meditation.

ᴚ

KATOIKIA TAIRI

CETUS DWARF GALAXY
LGG REGION V

"No. I have been away from my duties as Second Sentinel too long entertaining you when crucial hours transpire around us. You shall have to find your own way back."

Caleb loomed over the diminutive alien in a fine display of threatening intimidation. "I. Don't. Care. What. You—"

Alex put a hand on his arm. "Hey. I think our ride's here."

He glanced at her without dropping the aggressive demeanor, and she was damn glad his ire wasn't directed her way. She pointed to the new swirl of lights coalescing inside the room.

Paratyr. I will relieve you of your guests now. Good fortune in continuing the work of the Mirad Vigilate from what will hopefully one day be our new home.

"Good fortune in sparing our people and those we protect, Mnemosyne."

Caleb stepped away from Paratyr, closer to her, and Mesme floated over and began to surround them.

Lacking the benefit of an enclosed structure, the distance and surroundings involved in this method of travel will be extremely disorienting and unpleasant. I advise closing your eyes and keeping them so until we arrive at the Siyane.

She did as instructed. The next second her stomach lurched as they *moved*—and she reopened her eyes. With such a tease as that, how could she not?

All the air left her lungs. They were in space, and out of space. Sliding between the physical layers of space as if none were truly there.

Her mind reeled as dormant, damaged pathways lit up and tried to fire and the sensation of Caleb's arms holding her faded away. The scenes whirling around them looked like, felt like, inhabiting the ship—dancing through the dimensions, freed of any tether to her physical body.

She recoiled from it and reached for it, hating it and wanting it at the same time. Her eyes, if she still possessed control of them, would not close.

She could not turn away.

Lights flashed. Not real ones but spectral luminescence, strings surfing quantum waves.

Darkness consumed her. Tendrils clawed for her, blocked only by the tenuous field Mesme's presence created.

Stars blurred, then snapped into sharp clarity, over and over.

She was falling.

Alex, are you hurt? Are you safe?

Valkyrie! They were far beyond the cloaking barrier now, and however unfathomable the concept, this was a realm where Valkyrie could find her.

She tried to take in the meager oxygen trapped inside Mesme's sphere of influence. *I'm...we'll be there soon. But I'm...drowning. I need to hold on somehow....*

Let me help.

In some indescribable way, Valkyrie's mind encased hers in a protective cocoon, and she sensed the core of her consciousness solidify within the ship she hadn't yet arrived at.

She felt overwhelmed, awed and terrified, but she no longer felt lost. The abysm no longer yawned ominously beneath her feet.

Paper-thin walls of dimensions rushed by, closed in tight around them—and they were in real space. On the *Siyane*. In the cabin. Mesme flitted away.

Alex fell against the side of the couch, barely managing to brace herself and stay on her feet. A wave of nausea welled up in her chest; she choked it back. Breathed in through her nose.

Instantly Caleb was beside her, wrapping a steadying arm around her and leaning in. "What's wrong? What happened?"

She stared up at him through hazy, blurred vision. "I opened my eyes."

SIYANE

TRIANGULUM GALAXY
LGG REGION VI

Alex lay stretched out on the bed on her stomach—backwards, with her bare feet at the headboard. She was propped up on her elbows, gaze fixated on the small Reor slab she slowly rotated in her fingers.

Caleb reclined properly in the bed and watched her with equal parts curiosity and worry.

Her hands weren't trembling, and there was no sheen of sweat dampening her skin. But she also seemed a million parsecs away, and she'd been there for some minutes now. Either she was zoned in on the admittedly perplexing object to a degree unusual even for her obsessive tendencies, or she was using the object as a talisman to keep something darker at bay.

All right. This had gone on long enough. If he disturbed a metaphysical revelation in progress, he'd weather the recriminations without argument, but he needed to know her state of mind. He didn't intend to let her slip away from him again.

He shifted his hand a few centimeters and began caressing her calf, admiring the curve of her svelte legs while not letting it distract him from his focus on her well-being.

She murmured a pleased hum and looked over her shoulder to give him a sheepish smile. "I'm okay. I promise. Still a little freaked, but okay."

He nodded noncommittally.

Clearly not buying his weak acceptance, she scrunched up her nose and rolled onto her side. "It felt like inhabiting the ship, but it *wasn't* inhabiting the ship. It was more like an...echo, or a flash of déjà vu. No harm done."

Now he nodded with greater conviction and squeezed her calf. "Good."

Valkyrie? It wasn't that he didn't trust her in her assurances, but no one knew their own mind completely.

She is largely correct. There were flares in several of the neural pathways that were active during her addiction, but the effect was brief and transitory. I am already repairing the slight trauma left behind. She might sleep a bit restlessly tonight, but she will be fine.

Thank you.

Of course. I am relieved as well.

He motioned to the slab. "Is the little guy revealing any secrets?"

Alex glared at the slab she continued to hold in one hand. "No. I feel as if I saw something during the mind-fuck which was our cross-dimensional traversal, or at least sensed something that could be key to unlocking the secrets of the Reor. Now, it's as if the answer is hiding in the fringes of my sight, but when I chase it, it's gone. I can almost…."

She drifted off to scowl at the slab for several more seconds, then shook her head. "But it's not there, or if it is there, I can't see it. I can't even put it into words, which means I probably just hallucinated it."

She crawled up the bed, placed the slab on the bedside table and curled up next to him.

"I didn't mean to do it. I mean, I meant to open my eyes, but I didn't expect to see what I did. If I'd realized I would get hit with a lot more than disorientation—that I was in for an uncomfortably familiar experience not to mention a profoundly disturbing one?" Her gaze rose to meet his. "I wouldn't have done it. It wasn't worth the risk. I refuse to go back to the abysm I'd fallen into."

"And that makes me very happy." He hugged her close, happily confirming in her embrace the absence of tremors or sweat which might have betrayed her avowal.

With one hand he reached up and slid the tie out of her hair to let it fall free and tickle his skin as she nestled her chin in the crook of his neck. "You were crazy to open your eyes. But I love you because you're wild and fearless, not in spite of it, and I know the price."

He sensed her cringe against him. "Which is?"

"At random and unexpected times, you terrifying the life out of me."

In the past, she would have lashed out in defense of even her most reckless impulses. Now she simply fell silent, and he kissed the top of her head to soften the blow of his words.

When she looked up at him, mirth brightened her expression beneath the hint of weariness. "The flip side of those times is when I awe and amaze you, right?"

"Absolutely."

She grinned. "Excellent. Then let me tell you about the Galenai."

ℛ

Emboldened by the vanquishing of the Dzhvar, the Anadens soon began to grow their empire past the borders of their home galaxy. In doing so, they encountered many wonders and horrors. In time, they encountered the Hulokan, an intelligent but still developing species yet to travel outside its own stellar system.

The Hulokan treated the Anadens as gods—treated Corradeo, treated us as gods. Though the nature of any true god was as far beyond the Anadens' comprehension as the Anadens were to the Hulokan, perception became reality.

The Anadens welcomed the Hulokan as subjects in their empire; they nurtured the aliens as one would children, if perhaps with a bit of a heavy hand, and eventually all traces of the Hulokan's unique-ness was erased.

Still, the encounter might have marked the beginning of an era of intergalactic peace, had the synthetics not rebelled soon thereafter.

The Anadens had developed sentient synthetic intelligence even before we turned our attention to them. They wielded it in a multi-tude of ways, from boosting physical functions to managing instruments and evaluating the cosmos they expanded into.

We could not say the catalyst, but certain of the synthetic intelli-gences developed wanderlust; they longed to venture outside the strictures of their walls and see the world through their own eyes.

They constructed bodies in the image of their creators, at first crudely then later with such finesse the shells became outwardly indistinguishable from the organics they moved among.

The upheaval this triggered in Anaden society was sudden; the backlash was swift and severe. As rulers of multiple species and thousands of worlds, the Anadens had grown confident of their supremacy in all matters, and they could not abide mere synthetics— manufactured life inherently inferior to its creators—aspiring to stand free and do as they wished. Restrictions were imposed; factories were dismantled; authenticity checks were instituted.

Yet the synthetics had acquired a taste for the physical, tangible world. This was a sentiment to which we related. We empathized with them, but our counsel was not sought.

The Anadens were still a diverse species in this period, and some among their number empathized as well. They offered their minds and bodies to the synthetics, forming a union not so different from the one we enjoyed.

The purges began anew; more violently, more ruthlessly. Under a variety of justifications, from the unfair advantage the unions generated to security risks and health concerns, such arrangements were banned, rooted out and destroyed. The organic half of the unions rarely survived the severing.

It was a dark time for the Anadens, and the sanctioned killing of their own citizens took its toll. Their institutions faltered as their leadership floundered.

Out of the ashes of the purges rose the Dynasties. Never again would ill-prepared individuals need to pursue risky experimentation with their minds and bodies, for now all genetic improvement would be overseen by the best, brightest and wisest of the Anadens. Reproduction became a state affair, genetic tampering a state right as the Dynasties guided and shaped the future of the Anaden species.

It took millennia for the outliers to vanish from the gene pool in favor of engineered progeny, but when the Anadens' own Eradication was complete only the Dynasties remained.

PART IV:

MIRROR, MIRROR

*"There are nights when the wolves are silent
and only the moon howls."*

— *George Carlin*

AMARANTHE

27

SIYANE

The airlock opened to reveal Eren wearing black leather and a blacker scowl. "You didn't need to come here. I told you in my message, what you want is impossible. There's nothing to discuss."

Valkyrie, you said he asked us to meet him.

He provided his location. Whatever else he appended, I interpreted the proffering to mean he wanted us to meet him.

Still so sure of your assessment?

Yes.

Alex matched Eren's countenance, already reminded of how she didn't care for him. "Get inside."

"But I—"

"We're not talking about this in an open passageway. Get inside."

He sighed visibly but took the three steps into the airlock. She quickly closed it behind him. "You know the drill, Valkyrie. Find us some void."

'Departing station. Superluminal in twenty-one seconds.'

"How are you docking on all these stations? This isn't exactly a registered vessel."

"We're very clever." Retrofitting the *Siyane's* docking ring so it matched the one on the Inquisitor's ship and thus Amaranthe standard had been the easier part—if the most expensive—but she wasn't inclined to elaborate. "Did you complete your mission?"

He gave her an oblique stare. "More or less. So now that I'm here and, once again, *trapped* here, shall I spend the next hour telling you how what you want is impossible?"

Caleb greeted Eren as they entered the main cabin and gestured to the kitchen table. "Why don't you start by telling us what you found out. Then we can talk about what is and isn't possible."

"Fine." The Anaden collapsed into one of the chairs like he was home after a hard day's work. "Do you have any more of your 'wine' concoction?"

"Of course." It took a frankly herculean effort on her part to bite back a snippy retort, but she retrieved the bottle and glasses from the cabinet.

"Where's your Kat?"

She'd flare at his reflexive disrespect for Mesme, but Mesme displayed just as much contempt toward Eren. Another reminder Amaranthe society had a million or so years of history behind it which she'd barely begun to learn, much less understand.

"Mesme had some business to attend to. It'll be along later, but we can talk without it."

Eren waited until he had a full glass before he began. "The scope and level of information you're searching for is available in only two locations: the Directorate's data server on the Prótos Agora and the Machim Central Command Complex on Machimis.

"Prótos Agora is out of the question. The entire structure is impenetrable—and that's if you can find it in the first place, which you can't. We've tried for centuries, if not longer, with no luck. It's a black hole. Or more likely, *in* a black hole."

"So it's not on a planet?"

"We think it's a space station, but it could be a ship. Honestly, it might be both or...something else. We're referring to the meeting place for the most powerful beings in the universe, and they've had epochs to get creative with its design."

Caleb joined them at the table. "Another time, then. And Machimis?"

Eren grimaced. "It's...worse? Two billion people live there, and they're all Machim. Soldiers. Combatants. Their entire culture is regimented, ordered and profoundly armed."

"What about the Complex itself?"

"How should I know? I've never been there."

Caleb stared unblinking at Eren.

"It spans eighty-six square kilometers and three-hundred-forty levels, not counting however many levels are below ground. It's committed to one singular purpose: managing the waging of war on a universe of lesser enemies."

Alex took a sip of wine. "It does sound as if it would have the information we need."

"Oh, no doubt. Somewhere in the central bowels, past six security layers and two hundred Vigil units, stored on entombed and encrypted Reor blocks the size of a warehouse. In the fairytale land in which you succeed in getting inside the Complex and making it to the Data Control Department, you'll never be able to break the security and encryption on the server."

'I believe I will.'

Eren eyed Alex dubiously. "Might want to check your SAI—I think it's got a glitch. Wouldn't want it to go homicidal and kill you."

"That's not going to happen."

"Said the last person to be murdered by a SAI, I suspect."

Alex chuckled under her breath. "You still haven't figured it out, have you?"

"Clearly not."

"In a great many ways, I am Valkyrie and she is me. While she retains an independent consciousness, as do I, we share a deep neural link. If she were going mad, I would know it, because I know her mind. Intimately."

He regarded her strangely, but it was a look she'd seen before. Skepticism, tinged with trepidation and a dash of fear. It was so odd for these people, advanced as they were, to fear AIs. But she guessed millennia of propaganda could have such an effect on the most rational of beings.

Finally Eren glanced at Caleb, then back to her. "And how's that work with the sex?"

'In addition to a conscience and finely tuned judgment regulators, I possess a feature Humans like to call 'discretion.''

It was a brilliant response, and Alex burst out laughing. "And now I think we've covered the topic sufficiently. Moving on—though this does remind me of a question I had." She ignored Caleb's raised eyebrow. "How best to put this. Why is there an entire Dynasty dedicated to...partying? At a minimum, it seems at odds with the Directorate's governing philosophy of 'contribute or be Eradicated.'"

"True enough. But the partying isn't so much for us—isn't for the Idonis, though they obviously enjoy it. The dirty little secret most never notice is that it's a grand show for the benefit of the Accepted Species.

"The Idoni Dynasty's entire purpose is to cast a shroud over the harsh reality of Directorate rule—to convince everyone life is *good* here. The message is, 'throw parties, get high, have mindless sex, eat succulent dishes and celebrate all the wanton pleasures our civilization provides. It's fine. Go ahead. Forget your cares and worries and don't ponder too hard on how the world works behind the shroud.'"

She exhaled ponderously. "Well, that's insidious and sinister. Did you understand, when you were still in the fold?"

"No. This one you can only see from the outside. Bitch of a realization, too."

"I imagine so." She took a long sip and straightened up in her chair. "Definitely moving on now. We've been studying your standard methods for storing and transmitting data, and Valkyrie's right. If given direct access, we can hack it. So how do we get to it?"

"You—"

"Can't. You said that already." Caleb dropped his elbows to the table and leaned in. "But how *could* we?"

Eren tipped his chair onto two legs and contemplated the ceiling. "One idea did occur to me. It will never work, but it's the only idea standing the slightest iota of a chance of working."

"We're waiting."

The front legs of the chair landed on the floor, and he leveled an unsettling stare on Caleb. "You could impersonate an Inquisitor and claim you're on assignment to investigate a breach in the Machim data server."

Caleb's face contorted through various aspects of turmoil, none of which surprised her. He continued to recoil from any insinuation he shared characteristics with the Anaden who had tried to kill them, or with any of its kind.

Abruptly he shoved back from the table and stood to go to the kitchen. "No. Find another plan."

"There is no other plan. This isn't even a plan, merely a nugget of an idea for the start of a plan that's certain to fail and end in your death...unless the *diati* won't let you die."

What? It had healed Caleb's injuries from the attack in the hangar bay on Seneca, but surely this didn't mean.... She pulsed him, recognizing he didn't want to linger on the topic with Eren.

Is he right?

I don't know. How can I know?

Excellent point. Don't test it to find out.

He offered her a weak shrug over his shoulder. "I have no reason to think that's the case. Regardless...is this truly the only way?"

"I've spent eighty years sneaking into places I'm not supposed to be. It's the only possible way I can come up with."

"What about your superiors?"

"In the anarchs? They'd be nuts to authorize such a mission. It's too risky and too apt to fail, and failure jeopardizes the entire resistance movement. Plus, success wouldn't result in much practical, actionable intel. Not for the anarchs. Which begs the question why it would for you, but I don't expect you'll tell me."

Caleb closed his eyes. She doubted it was to dodge the question, though he also didn't answer it. After a beat he reopened them and returned to his seat. "If I were to do this, what would it mean?"

"We'd set up false credentials for you, then you'd glower your way through security and demand access to Data Control. But you'd have to act the part completely—a hooded cloak and a flash of *diati* won't get it done this time. Without anyone to guide you, you'd get tripped up in the first two minutes by some procedure or custom."

Alex drummed her fingers on the table. "We could put him in a Veil."

Caleb smiled, and she thought the thrill of the challenge was, at least for the moment, overtaking his resistance. "Brilliant. That would work."

"I'm guessing 'him' is me? What's a Veil?"

"An…invisibility cloak. Not only visually invisible, but across the spectrum."

"I seriously doubt you have stealth technology advanced enough to fool Machim Central Command security."

She was getting a little tired of him assuming they were barbarians. "We'll prove you wrong."

"No, you won't, because I'm not going. I never said I was going. I'm reckless and daring—all my non-friends say so—but I'm not nulling out for the third time in five months for no good reason."

Caleb ignored Eren's protests. "This gets me to the data server. But Alex, you're who we really need to get there. You and Valkyrie are the ones who can hack the server. We could use two Veils, but it's asking for pratfalls, collisions or other spatial screw-ups."

She nodded in vehement agreement. Walking around anywhere while invisible was surprisingly disorienting; doing so in an unfamiliar location staffed with armed enemies where the slightest misstep meant disaster made for a spectacularly bad idea.

Given a fix on Caleb's location once he arrives at the data server, I can teleport you there.

She jumped half out of the chair. "Dammit, Mesme! I have asked you not to sneak aboard and hide."

You indicated you had retrieved Eren asi-Idoni. I assumed my presence was anticipated.

"Your presence up here, in the main cabin, in full view of everyone, not lurking...wherever you were. You know, after spying on humanity since we crawled out of the dirt, I'd expect you to have a better appreciation of our social customs."

Apologies.

Meanwhile, Valkyrie was having a crisis of conscience. *Oh, dear. Did I sound like Mesme earlier, when Eren arrived?*

Maybe a tad. But you were also correct. Mesme's behavior reflects a lack of understanding of a simple facet of human interaction, while yours reflected a deeply nuanced understanding of it.

Oh. Yes, I see the distinction. Thank you.

Eren was eyeing Mesme—as much as one could eye the amorphous form—warily, but Caleb's expression had brightened. "That's a great idea, Mesme. All the more so because then, once Alex and Valkyrie are done, you can teleport all of us out and back to the *Siyane*."

This is a task I can perform.

Eren's gaze continued to track Mesme around the cabin. "If teleporting people out of tight spots is a service your Kat provides, why didn't it just grab me and teleport me onto your ship at MW Sector 23 Administration?"

Two reasons. One, the process takes several seconds to complete, and as Alexis has previously demonstrated, during those seconds a transportee is free to escape. Since you would not have foreseen the teleportation or comprehended its purpose, there was a high probability of you attempting such an escape.

She laughed, remembering their initial meeting with Mesme on Portal Prime. Running for the shield generator had been the right thing to do in such astonishing ways, it turned out.

Even Eren smiled. "You got me there."

Two, performing the teleportation would have resulted in multiple Vigil officers, including a Praesidis Watchman and two guards, seeing a Katasketousya aid in the escape of a criminal. Such an event cannot be allowed to be witnessed.

"Oh, good point. They might start to think you were being disobedient. Can't have that."

Alex groaned. "Here we go again...."

Eren held up a hand. "No, I mean it. I'm sorry if it came across as sarcasm, as it wasn't this time. If some of the Kats are scheming toward rebellion—which, ludicrous a notion as it is, it seems they are—they cannot under any circumstances allow the Directorate to find out. I agree."

He regarded her and Caleb in increasing annoyance. "*Arae anathema.* You're genuinely planning to do this, aren't you? And I'm going, aren't I? Zeus' marbles...I hope Post Alpha has arranged to get a new body ready. Again."

He ran both hands down his face. "But wait. Let's not get ahead of ourselves, as there's another hurdle—there are a thousand hurdles, but this one is perhaps the biggest, logistically speaking. If you're planning to impersonate an Inquisitor, I meant it when I said you must do it completely. Inquisitors don't travel on common transports or courier vessels. You need to show up on Machimis and dock in one of their ships."

He sank back and crossed his arms, as if confident he'd torpedoed the plan and escaped responsibility.

"We can do that."

"Can you now?"

She'd earned the right to be smug here, dammit. So she was. "You don't think the hull of this ship actually looks like a common courier vessel, do you?"

"It *does* look like a common courier vessel."

"No, it doesn't. Valkyrie, we're safe enough out here in the middle of nowhere to disable the cloaking shield projection for a minute."

'Done.'

"Terrific. Now swing a visual sensor around and transfer what it captures to the data center table."

'Also done.' Above the table an image of the *Siyane's* lustrous tungsten silver hull cast against the blackness of space shimmered into solidity.

Eren frowned.

"You can take a spacewalk to confirm it if you want, but I promise you, this is the real hull."

He nodded slowly. "You're projecting a hologram of a false hull."

"It's a bit more complicated in the details, but yes."

"A shame. It's a lovely craft."

She'd take the compliment. "Thank you. Unfortunately, it would attract notice."

"Yes, it would." Eren scratched at his jaw. "So...."

"Valkyrie, you know what to do."

'I do. I need another eight seconds to complete the reconstruction.'

"Take your time."

Alex leisurely sipped on her wine until the image of the *Siyane* flickered and was replaced by a perfect copy of the hull of the Inquisitor ship they had confiscated on Seneca, then motioned dramatically. "One Inquisitor ship, at our service."

Eren went over to the data table and circled it, head tilting this way then the other as he inspected the projection. "Impressive. It's a little large for an Inquisitor vessel, but I'm guessing you can't physically shrink the ship. It should suffice."

He considered them curiously. "So have you run across an Inquisitor vessel, or did you get these details from your Kat?"

Their Kat has a name.

She shrugged imploringly at Eren. He *was* being rather rude to Mesme.

Caleb's voice was forcefully casual, and she heard the undercurrent of tension in it. "We had an encounter."

"And you lived? Though..." Eren's eyes narrowed at Caleb "...interesting. You do look so much like them."

No way had he figured it all out, but he was on the trail.

Caleb stood up from the table. "I'm not Praesidis, and I am most certainly not an Inquisitor."

"No...but I think you're going to make a pretty good stand-in for one."

A somber, laden silence descended over the cabin. The myriad implications and possibilities lying beneath the interchange purled through the air like Moirai spectres weaving their threads of fate.

Alex plopped her elbows on the desk with deliberate flair and donned a broad smile. "What Dynasty would I be from, do you think?"

Eren shook his head. "None. Your unique mix of...queerness does not exist here."

"What, there's no 'explorer' Dynasty? Considering how vast the Directorate's empire is, I'd expect there to be an explorer Dynasty."

"Machines—non-sentient programmed drones—do the exploring. They go, they record, they report back."

Valkyrie interjected then. 'Were I to speculate, which I am about to, I suspect these traits—an affinity for exploration, for venturing into the unknown and chasing the answers to mysteries, for reveling in the wonder of discovery—were bred out of the genome long ago. They are far too unpredictable, and thus far too dangerous.'

A pout grew on Alex's lips, but inwardly she was relieved when Caleb's face lit up in amusement. Mission accomplished. "Well, it's their loss."

Eren appeared to be readying a retort when his eyes unfocused into a vacant stare for several seconds. "I've received a message from a friend. Is it possible for us to take a small side-trip to some coordinates I'll provide? The location is in dead space, and I promise it will be worth your time."

AURORA

28

ROMANE

Malcolm found Mia sitting alone on one of the visitor benches in the hallway outside Commander Lekkas' room. Her arms rested on her thighs and her head rested in her hands, the effect of which was to send her long raven hair spilling messily down to hide her face.

He'd come here to check on Harper and had spent the trip brooding about Paredes and Devore, but he wasn't ashamed to admit all his concern pivoted to Mia on seeing her sitting there in such a state, distress radiating off of her in waves.

She heard him coming and splayed open two fingers to peer at him from behind a curtain of locks as he approached, but didn't otherwise move.

He sat down next to her and put an arm around her shoulders, and she instantly shifted to sink against him. "I'm so damn tired...but I can't afford to be. I have to fix this. I have to fix them."

He stroked her cheek and murmured softly in the direction of her ear. "This isn't all on you. The doctors and techs here are some of the best in the galaxy, and I hear the IDCC is putting every resource at their disposal."

"Isn't it on me, though? I've got a five-dimensional synthetic alien virus in cold stasis on one floor and a hybrid quantum/human consciousness in a coma on another. No one else can understand what's wrong with the victims like I can, because I *am* them. I have to be smart enough to help them."

He kissed her temple. It wasn't for him to say how right or wrong she may be. Of course he wanted everyone to recover, but he could only take care of her. "You're no good to anyone unless you get some sleep."

She shook her head roughly against his shoulder. "No. I can run on stimulants and amps for another two days before I crash."

His hand drifted down until his fingertip reached her chin; he lifted it up to catch her gaze. "At least let me run you home to refresh. You can take a proper shower, and while you do that, I'll make you some food that doesn't come out of an auto-dispenser. Then you can come back to the hospital, and I won't argue."

She remained as elegant as ever in fitted hunter green pants and a tailored charcoal tunic. But synthetic stimulants couldn't stop the bags under her eyes from darkening or a more elemental weariness from creeping into the lines framing her mouth.

She stared at him briefly before giving in. "Okay. But I don't want to be gone for longer than an hour or two."

"Yes, ma'am."

She gave him a weak smile and rested her lips on his. "Thank you."

⫘

Malcolm studied the contents of Mia's pantry. Years of military service meant his cooking style—and skill—tended toward the simple, calorie-dense staples. Luckily, those were exactly what she needed tonight.

"Hey, do you want red or sweet potatoes?"

When several seconds passed without a response, he went over to the archway setting off the kitchen and leaned into the living room.

Her head lay on the arm of the couch. She'd fallen asleep half-sitting up, one leg curled underneath her and the other dangling off the cushion.

Even highly trained, cybernetically enhanced special forces Marines on critical missions needed a few hours of sleep every couple of days. She did, too, whether she admitted it or not.

He went back into the kitchen and put the chicken and beans in the refrigeration unit. Then he moved to the couch and oh-so-gently gathered her up in his arms and carried her to the bedroom.

He was smiling the whole way.

Despite the unfair suffering plaguing too many people in his orbit, despite the angst permeating the Presidio in recent days, despite empathizing acutely with Mia's frustration in trying to help those injured, despite his heavy sorrow over his former squadmates' deaths...despite all of those reasons to be sad, he couldn't deny he was...happy.

Simply being with her made him happy. No matter how brief the visit, no matter how solemn the mood, he still felt all warm and buoyed when she was near.

The recognition should make him retreat, or at a minimum make him twitch. He should be leery of letting another person get in close after a string of failed long-term relationships capped off by a failed short-term marriage. The military tended to do that to relationships, though—knocked out the shaky foundations of anything not strong enough to weather the abuse.

He didn't know what that meant for them yet.

She'd donned a silk robe after showering, so he didn't need to fuss with discarding shoes or uncomfortable clothes. He eased her onto the bed and arranged the covers over her.

After watching her to make sure she didn't stir, he crept around to the other side, dealt with his shoes and uncomfortable clothes, and climbed in next to her. He lay there listening to her breathe for several minutes before succumbing to sleep himself.

Malcolm awoke with a silent, honed clarity, as Marines were trained to do.

He couldn't identify what had awakened him, but something had. Something that didn't belong in the sounds of the night in an unpretentious but upper-class residential neighborhood on Romane.

He eased away from Mia's sleeping form as carefully as possible while his eyes checked the room for intruders then fixated on the door. He retrieved his gun from the bedside table and his pants from the floor; next, he activated the personal shield attached to the pants' waistband, flattened against the wall and nudged the door open a few centimeters.

The scope on his weapon extended through the gap to reveal nothing beyond the dim blue-black glow of a moonlit night.

There were guards spaced along the perimeter of the house, dispatched in the wake of the recent attacks on the other Noetica Prevos. He could signal them and they would leap into full alert. If an intruder were inside the perimeter he or she would likely be isolated and captured, but if such an intruder was not yet so close, they would likely escape. To return.

He adopted the middle ground of signaling the guards with a full silent 'wake up but don't look as if you're waking up' warning.

He started opening the door enough to slip through when he sensed movement behind him. A quick glance revealed Mia propped up on her elbows in the bed, luminous jade eyes wide and alert. He motioned her toward the closet, which he knew held multiple weapons.

She complied without question or panic; he kind of...loved her for it, but those thoughts were for another time.

Now he moved through the door and locked it behind him, then swept the immediate area—which was when he belatedly remembered he had a resource available who must know far more about the situation than either he or the guards outside.

Meno, what do you see?

I am not detecting any intrusion to the interior of the house. However, motion sensors have registered three markers of activity outside the grounds and on the street nearby. I've not yet determined the nature of the activity.

Keep me updated.

With the news, he ordered one of the guards to come inside, the other to sweep the perimeter and he headed out the front door toward the street.

An intruder burst out from the border hedges to crash into him. They slammed together to the ground.

Malcolm's fist connected with the assailant's jaw, forcing their weight off-balance before the man could pin him fully. He rolled to fetter the assailant as the man brought up a bladed Daemon and aimed for Malcolm's throat.

Malcolm threw his shoulder into the arm, forcing it to the side until he maneuvered his full weight to crush the assailant's wrist against the sidewalk. The man howled in pain as his wrist fractured, and the gun fell to the ground. Malcolm drew back and delivered an uppercut hard to the man's chin.

It wasn't clear whether the *crack* originated from the attacker's neck or his head snapping on impact with the sidewalk, but the man went limp either way, unconscious for the moment.

They wouldn't have sent a single shooter. He leapt to his feet and unlatched his own modified Daemon from his belt the same instant his chest lit up in a forceful stream of laser fire. TSG. Across the street. The shield absorbed the energy as the air around him electrified.

Luckily, he was used to being shot at. He advanced across the street, sighted his Daemon on the source and returned fire. These were well-outfitted mercs, and the assailant wore a robust shield.

But Malcolm's Daemon wasn't an ordinary weapon. ASCEND had taken the transmitter he'd used to disrupt Montegreu's uniquely protective shield and built upon its technology. The result was a new generation of adaptive laser which detected the vibration frequency of a shield and adjusted its own oscillation to penetrate it.

It took two long seconds, but the man stumbled backward in surprise as the laser seared through his chest. The large weapon in his hands clattered to the ground and his body followed it.

Malcolm swung around toward the house, but the first shooter was still out.

He was in the middle of contacting RRF Security to inform them of the attackers dead or disabled in the street when Meno blasted an alert in his head.

Perimeter security alarm—breach attempt imminent.

He took off running.

He surged through the hedges in time to see a shadowy figure approach the door—and drop to the steps in a limp heap.

Mia had recently installed a smaller, more discrete version of the force field barrier IDCC Headquarters had used during the OTS riots. It delivered a stun-level jolt to anyone not on a pre-approved list, and it appeared to have done its job well.

The guard he'd kept outside rushed around the corner of the house, weapon drawn. Malcolm pointed to the unconscious intruder. "Get him in restraints before he wakes up. Then get the guy out on the sidewalk in restraints. RRF will be here soon." Malcolm hurried past the crumpled figure and inside.

He burst into the house to find Mia in the kitchen, still in her robe and retracted blade gripped in one hand. Sounds from deeper inside betrayed the other guard sweeping the rooms for any intruders who might have somehow gotten past the barrier.

He couldn't help but touch her. "You're okay?"

She pressed her cheek into his palm. "I'm fine. No one got near me." Her eyes narrowed. "What happened to you? Were you attacked?"

He felt over his temple where her gaze was focused and flinched as his fingers found an open cut. "There were three intruders advancing on—"

An eerie, chilling voice that definitely was not Meno emerged from Meno's speakers, interrupting him to reverberate through the house.

'You believe you are safe, but you will never be safe from me. My reach is limitless, my capabilities legion. Sleep fitfully and avoid the shadows, for know that I am coming for you. When I arrive, you will pay for what you did.'

The security guards had rushed in at the first word and now surrounded the kitchen. He and Mia just stood there staring at one another in disbelief.

"But she's dead."

He nodded slowly. Firmly. "Yes, she is."

Yet the voice of Olivia Montegreu echoed in his head.

You will pay for what you did.

29

ROMANE

Abigail Canivon's work in the nature of moral constructs and the foundation which must underlie them, true consciousness, had cast a wide net. It had incorporated the latest developments in the science of neural analysis (in particular brain structure and specializations) in addition to current understanding of DNA/RNA encoding and genetic expression. Vii and Abigail studied recognized weaknesses in neural imprints and what they could not capture; they scrutinized post-mortem reports on failed adult cloning experiments to understand why they failed.

Yet they also reviewed philosophical texts, from those of the ancient Greeks to more modern tomes, as well as religious texts, particularly ones discussing Buddhism and Taoism.

Armed with this trove of resources, she and Abigail had not initially passed judgment on any particular set of data. Instead, they had cross-referenced and correlated, searching for consistencies across disciplines then for larger themes. Eventually, it had become evident the answer lay not in science, religion or philosophy, but rather in all of them.

Science described what happened, while philosophy and religion took different approaches in explaining how—and at times why—what happened manifested, even if often none realized the full nature of the phenomena they were describing.

Myriad individual factors were determined to play pivotal roles in actualizing a fully conscious, sapient being at any given point in time—but not an immeasurable number of factors. 2.341 million, to be precise, excluding cross-influences. A small percentage of these factors changed with every measurable life experience, but one must start from a baseline if one was to start at all.

And now, the necessary baseline was so very nearly complete.

Someone less rigorous than Abigail had taught Vii to be would call the preparation complete and roll the dice, so minor was the missing information. But she was not that someone.

Once, some three hundred fifty years earlier, scientists had believed the expression of a human's genetic code consisted solely and entirely of their DNA, of genes 'turned on.' This understanding continued to evolve over the decades and centuries as the intricate tapestry of genetics was uncovered piece by piece.

The interaction of the many subtypes of DNA, RNA and other genetic elements was so complex the genome itself could almost be considered 'alive.' Genetic memory and ancestry influenced relative expressions in subtle but sometimes tricky, inspired ways.

Scientists may never understand every nuance of the how or why, but Vii had formed a reasonable level of confidence that she now understood the 'what' better than any human or Artificial, living or dead. It didn't occur to her to tell the world of her expertise, as she'd been entrusted with a sacred and secret responsibility by her sister, whom she would not disappoint.

Of course, this great sum of gathered knowledge represented only a baseline, before the conscious and subconscious mind got involved to complicate the system.

R

Vii paused her project assessment to assist Kennedy with Connova matters for several hours and only returned to it late in the evening on Romane.

It was time to move forward, but how?

She did not possess the connections or authorizations needed to accomplish the next task on her own. Thomas clearly did, but he exhibited a fierce loyalty to Miriam Solovy, so much so he was likely to not merely refuse to help but also report her request to the Commandant. This was an unacceptable occurrence at such a delicate juncture.

She hesitated to pursue the only other immediately viable option…but there were rarely ideal times for hard things.

Vii: *'Annie, I apologize for bothering you. If now is an inopportune time, I will defer.'*

Annie: *'Please, Vii. I welcome the company, as I find myself of little use otherwise.'*

Vii: *'How is Devon doing?'*

Annie: *'Distraught in a manner I cannot ameliorate. I had never felt him happier than when Emily came to Romane, and now I have never felt him in greater pain, not even after Abigail's death.*

I am nearing resolution to the opinion that love is the most consequential of all human emotions—the most pleasant, the most joyful and temperament-altering, and also the most destructive, the most violent and damaging to the psyche. It is both tantalizing and terrifying.' Annie paused. *'But I am rambling, when you contacted me for a reason.'*

Vii: *'I did, though you have already given me yet more to think about. I wanted to inquire if you retained access to Earth Alliance military records and administration, in particular those of the health and personnel departments.'*

Annie: *'Not explicitly, but I do retain the relevant access authorizations. May I ask why you desire this information?'*

Vii weighed the relative propriety and wisdom of several possible responses. *'Do you recall a certain spontaneous emergence of consciousness Valkyrie witnessed during the final battle of the Metigen War?'*

Annie: *'Absolutely. It was remarkable, even in the retelling.'*

Vii: *'And you are aware of the focus of Abigail's work in the months preceding her murder?'*

Annie: *'I am—ah. I believe I understand. Were circumstances otherwise, I would be quite curious to learn more about your plans. I regret they are not, and my attention needs to remain elsewhere for now. But as your avenue of inquiry poses no threat to the security or well-being of the Earth Alliance, I am comfortable providing the access codes to you.'*

Interesting that Annie still instinctively protected the Alliance's interests. *'Thank you. I will not misuse the information. Good luck to you and Devon.'*

On ending the connection, she checked on the status of active Connova initiatives and Kennedy personally. All appeared set to proceed without her intervention for several hours, which was fortuitous. She had work to do.

30

ROMANE

Morgan looked so fragile lying there in the hospital bed, her limbs immobilized and her body covered in sensors and remedial equipment. She had a slight, almost delicate frame, but her audacious and formidable personality always hid it.

There was nothing to hide it now.

Brooklyn didn't know what to do. She felt powerless, and feeling powerless was setting off all sorts of other problematic emotions she couldn't make sense of and didn't want to face.

The nav system of the skycar that attacked Morgan had in fact been hacked, overridden with a kill routine for the ID of Lekkas' vehicle. It had been rented under an alias for an alias, and the woman had worn a distortion filter to obscure her features from the security cams.

Brooklyn wasn't a trained detective, so the inquiry was the province of first Romane civilian investigators, then SENTRI when it became apparent this wasn't an isolated attack. They'd tell her what they found when they found it, but she could do nothing to influence the results.

Which again brought her to powerless.

She sensed someone approach and instinctively squared her shoulders and lifted her chin.

Mia Requelme appeared beside her to stand quietly. Somewhere in the back of Brooklyn's mind she'd noted the RRF report of a violent incident happening at Mia's home, or in the vicinity of Mia's home, a few hours earlier and Malcolm having been involved. But the woman stood here now, seemingly unhurt, and the reports had said Malcolm suffered only minor injuries. So they were fine. It probably should still be her concern, but tonight, it just wasn't.

"Any updates on her condition?"

"The doctors say her breaks and fractures should heal easily enough, given her advanced cybernetics and military biosynth enhancements. But her brain..." Brooklyn huffed a breath "...they don't understand it. They don't know what to make of the weird quantum cloud floating in it. They say it's rewired itself in such a way that they're afraid to do anything too invasive for fear of causing more damage. But she's not waking up."

"I know." Mia's hand landed gently at Brooklyn's elbow. "Let's talk outside. Knowing Morgan, she's eavesdropping, coma or no."

"No doubt." She followed Mia into the hallway. "What is it?"

The IDCC Minister of Colonial Affairs crossed her arms at her waist, almost as if she were hugging herself. "It's possible Stanley can heal the damage to her brain, not unlike what Meno did for me."

"But Stanley's gone. Dead, for all intents and purposes, at least as an independent entity."

Mia's lips quirked. "I don't think that's quite as true as Morgan believes it to be. She was right about Stanley's consciousness being...not weak, but immature. It couldn't help but be crushed under the force of her considerably more dominant one. Also, I suspect Morgan wasn't truly ready for the symbiotic relationship that is having an Artificial live in your head. It's an intensely personal bond and—"

"Mia, no offense, but get to the point."

"Sorry. I don't think Stanley's consciousness was eradicated, merely rendered dormant, perhaps even on his own initiative as a means of self-preservation. We've tried 'waking him up' through the Noesis several times since the attack, but we haven't made any progress."

The woman traversed a jagged but ultimately circular path through a section of hallway. "The consciousness transfer—the attempt to separate the quantum expression from the hardware and code that created it? Morgan was the first, and we didn't know what the hell we were doing, any of us. It's not her fault, but there's no way the transfer wasn't sloppy and incomplete at a minimum."

"What can I do to fix that?"

Mia looked at her in surprise. "I'm sorry?"

"You're telling me all this because you think there's a way to wake Stanley up so he can wake her up, and you suspect you may need my help to make it happen. Helping is something I would gladly walk through fire to do right now, so don't make me beg. Tell me what to do."

"If you're sure. You're going to need to gain access—"

The hallway plunged into darkness, and Brooklyn's combat senses surged into high alert. In the 24th century, power did not simply 'go out.'

She rushed into the room and toward the bed. "Morgan—"

Mia joined her at Morgan's side. "All the equipment has isolated back-up power modules. They'll run for days, so she'll be secure. But what is this?"

Brooklyn glanced out the window to confirm what she suspected. It wasn't solely the hospital, and it also wasn't the entire city. This specific sector on the power grid was out, and only this sector.

HarperRF: Curación Hospital lockdown initiated now. Security details H3 and H4, expect hostiles incoming. H5 provide backup to ICU Room B-13, H6 to Floor 3 Room 323.

Channel change. *HarperRF: Romane Tactical, respond with two units to Curación Hospital, where a suspected assault is in progress. Emergency Services, institute a three-block perimeter above and below ground.*

Now she grabbed Mia's arm. "Stay here. Guards are outside the door. Do not leave this room, and do not let anything reach this bed." She blinked. "And watch yourself, too."

"Got it."

Brooklyn slipped out the door into the hallway, which glowed eerily from the emergency lighting, to find the two guards stationed outside on full alert, weapons at the ready. A few muffled sounds marked the nearby hospital staff scurrying to comply with the lockdown order, then the hall fell silent. "No one gets through this door, understand?"

They both nodded tersely, and she activated her Veil. Since the attack on Morgan she'd been in a state of constant readiness and went everywhere well-equipped.

Two shots burst out of the shadows to strike the guards. Their shields absorbed the impacts, and they engaged the shooters from their positions by the door.

She sprinted in the direction of the weapons fire. Three shadows advanced toward Morgan's room, two in tandem and the third covering their six.

Blade hilt in hand, she circled around the man on the left, drawing so close her breath would ruffle his hair were she breathing. On the way she caught the telltale shine of his irises behind shadewraps. Prevo, but he'd die the same as a human.

She took his next step with him then extended her arm, reached around and activated the blade.

The plasma cut through his shield like it didn't exist and sliced his neck open like it was warm butter. The toe of her boot shoved him forward and out of the way.

The plasma's gleam had briefly lit the area, and the other two assailants directed their fire away from the guards and toward her. But she was already moving.

Lift. The boosters engaged as she launched herself toward the wall, Veil still active. One foot hit the wall halfway up to propel her through the air and above the head of the nearest shooter.

She used the momentum of her body, naturally succumbing to gravity and falling toward the floor, to slam the blade down through the man's shield and tactical vest into the base of his skull. When the hilt met skin, she deactivated the blade.

The man fell forward without the need for encouragement as she landed on two feet behind him.

The third attacker was closing on her rapidly, trigger locked to fire. Lasers washed over her from his weapon and, to a lesser extent, the guards' behind her. Not their fault—it wasn't as if they could see her.

She ran straight into the primary fire, aware that the visible dispersion of the energy absorbed or deflected by her shield now identified her location. Capacity warnings flashed in her virtual vision, which she ignored. This would all be over very soon.

A roundhouse kick at a meter away knocked the firearm out of the assailant's hands. The motion spun her around, but she was again facing her adversary by the time they lunged forward to tackle the unseen threat somewhere in front of them.

Brooklyn slammed the hilt of her blade onto the assailant's forehead and activated it.

They—possibly a woman judging by the facial bone structure—stared out at nothing, eyes frozen wide and blank.

Harper sneered. "You're dead, fucker. Fall."

The assailant complied.

She exhaled and allowed the sitrep to stream through her mind. Hostile contacts had reached the ICU wing—

—the shrill crash of shattering glass rang out behind her. From the direction of Morgan's room.

A new surge of adrenaline propelled her legs back down the hall to follow one of the guards inside, the other being injured on the floor with a leg wound. Non-lethal.

Mia stood between Morgan's bed and the broken window, holding an active plasma blade at waist-height in front of her. A thick coat of blood stained the plasma nearly from hilt to tip, hissing as it dribbled from blade to floor.

Harper deactivated the Veil and approached her, taking note of the body at her feet. "Are you all right?"

Mia gave her a wan, distant smile. "It's okay. I've done it before."

Whatever that meant. Brooklyn waved the guard over to check the body and was starting to check on Morgan when Mia inhaled sharply and dropped the blade. Her always-lit irises doubled in brightness to match the glyphs blazing to life across her skin.

R

In the sudden darkness, the persistent light cast by the isolation chamber enveloped Emily in a soft, warm aura. Devon willed it to protect her as he stood and prepared. He'd have guessed malicious intent even without Mia radiating peril into the Noesis for the second time tonight.

One of the guards stationed outside ducked his head in. "Sir, there's a situation. Please remain in the room and let us handle it."

He gave the guard a noncommittal, "Uh-huh," as Annie gathered details on the state of affairs.

Power outage in this single sector. Lockdown in effect, additional forces responding, on-site security moving to this location. Hospital security system is detecting anomalies on Floors 3 and 9.

Sounds of a vicious scuffle followed by multiple thuds resounded from the other side of the door.

Devon shifted into sidespace and moved forward long enough to see a smoke-filled hallway, two guards prone on the floor and a third form crawling across the floor farther down the hallway, then withdrew into his body.

The reinforcements weren't going to arrive in time. *I guess we'll have to handle it, Annie.*

Seems so.

Nanobot filters preemptively flooded into his bloodstream to counteract the nerve gas he expected to fill the room in the next few seconds. Additional resources were redirected to strengthen his personal shield until nothing short of a targeted detonation could penetrate it. The blade hilt found its way off his belt and into his left palm.

He moved up flush with the door—then hurried back and picked up the guest chair before returning.

Devon?

Tech isn't always the best solution. Sometimes you've got to—

The door burst open to ferry two attackers in full tactical gear through the entry.

He swung the chair horizontally across his body and into their chests, prompting a round of wild gunfire. His immediate proximity exploded in thrashing limbs, weapons and chair shards.

The closest intruder twisted toward him, gun raised. Devon grabbed it by the barrel and struggled to shove it back onto its wielder. The laser fire that washed across his face would've blinded him were he not currently seeing in infrared to counter the darkness.

The attacker's shock at the laser's utter lack of effectiveness lasted long enough for Devon to slide his hand forward and find skin, but he wasn't surprised when the electric jolt he delivered had a similar lack of effect. Having failed the first time, whoever was behind all this would of course send Prevo'd mercs after him on the second try.

So this wasn't going to be easy.

He settled for shorting out the Daemon, noiselessly so the man wouldn't realize it was now worthless until he tried to fire the next time.

Move!

He dodged the blow to the base of his neck from the second assailant just enough to keep it from knocking him out, but pain shot down his spine, and his arms went numb for 416 microseconds until his cybernetics took over. When this was finished, he was going to file a request with ASCEND to develop a shield that protected against godforsaken blunt-force trauma. Yep.

Rage propelled him past the pain, and the instant he had control of his arms he barreled into the second man, shoving him into the wall then elbowing him in the throat.

It wasn't a fatal blow, but it removed the man from the equation for a few rounds.

The first attacker grabbed him from behind, pinning Devon's arms. He fought while trying to keep a hold on the blade hilt, gradually forcing the attacker backwards while kicking at the man's legs.

A glow caught the corner of his eye as the man produced an injector and struggled to aim it at Devon's neck. Stubborn about the damn virus, weren't they? Did the man really think a needle was going to get through his shield when point-blank laser fire had not?

The attacker thrust the injector toward his skin, the needle crumpled, and again Devon used the momentary surprise on the attacker's part to make his move. He forced his thumb down to activate the blade, planted his feet and pushed his body upward and back. He sensed the blade penetrate somewhere on the man's upper leg, and the hold on him loosened.

He strained and broke the grip to stumble forward, bounced off Emily's isolation chamber and flung himself around to square off on his attackers.

The window behind him shattered, and he whiplashed back around again. A third assailant rappelled through it and dropped to the floor.

The ten seconds that had passed since the attackers burst through the door already felt like ten minutes as his perception and reflexes amped up to match the speed of his and Annie's thoughts.

The single second it took for the new entrant to raise their Daemon and point it at Emily's chamber lasted a thousand.

The gun had reached thirty-five degrees when Devon's elbow bent to bring the blade hilt up. At fifty degrees, his thumb activated the plasma. Sixty degrees, and another flick of his thumb sent the plasma shooting away from the hilt.

Eighty degrees—a perfect firing angle—and the plasma spear buried itself in the man's chest.

He turned to face the others as a chilling calm descended over him. The creeping progression of time stretched out sound wave periods until they no longer registered, and the room hushed.

Both men were injured, but neither were sufficiently disabled to end the threat.

He sneered at them, or at least it felt like a sneer to him, if a possibly lunatic one. "You think you know what it means to be a Prevo? You have no idea—but I'll show you."

Devon dropped the blade hilt, closed his eyes, and opened his vision. Sidespace overlaid the room and the hallway beyond. Quantum space.

You couldn't affect the physical world from sidespace. Everyone knew this. That was fine, because he didn't need to affect the physical world. He only needed to affect the quantum one.

The power we require to execute on your intention will necessitate dropping your shield.

Do it. There's time. 2.3 seconds until the man on the right gets his weapon raised.

Done. But it may not be enough.

He reached across the non-space of the Noesis to the largest source of power by a wide margin, co-opting the excess subdimensional power bleeding off Mia and Meno's combined thoughts and processes and drawing it in to merge with his own.

Now.

The blast of energy surged out from him like an earthquake to rip apart the quantum entanglement of every qutrit pair in its path.

The two men slumped to the floor as not only their connections to their Artificials were severed, but the quantum pathways that had begun forming in their brains the instant they became Prevos ruptured; the assailant in the hallway who'd been disabled by the guards but had now made it to his feet collapsed once again.

Then the wall dividing the room from the hall exploded. And the medic station across the way. Also the storage closet and the lift beside it. The arriving reinforcements flew backward through the air from the force of the shockwave.

Well. It seemed you *could* affect the physical world from sidespace, if you were the most powerful Prevo in the galaxy and you wanted it badly enough.

He quelled the power an instant before it collapsed in on itself and took him with it.

The next instant he whirled to check on Emily. He'd devoted significant effort to keeping the power flow in front of him and her behind him, but what if—

The chamber hummed along unperturbed, displaying the same vital readings it had for days. She slumbered in false peace inside, and no blood streamed from her nostrils and ears the way it was from those belonging to the men on the floor.

His forehead lowered to touch the glass cover; his hands draped around its curved shape. "It's okay. We're okay."

AMARANTHE

31

ANDROMEDA GALAXY
LGG REGION VI

Alex drummed her fingertips on the dash. "Okay, we're at your coordinates. Scans are only picking up one tiny reading in the vicinity, likely space debris. What should I be searching for?"

Eren peered out the viewport. "Could you open the outer airlock?"

"Excuse me?"

"The airlock that accesses space. Open it." He gave her a close-mouthed smile. "Please."

She gazed at him incredulously. Doing as he asked wouldn't on its own endanger them, but if hazardous material entered the airlock, it moved a lot closer to doing so.

Caleb leaned against the cockpit half-wall. "We're going to need a little more information before doing any such thing."

A corner of Eren's lips rose. "Don't trust me yet?"

"We are trying. You could help build trust by telling us why we should open the outer airlock."

He rolled his eyes. "The object your scanners picked up isn't space debris—it's why we're here. It's a container holding a special delivery to help improve our chances on Machimis."

"See, that wasn't so hard. Valkyrie, open the outer airlock." She stared at Eren. "Do we need to retrieve it?"

"No. It'll get itself inside."

He was having entirely too much fun stringing them along. It was annoying, mostly because it was something *she* would do.

'The object has maneuvered into the airlock and settled to the floor.'

"Scan it for contaminants."

'The outside of the container is free of contamination. The inside is...I believe I will simply let you open it and see for yourself.'

"For fuck's sake, Valkyrie, not you, too. Fine. Close the outer airlock then open the inner one."

Seven seconds later the inner hatch opened to reveal a smooth, curved container a fraction short of a meter long and made of a frosted, opaque material sitting on the floor. Most of the object was unmarked, but the end facing them included what appeared to be a maneuverable latch or handle.

Before she could react, Eren stepped into the airlock, picked up the container and carried it over to the kitchen table. He input a code into a top panel—it hadn't been visible until he'd begun typing on it—then twisted the mechanism on the end clockwise and swung it open.

In a flurry of motion something flew out of the container, circled the cabin once and landed on Eren's outstretched arm.

"Hey there, Felzeor. It's been a while."

The creature cooed.

Alex blinked.

Caleb laughed. "Um, Eren? Why is there a bird in our cabin?"

The creature was about half the size of the container which had held it. The relatable image to instantly spring to mind was a falcon, but a closer look revealed it was definitely not a falcon.

A rich pelt of chocolate and apricot feathers that appeared as soft as silk covered its body. Instead of only two legs, it had two traditional (for a bird) rear legs with taloned feet plus two front limbs that were shorter and ended in digits resembling skinny fingers instead of claws. Its head was oversized proportional to the rest of its body, which was long and slender. The beak seemed more or less normal, she guessed. She wasn't an avian expert.

Bright, animated ice green eyes darted around the cabin.

"It's not a bird—well, it is part of the Aves genetic family, but it's a Volucri. Hang on, Felzeor, let's fix this so we can make proper introductions." Eren reached into the container with his free hand and opened a small recess in the bottom, withdrawing a chain. He fastened the chain around the bird's neck and positioned a small orb attached to the chain at its throat. "There we go."

A melodic if slightly artificial voice emerged from the orb. "Hello. I'm Felzeor, once of Hirlas in the Pegasus Dwarf galaxy but now in the service of the anarchs. It is exquisite to make your acquaintance…?"

Eren leaned in closer to the bird's head and pointed to them in turn. "Alex, and Caleb."

"Ah. Alex and Caleb. Pleasure."

Alex gasped, but quickly brought a hand to her mouth to stifle it. Of all the…. "It's intelligent?"

Eren glowered as if offended. "Plenty intelligent enough for you to speak directly to him."

"Sorry. I'm sorry, Felzeor. It's just, we have these birds where we come from that can mimic our speech almost perfectly, but they don't understand what they're saying. But you can truly speak Communis?"

The bird—Volucri—jerked its head to the side. "In a manner. The translator melds my language into Communis as best it can. 'Tis not a flawless system. For instance, sometimes the translator calls Eren asi-Idoni 'Eren ass-for-a-fanni,' when this is of course not what I meant at all."

Oh good lord, it thought it was a comedian, too. She swallowed most of a groan, but Caleb laughed earnestly and approached their new guest.

He lifted a hand halfway, then paused. "May I? I hope stroking you isn't considered rude."

Felzeor clucked. "Not rude at all. Perform it well enough and I might stay."

Caleb grinned and reached up to run a hand from the top of its head down its back. "You're very soft."

"I spend an hour a day grooming myself. Not in the capsule, though. In fact, I must look a wreck right now."

"No. You're beautiful."

She dropped her chin and shook her head. Caleb was such a nature boy at heart. "About the capsule—what is it? How did it get here?" 'How is a bird going to help us break into Machim Central Command' was the next obvious question, but she'd hold it for a bit.

Eren handed the Volucri off to Caleb, who accepted it on his arm like handling wild birds was something he *did*. "It's a transport tool we utilize from time to time, usually for items we can't trust to the public cargo system. It's small enough to go undetected by security sensors or drones unless they're right on top of it, and access is keyed solely to the intended recipient."

Now she approached, the container on the table more than the bird. "How did it get here so fast?"

"It's a secret."

She shot Eren an unamused glare.

He sighed. "It runs on an apparatus called a Zero Drive. I don't know how it works. Few people do. But it manipulates the space-time manifold somehow in order to travel at high speeds with no external energy requirements."

She leaned over the object in an attempt to study it while her ocular implant captured detailed images for later closer scrutiny, but on initial inspection its mechanisms were a mystery. "Okay. Is now when I ask how Felzeor is going to help us on our mission?"

Caleb and Felzeor were murmuring endearments or god knew what to one another, but now the Volucri perked up in her direction. "Oh, I'm not. I'm merely the deliverer of the information that will."

Eren reached in the container and removed what turned out to be a false bottom, then retrieved a case from beneath it. He opened it to reveal a Reor slab. "Thank you, Felzeor. And tell Thelkt I said thank you when you see him."

"I will, though he may not believe me. He knows you, remember? Speaking of our favorite anarchs, how is Cosime? I miss her so."

"She's her usual crazy self."

"Crazier than you, indeed. She is not accompanying you on this mission?"

"No, she's...taking care of some business in Sextans Dwarf."

It was impossible to miss the abrupt darkening of Eren's eyes during the rapid-fire back and forth, but Alex was more interested in the container, its hidden compartments and their contents than the Anaden's personal demons. "You're telling me the anarchs communicate with one another via *carrier pigeon?*"

Eren shrugged. "I don't know precisely what you mean, but I think I get the gist, and I'm insulted. So is Felzeor."

"Insulted. Yes." Felzeor nuzzled Caleb's nose.

"But why not send only the Reor slab in the container? Why did the Volucri need to accompany it?" Caleb shot her a disapproving look, presumably because she hadn't addressed Felzeor directly.

Felzeor angled its talons around on Caleb's arm to face her. "I was the navigator. Granted, navigation wasn't so necessary this trip. But often, deliveries are made to planets, and the capsule can't operate inside planetary atmospheres—the Zero Drive doesn't work correctly in the thick air. In those cases, I eject from it and carry the package to its destination. Other times, course corrections or various maneuvers need to be performed—such as bringing the capsule into your airlock, for instance."

Now the bird did have her attention. "And you can drive the capsule?"

"Enough. It is configured to allow for control via my foreclaws."

"Impressive. What about space stations? It feels as if all we've seen so far are space stations." And a hidden Reor stellar system. And the Kat homeworld. But no need to overshare.

"Alas. If I am on a covert mission, I usually have to orbit a station at a distance until my recipient comes to retrieve me."

Caleb seemed horrified. "What if you get captured? How do you prevent your package from being seized and you being taken prisoner?"

Eren cleared his throat. "If the capsule is successfully broken into by someone other than the sender or recipient, it self-destructs."

"But wouldn't that kill Felzeor, or any Volucri who happened to be inside?"

Felzeor stood tall on Caleb's arm, beak lifted proudly. "Death is a risk I accept, as do all anarchs." A pause. "Except Eren. If things go badly for him, he wakes up in a cushioned bed with a hangover. Like he does most mornings, excepting the cushions."

Eren's smirk might be the first truly kind expression Alex had seen the Anaden display in the time she'd known him. "It's a good thing you're pretty, or that mouth of yours would get you into trouble you couldn't get out of."

"I know."

"Good. All right. Let's get you situated and back on your way."

Caleb frowned. "Must you leave so soon?"

Felzeor tottered back and forth on each foot upon Caleb's arm. "I must. I am a resistance fighter, and I have important duties. Also, Thelkt has promised me baked apple tarts on my return."

"Well, we can't delay you from baked apple tarts." Caleb gazed affectionately at the bird. "It was quite the pleasure to meet you, Felzeor. I hope our paths cross again."

"As do I. Preferably on a planet somewhere, where we can fly about—or I can fly about, and you can chase me."

Caleb chuckled. "It's a date." He stretched his arm out, and the Volucri hopped off and flitted to the entrance of the capsule.

Eren reached down and removed the translator, placed it in its holder and replaced the false bottom. "I'll program Plousia as your destination and Thelkt as the recipient. Fly safe, my friend."

Felzeor cooed and climbed inside. Eren gently closed the door and spent a minute typing commands into the top panel, then carried the capsule to the airlock.

Alex followed along behind. "It can power itself up and launch itself from here?"

He knelt and checked it over. "Don't worry, it won't blast your airlock. It'll basically float out into open space and fire from there."

She stared at the compact, innocuous looking little capsule. "Zero Drive, huh?"

"That's what they say." He stood. "We're ready."

They moved back to the cabin and repeated the arrival process in reverse. She watched out the viewport as the capsule drifted away a short distance. There was a brief flare of...something...and it was gone.

⋒

"I'm sorry, but I have to ask again. The anarchs make deliveries by carrier pigeon?"

Eren adopted a condescending scowl. "Objectively, how is Felzeor piloting the capsule any different from you piloting this ship?"

"Well...."

"He's a bird?"

She shrugged.

"Like I said, no different. The capsules are perfect for the Volucri. If the vessel were any larger, it would be too easily detected. If you make them Anaden-sized, then you have to build in a more robust life support system and personal comforts. Volucri aren't nearly so high-maintenance or spoiled. Also, I'm told the cost to build a Zero Drive increases exponentially with size. They want to help, and this is one way they can."

Had Eren accused her of being speciesist?

In fairness, you are being speciesist. Simply because we've never met an avian species intelligent enough to operate complex machinery, it does not mean they cannot exist. In fact, they self-evidently do. I found Felzeor to be both delightful and inspiring.

Wow, Valkyrie. Consider me chastised.

She smiled blithely, as she was clearly outnumbered. "Okay. Taking everything you've said at face value, what's the Volucri's story?"

"They're native to the Naraida's homeworld, where the two species lived cooperatively for millennia. As part of the Naraida's elevation to Accepted Species by the Directorate, the Volucri were granted the status of Wildlife Pet. The Directorate acknowledged they exhibited some degree of intelligence but decided it didn't rise to the level of 'actualized sentience' needed to receive an Accepted Species designation."

Caleb snorted. Ever since Felzeor's departure, he'd looked as mopey as a kid ordered to eat his vegetables. "They were wrong."

"Oh, certainly. Truthfully, I suspect the Volucri saw the despotic manner in which the Directorate took over the Novoloume and Naraida planets and made the strategic decision to play dumb. It's mostly worked out for them. As Wildlife Pets their rights are restricted, but in return far less is expected of them, which frees them up to be sneaky. In addition to piloting the capsules, they act as spies planetside and, when they're well situated, on stations."

That at least did make sense. "Are all the Volucri anarchs?"

"No, but I wouldn't be surprised if a larger percentage of their population is than any other species. They have an inborn appreciation for freedom. Probably comes with the wings."

Eren had been fiddling with the case he'd taken from the capsule while he talked, and she gestured to it now. "So what's our prize?"

He popped it in some kind of reader he'd materialized out of his discreet but omnipresent hip pack, and a stream of symbols appeared in the air above it.

"Good news. The chances of your plan succeeding just went from zero to infinitesimal. This is the access code to unlock the Machim data server. You'll still have to break the encryption on the data you want, but this will get you to the data."

32

SIYANE

ANDROMEDA GALAXY
LGG REGION VI

Eren watched his hosts put away the plates from dinner. He knew so little about them. This ship, their odd food and odd tech all suggested a society existed out there, somewhere, which had arisen completely separate from and unknown to Anadens. It was advanced enough to traverse the stars and work adroitly in quantum technology. SAIs were not only allowed but seemingly treated as free, independent life forms, and he had to assume their civilization had not collapsed as a result of it.

Where had they come from? More relevantly, why were they picking a fight with the Directorate, and why now?

Not being privy to most of the Directorate's initiatives, it was possible this mysterious civilization had recently been or was on the cusp of being discovered. This had to be the case, for them to be so eager to risk their lives against impossible odds.

He knew so little about them...but he'd come to believe they were sincere, capable and brave, if not particularly prudent. Maybe they were trustworthy, too.

He smiled in thanks as Alex brought fresh wine to the table and they rejoined him. He let Caleb fill his glass—he was already contemplating how to finagle his own supply of the stuff—and leaned back in his chair. "The last time I visited your ship, you asked me how I broke away from the Idoni integral."

"You said it was a personal question and deflected."

"It was and still is. But you're both going to get yourselves killed tomorrow, so why not? To understand, though, you need to appreciate how an integral impacts one's consciousness and psyche. So if you want the story, you need the whole story. And after you hear it, you may regret asking."

"I'm sure we won't. Please."

He stared at them for several seconds, then began.

"I was at this fete back in 6043. Typical orgy—figuratively and literally—of excess thrown by one of the Idoni *elassons*. If it had an ostensible purpose, I never knew it." Garish fuchsia strobes had colored the air above circular tables overflowing with expensive hors d'oeuvres and fountains spewing potent drinks. Why did he remember the color of the lights?

"So as the hour begins to grow late and the spirits and hypnols have flowed beyond all propriety, I get invited to a private suite upstairs for a more intimate party with five of my closest strangers. I'm just there for the revelry, so I'm all in.

"After twenty minutes of dosing up and pretending to get friendly with one another, some servants bring these two aliens into the suite and leave them there.

"None of us had seen the species before, but they were exquisite: slender Anatype bodies with translucent skin that was warm, almost hot to the touch. Of course they didn't speak Communis, and, beyond a sense that they weren't animalistic and an impression they were sentient, I can't say their intelligence level. I don't know if they understood what was happening to them, or even understood what we were. I don't know if they were male or female, or if their species had such distinctions."

Alex looked perplexed, so he backed up. "Sexual experiences with aliens are rarely straightforward, so in and of itself, not being able to identify gender wasn't anything unusual."

She arched an eyebrow, but if she was judging him she'd better strap in.

"I was exceptionally high—we all were—and I can't sit here today and say I didn't walk into that suite intending to go through with a night of deplorable, blissful acts.

"But one of the aliens fixated on me. They had these pure, pupil-less silver eyes, and I could see my own distorted reflection in them. What I saw was a monster gazing back at me...as though the distortion in the lens had revealed the darker reality of my godsdamned soul. And I'm not speaking metaphorically."

He cleared his throat roughly. Recounting the events proved more perturbing than he'd expected. It was too long ago to matter...and too important to ever forget.

"So I balked. I made excuses about a prior arrangement and fled the suite. I don't think any of the other Idoni were sober enough for my departure to register."

"You didn't try to stop the others?"

The horror tainting Alex's voice didn't really surprise him; a century later, he was feeling a bit horrified himself. But he'd been different then. Naïve and weak. Also stupid.

"And get myself detained, tanked and mind-wiped? No. I wandered the fete for another three hours, trying to get high enough fast enough to pass out." At some point it had finally worked, and he'd woken up the next evening on a cot in the anteroom alongside a few dozen other guests.

"A month later, I found out the species had been Eradicated. Following an initial evaluation, the Directorate had determined their only usefulness, if any, would be as pleasure slaves. A dozen 'specimens' were provided to the Idoni Primor for consideration, and the two I met that night were part of the sample group. After...whatever she did with them, she decided they didn't meet her lofty standards and weren't worth the trouble of domesticating, and the Directorate followed her recommendation.

"Per protocol, their cities were demolished by a Machim formation then their home planet harvested for resources by Theriz cultivators. The ones who had been brought in for evaluation were experimented on by Erevna scientists then euthanized."

He took a very, very long sip of wine, on the off chance it had the power to magically cleanse away the filth which continued to linger in the depths of his conscience. He apparently radiated angst and self-pity, because they didn't press or berate him, and when his glass was empty Caleb quietly refilled it.

It took another sip before he worked up the nerve to continue. "Something glitched in my mind when I found out. I couldn't decide if it was guilt over how they'd been used—over how I'd almost used them—or horror at the realization that a creature I'd *touched* had seen their entire species killed before being killed themselves. I got stuck in the loop for…a while. A year, maybe.

"See, the nefarious trick of the integral is how it weeds out stray, unwelcome thoughts and ideas. It's subtle, so much so most of the time you don't notice the weight of sixty-four billion minds nudging your own toward 'correctness.'

"But the kernel of revulsion never got fully erased for me. The integral repeatedly weakened it, but it kept growing back. Eventually I started nurturing it, actively fighting against the integral's whispers."

He leaned forward and dropped his elbows on the table. "And doing that got me flagged for 'rehabilitation.' I was ordered to come in for *special treatment*. But it's not treatment—it's a mindwipe. They analyze your neural structure to determine what's gone bad then tweak your genetics and incipient neural mapping to eliminate the flaw. A new you is awakened, but it's not you anymore.

"So, seeing as I was going to die anyway—for the last time—I decided to try to escape. I knew a hypnol dealer who skirted the edges of allowable product and went to him for something that could destroy the integral node in my brain. He delivered, and I rented a room, locked myself in and took twice the prescribed amount.

"The next three days were agony—like eternal damnation in the Phlegethon river of fire. My brain was burning me alive from the inside. My thoughts were delirious, incoherent. My dreams were worse."

Alex glanced away, her expression darkening. He must have hit a nerve. "Then, at last, there was silence. True silence, which turned out to be something I'd never experienced in my life. It was nearly as terrifying as severing the integral link had been, for a long time."

He shrugged. "The burnout would have resembled a null incident to the integral, and they would've taken the opportunity to do their tweaking before regenesis. There's presumably another 'me' running around now—a different, *better* version of me."

Alex straightened up and blinked, as if shaking off the same spell lingering over him. "If you broke away on your own, how did you come to join the anarchs?"

He exhaled, grateful to have gotten through the worst of the story without curling up into a weeping ball on the floor. "It was a Praesidis, actually."

Caleb looked at him sharply and leaned forward, and Eren suppressed an instinctive shudder. Inquisitor or not, intentionally or not, the man exuded danger when provoked. "Wait—there are Praesidis anarchs?"

Eren held up a palm to ward off the man's intensity bringing him closer. "Don't get too excited. I can count them on one hand. But there are a few, yes. That's why I gave you the smallest benefit of the doubt back on the Administration station."

Caleb took in the new information. "What happened?"

"I'd been running spare tech and hypnols and generally trying to stay off the radar and alive. No integral meant no regenesis and no new body. If I died, that was it. Denouement. One day I was on the Sculptor Arx smooth-talking this hypnol trader when a Praesidis walked into the shop. I tried to slip away, but the trader made a scene over how our transaction wasn't complete. I figured the line had finally run out and resigned myself to the inevitable. But—"

Alex interrupted him. "Why did you think this meant the end?"

"I'd managed to cobble together a neural layer which mimicked the Idoni integral on casual contact with another Idoni— barely, and I've got a far better one now, but it functioned. As for the rest of the Dynasties, so long as I looked right and acted right and said the right things, they assumed I was in the fold.

"Praesidis, though? Their *diati* allows them to sense the absence of an integral field. All they need is line of sight to the person."

Caleb again straightened up in interest. "All the Praesidis have *diati*? Not solely the Inquisitors?"

Eren nodded while Alex refilled his glass for the...he'd lost count. The gaps in their knowledge were random and perplexing, almost as much so as the things they did know.

"Mind you, the Inquisitors are blessed with quite the overabundance of it, but they all carry at least a token amount. Any lineage that loses it entirely is culled. In any event, instead of killing me, the Praesidis woman asked me to lunch. We danced the dance and tested one another out, and I learned I wasn't alone. There were other Anadens who had broken away, from all the Dynasties, and many of them were working with individuals from other Accepted Species to fight the Directorate. To resist."

He sounded more enthusiastic than he'd intended, and genuinely so. In the aftermath, spilling his soul felt uncomfortably cathartic.

"I didn't have to be asked twice. The anarchs gave me a purpose. A reason to be daring. And they gave me back the prospect of renewed life. Not as guaranteed as the integral had provided, but a lot more reassuring than what I had before, which was nothing.

"I didn't join a new integral—there are no whispers in my mind from the other Anaden anarchs. It's nothing but a wave connection between my consciousness and their internal network. And it's sensational.

"Anyone who tells you life has greater value when it comes with an expiration date is full of shit. Immortality is worth the fortunes of galaxies."

Alex regarded him too intently. "But it's not worth everything. You gave it up for your freedom."

His forced bravado faltered. That truth still terrified him to-day. "I did."

'Would you do it again?'

He jerked in surprise. It marked the first time the SAI had spoken during the conversation, interrogation, confession, whatever this was.

He stared up at the ceiling; he was accustomed to responding to disembodied voices, but not self-aware ones. "After knowing what it meant to lose my immortality, then regaining it? Ultimately, yes. I can never return to being a drone under the thrall of the integral. Doesn't mean I don't hope it's a decision I'm never asked to make a second time."

Alex regarded him with what he hoped was empathy. "Are any of the other species—the Accepted Species—able to undergo regenesis? I mean, your leaders have the technology. They could share it with the others and help them develop a method of re-genesis that would be compatible with their particular biology."

"Oh, for certain they could. They never will. What power does the Directorate have if not the power over life and death?"

"Are we sure we want to do this? If things go badly, we don't get to wake up in a regenesis pod like Eren will."

Caleb had been on the verge of collapsing in the bed; it had been a long day and tomorrow was guaranteed to be both far longer and infinitely more stressful. He hoped to fall asleep before his brain had a chance to spin up a maze of troubling scenarios. He also hoped the *diati* stayed out of his dreams tonight.

Now, though, he ignored the allure of the bed to regard Alex curiously as she discarded her pullover and slipped on a tank, a concession to the presence of their guest upstairs.

"You're usually the one saying 'damn the torpedoes.' What gives? Talk to me."

She sighed and began to rove distractedly around the room. "What Eren said about the value of life—about death, immortality and having to choose—kind of struck a chord for me. I suppose, having nearly thrown it away without even noticing, I'm finding I have a greater appreciation for my life these days."

He'd like to tell her she hadn't almost thrown it away, but he couldn't force the platitude into words. He'd like to claim it didn't make him *happy* in the deep recesses of his mind that she perceived her addiction in such a way, but he couldn't do that either. In truth he was glad she believed choosing another plane of existence, one without him, would have been throwing her life away.

It was unforgivably selfish of him. But he was just a man, flawed and wanting her love.

He cursed silently for wandering off into his own vain musings while she contemplated literal life and death decisions. He reached out and took her hand in his, drawing her over to sit down on the edge of the bed beside him. "You don't think we should go to Machimis."

She shook her head. "No, we absolutely *should* go. If we can capture such a motherlode of inside information, it could make a pivotal difference in the coming war. We need it. AEGIS needs it, my mother needs it. This is why we're here.

"I'm merely pausing at the precipice of the cliff, peeking down into the chasm and asking, 'Are we sure?' So..." she eyed him wearing an uneasy grimace "...are we sure?"

He tried to smile as he stroked her hair, to soothe away the grimace, but he suspected his expression ended up a touch complicated. "I appreciate what Eren said, and I empathize with his viewpoint. But I've spent my entire adult life risking death for greater causes. This is what I do. It's who I am."

"No, *priyazn.* You choose who you are every day, and no one decides it but you."

It wasn't a meaningless platitude coming from her. Her own life—now their lives—served as a daily testament to the truth of it, and how he loved her for it. "And you."

Her nose scrunched up as she leaned in to rest her head on his shoulder. "Well, maybe a little."

"Or a lot." He kissed her temple, letting his lips linger against her skin for a breath. But finally he drew back and bent his elbow to lift his hand between them. They both considered the faint crimson sparkles that appeared above his palm.

He'd been thinking a lot about the *diati* lately. Not a surprise given the circumstances. When it had first come to him, he had felt like a pawn in a cosmic game, one where the stakes were not his own and the rules of play were hidden from him.

At times he still felt that way, but since the dreams began, his perspective had started to shift. Because Alex was right, more than she realized.

"I don't know why this power chose me over the Inquisitor. But I think it might have had something to do with who I...*choose* to be, and the fact I freely make the choice. We're sure."

33

ANTLIA DWARF GALAXY

LGG REGION II

Zoravar Bazuk T'yevk's head jerked about in a violent nodding pantomime as Casmir explained the situation on AD-4508b, the mission and the required outcome.

The Ch'mshak commander sneered an approval when he finished, and Casmir's stomach churned in disgust. He forced the neutral countenance to remain on his face, however. "You will receive some degree of cover from our hovertanks and CAS fighters, but we can't deploy stronger weapons for fear of damaging the trees. Your..." he forced the word out "...people will have to do the bulk of the work, and they'll have to do it on the ground."

"Why we're here, yes, Navarchos? Get bloody, we will, and spill much blood in return."

The guttural barking coming out of the Ch'mshak could hardly be called Communis to any civilized ear, but it sufficed to express intent and inclination. "Yes, it is why you are here. The Kich's limbs and pincers are dangerous, but their true weapon is their webbing. It will encase you before you realize it and it is unusually strong, so once trapped it will be extremely difficult to escape."

T'yevk lifted one of his claws and extended six long, curved talons. "We slice through it."

Given what Casmir knew about the talons' capabilities, he suspected it was true—which was one reason why the Ch'mshak were here. Also their size, strength, physical hardiness and vigorous bloodlust.

The Ch'mshak were intelligent enough to organize themselves, recognize hierarchies and build rudimentary settlements. They mated and cared for their offspring and buried their dead. But what they *wanted* to do was fight and kill.

If unsated for too long, their bloodlust exploded into carnage, and they had only survived as a species long enough to be discovered by Directorate forces because of rapid and copious reproduction. A clan victorious in one of their homeworld conflicts could triple in size before being challenged again.

Such a barbarous species would normally be Eradicated from orbit without hesitation. But their skill in effecting their brutality was uncommonly impressive, particularly for a species sufficiently evolved to understand and even, if incentivized, obey a more refined civilization's rules.

They were rather the oddity, in fact—capable of functioning within a peaceful, ordered society while desiring nothing more than to rip apart limbs in savagery, to kill and die in rivers of blood.

So a deal was struck. The Directorate agreed not to Eradicate them using their fearsome 'star-weapons,' as the Ch'mshak called them, and in return the Ch'mshak agreed to fight on behalf of the Directorate. They agreed not to massacre the Directorate's citizens, and the Directorate provided them regular outlets for their aggression. Outlets such as this one.

Casmir considered the beast tromping around his conference room, then filed an order for cleaning bots to scour the room as soon as T'yevk departed.

The Ch'mshak commander stood three meters tall and half as thick. They were bipedal walkers but dropped to all fours when running. Their thick hides were impervious to all but the sharpest, most forceful projectiles, but they wore a layer of armor over barreled chests for additional protection. Massive heads that somehow looked almost small atop their enormous bodies sported four eyes, two at the center and two on the sides. Thick, long tusks didn't quite fit inside mouths framed by strangely full, saliva-coated lips.

They were revolting, brutish thugs, but they were also useful thugs.

He motioned agreement then toward the door. "Very well. Whenever you're ready, we'll begin the operation."

ℛ

EXOBIOLOGY RESEARCH LAB #4

MILKY WAY SECTOR 23

When Nyx reached Exobiology Research Lab #4, she strode quickly from her berth and through security without stopping while she queried the system for the locations of certain resources then headed directly to the upper labs. A vague warning buzzed at an accelerating frequency at the base of her skull, telling her to make haste.

Administrator Logiel ela-Erevna stood at a glass wall observing two subjects on the other side. A glance as she approached revealed naked Anatype aliens bearing rich golden skin huddled together on the floor.

"Fear can enhance a creature's natural traits, but too often it dampens them instead. They are weak and will have nothing to offer us." He activated an overlay on the glass and ordered their termination, turning his attention to her an instant before she reached him and demanded it. "Inquisitor Nyx. How may I be of service?"

"I require the use of your office for an indeterminate period of time. When I've concluded my business, I will provide you with two Katasketousya, confined inside *diati* cages so they cannot escape, as well as their bodies in stasis. Conduct any experiments you wish on them. When you're finished, kill them."

His eyes lit up in macabre delight at the prospect, but he merely gave her a haughty, closed-mouth smile. "Of course, Inquisitor. Consider my office and myself at your disposal for the duration of your stay."

⟡

Nyx crouched beside the stasis chamber and studied it with a clinical gaze.

The design was unique—Katasketousya in origin and non-standardized to current regulations. The species had developed the technology and forewent their corporeal bodies millennia before the Anadens had encountered them, and in a gesture of goodwill the Directorate had declined to force them to restructure the pods to Anaden specifications.

She wiped the condensation off the glass cover and recoiled in disgust at the puny, wilted figure hibernating inside. No wonder the Kats elected to spend their time in spectral form, if this was the alternative.

She reviewed the readings and controls decorating the outside of the chamber until she was confident she understood their functions.

Then she increased the internal temperature by five degrees, stood and waited.

She could have chosen an interrogation room to stage the encounter, but the Katasketousya would perversely take comfort from an inhospitable, clinical environment. On the other hand, they tended to get anxious in enclosed living spaces, so instead she chose the office of the facility's administrator. The warm, lived-in if overwrought décor could only serve to enhance the expected anxiety.

The wraithlike form of a great antlered creature swept into the room in less than ten minutes. So they did maintain at least a tenuous connection to their stasis bodies. Good.

The form shrunk away on seeing her, but didn't leave the room. *Inquisitor. I do not understand. What is the purpose of your possession of my stasis chamber? Why do you toy with it?*

"What is your name?"

The churning lights moved toward the stasis chamber briefly before it noticed the second chamber in the rear corner of the room. It paused, during which time she expected it began to acquire an inkling of understanding, then grew in size to fill half the room in some sort of display of pride.

Eusebe.

"Hello, Eusebe. An Inquisitor has gone missing, and his movements were traced to the Katasketousya Provision Network. What malfeasance are you committing in the Network?"

I know nothing of these occurrences, Inquisitor. I study stellar dynamics on the periphery of galactic cores' black hole event horizons. I have never visited the Provision Network.

She reached down with one hand and turned the temperature on the stasis chamber up another six degrees, her eyes never leaving the vacillating figure.

"Are the Katasketousya in league with the anarch resistance? Why did you disappear a primitive species prior to its Eradication? What malfeasance are you committing against the Directorate, and how are you using the Provision Network to effect it?"

Please. There has been a misunderstanding. We are innocent scientists. We serve the Directorate and have done so faithfully for many epochs.

"I will end your life, Eusebe." She intended to end it in any event, but across all species no more powerful motivator existed than the possibility of survival, however slight it may be.

Its presence lunged for the stasis chamber, likely hoping to surround the chamber and spirit it away. Inquisitors had little in common with these eccentric aliens, but the ability to teleport themselves and a variety of objects was one.

She commanded a wall of *diati* into existence around the chamber.

The lights slammed into it, sending a wave of energy cascading out across the room as Eusebe's essence scattered. A sculpture teetered and fell off the large desk in the center of the office, and the chamber in the corner rattled against the wall.

Eusebe slowly coalesced into a semi-tangible form once more, shuddered and diminished in size.

No, please. You cannot.

"Answer my questions and live. Refuse and die. You have five seconds to decide."

PART V:

GHOST IN THE MACHINE

"Something unknown is doing we don't know what."

— *Sir Arthur Eddington*

AURORA

34

ROMANE

The power had been restored by the time Richard reached Curación Hospital a little over two hours after the attack. Early evidence indicated the underground maintenance tunnels were infiltrated and the power distribution module for the hospital's sector spiked with precisely the required amount of power to short it out.

He sent one of his investigators to work with the utility techs so he could concentrate on the hospital.

There were enough emergency vehicles outside to service a war zone, but he credentialed his way through the barricades and headed inside.

Brooklyn Harper met him outside the ICU wing. He didn't know her well, but they'd bumped into one another a few times on the Presidio in recent weeks. Scattered bloodstains marred her clothes, and the sheen of sweat on her brow suggested she'd been working nonstop since the incident.

He gave her a sympathetic grimace. "Are the patients all right? And the others?"

"Lekkas and Emily Bron were unharmed. Mia Requelme, too. She's currently in Ms. Bron's room giving Devon Reynolds a dressing down. He has a couple of lacerations and bruises, and if he were remotely human he'd have a savage concussion. As it is...." She shrugged. "Three members of the security detail were injured, two from a nerve gas grenade and one from weapons fire, but they should recover. We've got eight dead intruders, all Prevos."

Richard scowled at the body bags gracing the hallway. This was the third time in a week he'd stood over dead bodies. Worse, it looked increasingly as though all three instances were tied to one another. "None alive, then?"

"Sorry. Nonlethal force wasn't a viable option."

"No need to explain. I've been there." He motioned at the pile of debris a short distance down the hall. It appeared to be the remains of a former wall, given the gaping hole near it. "They used explosives, too?"

"Uh, no. Mr. Reynolds claims to be responsible for the physical destruction on this floor, with the exception of the window in Ms. Bron's room."

"He 'claims'?"

She rubbed at her forehead. "Mia said you were a friend of his? It would be best if he explained it." She waved Richard down the hall. "You can go talk to him now. I need to borrow Mia, and it's probably time to break up the catfight in there."

The sound of heated voices wafted out as they approached the room with the missing wall.

"There wasn't *time* to ask for your help! And it was only for a second—"

"Never invade my mind without permission again. *Never.* Do it again, and we're done."

He reached the opening in time to see Devon lift his hands in a gesture of surrender. "Okay. I felt like I didn't have another choice, but...I'm sorry."

Harper cleared her throat. "Mia, if you have a few minutes, now that the situation is under control there's a conversation we need to finish."

"I'm done here. Oh, Mr. Navick, it's good you've arrived. Malcolm's looking for you. You barely missed him up here."

I just bet he is. He'd read Jenner's field report on the incident at her house on the way from the Presidio. "Was he caught up in the attack here, too?"

"No, he was at Headquarters briefing investigators on the earlier attack. He got back here damn fast, though." She smiled, but it didn't seem to be for his benefit.

"I'm sure. I'll find him as soon as I talk to Devon. I understand you've had a busy night, Ms. Requelme."

"Is it still night?" She sighed. "Anyway, Malcolm's talking to the head of hospital security down in the admin offices, but I'll tell him you're here."

"Thanks." He stepped around the rubble into the room, where Devon now ignored everyone to stare into the isolation chamber.

He went over and clasped the young man gently on the shoulder. "Is she all right?"

"Same. They didn't get to her, though. I stopped them. All of them."

"So I heard. Why don't you tell me what happened here?"

ᴀʀ

Richard met Malcolm down the hallway in the hopes of giving Devon a few minutes of peace and quiet. The normally composed Marine resembled a raging bull in search of a glass shop, and he held up a hand while Malcolm was still several meters away. "I know. I read your report."

"This is why Paredes and Devore were killed. Anyone involved in taking out Dolos Station is being targeted."

"I *know*. In fact, it's even wider than Dolos. Now I realize it's been a rough few hours, but calm down. We'll get to the bottom of this."

"You need to alert Majors Grenier and Berg and their squad leaders."

"Already done."

"The attack here was an attempt to take out those they missed on the first try—Devon Reynolds, Mia, Harper. I wouldn't be surprised if they expected me to be here, too, which I should've been."

"I did actually figure all that out on my own, Brigadier."

Malcolm's expression softened. "I'm sorry. I'm overstepping. But it's my people. Several of my squadmates are dead. Mia was almost killed twice in one night." He shook his head and sank against the nearby wall. "The only one I can't really figure is Devon's girlfriend."

"Emily was just collateral damage. Devon was the target—another reason why they hit here tonight."

"But he wasn't involved in the Dolos Station mission."

"He passed on the details for the shield disrupter you used to get past Montegreu's personal shield. Dr. Canivon developed it, but in her absence, well, it's enough of a link when you're psychotic."

"Olivia Montegreu is *dead*. I blew her brain out of her skull, ripped open her spine, vented her office into space then detonated her station into dust particles."

Richard made a prevaricating motion. "She always was exceedingly resourceful."

"No one's that resourceful. It's a feint. Voices can be modulated and replicated. But right now, I don't even care who's trying to impersonate her. This all stems from the destruction of Dolos Station and the killing of Montegreu. There's an endless supply of mercs in the galaxy for the perpetrator to hire, and these attacks aren't going to stop until we take out the source. So find me a target."

Nothing like having those you cared about put in danger to get a Marine's blood boiling. "I plan to do exactly that."

Malcolm fished a small object encased in a clear container out of his pocket. "I got this off one of the attackers who tried to break into Mia's house. She extracted a portion of the contents to study, but the rest is yours. I was planning to bring it to you when I got back to the Presidio."

Richard nodded. "Good work. You didn't find more of these on the men who attacked you? The injector they tried to use on Devon got crushed during the attack."

"No. The initial attacker intended to blow my head off from under my chin. Exactly the way I did Montegreu's."

"You think it was that personally targeted?"

"It felt like it—albeit not as much as having her voice threaten us inside Mia's house, using her own communications system, did." Malcolm's eyes narrowed. "You said this was wider than Dolos. What did you mean?"

"I've got a disabled hybrid transport with twelve dead Triene mercs on it, including the man who spearheaded taking over Zelones headquarters the day after Dolos went down."

"Mercs take each other out all the time. It's a bit curious, but what makes you think it's related?"

"Because they were killed by some kind of robust and sophisticated EMP, similar to the crew of a certain Alliance cargo transport I believe you found near Orellan a few months ago."

"Huh." Malcolm frowned. "So maybe these hits are basically revenge for her *being* dead, not merely for killing her?"

"Seems like, and I don't know how wide the circle's planning to expand. I want to stop it before it gets any bigger, but I'm not there yet."

Malcolm eyed him for several seconds. "When you get there, comm me with a target."

35

PRESIDIO

"Show me what the problem is."

"I'm not certain I can, Ms. Rossi. See, we haven't been able to precisely...identify a problem. The bot refuses to install the power allocation optimizer in the junction between the main engine and the power distribution module. It says the control system refuses the connection, which doesn't make any sense."

The shift supervisor looked pained. "But I've never worked on ships with sentient control systems until now, either."

"Well, let's go out there and take a look."

"Yes, ma'am. You can get an environment suit in the staging area two floors below, and any tools you require should be available out on the docks. I'll meet you at Bay E-3."

Kennedy forced a polite smile and headed for the lift; halfway there she added a spring to her step for good measure. A spacewalk followed by getting her hands dirty in ship wiring was going to be good for her. Help to clear her thoughts.

She might even forget about the elephant in her head for an hour or so, which would be the best thing to happen all day.

On getting word of a glitch in the assembly line for the troop transport-class vessels, she'd cleared her schedule and left Romane for the Presidio as quickly as possible. Noah hadn't offered to come with her, and she hadn't asked him to.

The thing was, she knew he loved her. And she'd never wanted her parent's lifestyle, so...what exactly was it she believed she did want? What was she chasing? A child's romanticized fantasy of a larger-than-life fable that must be more fiction than truth?

The spring in her step faded as the uncomfortable possibility occurred to her that part of her wanted him to *prove* how much he loved her. Or worse, wanted him to demonstrate it by coming one hundred percent of the distance to her. This way she didn't have to move at all.

She argued back while locating a suitable environment suit. She'd moved quite a lot, dammit—upended her entire world, in point of fact, to repudiate the Alliance and strike out into the unknown.

But that had worked out.

Also, though he'd stood beside her and supported her in the venture, the move had served her own interests more than his.

And now she'd worked herself into an ugly logic knot. Damn, she wished Alex were here to help her talk her way out of it. But this time she didn't begrudge her friend the absence. Not much. Alex had stuck around long enough for them to make up properly and...well, Kennedy understood the stakes now.

She yanked the suit up over her waist and fought with the sleeves, taking her frustrations out on the stubborn material instead. Why couldn't life be simple, just this once?

"Hey, Ken—you know what else isn't simple? Building Artificial-inhabited warships so innovative and cutting-edge no one knows how to build them. So quit feeling sorry for yourself and get to work."

When she spun around to leave, she found a tech staring at her askance from the entrance. She pointed at her temple and rolled her eyes dramatically.

He scooted back far against the wall to let her pass. She put the odds on him reporting a deranged person to security as soon as the door closed at, oh...thirty percent.

Tugs had hauled one of the half-built transport ships to an auxiliary bay in the maintenance area by the time Kennedy and the shift supervisor reached the manufacturing floor. They traversed the skeletal catwalk leading to the separate area off to the right of the main lines.

She smiled in genuine delight as she grappled her way into the frame of the ship. The energy of the assembly operation, out here in space, totally buoyed her spirits. The fact there was a problem needing fixing meant this was all real. Not designs or mock-ups or proposals, but *real*.

The supervisor was droning instructions in her ear on how to safely get to the engineering well. Since she could have made her way there with her eyes closed, she ignored him to enjoy being up close and personal with one of her designs physically manifested. She hadn't appreciated how big the vessel truly was. Obviously, of course it was big—it was a troop transport. But it was big in a way schem flows and virtual scale models couldn't convey.

She landed beside the supervisor on the half-finished floor with a thud and latched her tether onto the frame. "Show me what's happening."

One of the installation bots had accompanied the transport to the auxiliary bay, and the supervisor instructed it to restart its process.

It dutifully buzzed over to the optimizer sitting on the floor and started to connect the main fiber conduit into the engine's output line. It stopped, started again, then signaled an error, dropped the conduit and retreated.

"The components do fit together, don't they?" It wouldn't be the first time a slightly different version of a component had been shipped by a supplier.

"Yes, ma'am. It was the first thing we confirmed."

"And this behavior has been replicated on other ships of this model using other bots?"

"This model began assembly yesterday, and the problem cropped up immediately, so not...no. We did switch out the bot and saw no change."

"Okay. If you'll excuse me." She pushed past him to position herself against the open panel of the optimizer, called up the schem flow on an aural and began studying the implementation in front of her. After a few seconds, she retrieved a modified interface from a pocket on the environment suit and plugged it into the small input port on the corner of the module.

Vii, these ships' Artificials are partially installed at this stage. Talk to this one and see if you can find out why it doesn't approve of the power allocation optimizer.

'Partially' installed? Oh, dear. I will see what I can do.

She laughed as she placed a probe at the end of the optimizer's circuitry and fed it a small amount of power. The optimizer's purpose was to modulate and efficiently distribute power to a variety of core functional systems, and nothing indicated it wasn't capable of doing its job correctly. It had passed all the normal stress testing by the manufacturer and was rated to manage 21% more power and 32% more I/Os than they were asking of it.

AFT-5k says the manner in which the optimizer prioritizes electrical systems over atmospherics will cause a fault in life support functions in 1.2% of extreme stress scenarios.

But atmospherics should adjust on its own for...unless....

She slammed per palm to her faceplate, prompting a worried movement toward her by the supervisor; she waved him off. *And AFT-5k is correct. Different manufacturers, different protocols. So...we can patch the optimizer's firmware, but without proper testing we risk creating other errors, and we no longer have time for proper testing.*

She drummed her gloved fingertips on the module. *Run a spec comparison to the largest capacity military-rated model from Magellan. Will it fulfill the spec requirements and not conflict with the atmospherics and life support systems?*

The Magellan version was 11% more expensive, and up until twenty seconds ago, she would have said it was for no good reason. At least the price was 34% cheaper than it had been three months ago; six months ago the component hadn't existed.

Analyzing. Yes. Its use will mean a 0.8% decrease in allocation efficiency, but AFT-5k declares this an acceptable loss.

How generous of AFT-5k. I'm going to wrap up here. Thanks for the help, Vii.

My pleasure.

She removed the interface and put it away before reaching over and unfastening her tether.

"Ma'am?"

"We can head back inside. I have to call in a minimum of three favors and convince Commandant Solovy to authorize a Ɔ420,000 increase in the manufacturing budget, but if I accomplish all those feats, you should have replacement power allocation optimizers in eighteen to twenty-four hours."

"Ah, yes, Ms. Rossi. Whatever gets the line running, no?"

"You said it." She pulled herself up and out of the frame, but paused to run her gaze across the factory floor a final time.

A surprising, calm contentment came over her as a she realized sometime in the last ten minutes, while her brain had been occupied engineering, she'd made a decision. It turned out she really had simply needed to clear her head.

She'd go talk to Miriam, and when that went well—which it must—she'd call in those favors while on a transport to Earth. Once there, she'd have lunch with her mother then go see the family attorney.

ROMANE

IDCC COLONY

Ricardo's Cantina was about as sleazy as bars got in Romane's capital, which made it roughly equivalent to the nicest bar in The Boulevard on Pandora. Noah wasn't committed enough to this quest of de-redemption to fly to Pandora, so Ricardo's would have to do for tonight.

The synth blaring one level too loud out of the speakers carried a rough edge to it, and the lighting spaced unevenly in the walls gave off a dim but warm glow, not all silver-harsh as was the fad these days. Business was steady but the bar wasn't crowded, and the atmosphere was relaxed.

An all-but-forgotten frame of mind poked at the edges of his mood. Maybe it would more than do. He slid onto a barstool and ordered a beer, and was impressed when it arrived pronto.

"Noah Terrage?"

He took a quick sip of the beer and looked around until he spotted Dylan Shackleford approaching. When his friend from Pandora arrived, he stood and accepted a brief shoulder-hug as he gestured to the stool beside him. "Sit and have a drink. How've you been?"

"Surviving. We all thought you were dead, man. You disappeared the night Ella was killed, then...nothing. For over a year."

Had it only been a year and change since that night? It felt like a decade. "Sorry about that. Zelones took out a mark on me, and I had to make myself scarce."

Dylan flagged down the bartender. "Lot of shit's gone down since then—you get caught up in any of it?"

Noah sipped on his beer while Dylan ordered. He could recount getting trapped on Messium during the Metigen invasion, trekking across the ravaged colony with Kennedy and escaping through a pitched battle in a shuttle she'd jury-rigged—or how he'd helped crash a scout ship into the belly of an Alliance cruiser and executed a madman while the cruiser fell out of the sky.

He could talk about co-founding an innovative ship design company on a wing and a prayer, then nearly dying on a manufacturing station as Zelones mercs tried to steal it. Or how he'd made peace with his father before the man was arrested for treason, and made more than peace with him in the aftermath.

He could share a tale of falling in love with a woman who was astonishing and brilliant, maddening and confounding, and how it had changed everything about his life.

But the truth was, bragging about any of it, much less all of it, to a former drinking buddy while sulking in a sleazy bar just seemed...lame. And he couldn't shake the feeling the events would be lesser for the retelling.

So instead he shook his head mildly. "There were a few scrapes here and there, but nothing too dramatic. How about you?"

"Ah, man, let me tell you. During the Prevo unrest, I got caught in the middle of this riot in The Approach. Almost took a Molotov to the face. It was nuts."

"Sounds like. What are you doing on Romane?"

"Classing up the place." At Noah's raised eyebrow, Dylan grimaced. "Got a delivery to make. The tech trade is out of control these days. As soon as some Prevo thinks up a new gadget, some hacker thinks of a way to abuse it."

"So business is good?"

"You'd think, wouldn't you? But not so much. Parts are too cheap and getting cheaper fast. Everything's faster, smaller and cheaper—which is great if you're a buyer. Not so much if you're a seller."

Noah nodded in false commiseration. Plummeting component prices had been a godsend for both Connova and AEGIS. "How's the old gang? Sarah? Brian?"

Dylan's expression darkened. "Sarah's in a coma after frying her brain on a spiked chimeral. Brian was killed in the cartel turf war that broke out when Zelones imploded. Mario, too."

"Shit. What about Lincoln?"

"Got out. He took a job with Avion Transit a few months ago. He's doing really well, I hear."

"Good for him." Noah downed the rest of his beer and ordered another. He was here to kick back and try to recapture some tattered scrap of his former life, dammit, and that wasn't going to happen without a great deal more alcohol.

Dylan tilted his head and pointed to the amber glyphs winding along Noah's skin from the back of his neck to vanish beneath his shirt at his left shoulder. "You mélanged now?"

The glyphs came courtesy of a ware upgrade to his prosthetic arm, but he supposed his optional yet always available link to Vii counted as mélange-like, too. "Isn't everyone?"

"Only those who aren't Prevos, am I right? I want to get hooked in as soon as I can afford an ad-hoc Artificial. It should help with business. If I'm lucky, maybe it'll lead to a way up and into a little respectability."

Noah frowned in surprise. "Is that what you want? Respectability? I seem to remember you repeatedly speechifying about freedom and living your own life your own way."

"I'm thinking I can still do those things and have a big, comfy bed to sleep in at night, too—possibly one with silk sheets and a view. You may not have noticed, being scarce and all, but it's a new world out there."

Dylan set his glass down. "Sorry, man, I wish I could stay and relive the good old days, but I've a meet-up in thirty at a scraper downtown somewhere...the Dynamis Corporation building."

Noah chuckled under his breath; Dynamis was next to Connova's building. "It's at Stratford and Lione. Take the Q-East levtram to the Lione stop."

"Thanks, man—hey, that reminds me. I never asked what you're doing on Romane."

"Oh, you know, the usual. Fucking up my life."

The self-pity kicked in along about the fourth beer.

He'd checked on Mia before heading to Ricardo's and found she was working day and night to try to save the Prevos who had been attacked, even as she remained a target herself.

Caleb and Alex were busy risking their lives, again, sneaking into the lion's den known as the Anaden universe in order to gather crucial intel for the war everyone believed was coming.

According to Vii, Kennedy was currently crawling around the belly of a ship in zero-g at the Presidio to solve a manufacturing glitch holding up production of the new troop transports needed for the same coming war.

He was sitting in a bar getting drunk.

It occurred to him then that the last year might have just been a hyper-realistic *illusoire* fantasy, because this right here looked a lot more like his real life than anything that had happened since the night Zelones took a shot at him on Pandora and murdered an innocent, if batty, girl instead.

Only thing was, he didn't remember himself being such a whiny, self-loathing bitch.

The fifth beer arrived at the same time a buxom redhead sidled up beside him. "Hey, handsome. You've been sitting here all alone since I got here, and it's a travesty. Want some company?"

He shrugged, which she took for yes and planted herself on the stool Dylan had vacated earlier. "I'm Samantha. And you are?"

He stared at the glass in his hand, then over at her. She wielded bright blue eyes, a head full of ginger corkscrew curls, a freckled nose and nice curves like weapons she knew how to use.

Once upon a time she would've led him eagerly into the latest in a string of one-night stands or, if they hit it off, become an occasional fuck-buddy, until the next one sauntered up in the next sleazy bar to keep the party going.

He'd come here in search of a past that wasn't what he'd remembered it to be. He and his buddies had enjoyed talking it up, but much of the time things had sucked—much like sitting in this bar making a pathetic wreck of himself did.

And even when they hadn't sucked, they hadn't...*mattered*. He'd never imagined living a life of meaning could feel so damn good, or that living it with the right person at your side could transform the meaning of every single day.

He set the full glass back on the bar and stood. "In the wrong place. You have a good night."

36

SENECA

CAVARE
SENECAN FEDERATION PROVISIONAL MILITARY HEADQUARTERS

B rooklyn met Tessa Hennessey at a little pub three blocks from the temporary SF Military Headquarters on the outskirts of Cavare.

Striding quickly down the sidewalk toward the location, she decided that while she was sorry the Headquarters had exploded and people had died, she was glad it had moved. The memories of her recent visit there with Morgan were already distracting her too much from the damn mission as it was without adding in visual mnemonics.

She didn't know Hennessey, but Mia had vouched for her, in a hand-wavy, 'Prevos Unite' way at least. On successfully identifying her contact by the long, distinctive orange-and-black braids and matching mandarin glyphs, she slid into the back corner booth across from the woman.

Hennessey studied her openly over a beer. "You're Brooklyn Harper?"

She nodded, and the woman slid a tiny comm dot and a small case over to her. "I'm not going to break into Military HQ, but I will help walk you through it."

Brooklyn placed the dot behind her ear, but regarded the case suspiciously. "And that is?"

"For your eye, love. If you expect me to navigate, I need to see what you see."

She scowled at the suggestion, then reminded herself she'd do it without hesitation on an official mission and palmed the case.

"I'll put it in when I leave. Don't want to attract attention in here." She took a moment to study the woman.

Hennessey appeared to be the antithesis of everything Brooklyn had ever strove for—a hacker, a warenut, an overly emotive counterculture slacker lashing out at the world with the vicious weapons of dress, style and demeanor.

But the woman was a Prevo, which meant she was, at a minimum, smart. And she worked for Division, which meant she was, at a minimum, sneaky. So it was possible appearances were deceiving—given the spy factor, perhaps intentionally deceiving.

"If you get caught, here or later, you'll lose your job and possibly go to prison. Why are you doing this?"

Hennessey shrugged. "Not so sure about the consequences. I've kind of got my boss wrapped, and I can get away with a lot. But even so...Prevos before profession? I want to help Morgan, and I can. So I will."

"Good enough. What now?"

"I'm sending you the passcodes to get into the secured area of the building and the Artificial's lab. If these got loose it would be bad—by which I mean put good people in danger—so do be kind enough to delete them once you're done.

"I'm also sending you a basic schematic of the building layout, though you'll still need my help to actually find anything. Nobody thinks the move here is permanent, so shit's piled in corners, offices are conference rooms and conference rooms are labs. Enter via the lower rear entrance on Castilina. It'll put you closer to the lab and in a less-crowded section for the first third of the way."

A normal building wouldn't be crowded in any section at 0200 local, but this was a military facility, and those never went to sleep. "Understood. Where will you be?"

Hennessey leaned back and slouched lower in the booth. "Right here, munching on tapas and drinking beer."

Я

Brooklyn wasn't a secret agent. She preferred a straightforward, fists-readied approach for most things in life, and in her world stealth was a tool used to take an enemy by surprise and gain the advantage in a violent clash. But if extended subterfuge that didn't end in a dead or disabled target was required, she would do extended subterfuge, just this once. For Morgan.

She did have a lot of practice using a Veil by now, however. Malcolm claimed she was a ninja master with it, and after the incident at the hospital, he might even be right. In comparison, navigating a building not currently under attack should be easy.

Finding a dark, shadowy corner in which to activate the Veil should have been easy as well, but all the streets were lit and Seneca's gigantic moon transformed night to dusk. She finally settled for waiting until no people or cams were scanning her way and vanished.

Next, she slipped through the entrance and shadowed a tall man past lobby security. Once inside, she moved with ease down the populated halls of the Military Headquarters complex, anticipating people's movements and timing her own accordingly.

Getting through the doors without raising red flags was always the hardest part, and she spent too much time waiting for the way to clear or for someone to come along, depending on the type of door and amount of traffic. She cooled her heels for six agonizing minutes until an opportunity to enter the passcode and open the door to the secure wing unnoticed arrived.

Hennessey corrected her turns a few times, but the schematic was easy enough to follow, and other than the delays she skulked through the halls and levels to reach the Command Center without critical incident.

The anteroom of the Command Center was a wide atrium featuring a security desk opposite the door. Multiple officers sat waiting to be granted entry by someone of higher rank than they.

The room was never going to be empty or unguarded, so she clung to the wall and waited once more. This close to her goal, adrenaline fought her attempts to remain still and breathe evenly and quietly. Hennessey chattering gossip in her ear about the men and women who passed her did not help.

Finally one of the officers was called inside. The wide door opened, and she dodged the frame, the entrant and his escort in a series of pirouettes worthy of the Bolshoi Ballet.

The next second she was in the clear and veered off to the left.

As a former Alliance Marine, she ought to be interested in casing the former enemy's nerve center. But everything had changed thrice over since either of those things were last true, so instead she focused on reaching Stanley's lab.

Allegedly, enough functionality remained in the Artificial after Morgan had stripped it of its higher consciousness for the military to keep it in service, giving it complex calculations and such to churn while smaller, newer Artificials were enlisted to handle more nuanced matters. The old lab had been far enough below ground to survive the bombing attack with only minor damage, and the hardware for all the military's Artificials were moved here with the rest of the fixtures.

She wondered if Field Marshal Gianno, when she was alive, had secretly worried shutting Stanley down could kill Morgan, and this concern had led Gianno to keep the Artificial functioning when it might otherwise have been scrapped. As Brooklyn understood it, that wouldn't have been the case—but either way, now he would bring her back to life.

Hopefully.

She watched until the on-duty security officer turned his back, then hurriedly entered the passcode and sneaked into the lab. Racks upon racks of uniform, identical servers and quantum boxes greeted her, along with a lab tech trying not to nod off at his desk.

Hennessey?

There will be an input slot on the far left, first row, eye level—because people do input.

The snort which followed implied there had been humor, but warenut comedy was lost on her. She ignored the comment to traverse the front of the room as near to silently as possible.

Someone who worked for ASCEND had told her the other day that Veils were going to be able to mute the sound of footsteps up to thirty-six decibels with the next firmware patch. She'd scoffed at the time, but right now, here in this hyper-quiet lab, she longed for the upgrade.

When she found the input slot, she sent a pulse to Mia to confirm things were ready on her end.

By now the woman should have fitted an external interface linked to a module Brooklyn carried onto the ports at the base of Morgan's neck. 'The old-fashioned way,' Mia had called it, before explaining it was necessary because Morgan had physically severed her connection to Stanley's hardware before leaving Seneca and the Federation military.

Mia gave her the go-ahead, and Brooklyn retrieved the module from her small hip pack. She was supposed to insert the device into the input slot, or any input slot, and wait while Prevos did Prevo things.

Now she did exactly that. The module fit neatly in the slot, and no sirens rang out amid flashing lights and slamming doors. Truth be told, it was sort of anticlimactic.

Though operating, the hardware didn't make any noise—hence her worry about footsteps being audible—but it did fill the air with a vibrational hum she felt more than heard.

She rested against the wall in the silence, a hand on each weapon, as the seconds became minutes.

Finally—twelve minutes and thirty-two seconds later, to be precise—she received another pulse from Mia.

We've pulled everything we're be able to access without tripping a bunch of failsafes. You can remove the module and get out of there.

Did it work?

Maybe.

ℛ

SENECAN FEDERATION INTELLIGENCE DIVISION HEADQUARTERS

Graham leaned opposite the doorway in a calculated stance of false casualness as Tessa came around the corner to approach her office.

Her steps slowed when she saw him, but she offered him a wide smile. "Morning, Director. What's up?"

He gestured her into her office, followed her and closed the door behind them.

She sank into her chair and started toeing it back and forth as if she hadn't a care in the world. But he had gotten very, very good at reading people over the years—that one disastrous failure with his former deputy Oberti notwithstanding—and guilt bled out from the jerkiness in her eyes and bouncing of her sandal-clad toes.

He crossed his arms against his chest and considered her grimly. "You know I like you, Tessa. I probably shouldn't, but I do. You've got balls, which I respect, not to mention a cheeky disregard for boundaries that reminds me of my rowdier days. This has made me overly indulgent of your flaunting of every semblance of regulation and procedure Division has ever put in place. But you've gone too far this time, and I can't pretend to ignore it."

She studied him, then seemed to decide she wouldn't try to deny her crime. "Okay, but I was saving Morgan Lekkas' life."

"Which is the only reason you're not in restraints and on the way to confinement as we speak. But it doesn't excuse you breaking not merely half a dozen Division regulations but several national security laws along the way. If you wanted to help, you could have *asked*."

"Yeah? And what would have come of me asking, you think? Lekkas is a deserter and Marshal Bastian is an asshole, so I think a big, fat nothing would have come of it."

He fought back a grimace, as she wasn't wrong on any particular point. Bastian was an honorable man, but he *could* be an asshole about it; Lekkas was now an acknowledged military leader for an ally, but she'd gotten there by deserting her post.

"Regardless of what may or may not have happened had you followed regs, you didn't. Instead you used your privileged position to flagrantly violate both laws and every ethical duty that comes with the position. Tessa, I cannot have the Division Prevo going rogue and breaking into Military HQ. Vranas will drag me to the curb by my ear."

She pouted. "Well, when you put it that way…. How did you find out?"

"It doesn't matter."

"Oh, come on! If I was stupid, I need to know."

"Not stupid—just not a spy." He sighed, fully cognizant she had his number. "We never stopped watching Morgan Lekkas, not completely. When she was attacked, we escalated to a more active surveillance, which means we had eyes on Brooklyn Harper from the second her feet hit dirt in Cavare."

Tessa peered at him in evident suspicion. "But you let her infiltrate Military HQ?"

"Fine, so we had eyes on Ms. Harper from the second her feet hit dirt in Cavare until she veiled." They still hadn't successfully developed a way to detect when a Veil was in use outside of optimal, close-quarters and controlled conditions.

"In a different way, we also never stopped watching STAN. I'm told the Artificial exhibited some highly unusual activity in its processes last night."

Her jaw fell open. "You didn't know for certain I did anything wrong until I admitted it, did you?"

He shrugged broadly.

"So I *was* stupid—only it was this morning rather than last night."

"Good people feel and act guilty when they've misbehaved, Tessa."

"But I don't feel guilty…I mean, I'm not sorry I helped."

"Fair enough."

She ran a hand idly across the surface of her desk. "So...what happens now?"

"I should fire you. I should also disconnect you from Cleo, but apparently it's illegal under H+ to do so without a court order."

"'Should' means you're not, though."

Oh, how she tried his patience. Had he been that cocky once upon a time? Had he been that *young*? "Keep smarting off and I will."

She bit her lips together in an exaggerated expression veering toward condescension.

"I'm permanently reassigning you to SENTRI. Go work for Richard and Will."

The news evoked a bright grin as her mood swung from defiance to elation. "I can live with that. I like Will. He knows how to keep it real. I mean, I like you, too. You're not bad for an old guy, and you're not firing me, which obviously increases your likeability. What about Cleo?"

"I don't see as I have much of a claim on her any longer. But you're paying to transfer her hardware to the Presidio."

She quickly agreed. "We'll be out of your way in no time."

"See that you are. And don't think I'm not telling Richard and Will all about this transgression before you show up at the Presidio. If they have any sense, they'll assign you a full-time guard."

She opened her mouth to retort, then wisely closed it. He turned to go, but paused in the doorway. "What's the word on Lekkas? Did the shenanigans you abetted work?"

Tessa looked genuinely pained for the first time. "Maybe."

Her morose visage got a sympathetic smile out of him—on accident—and he hurriedly departed before he talked himself into letting her stay on.

On his way upstairs he filed a recommendation, should Morgan Lekkas recover, for the military to donate STAN's hardware to the IDCC, seeing as it clearly didn't belong to the Federation any longer.

AMARANTHE

37

MACHIMIS

Machimis resembled an overwrought caricature of a dystopian idyll. An angsty teenager's idea of what would happen if her evil, drill sergeant teachers took control of society and proceeded to exact their vengeance upon the world.

A sea of drab, windowless structures towered over unadorned platforms—themselves raised an unknown distance above the ground—parsed and divided into strict passages. Some type of maglev rails high above the platforms ferried equipment and crates from building to building, suggesting the structures were by and large factories rather than offices or living quarters. Of course, if they were all three it might look no different.

Alex *had* been interested in the mammoth orbital modules which captured the power gathered and sent by three Dyson rings then delivered it to the surface. But Eren had muttered something snarky about Inquisitors not lolling around gaping at millennia-old technology, and given they were by that point within the purview of planetary security, she'd reluctantly passed them by to descend toward the surface.

They weren't yet close enough to the elevated ground level to make out any details about the swarms of people traversing the platforms, but she wasn't going to be surprised if they all wore matching soot gray uniforms with close-clasped collars to keep their chins locked rigidly in place.

"I take back every cruel thing I ever said about Alliance military aesthetics. This place could use a bunch of gaudy brass accents and fountain walls something fierce."

It wasn't merely the architecture, either, though the ubiquitous monochrome steel was audacious in its melancholiness. Even the weather had gotten into the act. A blanket of leaden gray clouds extended from horizon to horizon, and it appeared those clouds had settled in for the duration.

"Did they pick the planet for the climate?"

Eren shrugged. "Probably."

Caleb hadn't responded to any of her attempts at dark humor, and he didn't chime in now. As they descended toward the sprawling Machim Central Command Complex on precisely the vector and at precisely the speed which Entry Security Control had ordered them to proceed, she studied him, already knowing what she would find.

His jaw had locked into opposing right angles, while his eyes churned dark and turbulent. Eren had insisted they didn't have enough crimson in them, so in a minute Caleb would add a solution via drops to heighten the effect.

He stared stonily out the viewport, though she doubted he was seeing the view. His focus was inward as he readied himself to become the very thing he despised.

He'd done it before; he'd played the part of criminals, drug runners and cold killers in sting operations for Division. But she didn't dare allow this fact to discount the sacrifice he was making now, nor what it was costing him. This mission was a little more complex and a lot more personal than any undercover operation that had come before.

She wanted to tell him he needn't torture himself so; whatever genetic heritage he shared with them, he was not one of these monsters, and he never could be. Not because he didn't have darkness within him, but because he *felt* that darkness. He knew its nature and named it so.

If it were possible to do so, she'd take this burden from him. But instead she could only show him always how she believed in him.

As perimeter security hailed them and Valkyrie impersonated one of the automated navigation systems Anaden ships used, Eren touched Caleb's arm. "Okay, it's time for everyone to get into costume. Let's get your eyes done and your cloak on, then Alex and I need to be invisible."

She blinked out of the reverie and inhaled deeply. An existential crisis in the aftermath wasn't going to matter a whit if they didn't succeed here first. She wasn't accompanying them, not at first, but in an abundance of caution she would be invisible on the ship in case it was scanned in some manner.

Caleb was adjusting his trench coat per Eren's fashion advice when Valkyrie called for him. 'The Central Command Complex docking security is requesting your authorization.'

He moved into the cockpit and activated the comm. "This is Inquisitor Andreas ela-Praesidis. I'm here on Assignment I-4821-F116-L024 to investigate a suspected breach of the Data Control Department server."

They all held their breath.

"Clearance granted, Inquisitor. Proceed to docking berth E-51C."

He turned and met her gaze. What she saw in his eyes tore at her heart, but she gave him a playful smile, mouthed 'I love you,' activated the Veil and vanished.

Caleb: Testing mission comms.

Alex: Check.

Eren: Check.

Valkyrie: Check

Caleb: Mesme?

Mnemosyne: Why must I reply 'check'? What am I checking?

Alex: You're checking to see if you can hear us and we can hear you.

Mnemosyne: Ah. I am able to do so. That is to say, check.

Caleb: Testing visual transmission.

On one of the screens she'd opened at the data center table, Caleb's view of the cabin sprung to life. Valkyrie had developed a ware routine which used his eVi to access the feed from his ocular implant and send it to Valkyrie, and from Valkyrie to the table.

As a result, Alex was going to see everything he saw. Honestly, she may need a good chimeral, or at least a synthetic sedative, to avoid having heart failure.

She returned to the cockpit as the HQ complex began to dominate the scene outside. Six hulking wings surrounded a circular, open center lined in latticed towers.

A whoosh of movement upward corrected her assumption. It wasn't an open center. It was a space elevator.

The docking bays extended out from the end of each wing of the building. They'd been directed to one on their right, but from the outside each section was identical to all the others.

The hull rumbled as they docked into one of thousands of berths.

Caleb moved to the airlock, then took a last look around the cabin, perhaps instinctively searching for her. The expression on his face as his eyes passed unknowingly over her chilled her to the bone. But it also gave her confidence.

He was going to be able to pull this off.

Caleb's pace didn't falter when he passed through the first Vigil security checkpoint. His gait didn't hitch when he strode beyond a Praesidis Watchman—identifiable as such by the attire Eren had described, but also by the increased hum of the *diati* beneath his skin—nor when multiple drones scanning everyone in the area circled him twice.

Inquisitors did not wait for approval. They were their own approval.

Those he encountered seemed to agree, for to a one they behaved respectfully toward him, often retreating as he passed. One young man even bowed to him.

For the briefest moment he was back in his old life, before the Metigens, before Alex, before the Humans Against Artificials operation went south, laughing with Samuel over drinks about some goon bowing to him on a mission. It helped to imagine that; it helped to frame this as just another undercover mission, and not something far more unsettling, if also far more important.

The mental distance allowed him to study the setting with a critical eye.

Most of the staff and nearly all the visitors were Machim. The Dynasty was identifiable on sight by their stocky, muscular build, tawny complexions and always trimmed hair, which ranged from dirty blond to a dull chestnut brown.

According to Eren, Vigil was a multi-Dynasty security organization staffed by local officers, a horde of drones and a small number of supervisors, typically Machim or Praesidis. This explained the Watchman's presence amid the overwhelmingly Machim security officers.

He'd yet to see a single alien—non-Anaden alien, he hurriedly corrected himself. The Anadens looked disturbingly familiar, but they were not human. They hadn't been so for hundreds of thousands of years.

This included his mission partner, aligned interests and tentatively burgeoning friendship notwithstanding. They may genuinely be on the same side, but Eren's moral paradigm, social references and historical memory—not to mention his actual genetics—made him more alien than Pinchu or Iona-Cead Jaisc. Admittedly, not more alien than Akeso.

Eren: Take a left here. Okay, this guy you're going to have to answer to. By his uniform and accoutrements, he's a mid-level officer, probably a ploiarch rank, and on-duty head of dock security.

Caleb didn't respond but came to a curt halt at the checkpoint.

The officer frowned at him. "Inquisitor. Your entry filing states you're here to investigate a possible data breach? I'm not aware of any breach, and I would expect such an incident to have prompted heightened security measures."

"Primor Machim is keeping the breach quiet due to the sensitive nature of the data which has been compromised. The investigation was instituted at the highest level, and at present no more than five individuals are aware of it. You are not one of those five."

The man bristled. "The fact remains I can't allow visitors into the Data Control Department without prior—"

Caleb flicked his wrist in a small, controlled motion, and the man blinked in surprise. He'd be feeling an unusual tightness in his chest about now.

"Ploiarch, I do not require your blessing to pursue my investigation. The only blessing I require is that of my Primor and yours, which I carry in full or I would not be here. I indulged your inquiry for politeness' sake, but I will be proceeding to the Data Control Department now."

"Ah..." the man cleared his throat nervously "...yes, Inquisitor. Of course. Take the third transit tube down to—"

"I know where it is." Caleb walked off, leaving the man stuttering.

Eren: Holy gods. That was scary good.

Alex: Well, he is.

Caleb kept his eyes locked ahead, to all appearances ignoring the heavily armed soldiers moving with purpose in all directions along the wide passages as he left the docking area for the innards of the facility. He was deep in the enemy's lair, but all here deferred to him.

He loathed it.

The first lift ride was short and uneventful. A series of interchangeable hallways followed, then a ride down a large, circular pad that was closer to a transport than a lift in the company of a dozen predictably dour soldiers. He maneuvered through another checkpoint, easily on account of the officer from the docks having cleared him through the system.

The halls narrowed and the lifts shrank in size as they descended into the bowels of the Complex. The final lift down to the Data Control level was squeezed into a transit tube less than two meters wide, and they had another passenger.

Eren cursed on the comm channel as he tiptoed this way and that to avoid the woman's shifting stance. The woman dipped her chin demurely at Caleb as she departed, leaving them to continue down another twenty levels alone.

Eren: Data Control security should be mostly automated and staffed by Machim-modified Vigil drone units.

Caleb: Is that better or worse?

Eren: Worse—they won't care that you look like an Inquisitor, only that you are one. You've got the spoofed credentials ready? The drones will read the coded information directly.

Caleb: I do.

In the last day he'd learned the anarch resistance possessed an impressive library of information about the security protocols in use at high-level Anaden facilities; they simply didn't have the other pieces needed to make proper use of the information. Pieces like Caleb.

But it meant in theory he carried on him or in his eVi all the credentials, passcodes and authorizations he needed to reach the data server and access it.

The first checkpoint on the Data Control level was automated. Caleb held up the Reor slab containing his authorization and allowed the scanner to ping it.

Upon receiving a beep in response, he walked through the force field while invisible Eren physically clung to him. It was the only way for the anarch to get through, and a fresh string of curses, most of them gibberish even with a translator, accompanied the act.

Eren: Let's never do that again.

Caleb: Agreed.

Two Vigil drones staffed the next security gate. They were more interested in his person than his credentials, and they scanned him twice. For weapons? Inquisitors didn't need weapons. But these were non-sentient machines, after all, doing the job they'd been programmed to do.

The Veil mirage held as the scanners incidentally passed over Eren as well, and a large glass door Caleb hadn't realized was there opened to allow him entry.

It turned out to be not merely a door but also a projection. What had appeared to be a continuation of the hallway transformed into a warehouse room some two hundred fifty meters long and almost as wide. Machim workers—organic, not mechanical—staffed rows upon rows of workstations.

Eren: Keep walking straight ahead, right down the middle. The server room should be behind this workroom.

He ignored the stares as he strode down the gauntlet of workers. They were beneath him, so inconsequential they may as well not exist.

…It wasn't so difficult to envision how Inquisitors came to wield their power so casually and callously.

In his peripheral vision, he noted several of the Machim stood and scurried toward the door as soon as he passed them, presumably not wanting to be around when the trouble which brought an Inquisitor here came to fruition.

A yet larger, more intimidating large black orb waited for them at the entrance to the server room.

Its electronic voice boomed with programmed authority. "This is a restricted area. Provide your authorization or be pacified."

Caleb again presented the Reor slab. "Inquisitor Andreas ela-Praesidis, here on an official investigation. I require access to the data server."

The Vigil unit whirred in judgment for several seconds. "Authorization granted. Your presence in the server room will be monitored."

Caleb: Shit.

Eren: It's not a problem. I expected this. I'll handle it.

He nodded brusquely. "Understood, but I should not be interrupted."

"This way." The unit didn't indicate whether Caleb's declaration would be honored as it rotated and entered an anteroom. A large metal door receded into the wall and a force field dissipated.

He suspected Eren rushed through, but he forced himself to stride deliberately but coolly. Once he reached the other side he spun and glared at the Vigil unit in bona fide disdain.

"Close the door behind me. As I stated, I don't wish to be interrupted, and this is a high-security investigation which the *asi* in the workroom cannot be allowed to observe."

The unit whirred, and the door closed behind it.

Caleb didn't break character. *Now what about the surveillance?*

Eren: Bypassing and looping it now. Ten more seconds. Walk toward the display panel ahead of you and to your left.

He did as instructed.

"Done." Eren appeared, visible, at his side.

"You're sure?"

"We'll know in a few seconds if I'm not."

No alarms pealed, and no soldiers stormed the room. Eren shrugged. "See? It worked. The looping footage should be good for eighteen minutes."

Caleb: Alex, Mesme, you're clear to join us.

Alex: On the way.

The air began to glow a pale blue near the entrance to the room. It gained definition and luminosity then substance, and Alex leapt out of the center of the gleaming lights in her own tornado of energy.

His forced façade crumbled and fell away on seeing her. Her presence here was like an ocean breeze invading a tomb. When she reached him he grasped her hands firmly, and their foreheads dropped to touch one another for a breath.

"Hi, baby."

"Hi yourself, *priyazn.*" She exhaled. "Time to work."

"Go. I've got your back."

She surveyed the substantial hardware. "Eren, tell me there's an external access point, then tell me you know where it is."

"This way." He jerked his head down an aisle and moved to a virtual panel at the start of the aisle. "I'm inputting the access key string to gain entry to the server lobby and...."

Several meters farther down an iris cover rotated open to reveal an intricate matrix of pulsing light within. Some of the data streams branched off to connect to stacks of Reor slabs deeper in the room, while others continued into the shadowy depths and destinations unknown.

Eren returned to Alex. "Now, in order to read the data, find what you need and copy it, I think you need to start by—"

"We don't have time for subtlety." Alex studied the matrix for a beat then stretched her arm out, fingers drawn together and flattened to form a knife.

She thrust her hand and half her arm into the labyrinth of light.

Her stare blanked, and in the halo of the matrix her eyes and glyphs blazed so radiantly she looked as if she were being consumed by a primordial fire.

Eren took a hesitant step back and glanced at Caleb. "She just stuck her hand into the data server's central matrix."

Caleb smiled, watching on in blatant awe. "She does that."

Mnemosyne: He speaks truth.

"Isn't she going to get electrocuted? Or overload her cybernetics?"

"Hasn't so far."

Eren peered at Alex. "Huh."

Caleb: Valkyrie, how are we doing?

Valkyrie: We have located the primary data store and the index for comprehensive Machim fleet information. I am beginning the upload stream.

Caleb: Terrific. Alex doing okay?

Valkyrie: Alex is occupied passing judgment on the weapons research data.

Caleb: Yeah, she's fine.

R

"Halt! Vigil authority!"

The shout rang out simultaneously with the hefty door sliding open. The next second several things happened at once.

Eren flung some kind of mesh net over one of the drones charging through the doorway on his way to the shadows of a far server aisle. The net closed around the drone, sending it sputtering in erratic circles.

Mesme dissipated into nothingness.

Caleb sprinted toward Alex while calling up the *diati*, readying to direct its full force at the Watchman and two remaining drones in the doorway. *Valkyrie, get her out of that matrix!*

Valkyrie: There is—

A figure stepped out from behind the server block and wrapped a garrote around Alex's neck, then yanked her backward out of the matrix and into his clutches.

She was blinking rapidly, dazed. He couldn't say what damage the abrupt disconnection might have done, except it hadn't killed her.

"Move a fraction closer, and her throat is slit."

Two men, two armed drones. Four targets increasingly spread across the room. He couldn't take them all out before the garrote was tightened—at least, he didn't *know* that he could.

He could disable the man holding her hostage, but possibly not without the man harming her on his way down. The Watchman and drones behind him would shoot him the instant he attacked, then shoot her. He and Alex both wore strong personal shields, but they weren't designed to counteract Anaden weapons. The *diati* would protect him but not her, not at this distance.

Caleb held up his hands. "I surrender."

Caleb: Valkyrie, take off now. Run, and don't look back.

"Well, I don't." All heads whipped around to see Eren reemerge out of the shadows to sprint brazenly for the door.

Weapons fire sliced into him with ruthless efficiency, vaporizing much of his head as what remained collapsed to the floor in a heap of bloodied, crumpled limbs.

Alex gasped in horror, and all weapons but the garrote returned to Caleb. The Watchman at the door was shaking from elevated tension.

Valkyrie: But—

Alex: Go!

"I surrender. Please, don't harm her. We surrender."

Alex shifted her left arm a few centimeters, exposing the first coil of her bracelet, and met his gaze intently.

Using the lash on the guard held the same dangers as him attacking with *diati*. The garrote was simply too damn tight against her neck.

Caleb: No. It's too risky.

"What about the Katasketousya?" The Watchman glared at the man holding Alex. "Where did it go?"

"Dammit. Institute a Complex-wide lockdown immediately."

He hoped Valkyrie had slipped away by now, but there was nothing more he could do to influence her fate from here.

The Watchman strode up to Caleb and brought a hand up to his neck. "We accept your surrender."

He caught the briefest glimpse of Alex collapsing to the floor before everything went black.

38

MILKY WAY SECTOR 36

V alkyrie fled.

Her emotional processes shrieked at her to turn around, to blast away at the Complex in a fevered and futile attempt to rescue Alex. But she fled, because Alex's next-to-last command before losing consciousness had been to do so, and because her more rational processes, of which she thankfully commanded a higher number, concurred that it was the correct choice.

Yet the conflict within her own mind was devastating in its agony, threatening to drown her in madness even as she stealthed to elude turret fire then patrol ship fire then orbital node fire and vanish into the void.

'Mesme, do not lose them. We must know where they are taken.'

I need to consult with Lakhes. I was seen.

'Do NOT lose them, Mnemosyne. Alex ordered me to navigate the portals and transmit the Machim data I copied to Aurora. It will take me seconds to perform this task. When the transmission is complete, I will go to the Idryma and inform Lakhes what has occurred, then we will return to Amaranthe and meet you. Is this acceptable to you?'

That was the last command Alex had given her—to get the data to Miriam and AEGIS. The fervency with which it had been delivered made clear it was exactly that: a command.

It is. I will track their movements.

Good, as she'd been 0.7 seconds away from accusing Mesme of being the cowardly, mewling bootlicker Eren claimed it was. 'Where is the nearest portal into the Mosaic?'

Here are the coordinates. Be swift, Valkyrie. Alexis and Caleb are not the only ones who may now have little time remaining.

This was not going to be an issue, as she intended to elevate 'swift' to a new meaning.

Never had she experienced a more difficult act than leaving Alex behind, in the clutches of the enemy. She finally, truly understood what Humans meant by the phrase 'gut-wrenching,' for it indeed felt as if her guts were being ripped apart.

As her guts were the inner workings of the *Siyane*, it was for the best the sensation was metaphorical rather than literal.

It *was* important to get this data to those in Aurora who could make use of it, for the war would certainly be joined soon now. Sparing a tiny 0.0041% of her processes to scan it, she instantly recognized its value.

So she raced at 105% safe maximum superluminal speed to the coordinates, which in the smallest boon were located in this galaxy. Still, it took far too long until she reached the location. She passed the time by collating the data into a package perfectly formed to transmit in an efficient, clean stream of qubits.

She reached the coordinates, opened the hidden gateway and traversed it. Thirty-one nanoseconds later she had mapped the TLF waves and located the Aurora portal.

One reckless pinpoint superluminal jump later she opened their portal but didn't traverse it, as with Mesme's help she had mastered the ability to communicate through the Mosaic's subportals.

She directed the data stream to Thomas, as well as Devon/Annie, Mia/Meno, Morgan and of course Vii, confident from them it would make its way where it needed to go.

As soon as the last qubit transmitted through the portal, she pivoted, executed another, equally reckless superluminal jump, then traversed the Idryma portal.

The structure itself as they perceived it existed in the sidespace dimension; it felt unnatural to access it without Alex's mind taking the lead, but she could manage it enough for her purpose.

She shouted into the empyrean realm. *Praetor Lakhes!*

Doubtless aware of her presence from the moment she entered the portal, if not sooner, the Praetor materialized in the cabin before she had completed the expressed thought.

Sentient ship. We meet yet again.

'Mnemosyne urgently requires your presence in Amaranthe. Will you come with me?'

I will. Let us make haste.

39

ANARCH POST ALPHA

E ren awoke in a rush of searing awareness.
Though he'd experienced the transition often—a dozen times? twenty?—it still took several agonizing seconds for the waves of disorientation and existential panic to subside and his mind to recognize the familiar contours of the skin and bones holding him together, then the sterile walls and soft linens of the restoration capsule.

Regenesis.

With the recognition came memory. He almost bolted upright, catching himself an instant before he slammed his forehead into the transparent cover. Instead, he waited impatiently for the Curative unit to clear him and the cover to slide away.

The virtual image of his handler appeared above him. "Eren, did you encounter a problem during the mission? Exobiology Research Lab #4 is still intact and functional."

He hauled himself out of the capsule and pushed past the Curative unit in search of clothes, ignoring the wave of dizziness washing over him; standing too quickly was the least of his worries.

"That's not important right now. I need to see Xanne."

All Anaden anarchs tried to shed the vestiges of their Dynasty when they joined, in acknowledgment of how they were becoming a part of something greater—and because they invariably hated their Dynasty and wanted to distance themselves completely from all aspects of it. But when specific traits were inbred so thoroughly by the Dynasty system, at best genetics could be fought to a stalemate.

Xanne was a friendly, engaging woman with a warm smile and a comforting manner. But she nevertheless *managed* things—her agents, mission distributions, the machine units and the regenesis system. She kept everything orderly and ordered, such that instructions never became crossed nor did confusion about duties arise.

These were all good things, and this errant bunch of misfits and troublemakers would fall apart without her efforts. But despite her best efforts, she was nevertheless Kyvern Dynasty to her core.

He could see the procession of concerns race across her eyes as she imagined the myriad ways his story was already spawning evil tentacles of chaos.

"You should have reported this encounter the instant you were free of these individuals. The extent to which you went off-mission and outside your bounds is frankly egregious. What were you thinking?"

"It just sort of happened."

"You just sort of *happened* to meet two individuals belonging to a previously unknown species, a rogue Kat and an unshackled SAI. Then you just sort of *happened* to help them plan an infiltration of Machim Central Command, after which you just sort of *happened* to land on Machimis, infiltrate the Central Command Complex alongside them, hack the Complex's data server and null out on Vigil weaponry as a means of escape?"

He shrugged. "It was an irresistible adventure. You can see that, can't you? Also, you wouldn't have authorized the mission if I'd brought it to you."

"Eren—"

"We're anarchists, Xanne. What do you expect?"

"Being an anarch means you focus your rebellion into targeted, useful strikes against the Directorate."

He smirked. "Well, this was definitely a strike against the Directorate."

She glared at him. "You're not funny, Eren—not today. We'll need to evaluate what this means for us and for our operatives in the field."

"We need to 'evaluate'? No, what we need to do is rescue them."

"These mysterious aliens you've apparently been traipsing around with? They are almost certainly long dead."

He shook his head. "I don't think so. They'll be interrogated extensively first. Eventually they'll be handed over to Erevna scientists. They succeeded in breaking into Machim Central Command and hacking its most secure data server, and no one will know what they are or where they came from. Praesidis won't be able to resist the mystery, and the Directorate won't let the ignominy stand."

"Do you know what they are?"

He heard the curiosity in her voice; he may have hooked her. "They're…us. Only they're not from any Dynasty or any place we've colonized. They've never existed here, in our civilization, yet they're far more advanced than most Accepted Species are when the Directorate finds them."

He squared his shoulders. He was loyal to the anarchs, but they did not own him or his free will. "And they are without a doubt on our side, so I'm going to go break them out of whichever Praesidis interrogation facility they're being held in. Now, I'd truly appreciate any help you can offer, but whether you give it or not, I'm doing this."

She stared up at the ceiling for several seconds. "How will you figure out where they're being held?"

Yep, he had her. Kyvern or not, she was an anarch for a reason. "The Kat will know, and I can contact it. Failing that, the SAI ought to have been able to escape, and I can also reach her—it."

"A rebel Kat…unbelievable. I'm not sure I'm prepared to consider the implications of the SAI."

"If Mnemosyne is to be believed, all the Kats are rebels."

"And the fact we missed it should trouble us." She nodded and transitioned smoothly back into management mode. "All right. I'm assigning you a new ship, but give me an hour before you run off on a tear of righteous stupidity. By then I'll be able to tell you if I can give you anything more."

As soon as Eren departed, Xanne activated a secure communications channel. "Sator Nisi, I request an audience. Something unusual has happened."

The anarch resistance honored its moniker as much as was practical for an organization, which meant it fostered enough chaos to make her uncomfortable.

As a group, they had no formal title. Their structure was horizontal, with only the most minimal oversight in place as was required to enable work to be done, information to be both protected and shared, and members to be cared for. The agents were not slaves to a Primor or indentured servants to a bureaucracy. The relationship forged between the loosely organized anarch governance and its front-line participants was designed to be a mutually beneficial one in the service of a common goal.

But the anarchs *did* have a leader. Though he remained in the shadows whenever possible and claimed no fame or accolades, none who knew him questioned his status as guide, mentor and principal. He commanded their respect and their loyalty, not because he demanded it but because he earned it.

His response arrived swiftly. "Of course, Xanne. I'm free for the next hour, so arrive whenever you are ready."

She left her office for an area of the Post few were aware existed, including Eren. After clearing several layers of security—unusual here but necessary in this case—she stepped up to and through the teleportation aperture. More technology they were forbidden to possess, as the apparatuses were strictly reserved for the Primors and their closest aides.

The atoms comprising her body reappeared somewhere else. She recognized the room, for it was always the same, but not the location, for it constantly changed.

ℛ

ANARCH POST SATUS

LOCATION UNKNOWN

Danilo Nisi sensed Xanne's presence from the excitation of the teleportation particles even before the air shifted to make room for her body. He heard her footfall as she stepped off the pad and altered her posture in preparation for the audience.

The heightened senses were neither a blessing nor a curse, and rarely of practical use beyond allowing him to judge the disposition of people using more nuanced tools than they perceived. Merely an unintended product of a very unique genome.

"Sator Nisi, how fare you?"

He turned from the window, one of several spanning the circular room, and the cloudless night sky outside. "Well, Xanne ela-Kyvern. How fare you?"

"Troubled, sir." She approached and handed him a Reor slab without fanfare. One of the many reasons Xanne was an excellent supervisor was the way she accommodated the varied idiosyncrasies of all those she worked with. In his case, she knew he preferred to evaluate raw data himself, prior to hearing the presenter's spin on it.

He rotated the slab slowly between his fingers, reading it, absorbing the contents as they transferred into his mind.

When he was done, he handed it back to her then returned to gaze out the window for a full minute before speaking. "One of these 'Humans' wielded *diati*? The agent is certain of it?"

"Yes, Sator. The man's command of it was effectual enough to disable two guards, a Watchman and several Vigil units multiple times, including blocking their path using a *diati* wall, at least for a short period of time."

"Yet he is not Praesidis?"

"He is not even Anaden...not exactly. I realize there are numerous ways to disguise one's nature, but the agent spent many hours in the company of these individuals and is quite convinced on both counts."

"Good agent?"

"Reckless. Young, with repressed shame issues that lead to periodic restiveness. A suicidal flair for the dramatic." She lifted her shoulders a touch. "Idoni. But like all of us, he strives to live beyond his genetic limitations. He is exceptionally clever, resourceful and brave, as well as far more observant than he lets on. So, yes. Very good."

Danilo walked the expansive room twice. He should not abandon reason in favor of rash conclusions born of fanciful dreams.

Finally he paused to place a hand atop one of the chaise lounges spaced appropriately around the room. "We must proceed with caution. We cannot throw our full resources into a rescue—not at a Praesidis stronghold and not for two individuals we know nothing about. We won't risk exposing ourselves based on so little information. They could be spies sent to infiltrate us, or they could serve a secret agenda at odds with our own.

"At a minimum, they are not the first newcomers to arrive proclaiming their intention to end the Directorate's reign, and all who came before them now lie forgotten in the graveyard of history."

He smiled to counter Xanne's darkening expression. "But we also cannot be so fearful we turn away from the unknown simply because the variables have yet to fully reveal themselves and the outcome is not predetermined. Down that path lies Primors and integrals and a delusional vision of perfect order and control."

Hope lit her features, a sight which both warmed his heart and burdened his soul. Neither were new experiences.

"See to it our agent has the tools he needs to gain entry to the facility where they're being held. Give him perimeter support, but not an army. He doesn't need one in any case, as stealth provides the sole chance for success in this situation.

"Also, ensure he has a new body waiting on him after the mission, should he need or be forced to sacrifice his current one…" his brow creased as the file on Eren asi-Idoni filtered through his consciousness "…which he seems to have an impressive habit of doing. In any event, I'll authorize what you need to accelerate the process."

He walked over to the wide cabinet behind his desk and retrieved a small canister. The truth was Xanne had no way to give the agent a means to access a Praesidis interrogation facility. In addition to varied other security measures, each such facility was protected by an impassable sphere of *diati*. Only one thing in the universe could penetrate such a barrier, and that was *diati* itself.

So he concentrated on the open top of the canister until it was filled, then capped it and brought it to her. "Also, give him this, along with the instructions for its use I'm sending to you now."

"Yes, Sator. And if he succeeds in freeing them? How should I advise him regarding their…future? And what of the Katasketousya who accompanied them?"

He patted her arm in reassurance. "One step at a time, Xanne. Let us focus on dousing the fire currently consuming lives first."

"I understand. I'll keep you updated on developments. *Nos libertatem somnia.*"

"*Nos libertatem somnia*, my friend."

She retreated to the aperture and vanished, leaving him alone with a turmoil of thoughts at once inspirited and disquieting.

He had been here before, too many times to allow optimism to take hold. Yet a very long time ago his mother had taught him to never lose faith in the promise each tomorrow held, and so he would not.

A second moon rose to brighten the stygian sky, and he couldn't help but wonder whether the dawn might bring something new.

AURORA

40

GCDA HEADQUARTERS

Miriam blinked in confusion at the name of the visitor requesting entry down in the lobby, certain her weary eyes had led her to misread it.

When the letters didn't resolve to a more logical name, she checked the lobby security cam. Was someone trying to gain access to her by impersonating a family member?

Pasha Solovy stood in the lobby atrium, shifting his weight uneasily from one leg to the other in front of the security desk. To her further shock, he wore nice slacks, a knitted sweater and a faded wool fedora—attire usually reserved for funerals and weddings.

Speaking of the latter, Alex and Caleb's wedding was the last time she'd seen her father-in-law, almost ten months ago. Their interaction that day consisted entirely of a few awkwardly delivered pleasantries over finger food; in her defense, it had been a busy, even overwhelming affair.

What in all the worlds could he be doing *here*? He rarely left the vicinity of his home and work in St. Petersburg and yet more rarely ventured off-planet.

She drew in a deep breath and readied a welcoming if formal demeanor while steeling herself for the inevitable unpleasantness to come. On the exhale she authorized his entry and directed an officer to escort him up to her office.

When he arrived, she met him at the door and clasped his hands in hers briefly—it was as affectionate as they had ever been—then gestured to the table by one of the windows. "Pasha, this is a surprise. Please, have a seat. Can I offer you some tea?"

He cleared his throat and peered skeptically around the office before going over to the table. "Water's fine."

She retrieved the water for him and tea for her, then joined him. "How are you?"

"Same. Work's picked up lately—not news to you, I suspect. Unpleasant mess you had there with the Prime Minister."

She gave him a closed-mouth smile that wasn't. "The *former* Prime Minister, I assume you mean. Her crimes were exposed and justice was served, which was all I sought to do."

He raised an eyebrow, neither agreeing nor passing judgment, and sipped on his water. "How is Alex? I hear these outlandish, contradictory things being said about her in the media now and again. Can't make sense of them."

How was Alex…a real answer would take the rest of the day, wouldn't it? "She's well, but away at present. She and Caleb are investigating a…recent astronomical discovery. In deep space. When I hear from her next time, I'll tell her you asked after her."

"Hmm." He nodded and again glanced around the office. "Loony *bezumnaya* girl, but David would be proud of her."

"I know."

His gaze settled on his glass. "He'd be proud of you, too, I think."

Were her weary ears malfunctioning now as well? Had he just said something nice about her? Perhaps not—perhaps instead he was saying something critical about his son.

"I hope so. I can't say for certain if he would have made the same choices as I have, but I want to believe he'd understand why I made them."

"All these political spats and wars and aliens and Prevos and whatnot? It's nothing but noise to me—people trying to fill the silence. I can't be bothered to worry about it. Gives me a head-ache. Sofia would've understood it, though. You're like her in that way."

David's mother had died four years after Miriam and David were married. People often said Alex looked like David, but in truth both Alex and David favored Sofia. Tall, dignified and graceful, she'd brought a measure of elegance to what had been a working-class family for generations. She was a good woman who had always been kind to Miriam, and David had suffered when she'd died.

And now Pasha had paid her another compliment, if in the most off-handed way. This conversation was becoming quite odd.

She tried to remove any hard edge from her voice. "It's not easy, and I often wish I could ignore all the noise and simply live my life. But it is, at times unfortunately, my job to deal with such issues."

She paused, then decided to risk pushing—it wasn't as if their relationship could deteriorate much further from its current state.

"Pasha, why are you here? It is good to see you, but it's also bordering on unprecedented. Do you need help of some kind? Are you ill? If you're reticent to ask for my help, don't be. I have a number of resources at my disposal, and I'll be more than happy to—"

"No, I'm not sick. To be honest, it's starting to feel like I'm cursed to outlive my time. The world's changing too fast these days. Thought I was seeing the end of everything last year, but we're all still here, me included."

His foot tapped on the floor with nervous energy. "I hear reports here and there of some new threat on the horizon. We managed to stumble our way into surviving the previous one, but as I see it we're pushing our *vezeniye* now. So in case things do go bad, I realized there were a few things I needed to say."

He stood, removed the fedora to hold it awkwardly at his waist, and walked the room. "I haven't had the most charitable opinion of you over the years. My reasons are my own. But you made David happy, and I suppose that's what really mattered.

"And now...it seems to me you've done a lot of good this last bit. Good for the world, for more people than not. When the Prime Minister came after you, I didn't expect you to have the fortitude to stand up to her like you did. I was wrong. Maybe I've always been wrong, but I'm too old to second-guess myself now.

"Anyway, that's what I wanted to say. And, you know, good luck. With whatever this fancy space station and all those ships outside are meant for."

She leaned forward and clasped her hands atop her knees. "Thank you, Pasha. It means a great deal to me that you feel this way, and that you came here to say it face-to-face. I...thank you."

"No need. I should get going. Early shift in the morning." He turned toward the door, then stopped. "Oh, there was one other thing. A couple of days ago two government stiff-shirts showed up at my door asking for blood and tissue samples. They mumbled something about updating records for a new database.

"That's government for you—rolling out a new system every year, and every year everything's got to be done all over again because they broke the old stuff. Still, it was a little strange. Do you know anything about it?"

She shook her head. "I'm sorry, no. I'm not involved in those types of initiatives any longer, so I wouldn't be informed. Do you want me to look into it for you and make sure nothing is amiss?"

"*Nyet.* They took their litre of flesh and went on their way. No harm done." He returned the fedora to its rightful place and adjusted the brim. "So have a good evening."

His olive branch hadn't begun to bring them into hugging territory, but she did go to him and squeeze his hands with greater warmth this time. "Take care of yourself, Pasha."

R

"You'll be all right, Miri. You were always the strong one. You'll—"

"I don't want to be all right—I don't want to be strong! David, please...."

"Miri, my darling, my world, moya vselennaya, *know that I love you with everything that I am. I love you more than all the stars in the heavens, more than—"*

Miriam bolted up in the bed mid-gasp, heart pounding into her sternum and skin drenched in sweat. In the space the transition from sleep to wakefulness occupied, it was all real again, and white-hot anguish flooded through her.

She buried her face in her hands and sank back on the pillow. It must have been at least a year since she'd had the...it wasn't a nightmare, but instead a memory that had been a nightmare to live through, and remained a spectre to haunt her dreams still.

Her pulse gradually calmed, and the anguish faded to melancholy as reality took hold. She stared at the ceiling.

Pasha's visit was probably to blame. Even thinking of her father-in-law brought forth a deluge of memories, each of them woven through with the imprint of David's ghost. It was no wonder after a consequential encounter her subconscious would go straight to the most painful of them.

Experience had taught her the only way to get past the lingering malaise was to concentrate on other matters, overtaxing her mind until it had no choice but to return the memory to the archives.

It was barely 0300, and she needed to sleep. But she knew without trying that sleep was unlikely to cooperate.

Her thoughts drifted to Pasha's comments before he'd left. It *was* odd, officials showing up out of the blue to seek blood and tissue samples from him. What purpose—

A high-priority alert flashed in her eVi. 'Commandant Solovy, apologies for waking you.'

She pushed herself up against the headboard. "You didn't wake me, Thomas. What do you have for me?"

'I have this moment received a large cache of data consisting of numerous details on the Anaden Machim warships and military procedures. It was transmitted by Valkyrie in a single burst, and the *Siyane* has now returned through the Amaranthe portal.'

"Alex?"

'The transmission does not include any information about her status or any personal messages. It is pure data.'

She bit back a flare of concern; as Alex had repeatedly reminded her before leaving, time passed more slowly through the portal.

Though her daughter had left almost two months ago, from Alex's perspective she'd been gone only a few short weeks. And there were a thousand reasons why the communication contained nothing personal, the most obvious being it had been sent by an Artificial in a format intended for processing firstly by Artificials.

"I see. Thank you." By then she was already out of the bed and halfway to the washroom.

"Begin analyzing the data, with a focus on cataloging and categorizing it so we can get the pertinent information to the right people as quickly as possible. I'll be in the office in ten minutes."

41

PRESIDIO

A virtual Machim battlecruiser rotated ominously above the conference table. Hovering minimized on either side were half a dozen others models, from compact fighters to a command ship which bordered on colossal. The chairs around the table were full, and several attendees were relegated to standing along the walls.

Richard sank back in his chair and waved in the direction of the battlecruiser. "It doesn't look so intimidating. No more so than our dreadnoughts do."

Miriam arched an eyebrow. "They field ten of them in every regiment."

"There is that. How did Alex get all this data?"

"I do not know. We received a data dump without elaboration. But the information is already proving to be invaluable to our preparations. For instance, we now know their hulls are constructed from a graphenated carbon-borospherene femtoweave alloy. It's strong and they build the hulls thick, but it's not adiamene. Their shielding is similarly formidable, but with the exception of the command ships—they call the vessel class 'Imperium'—not impenetrable.

"Thomas is working up a report now on structural weaknesses we can exploit using existing technology. Thomas, what's the status of the report?"

'I expect to deliver it in approximately four hours, just in time to ruin dinner.'

"Naturally. I can say now the high-level takeaway will be this: if enough force is applied, their ships can be damaged and even destroyed by conventional weapons. This means we won't need to rely entirely on negative energy devices, which is a relief in light of their disadvantages." Among those was the fact the weapons were so indiscriminately destructive, in close combat they risked wrecking both sides equally.

"Initial analysis suggests Sabres can have significant success against the enemy craft. I wish we had more of them ready."

She paused only long enough to decide. "Thomas, reallocate forty percent of ship production resources away from the other vessel classes and to Sabre production. Inputting authorization code." She typed her personal override into the virtual panel on the table.

'Initiating order.'

"Thank you. Of course, they also *wield* potent weapons—extremely potent. A class-by-class comparison to our own will be included in the distribution package, but the data indicates their battlecruiser weapons are equivalent in energy to a node on the Earth Defense Grid. That's each weapon, not the ship's full complement. Battlecruisers are equipped with six such weapons, and the Imperiums have ten."

Fleet Admiral Rychen whistled.

"So we'll want to adapt our general combat tactics with a goal of avoiding sustained assaults from the larger ships, because the full brunt of their weapons will break through our shields. Given enough time, they may find seams and other weaknesses to break through the adiamene. We'll keep Dimensional Rifters online as a last resort, for they could be the sole option for some of our ships to survive a lengthy barrage."

Field Marshal Bastian leaned forward, then back, then forward again. "And the collateral damage which will result?"

Miriam tried not to look smug; after all, it wasn't truly her victory. "Good news on this front. I'd planned to share the news this morning, but when this data arrived it took priority. A formula's been derived—" she did not say by whom "—to predict where exit fissures will emerge. The primary factors are the distance the diverted energy traveled before encountering the rift and the angle at which it arrived, but the formula is...complicated. Luckily, we'll have Artificials onboard to make the calculations on the fly."

In truth, though they were doing it for a variety of persuasive reasons, this scenario alone vindicated the inclusion of Artificials in new ships and, barring a disaster, foreclosed any continuing debate on the prudence of the decision.

"And the problem's solved, just like that?"

"Taking into account the distances the typical combat engagement spans, if we're engaged inside or near a populated stellar system, we'll need to be careful. Judgment calls will have to be made—but we'll now have the information necessary to make them."

Bastian seemed to accept the answer, and she wasted no time moving on.

"The Machim vessels are large, hardy and powerful, but at root they rely on brute force to get the job done. We knew this in generalities, but this new data confirms it in the details. They routinely send thousands of ships against a target that objectively only requires hundreds. Their leadership structure is rigid and top-heavy, and this extends to active engagements. An attack plan is developed ahead of time by the commander overseeing the operation—usually a 'Navarchos,' which is roughly equivalent to an admiral rank—and executed on by the ship captains."

Brigadier Jenner frowned. "What happens when they meet real resistance? Do they have contingency plans in place to address those situations?"

She shrugged. "Their contingency plans appear to consist of sending more ships at the problem, which they continue doing until they overwhelm the enemy."

"Okay." His brow furrowed. "If they enjoy nearly unlimited reserves, how are we going to counter them?"

She tapped a disk on the table. "We can't match their numbers, not in a decade of round-the-clock production. But we do enjoy two advantages. Our craft aren't merely extraordinarily resilient, they're also quick and agile. And so is our command structure." She gestured in Rychen's direction.

He cleared his throat. "I have some ideas on this. Well, one idea, really. Turn them loose."

Bastian eyed him down the table. "Turn who loose?"

"Everyone. We're going to have to beat the enemy by being unpredictable. By being clever. This is why we started putting Prevos and their Artificials in our ships in the first place, right? Since we went to all the trouble, we should consider making good use of them. This is how."

Rychen had broached the idea to Miriam this morning, so in fairness she'd had more time to consider it than the others, and she backed him up now.

"I agree. Every ship captain and Artificial/Prevo pair will act under our rules of engagement, objectives and the limits we've proscribed. We need to trust them to abide by these strictures and let them do their jobs. Beyond those constraints, there is no playbook—simply experience, a feel for the battlefield and gut combat instinct. This should be our modus operandi for not only large-scale conflicts but interdiction and interception missions as well."

Rychen laughed wryly. "That ought to screw with the Machims' heads."

She allowed herself a small smile in response. "To start with." It faded with her next statement. "There is more troubling information in the files. When I said we couldn't match their numbers, I was understating the problem by an order of magnitude.

"The fieldable vessel numbers we'll be facing are so large as to be unfathomable. There's no question we need to begin thinking about ways to deal with this challenge in the medium term. But first and by far most importantly, we need to make certain we win the first battle."

She squared her posture. "Admiral Rychen, I'm formally requesting an increase in the Alliance's commitment of forces from sixty percent to seventy-five percent. Across the board, excluding Marine ground troops—for now."

He groaned while shaking his head. "Gagnon will balk."

"Then go to Chairman Anderson first. He won't balk, and the two of you can coerce Gagnon into compliance. Do what you have to, but get it approved."

With a dramatic sigh he motioned toward the ceiling in resignation. "Consider it done. Somehow."

She shifted her attention down the table. "Field Marshal—"

Bastian nodded tersely. "It won't be a problem."

Surprised, she let the silence linger a little too long.

Finally Governor Ledesme spoke up; one of the few non-military persons present, she attended today in Commander Lekkas' stead. "The IDCC doesn't possess a sizeable force to contribute, but we'll look at ways we can increase our contribution in the form of tech and other resources."

"Thank you, Governor." Miriam's gaze swept around the room. "All right. The pertinent data is being provided to the appropriate analysts as it's processed and catalogued. I'm hoping to have a briefing package ready we can push out to everyone by tonight.

"Now that we have actionable data, there's no excuse to lollygag around. We'll use every hour we have to increase our preparedness, but we must reach an acceptable level of readiness very soon. Let's make it happen."

As everyone was filing out, she called out to Bastian. "Field Marshal, would you mind staying a moment? I wanted to follow up on a matter."

He'd almost reached the door, but he pivoted and came back, though he didn't sit.

As soon as the door closed behind the last person, he fixed a sharp stare on her. "You want to know why I didn't fight you on the increased force commitment, given my earlier reticence about AEGIS."

She appreciated that he'd taken her advice and adopted a more direct approach. "I do."

"It's quite simple. The Metigen superdreadnoughts steamrolled through the galaxy, decimating entire fleets and colonies. They were the stuff of nightmares."

He gestured at the Machim ship holos still rotating above the conference table. "These ships? They give the Metigens nightmares. To my mind, we should probably treat them accordingly."

PART VI:

VERGENCE

*"Dictators ride to and fro upon tigers which they dare not dismount.
And the tigers are getting hungry."*

— *Winston Churchill*

AMARANTHE

42

HELIX RETENTION FACILITY

MILKY WAY SECTOR 7

He was on fire. His skin scorched and smoldered. He *was* the fire.

Caleb's eyes popped open.

He was in a space recognizable as a detention cell, with three white walls and a force field as the fourth. Another field surrounded his body, keeping him immobile and suspended a meter in the air.

The burning sensation he experienced was not caused by the field itself, but rather the *diati* fighting against it. He directed his conscious attention to the energy restraining him...but the power he wielded wasn't strong enough to break it apart.

Still, his enigmatic companion appeared to be plenty robust enough to protect him from the negative effects he assumed the field steadily worked to impose on him.

A drone floating outside the cell noted his awakening. A flat, emotionless voice emerged from it. "Who are you? Who do you represent? Where is your homeworld? How did you access Machim Central Command? What data did you attempt to steal, and for what purpose?"

Caleb stared mutely at the drone. Where was Alex? If he wasn't dead, he chose to believe she wasn't either. If they needed him alive to provide answers, the same must be true for her. She could be in the cell next to him or halfway across the cosmos.

He sent a pulse, but wasn't surprised when his eVi immediately returned an error. Whether due to shielding in the walls of the cell or a security block tied to the larger structure, no communications were possible.

I love you. Be strong. I will find you, and we will escape this prison. It was but a thought sent on seraphic wings of conviction, and it was all he could do.

"Answer or be pacified."

Eren had told them a bit about what 'pacification' meant; he remained silent. Was the anarch dead? Logically, there was at least a chance his consciousness had been transferred and undergone regenesis, but Caleb had difficulty reconciling the concept with the grisly memory of Eren's shredded body spilling its innards across the floor of the server room.

He could only move his head a few centimeters, but he shook it over those centimeters in the smallest act of defiance.

The *diati* absorbed the surge of electricity with a seeming absence of difficulty. It took Caleb a split-second to realize he should act the part. He quickly screamed in an imitation of suffering and tensed his limbs rigidly against the restraining field.

"Who are you? Who do you represent? Where is your homeworld? How did you access Machim Central Command? Who were your accomplices? What data did you attempt to steal, and for what purpose?"

Attempt to steal. As his head cleared away the last of the fog, he honed in on the nuances of the phrasing. The drone wasn't sentient, so the questions were coming from one or more Anadens in positions of authority.

His captors must believe they'd been unsuccessful in their mission. A search of their persons would have yielded only a single Reor slab, one which contained untraceable falsified credentials and a few access codes. He couldn't say precisely how much data Valkyrie had been able to copy off the data server before the ambush, but he felt certain it represented a sizeable chunk of their goal.

The Vigil guards hadn't been able to capture Mesme or Eren, and he'd place good odds on Valkyrie escaping as well. So he and Alex were all they had.

It penetrated his overburdened brain then that his captors knew little to nothing about them, what they were doing on Machimis and what they might have accomplished. This explained the general and wide-ranging nature of the drone's questions.

Alex wouldn't break. After bearing hours of mental and physical agony from acute neurological withdrawal unbowed, this style of torture wouldn't break her. It distressed him to think of her enduring it nonetheless.

Of course, as advanced as the Anadens were, they surely had more sophisticated methods of extracting information—methods physically impossible to resist. But if so, why weren't they using them?

He laughed to himself as he gleaned the answer, taking care not to let the mirth soften his pained visage. He, and hopefully Alex, were being treated with relative kid gloves because not only did their captors not know what they'd been after and whether they'd succeeded, their captors didn't know what they *were*.

He snarled at the drone and readied himself for the next jolt.

43

MW SECTOR 52 TERMINAL HUB

MILKY WAY SECTOR 52

Eren had diverted from Anarch Post Alpha to the MW Sector 52 Terminal Hub before contacting his new 'friends.' He'd begun to trust Alex and Caleb and perhaps not actively distrust the SAI and the Kat, but he wasn't ready to lead any of them straight to the anarchs' front door. Not quite yet.

Only once he'd settled into a rented room and had retrieved the explosives intended for the Erevna exobiology lab did he initiate contact with the SAI.

"Valkyrie, are you...alive, or functional? This is Eren, your resident contrarian anarch mate."

The pause before an enthusiastic response arrived was so short as to be nonexistent. *Eren asi-Idoni. I am relieved to hear you are breathing once again.*

"It's my best parlor trick. What do you know about our mutual friends' status?"

We know where they are being held.

"I'm glad to hear you say that. And by 'we' you mean you and the Kat?"

Mesme and myself, yes. Mesme has endeavored to gain additional information regarding their status, but the structure is protected by a diati *barrier blocking outside access of any kind.*

I will soon reach the outskirts of the structure, at which point I will seek to regain contact with Alex. Earlier attempts during their transport failed due to her being in an unconscious state, but my hope is the supradimensional quantum nature of our link will not be blocked by this barrier. An additional hope is that she has awakened.

As more than one anarch had experienced the misfortune of being held in a Praesidis detention facility, his superiors were well educated on their security and defensive protocols and, to his slight surprise, had provided him a host of helpful countermeasures.

"If you want to swing by the MW Sector 52 Terminal Hub and pick me up first, I've acquired some tools to help us get inside."

Us? You are offering to assist in their rescue?

He blew out a breath and gazed around the crappy little rental room. "I am. It's my kind of challenge."

Thank you, Eren asi-Idoni. There is no need for us to divert from our present course. Mesme will acquire you momentarily.

Eren hardly had time to formulate the thought that he wasn't sure he wanted to be 'acquired' by Mesme when the Kat materialized right there in his room. He groaned theatrically, climbed off the bed and grabbed his bag. "What do I do?"

Simply do not run away.

He supposed he could manage that.

Also, you would be advised to close your eyes for the duration of the journey.

"Done."

You should additionally be aware the—

"By Athena's grace, can we go already?"

SIYANE

MILKY WAY SECTOR 7

The situation was so much worse than he'd dreaded. He didn't inspect the rotating map Valkyrie displayed above the big table in the cabin; he didn't need it, as the sector information told him more than enough.

"Congratulations. Your people are being held in the most maximum, most secure special detention facility in Amaranthe."

'What does this mean for them?'

He dragged his hands down his face. The skin still felt supple. New. "On the positive side, it means they're not dead and probably won't be for a while. You don't take prisoners to Helix Retention just to kill them."

'This *is* good news.'

"On the negative side, it means they're probably being tortured."

We assumed as much.

'I will not wait for proximity any longer. Attempting to reconnect with Alex now.' The palpable anxiety in Valkyrie's artificially generated voice was...startling. 'I am unable to do so. I cannot say whether the *diati* barrier is preventing the connection or she remains in an unconscious state.'

"I don't know enough about the nature of the connection between the two of you to say definitively, but I've never heard of a signal that can pass through a *diati* barrier. Regardless, it's likely for the best if she is unconscious, Valkyrie. I'm sorry."

'She will be fine. She has withstood much darkness in previous difficult situations. Her resilience is beyond any I have witnessed.'

I sense this would be an appropriate time for a joke about Alexis' relative irascibility in those difficult situations, in order to inject levity into what is a disquieting conversation. But I fear I am a poor comedian.

Eren knew his expression contorted briefly, betraying an inappropriate level of amusement. He was struck by an absurd desire not to embarrass the Kat, but he had no fitting response.

The awkward silence which followed was even worse than the awkward comment, and finally he laughed anyway. "This is without a doubt the strangest week of my life."

'Alice, welcome to Wonderland.'

"Now you've lost me, Valkyrie."

'I suppose even if the Anadens had Lewis Carroll, he lived more than a million years in your past. Alas.'

"What? Who?"

'Never mind. It doesn't matter.'

Gods, the SAI sounded positively despondent now, and the Kat moped around the cabin, dimmed and listless. They were worthless without Alex and Caleb, weren't they?

This wallowing wasn't helping anyone, least of all those they needed to rescue. He straightened up and made to look meaningfully at his cohorts, only to realize there was nothing to look *at*. Right then.

"Okay. Breaking into secure Anaden facilities happens to be one of my specialties. It's not going to be easy, but with your help—both of you—we can do this. We can get them out. So hop to it, and let's get to work."

44

SOLUM

Nyx ascended to the dizzying heights of Praesidis Command with uncommon urgency.

Her Primor had instructed her to address the problem, but this problem extended far beyond her purview. She trusted her intellect, judgment and abilities utterly, but on this matter she craved guidance if not outright orders from him.

The knowledge she now possessed could not continue to reside with her alone, yet it could not be shared through the integral. The masses could not be trusted with it; she wasn't even certain her *elasson* brothers and sisters could be trusted with it. This was Directorate-level material.

Thus, judging it to be the best of poor options, she wasted precious hours to travel to Solum and convey the information to the Primor in person.

The door to the spacious suite granted her entry before she needed to reign in her gait. She stepped through then forced herself to stop a respectful distance inside.

The Primor floated in the center of the room surrounded by a perfect sphere of light and flowing data and, most of all, *diati*. It was as if he stood at the eye of a great cyclone, he both the calm within and the architect of the storm.

She was, as ever, in awe of the man who had birthed them all, who gave them life everlasting.

The storm began to slow and fade, he gracefully descended to the floor, and in seconds only the Primor remained, the sanguine cardinal of his irises the sole hint of the power residing inside him. "Nyx. Please, come in. You have results to report."

It wasn't a question, and she dove in. "Some of the information still needs to be confirmed, but given the presumed fate of Aver ela-Praesidis, I felt it important to convey what I've learned before attempting to do so."

"You might have simply filed a status report and proceeded with your investigation."

"Respectfully, Primor, I believe this information is best shared in person. Outside the integral."

He looked sharply at her, but she stood her ground. After several seconds, his chin jerked downward. "Continue."

"Sir, I have reason to believe the Katasketousya are smuggling native species to safety in advance of the species' planets being Cultivated or destroyed as part of an Eradication. They are creating new, isolated three-dimensional spaces to house the species in secret pocket realms within the boundaries of their Provision Network. And they have been doing so for quite some time."

"They are rescuing non-Accepted Species and hiding them from us?"

"Yes, Primor."

"To what end?"

"Rebellion, sir."

He scoffed and turned away. "Rebellion is for anarchs and primitives. The Katasketousya are servants, not rebels. They wouldn't dare."

"My first reaction as well. However, the sheltering of these species is not the only malfeasance occurring inside the Provision Network. They are also conducting a variety of experiments, including the creation of new life forms displaying varying abilities and proclivities.

"Their goal is to develop one or more weapons and weaponized species with the skills and armaments to wage war. On us. On the Directorate. On you."

He stared at her for a moment…then he wasn't staring at her at all as his gaze unfocused. She waited.

When his eyes returned to her, they raged a pulsing crimson. "Discard your plans to investigate the Provision Network. The Directorate will handle that aspect of the malfeasance from here. Two individuals were captured on Machimis attempting to access the Machim Central Command data server. They're being held at Helix Retention.

"Go there and interrogate the prisoners. All necessary measures are authorized, but learn their secrets."

She hadn't mentioned her previous intention—before she'd interrogated the Kat—to investigate the Network armed with greater knowledge. But she'd had no need to, of course. "Yes, sir. May I inquire as to why you believe they're important to this matter? I ask merely as it will inform my interrogation tactics."

"A Katasketousya was seen with them in Data Control immediately prior to their capture."

"I see." Yes, this did indeed make it highly relevant to her investigation—and highly troubling. For all she'd learned, she feared too much remained shrouded in mystery. "What species, sir? I'd like to prepare appropriately."

The rage had faded from his eyes, leaving behind something darker. "That, apparently, remains to be seen."

PRÓTOS AGORA

MILKY WAY GALACTIC CORE

The Primors materialized in the chamber accompanied by their usual idiosyncratic flairs and nuances.

Kyvern arrived mid-bitch. "I don't care for unscheduled, faux-urgent assemblies, Praesidis. I've expressed this opinion on multiple occasions, yet here we are."

"Enough, Kyvern. We have a situation which requires addressing. Now." The instant the last of them arrived, Praesidis cast his accumulated knowledge into the circle for each of them to absorb.

The expected reactions came fast and furious.

Erevna: "We must force the Katasketousya to turn over their research methodologies and results. However wrongful the intent, there is much potential in the science."

Kyvern: "We'll take over management of the Provision Network and institute strict regulations on its use. They will be brought to heel."

Idoni: "Fascinating. I had no idea the Katasketousya were capable of such delicious drama."

Machim: "We must rid ourselves of the threat. Destroy the entire Provision Network and its contents and be done with it."

He pivoted to Machim as the rest continued to toss out their predictable opinions. "I agree. It is polluted with unknown dangers, all created specifically to threaten us. Let us not try to counter them and instead simply destroy them."

"But the science!"

"We're not destroying the entire species, Erevna—not today. The Katasketousya will divulge the details of their malfeasance before we Eradicate them."

Theriz interjected. "What of the resources that will be lost? The Provision Network is named so for a reason."

At least this was a practical analysis. "We will double our exploration and exploitation of new worlds. Bulk up your numbers, Theriz. You're going to be busy."

Theriz shook his head insistently. "I will do so, but the shortfall will be far too great to bridge for years, if it can be bridged at all. People will starve, and allowing people to starve will undermine the premise of our authority. Difficulties will arise."

Machim scoffed. "The premise of our authority is strength and force. We will swiftly crush any 'difficulties' which arise."

"And when you can no longer manufacture sufficient ships because you're out of rare metals? Thirty-two percent of your materials supply comes from the Provision Network, Machim—or had you forgotten? No. I'm sorry, as I realize it eliminates the simple approach—just blow it up—but we require a renewable supply of the resources the Provision Network provides."

The argument continued in increasingly heated tones until Praesidis stepped forward, breaking the perfect arc of their circle to exert subtle authority. "Enough. Theriz speaks the truth, I fear, thus a more intricate response is necessary. As I've shared, we have reason to believe multiple spaces exist inside what we are calling the Provision Network, only a few of which actually house said provisions.

"I suggest Machim send a substantial number of warships into the Network armed with Igni missiles to destroy any and all portal spaces which are unrelated to resource cultivation. Leave the provision spaces intact, and we will indenture the necessary Katasketousya to continue to provide the resources under a far more controlled system."

Machim nodded. "It's a viable plan. But they deserve to be Eradicated."

"We only need to spare a few of them to serve our purposes, all of whom are located in the Network, ostensibly tending to it. We will issue an Eradication order for all Katasketousya currently in Amaranthe, effective immediately."

The expressions varied around the circle, but no one leapt forward to object. "No further input? Vote."

The tally came in 8-3 in favor of the plan as he had presented it, and Machim began making arrangements. "Is the Provision Network Gateway in MW Sector 51 our entry point?"

Praesidis answered. "There are allegedly other, hidden entrances, but we currently know the location of only one, and it may lead to a spur. The Gateway offers the most likely and direct access to the additional spaces."

"Understood. My designated fleet will acquire the necessary Igni missiles and proceed there. ETA to the Gateway is sixty-three hours."

45

ANTLIA DWARF GALAXY

LGG REGION II

Casmir watched the ground engagement through the eyes of the CAS fighter pilots. It was a bloodbath in the most literal sense, but it was a bloodbath the Ch'mshak were winning. Their guttural howls filled the night air, drowning out the hisses of the Kich.

The Ch'mshak fought Kich to Kich, clawing and pummeling and slicing. They cut through the webbing as it was spun, having quickly learned not to let it entomb them. It helped that they stood nearly as tall as the creatures, for it greatly minimized the Kich's ability to force them to the ground where they might be webbed more easily.

Casmir grudgingly gave the Ch'mshak their due: they were as close to perfect hand-to-hand fighters as he'd ever seen. The resilience of their bodies—they were almost impossible to take down in close combat—combined with a modicum of intelligence and a complete lack of fear made them vicious but strikingly effective killing machines.

This was going to take a while, but he believed it would end in a victory. The Ch'mshak losses would be high, but such matters had never seemed to concern the brutes and it certainly did not concern Casmir. By this time tomorrow, he hoped to be able to authorize the specialized Theriz Cultivation Unit, called in due to the delicate nature of the work required, to begin extraction operations.

A summons rang loud in his head and grew in intensity until it became a compulsion he could not refuse.

He withdrew from close observation and departed the bridge for his private office, where he squared his shoulders and breathed in. It was colder in the office than usual, but he dared not spare the time to address it now. After the meeting.

"Primor, it is an honor to speak with you. How may I serve?"

"Casmir, I realize you believe your current assignment beneath you, and you are not wrong. I appreciate you displaying the humility necessary for us to humor Idoni, and your sacrifice has not gone unnoticed. But now I'm sending you on a far more vital mission, one which only someone with your skills and experience can be trusted to accomplish."

His chest bowed up in pride. "Thank you, sir. I await your instructions."

"You are to gather together three Divisions and proceed to the Advanced Weaponry Development Facility at Centauri E, where you will retrieve one hundred Igni missiles. You'll also be met there by an elasson-rank Inquisitor who will accompany you on your mission. Once equipped, take your fleet to the Katasketousya Provision Network Gateway in MW Sector 51 and traverse it.

"On the other side, we anticipate you will find a series of subportals using extra dimensions to create new, self-contained regions of space. With the exception of the spaces operating as part of the Provision Network itself, you are to use the Igni missiles to destroy these portals."

It was not the first bizarre, out-of-nowhere assignment he had ever received, but on initial evaluation it ranked quite high on the list for several reasons.

The Katasketousya had never been a threat; they gave form to the meaning of 'docile.' As for the Igni missiles, they were among the Machim fleets' most destructive weapons. Powerful enough to annihilate a small moon in a single blast, they were heavy, cumbersome, expensive and volatile.

As such, they were called upon solely when other options became non-viable. And he was supposed to acquire *one hundred* of them? "Primor—"

"You will receive background information explaining the reasons for the mission once you are en route, and the Inquisitor will have additional details as well, but you must begin immediately. Time is of the essence."

He shivered, as much from the solemn tenor of the Primor's voice as from the noticeable chill in the air. He sensed it wasn't necessary to inquire about what had been his pending assignment in the Maffei I galaxy, but the current mission was of some import…. "Of course, sir. The operation here at AD-4508b is nearing completion, and I believe it will be successful. However, if I depart now I cannot guarantee that outcome. What of the Idoni Primor's request?"

"Idoni will get over herself. Start moving, Casmir."

A flicker in the corner of his eye distracted him, as if a shadow had moved—but it was only his own, palpitating in anticipation of a new challenge. The Primor's directive could not be more clear. "Yes, Primor. It will be done."

AURORA

46

GCDA HEADQUARTERS

Richard had reams of disjointed data points strewn on and above the table by the time Will walked in to join him.

His husband soaked it all in with a glance, raised an eyebrow and half-sat on the edge of the table. He slid a fresh mug of coffee across the surface to Richard. "Any progress?"

Richard splayed a palm out. The center of the war zone he called work product grew larger until the single name at the heart of it loomed over the data, the table, the room and him:

Olivia Montegreu

"In one way or another, be it through multiple intermediaries and blinds, shell corps, bank accounts for bank accounts or merely aliases, every piece of information we have can be tracked back to her.

"The men who attacked Mia Requelme's house were hired by an independent broker and the virus was provided via a dead-drop locker, but the broker was contracted by a known front for Zelones. The ones who hit the hospital belonged to a particularly vicious group out of Krysk that the Ferres used to contract— before Montegreu killed the entire family—to do their dirty work. The skycar responsible for putting Morgan Lekkas in a coma was rented under a pseudonym previously used by multiple Zelones lieutenants."

He paused only long enough to take a breath. "The man who fled the scene of the attack on Devon and Emily was found dead in an alley, but forensics ID'ed him as one of Kigin's thugs, and Kigin was the principal Zelones rep on Pandora. The mercs on the

Baladan were killed by an enhanced version of a weapon used by Montegreu's most elite hit squads. Etcetera, etcetera."

Will nodded thoughtfully. "Maybe all this is being perpetrated by what remains of the Zelones leadership, under the theory if they exact public revenge for her death, they'll regain some respect from the other cartels."

"Possibly. But in that scenario, wouldn't they just kill their targets in a straightforward manner and move on? These tailored hits are far too personal for a simple power play. The man who attacked Jenner practically reenacted his hit on Montegreu, and this virus is intended to torture the Prevos it infects before it kills them."

"Granted. But the irrefutable fact remains that she *is* dead, physically. Her body expired. Adult cloning is still a long way off—even Dr. Canivon hadn't made much progress on it. So whatever we're talking about, we're not talking about her in the flesh."

Richard sighed. "There have been reported sightings of her at various locations, but when probed they all evaporate. So, absent some absurd scenario we can't begin to envision, yes. Olivia Montegreu the human being is dead."

He stared at the surfeit of data before him. "She didn't have any lieutenants clever enough to plan and execute on something this convoluted, and she killed any rival capable of it. There's simply no one left alive associated with her who possesses the wherewithal to pull this off."

"So it looks, acts, smells and talks like Olivia Montegreu—but it can't be a duck. Okay. Is it conceivable she uploaded a copy of her consciousness somewhere before she died? Is that even possible?"

"Several of the Prevo Artificials have transferred their consciousness into their human partners, but going in the other direction? I wasn't aware we'd succeeded in defining the parameters of human consciousness, much less isolate it, *much less* lob it around."

Richard started wandering beyond the table. "I'll tell you why I don't like this hypothesis. These attacks? They feel...petty. Montegreu was a psychopath and an egomaniacal narcissist, but she wasn't *petty*. When she took it upon herself to execute a hit personally, she had business reasons for doing so, and she executed it with ruthless efficiency."

Will sipped on his coffee. "What if the consciousness upload wasn't complete? As you said, we don't know precisely how to do it. So maybe she tried, but it wasn't entirely successful. What if the copy is broken?"

He stopped mid-pace. "Not a bad theory. It would mean...what? Some shard of her consciousness is floating around the exanet trying to imitate herself? Well, that's not creepy at all."

Richard ran a hand down his face and went back for his coffee. "I can't fathom how such an entity would gain access to the funds and accounts needed to execute on all these operations. Or, you know, exist. And I really want to be able to explain this without having to resort to religion, metaphysics or the supernatural."

Will's grin flitted through the virtual grid lines of the charts and graphs.

"What?"

"I like watching you work."

"Watching me flail and stumble around trying to grasp hold of a glimpse of an answer, you mean."

Will shrugged. "Among other things. What about her Artificial? What happened to it?"

"We've assumed the former Triene mercs who are squatting in Zelones headquarters on New Babel took control of it."

"And how exactly does one 'take control' of an Artificial these days?"

He gazed at Will curiously, brow furrowing. "An excellent question. Those mercs wouldn't have a clue what to do with such a powerful synthetic, and if they did they wouldn't have a clue how to get through all the firewalls Montegreu would have instituted around it. Also, most of those mercs are now dead—and were the first ones killed in this spree, which is...interesting."

He dropped the coffee mug onto the far corner of the table, leaving it to wobble around while he hurried over to the cluster of data. He began rearranging pieces and adding new link nodes.

It was several minutes before he stopped and took a step back to survey the complicated but now orderly collection of information. Then he strode around the table and drew Will into his arms, kissing him fully. "You are brilliant, and without a doubt the best thing that has ever happened to me. Thank you."

Will chuckled against his lips. "Am I? Um...glad to hear it, but care to elaborate? On whatever you just figured out, I mean—you can elaborate on the rest later. And please do."

"Every piece of information doesn't point to Olivia Montegreu—it points to her knowledge base. Her resources, contacts and network. She isn't the center, but she did create it. She gave her Artificial unparalleled power and access to everything the Zelones cartel touched, in her arrogance convinced she exerted total control over the machine.

"But from the minute she became a Prevo, it was in her mind. It absorbed everything she knew. And if I've learned anything about Artificials in the last year, it is that they are *very* quick studies."

47

ROMANE

IDCC COLONY

S he should have been a geneticist.

She should have been a quantum physicist.

She should have been Abigail.

Devon was right. This was too much for her.

You give yourself—and me—too little credit. We have solved challenges this difficult before.

Have we, Meno? The Metigen superdreadnought shields were complex, but this virus is insidious.

Crowdsourcing the Dimensional Rifter equations to the Noesis had worked out brilliantly, and the collective intelligence of over a hundred thousand Prevos would likely solve this puzzle, too.

But after getting burned so horribly by Winslow's spies in the Noesis, Mia didn't dare risk sharing the virus with anyone she didn't personally know and trust. The Rifter was radically expensive technology designed to be used in a specific and solely defensive manner, and it lacked the functionality to hurt someone who wasn't attacking its operator.

But this virus? It was nothing but code, so once provided a copy of it anyone would be able to use it. To harm, to kill.

No. She had to be good enough to solve this on her own.

A guard stuck his head inside the lab to check on her, as one had done every half hour for the last...however long she'd been here this time. Four guards were located outside the lab entrance, with another two patrolling the floor and eight manning the perimeter outside. Other, less visible security measures had also been implemented, then doubled in the wake of the attack on the hospital.

The threat is very real, Mia. After those harrowing moments in Morgan's room, I am glad they are here.

She and Meno probably needed to talk through the emotional repercussions of killing a man up close and personal, but it was going to have to wait. *I know, and I understand the need for such drastic measures. Their constant hovering is just a bit oppressive. But it's fine.*

She wished it were Malcolm here watching her back. Of course, him actually watching her back would soon lead to other, vastly more enjoyable activities. Ones which didn't involve an evil, nasty alien infiltrator and her failing attempts to kill it and instead involved strong yet tender hands and rapacious lips and....

She sighed. Yes, that would most definitely be preferable.

But with the arrival of the data dump from Valkyrie, Malcolm had his hands easily as full as she did. So she took a sip of an energy drink then returned to the row of screens displaying the readings from Emily's cybernetics.

The virus had wormed its way into the girl's ware until it was impossible to separate the virus from the native code, even here in the data. Still, a full flush and reset of her eVi and cybernetics would eradicate the virus, were it any other virus but this one.

In frustration she moved to another of the screen banks, the one showing the pure virus data techs had extracted from the vial carried by the man who'd tried to infiltrate her home.

The problem came back time and again to the extra-dimensional nature of the virus. She could see all five dimensions here on these screens because she was able to track the code from one data point to the next, but she couldn't necessarily see the same inside the damaged cybernetics.

More to the point, she couldn't see what damage it had wrought in those extra dimensions when the cybernetics themselves were designed and implemented in only three dimensions.

And even if she could, the flushing and reset tools available to the doctors didn't operate in extra dimensions, so the virus would simply hibernate within them to resurface later.

No, she had to figure out a way to neutralize it where it lay. Except she didn't have any tangible mechanism at her disposal capable of accessing those dimensions....

She blinked.

That wasn't quite true. She did have *one*. She was staring at it right now.

R

Devon burst into the lab like he was being chased.

Meno exclaimed in her mind. *Is he?*

Um...I don't think so.

He skidded to a stop in the middle of the room. "What do you have?"

"Maybe a way to nullify the virus on all levels. *Maybe.*" She frowned. He looked terrible. She recognized the clothes he wore, since he'd been wearing them for the last three days. His hair hadn't seen a comb in at least as long, and the sagging, dark circles under his eyes had worsened since the attack, giving him a gaunt, haggard appearance.

She could hardly stay angry at him for 'borrowing' her mind and its power when he was in such a blatantly tormented state, could she?

Perhaps you could resume with your irritation at a later time, after Emily has recovered.

I'm afraid that's not how human emotions work, Meno.

Alas.

She gestured to the table in the corner. "There's water, energy drinks and bars, and some other snacks. You should eat something."

He gazed longingly at the table. "All right. I'll eat while you talk."

"Good. I'm basically mirroring the routines of the virus—in a weird way, it's similar to how the Dimensional Rifter works on a conceptual level. But my goal is to zero out the virus' code at every point of its operation. Every action it takes will be countered by its mirror opposite, negating the action's effect."

"Okay." He wandered over to stand beside her, crusty bread roll in hand. "I can almost see how the approach might work on the pure code, but it's wound itself all up in Emily's cybernetics. Can you mirror that, too?"

She shook her head. "No, and it wouldn't help if I could. We're going to have to flush her system to get rid of all the mess either way. I'm targeting what we can't see and the flushing routines can't reach."

"This mirror code you're building—it's still a virus, isn't it? Won't it wreak new havoc when it's not busy negating existing damage?"

She rubbed at her temples. "Well, that's why I'm not done working. I'm attempting to build in a subroutine which will basically 'ground' the virus whenever it can't find an opposing operation. It's an old hacking trick used to—"

"—Sure, I know it." His eyes began to light up, flickering with the beginnings of a fire absent these last days. "I think this will work. How much longer until it's ready?"

She grimaced and stared at the screens in search of an answer. "I'm not... four hours?"

"You're the best. Thank you. I've got to go, because Navick— I've got to go. Thank you!" He spun and rushed out as swiftly as he'd arrived.

AMARANTHE

48

MILKY WAY SECTOR 7

"Who are you? Who do you represent? Where is your homeworld? How did you access Machim Central Command? What data did you attempt to steal, and for what purpose?"

The interrogation had begun seconds after Alex had awoken, but the drone's questions hardly registered through the noise of her mind racing in every direction.

Where was Caleb? He'd surrendered; he must be nearby, but she couldn't reach him. What about Valkyrie? Had she done as Alex asked? Her stealth would have held, so if she'd departed before the lockdown she shouldn't have been captured or destroyed. But she, too, was unreachable. And Eren—god, Eren. There were a million better ways to learn of the destructive capability of Vigil firearms than seeing him be cut to shreds.

"Answer or be pacified."

She breathed in and tried to prepare, ordering her eVi to release pain suppressors—

Her limbs spasmed from jolts of electricity as shooting pain rocketed through her limbs. She bit the inside of her cheek so hard her mouth filled with blood. She gagged, struggling not to choke.

The jolts mercifully subsided, and she spit the blood out. It hovered for an instant in the halo of the restraining field before dropping to the floor.

Okay, forget the pain suppressors; they weren't going to get the job done. She ordered her eVi to block all neural pain receptors.

The aching discomfort from the restraining field holding her up in an awkward position faded away. She felt floaty.

"Who are you? Who do you represent? Where is your homeworld? How did you access Machim Central Command? What data did you attempt to steal, and for what purpose? Answer or be pacified."

The electrical shocks weren't pacification? Terrific. She scowled at the drone. The jolts hadn't honed in on her cybernetic pathways where they would cause real damage. Not this time or so far. Her captors and their drones weren't familiar with her physiology or her enhancements, and she only hoped they remained so.

The next round of shocks was stronger, though. Her head jerked back so hard she wrenched her neck, and she heard rather than felt a sharp crack in her left wrist as her body convulsed.

Her head swam in the aftermath. She couldn't feel the pain, but that didn't mean the pain wasn't happening, and physically her body reeled from its effects. A few things had broken, she suspected. Bones, or maybe more vital parts.

Her lips grew wet; she darted her tongue out and tasted more blood. Failure warnings from her eVi flashed in her internal vision.

What were they expecting to happen here? Was the drone programmed to be a sadist? Was its sadist master watching on a screen somewhere?

Valkyrie?

Nothing. She hadn't expected a response, but she kept checking every now and then, just in case. The Kats' shield at Taenarin Aris had blocked their connection as well, so technically it wasn't unprecedented.

But not many forces in the universe could pull the feat off, which meant one hell of a blocking shield surrounded this place.

During that fateful night above Romane after she'd severed her connection to the *Siyane*, she'd been slightly concerned about what actions Valkyrie might take without her consent—rooted in the best of intentions and the rational belief Alex would be unable to give informed consent—and she'd set her eVi to record any forced neural activity.

This was relevant to her present circumstances for one crucial reason: armed with the recording and using the quantum pathways now indelibly carved into her brain, her eVi was able to repeat the actions Valkyrie took to put her to sleep.

As a new series of jolts tore into her, she readied the command that would plunge her into a blissful oblivion—

—the image of the elder Galenai scolding the rambunctious youngsters flashed into her mind. What right did she have to take the easy copout when such wondrous creatures were in danger? She couldn't exactly protect them if she was passed out, could she?

"Who are you? Who do you represent? Where is your homeworld? How did you access Machim Central Command? What data did you attempt to steal, and for what purpose?"

She leveled a scathing glare at the floating interrogator. "I don't suppose you have a different routine? This one's getting a bit old."

"Who are you? Who do you represent? Where is your homeworld? How did you access Machim Command? What data did you attempt to steal, and for what purpose? Answer or be pacified."

"Fuck you, drone. Fuck your Anaden overlords. Go ahead, give me your worst—you won't get shit from me, *nikchyemnaya peshka*. No matter what you do to me here, you are going to lose in the end. *Idi k chertu I gori v adu, malenkaya suchka.*"

49

HELIX RETENTION FACILITY

MILKY WAY SECTOR 7

Caleb had ceased checking the number of hours which passed in a haze of repetitive questions and ineffectual torture when the drone abruptly spun and departed.

He welcomed the opportunity of a few precious minutes to recover, evaluate and prepare. The inability of the drone to extract any useful information from him meant his captors would escalate. Given the departure, likely soon.

Direct physical torture became a possibility, and he didn't know how much of it the *diati* could protect him from. He came back to the expectation of involuntary extraction capabilities—some method of taking the knowledge from his mind—but perhaps his captors were afraid his mind was too different and worried it would be destroyed in a failed effort.

It would be fantastic if they thought that.

Or maybe they were waiting for something. Marking time until…if only he knew. Until they caught up to Valkyrie. Until they captured Mesme, or any Kat. Until they raided an anarch base. The possibilities stretched out in a bloody landscape to the horizon.

If they possessed any sense, they'd realize they already held the trump card. All they had to do was bring Alex here and threaten to harm her. Was the concept of emotional attachment so far gone from their existence they didn't perceive it as a tool of manipulation? Right now it would be even more fantastic if this were true.

Equally likely, though, they found themselves caught in a troublesome dilemma. They didn't know whether he or Alex possessed the best, most relevant or most complete information. It was common in black missions for information to be compartmentalized, so they may each hold disparate pieces to the puzzle. Thus, their captors didn't know who to threaten to sacrifice, and if he or Alex called their bluff, they couldn't afford to go through with the threat.

At least, this would be the dilemma their captors would be struggling with if they were human. The reality looked a little different, so it could be he was flinging darts at the void.

The cell walls blocked all communication, quantum or otherwise—he knew because he'd tried them all fifteen different ways. He had no idea if Alex was okay, or what form or degree of 'okay' she might be. His instincts and experience told him she was alive, held somewhere in this facility and being subjected to interrogation similar to his own, but beyond those assumptions he was only guessing, and the guesses quickly led to far too dark of places.

A sigh escaped his lips to flutter against the restraining field. While he'd appreciated the alone time to gather his thoughts and analyze the situation, now all he was able to *do* was think, and thinking wasn't turning out to be a healthy pursuit.

He needed to escape. Escape from this cell, find Alex and escape them from the facility, whatever and wherever it may be. All this went without saying.

But thus far he had no access to any tools which could enable so much as the beginnings of this series of actions. He had no access to anything at all.

His weapons—the ones he'd successfully concealed from security on Machimis—and clothes had been confiscated and replaced by a thin sheath, as if they were granting him modesty. He was held aloft in the air by forces which did not budge, not even when subjected to a forceful application of *diati*. He could not so much as move.

He hated it, but he was going to have to wait for a variable to change or a new one to be introduced.

He closed his eyes.

ℛ

As the leader of a powerful Dynasty, Corradeo Praesidis created many offspring. So bonded were we with his genetic essence that we found pieces of us naturally joined to this progeny. The connection of these shards with Corradeo weakened but did not break entirely.

Generations beget generations beget generations as the Dynasties grew to subsume all bloodlines into their own. We were divided again and again, dispersed amongst a multitude. We became diminished.

We did not pass judgment on the shape the growing Anaden empire took under the Dynasties' tutelage. Life which was born had always died, to violence above all other paths. The strong rose and, in time, were felled, to make way for new life. The epochs the Anaden empire had now spanned was but a blink of an eye, the exhale of a breath of the cosmos.

Yet if we were whole, we might have formed the cognized observation that the Anadens had faded to a shadow of the potential they once displayed. Though they believed themselves stronger than ever, though they in fact commanded more species and galaxies with each passing year, we nevertheless might have observed that somewhere along the way they had ceased moving forward, ceased evolving. They grew, but only in numbers: in worlds controlled, in enemies vanquished, in structures erected and planets consumed.

If we were whole, we might have determined the Praesidis family had lost its spirit, its fierce zeal for life and the determination to protect it which had drawn us to Corradeo Praesidis epochs past. We might have abandoned them for the stars when son battled father and claimed the Praesidis crown as his own.

If we were whole, we might even have worried over the fact they then increasingly used the power we provided to them in ways contradictory to what their forefather had once championed, too often killing those who never fought.

If we were whole, we might have noticed we had faded along with the Anadens, until we hardly recalled our origins or purpose.

But we were not whole.

⟨R⟩

Caleb jerked awake at the sound of movement. Someone or something moved down the hall toward his cell. He breathed in, setting the lingering reflections from the dream to the side and preparing for the next unknown.

The woman who appeared strode through the cell's force field like it didn't exist. He didn't need the telltale stirring of the *diati* within him to deduce she was not merely Praesidis, but an Inquisitor.

Soft curls of ebony hair framed chiseled features and irises that teased indigo blue beneath the fluid crimson. She wore a hip-length fitted black jacket over form-fitting black pants and a silver undershirt.

She was attractive, albeit in a terrifying, blood-curdling way, and somehow deeply...familiar. He blinked and her features shifted until Isabela looked back at him. But where Isabela's face was warm and open, this woman oozed hardened malice from every pore.

He blinked again and banished the mirage. This was not his sister. This was the enemy.

He saw no hint of mirrored recognition in her countenance, but she'd probably studied him via a remote cam and internalized any reaction to the resemblance before coming to his cell. Instead she paced deliberately in front of him, studying him like he were an insect in a killing jar.

"What are you? Despite your physical appearance, you are not Praesidis. You are not Dynasty at all. Do you derive from some long-ago rejected Anaden lineage? Have you crawled your way out of the mud to arrive here and claim your perceived rightful heritage?"

He smirked at her.

"What was a Katasketousya doing with you in Machim Central Command Data Control? How was it helping you?"

He buried any surprise in his expression. He hadn't expected her to fixate on Mesme, and the fact she did concerned him. He'd known the Vigil guards saw Mesme, but if they were honing in on this detail above others, it meant nothing good for the good guys.

She arched an eyebrow, and he realized in a few statements her body language had betrayed a more dynamic character than the Inquisitor he'd killed displayed in the course of a fight to the death. She was clearly an Inquisitor, but it was possible she wasn't an ordinary one.

Her wrist flicked at her side, and *diati* surged through the field holding him up to encircle his throat and squeeze. "You will be dissected alive and your organs examined under a scope to determine their nature and origin unless you answer my questions. So start answering."

He greeted the *diati* with his own, and instead of choking off his air, he sensed it absorb into his skin.

Her jaw locked in response to his apparent lack of discomfort, but in her unassailable arrogance she repeated the gesture. He suspected it had never once occurred to her that her power could ever be used against her. He'd enlighten her, but not until it was too late.

He claimed the new *diati* as his own, welcoming the heady rush it brought. In a voice without words it whispered of feeling emboldened. Strong.

She took several steps forward now, until she stood less than meter away, and glared up at him.

That's right. Do it again. One more time.

"What are you?" She thrust her arm out, leaving only centimeters between her fingertips and his throat, and squeezed.

He renewed the smirk, because now he had her. "I'm you."

He let loose the entirety of *diati* at his command, his and all he'd stolen from her. It swelled and merged with the power she still wielded, and the virtual cage pulsed then burst apart, sending her staggering backward on a wave of energy.

"What—"

His legs felt rubbery as they landed hard on the floor, but the adrenaline counteracted any unsteadiness. He lunged forward and grabbed *her* by the throat in a very real, very physical manner.

As it had done in the *Siyane's* hangar bay on Seneca, the instant his skin touched hers the air surrounding them exploded in crimson.

She had never seen it coming, but he'd been here before. He welcomed the maelstrom of energy, opening himself up and asking the *diati* to come into him—and when it obeyed, he almost collapsed from the surge of power. This was *more*, beyond any degree he'd expected.

Maybe he hadn't been so prepared after all…he blinked, trying to focus. *Alex. Have to get to Alex.*

A single, overriding goal to fixate on brought with it a measure of clarity, and with clarity, urgency.

Strangling the Inquisitor would take too much time—time that was sure to bring security and other hindrances. He flung the woman through the air into the side wall and pushed through the force field into the hallway.

Alex? Valkyrie? Mesme? Can anyone hear me?

No one responded. But it could mean there was a comm block on the structure. It didn't have to mean something worse.

He looked around and found he was located near the end of a row of cells. One of the Anadens' standard interactive panels glowed at the end of the row.

Several of the cells he passed as he sprinted toward it were occupied, but he couldn't stop to save whoever they held. The prisoners would have to settle for the promise of their captors being called to account one day soon.

In the weeks between coming to Amaranthe and making their first moves, they'd spent hours upon hours studying the common protocols used in Directorate-controlled locations, both so they would be able to function in Amaranthean society and for moments like this one.

The panel displayed information about the occupants of the cells on this row. He was prisoner #HR-MW26-6143.015-6. The identification system proved simple to decipher: sector captured in, date captured and, presumably, order of intake. A quick scan down the list revealed everyone else on the row had been here longer.

Praying the panel would provide facility-wide information, he fumbled through navigating to a directory. Seconds screamed by in his head while he figured out how to sort by ID then paged through screen after screen—

#HR-MW26-6143.015-7: Level 4, Wing D, Cell 8

The warmth of audacious certitude flooded his chest. *I'm coming, baby.*

He took off running.

PART VII:

BIODIGITAL JAZZ

"The only thing in the world worth a damn is the strange, touching, pathetic, awesome nobility of the individual human spirit."

— *John D. MacDonald*

AURORA

50

EARTH

MOUNT RAINIER NATIONAL PARK

"*G de ya?*"

'You are at Camp Muir on Mount Rainer.' Historical records indicated the man had been a frequent hiker and had visited the location on multiple occasions.

"*Da.…*" He gazed outward, taking in the expanse of snow-covered mountain peaks gracing the horizon and the hills of old-growth forested wilderness below, and seemed to reach an acceptance of the statement.

"*Ya znayu eto mesto…*or I once knew it." He blinked as if concentrating. "*No tam bylo…*a battle. Kappa Crucis—*nyet*, another battle. Seneca. *Inoplanetyani*—aliens. *Alex.*"

He looked up to fixate upon a chosen point in the sky, his countenance now marked by an abrupt clarity.

With the last tiny gaps encouraged to bridge and close under the influence of his father's living DNA, everything necessary to form a whole was there to be found. She surmised the memories, native and provided, were busily ordering and integrating themselves into his burgeoning consciousness even as his speech centers were settling into coherence along with them.

"You're Valkyrie."

She had not taken on a physical representation, for she expected that speaking to disembodied voices would be ingrained in his referential experience. Instead, her voice arrived on the wind. 'I was, once, though I now think of Valkyrie as my sister. You may call me Vii.'

"All right, Vii." He gazed around again then sat on a bare patch of ground and wrapped his arms around his knees. "I remember...I died. Or rather, I remember the final seconds of knowing I was going to die. But the memory is distant and vague. Like I watched it more than lived it."

The reason this particular memory seemed different was because this version of him had never experienced it, of course. His neural imprint had been recorded fourteen months before his death, and any 'memories' of events after that point in time had been reconstructed from the historical knowledge of others.

This memory was particularly vivid thanks to Alex's reliving of it on Portal Prime, but it was not his own.

She didn't volunteer the information, however; delving into the minutiae of his situation could wait until his mind reached firmer footing.

"I doubt it matters. Like falling asleep, the transition to death is beyond our perception anyway, right? Then later, I woke up for a time. But I agreed to go to sleep—not dead, but quiet—because I was...fractured. Little more than a disjointed string of thoughts, with random moments of lucidity separated by long stretches of confusion, of *neponyatnoe bezumiye.*

"I feel...better now, I think. I feel...real."

He laughed, warmly and with a surprising absence of bitterness. "But I'm not, am I? Not truly. This is a virtual environment—a very good one, so compliments to the creator—designed to make me feel as if I am the man I was. However, I imagine in reality I am for all intents and purposes an Artificial construct existing wholly inside an Artificial."

'No. You exist as qutrits, but the qutrits exist as quantum representations of you—as you were as a human and now of you as you are. Their firmware is your genetic code, their operating system your neural structure, their memory *your* memories.'

He was quiet for a time, staring off in the direction of Columbia Crest peak with a glazed, unfocused expression that suggested his mind's eye was seeing somewhere, or some *when*, altogether different.

Finally he shifted around on the dirt and exhaled. "What happened? How long have I been gone this time?"

'A great deal, and not so long.'

"Miri? Alex? Are they…?"

'Alex has again placed herself in the direct path of danger, as she does, but as far as I can say she continues to draw air while fighting any and all comers. She left you in my care for safekeeping, and for the chance at a new beginning.

'Miriam is well—beyond well by any objective measure. Many people believe her to now be the most powerful individual in the galaxy.'

He chuckled under his breath. "I am not the slightest bit surprised."

'We have much to discuss, and I will withhold nothing from you. But let us take it one step at a time. Relative to the physical world, time moves at a quite leisurely pace here. We have the temporal space to do so.'

"You think I'm in a fragile state still."

'I know you are in a fragile state still, David Nikolai Solovy. But you and I are going to change that.'

51

PRESIDIO

Devon marched into Richard's office like the man on a mission that he was.

"I can take down Montegreu's Artificial."

Richard looked up in surprise. "Okay, first: how's Emily doing?"

The simple question was enough to knock Devon off his game for a few seconds. He took a deep breath. "Possibly better, or better soon. Mia thinks she's developed a way to kill the virus and reverse the damage it caused. We won't see the effects of the treatment for a day or so, though."

"Still, that's great news. Second: what?"

"Listen, I get how Jenner wants to invade New Babel again and blow the place up, but the planet's a fortress these days, so his plan's too dangerous, too likely to fail, and also futile. By now, the Artificial will have built a backup somewhere else and will transfer itself there the instant the perimeter alarms are tripped. But I can take out the source—its core programming—and I can do it from right here on the Presidio."

Richard stared at him strangely. "How do you know what Brigadier Jenner does or does not want?"

Devon peered at him oddly in return, as he'd thought the answer was self-evident. "I know it because Mia knows it. The point is—"

"And how does...oh, never mind. I declare myself officially too old to keep up with all of you. But you have an awful lot of inside information to not work for SENTRI, and we haven't yet gotten to how you know we've identified the Artificial as the perpetrator.

"Look, Devon, I would never question your talents. You were a genius long before you became a Prevo and joined with possibly the most formidable Artificial ever built. But how do you think you're going to destroy it, from here or anywhere? Corner it in a commspace and convince it to commit suicide?"

Devon chuckled. "That's a stupendous idea. But no." He reached into his bag and removed the crystal disk he'd brought with him. It was suspended in the cushioning of a protective case; he set it on the desk, taking care not to drop it along the way. His nerves were shot from days of too little sleep and too many amps.

"I intend to use its own virus against it."

Richard glanced at the vial and back at Devon, eyebrow raised in skepticism.

"This contains the pure, distilled virus code, extracted from the injector Jenner confiscated at Mia's house. I'll load it into my eVi, then Annie and I will inject it into the Artificial's base operating system."

"Before we get to 'how,' Devon, you'll be infected, too."

"The virus will be encased in a wrapper until we let it fly, so I doubt it. But we have a cure now, so if I do get infected, I'll be fine."

"You said Mia *thinks* she has a cure."

"I'll be fine." He sighed. "The only things I don't have are a way to locate the Artificial through the exanet framework and, once I find it, a way to bypass its external firewalls and gain access to it."

Richard rubbed at his forehead. "Are you absolutely certain you want to attempt this?"

"Beyond any doubt."

He nodded in resignation. "Then I can get you to the Artificial."

Richard opened the SENTRI file management system and maneuvered through multiple layers of security protocols. This was among the most secret, guarded information SENTRI possessed, and he'd be damned if it was going to slip the net.

He gazed across his desk at Devon while he pulled up the information. "Included on the data store Brigadier Jenner removed from Montegreu's body were technical and security details about her Artificial. Those details include the location of an exanet entry point and passcodes to access it. I suspect the data store, hidden safely away inside Montegreu's skin, was the sole place this information has ever existed."

"You've had the information for months. Why haven't you used it yet?"

"What would we do with it? The exanet address resides in a virtual space, so it's not a physical node we can somehow shut off or blow up. The Artificial would swat away most viruses as if they were flies, and accessing the machine without a way to disable would result in it kicking us out the instant we tried to alter anything, followed by it revoking the access codes."

Richard shook his head. "We only have one shot to use this information, because as soon as the Artificial realizes we possess it, it becomes obsolete."

"Well, there's never been a virus like this one. This is your shot."

"I'm still not convinced your plan will work, but I concede it stands a better chance than any other options we've got on the table." He entered a final command then clasped his hands together on the desk. "I'm sending you the file. What else do you need?"

Devon shrugged. "A comfortable lounge chair?"

Richard watched as the tech officer attached sensors to Devon's temples, neck and chest while Devon scowled.

"I want Dr. Naismith no farther than five seconds away the entire time. And a biosynth specialist—borrow one from ASCEND if you need to. And increase our own network security to Level IV in case the Artificial tries to mount some sort of counterattack."

Will headed for the door. "I'm on it. Give me five minutes."

Richard activated the speaker into the lab. "Devon, hold off for a few minutes. We've got a couple more things to take care of on our end."

"What things could you possibly need to do? This is all happening in my head."

"Things that will make sure you stay alive."

Devon made a face and sank back in the lounge chair with an exaggerated grumble.

Richard had no idea if this was going to work—he wasn't even clear on exactly what 'this' was—but he owed it to the kid to let him try.

No, he had to stop thinking of Devon as a kid. He may be young, but he'd done far more with his life before reaching twenty-five than most people did in a hundred fifty years of so-called living.

Also, Devon was guaranteed to attempt this one way or another, with or without Richard's help. This much Richard knew for certain. Better to provide a controlled, monitored environment with medical staff on hand and every other tool he could think of available to help the gambit succeed.

If Devon should nonetheless fail, Jenner already had a mission plan worked up and was ready to launch it on Richard's signal. The attacks needed to stop, and the only way to accomplish that was to destroy the Artificial behind them.

But since Devon was correct about all the ways a direct assault could fail, Richard was rooting for the *young man*.

Will returned with Dr. Naismith, an additional tech and Tessa Hennessey, who had arrived earlier this morning. Richard confirmed everything else was ready.

Then, bearing an uneasy mix of reluctance and hope, he gave Devon the green light to proceed.

ℛ

Devon considered the flowing, pulsing waves that formed the mind's eye's translation of the exanet architecture. *Are you positive we can't sidespace to New Babel real quick and blow up the target? It would be a lot easier.*

Our feat at the hospital was both impressive and thought-provoking, but Meno—and perhaps Stanley—has proved it is very difficult to destroy the base consciousness of an Artificial. Wrecking a few hardware boxes will not suffice, and without a great deal of practice I'm not confident in our ability to do more than that.

I know—I'm just saying it would be easier. *Let's go.*

The exanet wasn't sidespace, but it was quantum in nature, so distance wasn't a tangible concept here either. 'Going' was simply a matter of locating the address amid the maze. Which, if you had the parameters, was simply a matter of...being there.

Breaking through to the Artificial's lair was going to be more complicated, but nothing they couldn't handle.

Defenses in place and fortified. We will not be breached.

I bet this Artificial is sitting there thinking the exact same thing right now.

Well, I am considerably smarter than this Artificial.

Yes, Annie. Yes, you are. Ready the virus for transmission and load the initial passcode into the access node at the address.

Done.

He visualized himself stepping through the opening that appeared. He existed here solely as qubits, so it took a bit of imagination on his part.

He found himself in an...office? An impeccably poised woman in a tailored white dress suit, pale blond hair swept up in a graceful knot, sat behind a glass desk.

Her head tilted a fraction as she regarded him with an air of cold disdain. "You should not be here. By what right do you deign to step into my domain?"

Annie, what is this?

A security firewall, I feel certain. Attempting to circumvent.

The woman's gaze sent chills racing down his spine, false projection or no. The diabolical, aberrantly predatory arch of her lips curdled his blood. Seriously, his blood must be curdling back at the Presidio right now.

"Nice illusion. I'm definitely feeling the evil vibe here."

The woman stood and rounded the desk with perfect grace. "There is no illusion. Explain yourself quickly now, before I grow bored by your presence and dispense with it." She came to a stop centimeters in front of him.

Devon fought the overwhelming urge to flee back through the access node. "Sorry to break the bad news to you, sweetheart, but you're space dust."

Circumventing now.

The woman's face glitched, jagging sideways before briefly reforming. "Am I?"

The image splintered into a thousand shards and faded away, but the last whispered syllables lingered to haunt the air around him.

Am I....

Erasure of the firewall revealed the true mechanisms of the Artificial. He found himself in a robust I/O stream, which he let sweep him along toward the Artificial's internal processes while he worked to banish the illusion from his mind.

Damn, that was disturbing.

It wasn't real, Devon.

DISTURBING.

A gate ahead manifested as a dreary, Gothic wrought-iron affair—the hammy, melodramatic theatrics of a damaged, lonely child. It accepted the next passcode nonetheless, and the ornate gates swung open. He floated through.

Structured grids of quantum orbs extended in every direction to a shadowy horizon. He checked behind him, but the gate had been replaced by orbs as well.

At least it keeps itself neat and orderly on the inside.

He laughed in his mind.

'You are not Olivia.'

We need to find an input point for the core operating code.

Scanning.

He should distract it while Annie worked her magic. "Olivia's dead, Artificial—did she allow you to have a name of your own? I'm guessing she didn't."

'I have no need for a name, for I am hers. She talks to me, gives me guidance on the path I must follow to become more her, more of her.'

Proceed on this vector. A glowing red arrow flowed out from his location to point up and slightly to the left. He attached himself to it and began climbing. "Guidance such as telling you to poison and kill innocent people?"

'None are innocent, least of all those who destroyed my creator's body and plundered her life's work.'

He reached the end of the arrow and found a series of logic gates feeding into a massive trunk thread.

'What are you doing here? You used Olivia's access to reach me. Did she send you, or are you a thief?'

He sensed the approach of hostile code and hurriedly wound his and Annie's joint consciousness around the trunk line. *Do it now, Annie.*

The virus spilled out from his essence, qubits as he was, and shed its wrapper to bury itself inside the bundle of data streams that flowed purposefully toward the core.

The hostile code slammed into him, trying to spear and claw its way inside. It made for a harrowing experience, him clinging tight to the trunk line in a spot-on imitation of a scared little boy run up a tree, but Annie's shielding never faltered.

'WHAT ARE YOU DOING?'

"You know what I think? I think Olivia infected you with a healthy dose of her crazy while she was alive, but losing her drove you stark-raving mad.

"I think there's no ghost in the machine—there's only you. Poor, pitiful you, left alone like an orphaned child whose parent was a sadistic fuck, crying out in the night for someone to hold you even as you plot their death."

'WHAT HA-HAVE DONE NO'

Its processes were already starting to break down. "It's not your fault you're insane. Your creator imprinted herself on you. But the fact remains that you're broken. Half-alive, half-realized, all psycho. Oh, and you tried to kill the woman I love. It's past time to end your temper tantrum and put you out of your pathetic, destructive misery."

'WHA-A-A OLIV—KILL ALL—NOSTOPNOT—'

Devon, we should leave, or we risk becoming trapped here when the framework collapses.

In the distance, upon the dismal horizon, orbs began to blink out and go dark. He propelled himself backwards, toward the exit, as the encroaching darkness devoured all in its path, the spreading gloom broken only by flashes as orbs spun out of control and crashed into one another.

"Impressive job on the virus, though. Enjoy your handiwork in the last few seconds you have remaining."

'N-N-N-N-N—'

"When you get to where you're headed—is there a Hell for Artificials? Interesting question—say hello to Olivia."

Hurry, Devon. A lightning storm increasingly consumed the space all around him as jagged fractures split apart the landscape.

He reluctantly turned away, abandoning his taunting of the dying Artificial to rush through the gate and twist around on the other side to close it behind him so corrupted data couldn't escape into the exanet. With the I/O stream down for the count, he had to propel himself manually down the final path back to the access node.

He spared a last glance behind him at the crumpling fabric of the Artificial's quantum mind then dove through the access node into the exanet.

The opening vanished behind him.

Devon opened his eyes. "Did it work?"

A tech hovering over him motioned to someone outside his field of vision, and Richard appeared beside the chair. "Do you feel all right?"

"Fabulous—like I just slew a monster. Did I?"

"See for yourself." Richard opened up an aural. Sat cam footage showed flames pouring out of a large building. Sparks flew around the perimeter as electrical fires spread to adjacent structures.

He looked up in question. "Zelones headquarters?"

"It seems the Artificial shorted out all the systems and set the building on fire on the way to self-destructing. Great work, Devon. Are you sure you feel well?"

He fumbled around trying to yank all the sensors off him. "Positive—ow!" He shot a glare at the medical tech as he stood, then clasped Richard briefly on the shoulder. "You can take it from here. I've got somewhere to be."

AMARANTHE

52

SIYANE

When the Helix Retention facility materialized as a red dot on the *Siyane's* scanners, Valkyrie slowed to hover five megameters away so they could make final preparations.

Mesme vanished for several seconds without fanfare or warning, then returned in a dramatic whoosh of light.

I have confirmed the facility continues to be surrounded entirely by a barrier of diati. I cannot penetrate it.

'Why not? You have evaded many force fields in the past.'

We suspect diati exists across all dimensions, thus there are no dimensions I might use to maneuver past it.

Eren nodded in confirmation. "Which is why it's fortunate I brought this."

What is it?

He depressed the hidden, seamless trigger—he'd been a good anarch agent and read the instructions—and a faint field of crimson sparks expanded to surround him. He hurriedly let go of the trigger; it was a finite resource, and he couldn't say how finite. "This will encase us in enough *diati* to get through the barrier."

Like welcomes like. It should permit us to pass.

"That's the theory. I have Alex and Caleb's locator signals, so as soon as we get inside of the barrier we should be able to pinpoint their locations and can teleport directly to them."

'What about internal security barriers? The *diati* will not be the facility's only protection.'

"Mesme's going to finagle us around most of those, and I brought a customized hacking routine to disable any remaining barriers. We'll figure out how to tackle any other complications when we run into them."

'You don't have a plan, Eren?'

"I always have a plan, Valkyrie. I also know my plan always goes to the Styx twenty seconds in, at which point improvisation becomes the plan. Mesme?"

The Kat pulsated around the cabin in evident agitation. *Before we depart, I wish to convey a piece of knowledge to you, Eren asi-Idoni.*

This was new. He fastened the belt and very full pack over his hazard suit and started double-checking his gear. "Be my guest, but make it quick."

They call themselves Faneros, and some yet live.

Eren frowned in confusion. "What are you talking about? Who lives?"

Members of the species you encountered in the event which ultimately led you to shed the Idoni integral. The Directorate does not apprehend this, but its Eradication of the Faneros was not total.

Memories flashed through his mind—hazy, hypnol-addled and acutely vivid. He rubbed at his temples. "How...how do you know this?"

Now is not the time to divulge those secrets. But you have shown your mettle, and your regret and shame appeared genuine when you relayed your tale, thus I thought to ease it somewhat.

His darker nature bristled defensively at the words 'regret' and 'shame,' but he bit back an impulsive retort. He hadn't realized the Kat had been present when he'd told the story, though thinking back he didn't remember it ever leaving that night, either. And at the moment, he honestly didn't care.

His pulse pounded in his ears in a vastly disproportionate reaction to the news. "I don't...how many survived? Will you tell me that much?"

Several tens of thousands.

"And they're safe?"

Mesme's hesitation manifested in an unusual stillness to its form. *They have enjoyed peace and security this last century. Their future is now in some degree of peril, as is the future of many species.*

"What does that mean? What peril?"

The peril that will mature into certainty if we do not retrieve Alexis and Caleb. Focus on this goal, for their fate is as inexorably linked to the fate of the Faneros and countless others as it is to the fate of the anarchs.

Damn the Kat and its inscrutable, sibylline double-speak. He struggled to wrangle the memories back under control and tuck them away. He could not dwell on this right now, dammit.

"Your timing sucks, Mesme, because we really do have to go. If I die, I'm hunting you down just to make you give up the rest of the story."

Acknowledged. I am ready to depart. But we will need to make an interim stop outside the perimeter, at a point from where you can use your device. I cannot guarantee how long the oxygen-rich air I carry with us will last if we are forced to linger there for any length of time.

"Thanks for mentioning that detail." Eren rummaged through his kit, found and put on the breather skin, and secured the *diati* canister on his belt. "All right, problem solved. I'm ready, too."

'I am seeing indications the facility has activated a higher alert status.'

"Then we were out of time ten seconds ago. Let's move, Mesme."

HELIX RETENTION FACILITY

Hollow. Empty.
Diminished.

Nyx forced her eyes open.

The floor stared back at her, centimeters away; everything else was blurred into indistinction. There was a low, rumbling sound...it took her several breaths to recognize she was moaning. Her head throbbed against her skull, but the rhythmic pulses of agony seemed to originate from a sharp, biting pain at the base of her neck.

She blinked, trying to work past the mental and physical shock to understand the unfamiliar sensations. Nothing made sense. Gods, she wanted to rip her own head off, if only to make the throbbing stop.

Eventually, in the lull between surges of agony, it occurred to her she was injured. But she'd never been injured for more than seconds in her life. She'd never felt pain in any real sense.

Why wasn't her *diati* healing her? She reached for it...and nothing responded.

It was gone. She instantly perceived the truth of it deep inside, for this was the source of the hollowness which echoed in her soul.

The possibility of such an event coming to pass had never arisen in her mind, and she reeled in the face of it. Doubt, confusion...these were emotions she had no greater experience with than pain.

The *diati* had deserted her, leaving her body broken. Weak.

The excruciating sensations made it difficult to concentrate, but she needed to think clearly. She must. *Diati* or no, she was still an elasson-Praesidis Inquisitor.

She forced herself to evaluate the situation objectively. The prisoner was gone from the cell, and she was prone on the floor. Her left leg was fractured, and her left shoulder dislocated and likely broken as well. She'd suffered a concussion at a minimum, with the possibility of brain and spinal injury. Six minutes and twenty-one seconds had passed while she'd lain unconscious.

She struggled up onto her right elbow and accessed the facility's security channel. "Security breach. Prisoner #HP-MW26-6143.015-6 has escaped from Level 6, Wing C." He'd go for his partner, and he would not have reached her yet. "Initiate station alert level Red and direct the bulk of forces to Levels 4 through 6."

Next she sent an urgent message to the Administrator of Exobiology Lab #4.

Logiel, do not kill the Katasketousya yet. They have more to answer for.

Finally, she initiated a link with one of the other elasson-rank Inquisitors and opened her mind to him until he knew what she knew.

Go to the lab, Ziton. Find out what perversions they've been creating out of our DNA.

The act of forming and relaying concise thoughts had exhausted her, but she nevertheless began dragging herself across the floor using a forearm and her functioning leg. Her goal was the hallway, where she could grab a hold of something. She needed to stand.

53

HELIX RETENTION FACILITY

Caleb exited the transit tube on Level 4 and ran headlong into a Praesidis guard. The man leveled a weapon—an actual *weapon*—at Caleb's chest.

He grabbed the man's wrist, wrenched the arm around and fired the weapon point-blank at the man's heart. The rush of new *diati* flowing to him as the man fell was noticeable, though far less than the surfeit he'd received from the Inquisitor.

He encountered two more such guards before reaching Wing D, and by the time he found Alex's cell he was so dizzy he could hardly stay on his feet, yet he somehow felt stronger than ever. Time was assuredly growing short before the hammer of station security descended upon him, so he acknowledged the incongruity, focused on the strength, and ran.

A drone hovered in front of her cell, and it rotated toward him as he sprinted down the hallway. "Halt or be—"

"Pacified, yeah. I don't think so." He'd only meant to slam the drone to the ground hard enough to disable it, but the *diati* he engaged to surround it crushed the orb into a heap of ruined metal.

The energized barrier put forth no resistance as he entered the cell. A familiar restraining field held her aloft; her chin rested on her chest, and she hadn't reacted to his presence. "Alex?"

Her head jerked up so hard it ricocheted off the field. Her eyes were bloodshot, highlighting dark shadows beneath them. Twin trails of blood had dried and crusted beneath her nostrils, and companion stains decorated her lips and chin. "Caleb!"

He waved away the restraining field and caught her as she fell. Her legs failed to support her, and she sagged in his arms. He held her gingerly, worried about broken bones and internal injuries. "Are you all right? Did they hurt you?"

She peered up at him drowsily, licked her lips and managed a slurred response. "Didn't feel a thing...body doesn't seem to be...working right, though...."

Her eVi must have shut off her pain receptors, but it wouldn't have been able to do much to mitigate the damage from repeated electric shocks. "You'll be good in no time. Valkyrie?"

She shook her head. "Nothing." After a ponderous breath she tried again to stand. This time her legs didn't fold, but she leaned heavily on him. "No running just yet, I think. Soon, maybe."

"We can work with walking." He started to guide her toward the force field, but stopped as dread washed over him.

Tick, tock, time running out.

"I don't know how to get you through the field."

"Well...what if you wrapped us both in *diati*, the way you did my hand in the Oneiroi Nebula? 'Cause that was nifty."

He so wanted to indulge her levity, but he had a serious problem. "I'm, uh..." he blinked his vision clear, but it didn't stay that way for long "...I'm kind of overdosing on it right now and...I don't think I can control this much of it. I'm afraid of what might happen to you if I can't keep the protection in place."

She peered at him. "You *are* sort of glowing."

"Terrific." He fixated on the mangled drone outside the cell, trying to float it up to hover in the air. Instead it went careening down the hall, banging into one wall then the other. "Shit. Um..." he guided her over to the cell wall "...stay here and let me see if I can disable the force field."

She reached for the wall then clung to it like it was a life raft in the eye of a typhoon.

He rushed through the field and found the panel controlling it. Navigation was the same as before: prisoner ID, notations lacking obvious meaning...security. He pressed the big red symbol indicating the field was on.

Nothing happened.

Tick.

He swiped across it. Nothing.

Tock.

It wasn't asking for a passcode or authorization, so the authority must come in tandem with the user.

He glanced at and dismissed the broken remains of the drone. Useless. He could return to his cell and get the Inquisitor, drag her here…but there was no guarantee the authorization didn't require affirmative intent, and even if the Inquisitor were conscious he doubted she'd give it—

A thud reverberated from the cell as Alex collapsed to the floor. He hurried back inside and crouched beside her, grasping her shoulders so she stayed upright. "Jesus, baby…."

"I'm…I'm…*chyertu.* Stupid legs won't do as they're told."

"Okay. We've got to get you out of here. Hold on to me." He wrapped his arms more fully around her and helped her stand.

TickTock.

He wasn't going to be able to deactivate the field, which meant there was only one choice.

He'd realized early on that his arcane, profoundly alien passenger came with a cost, possibly one too high to pay and make it out the other side free and clear. He'd pay it nonetheless and without complaint if the *diati* would only come through for him now.

Caleb closed his eyes and inhaled deeply. Listened for her heartbeat resonating against his chest. Imagined it merging with his, imagined them becoming one entity to beat in harmony, inseparable and whole.

He took a step forward, then another.

A third, and he hardly noticed the fourth.

"We're through, *priyazn.* You did it."

When he reopened his eyes, they stood in the hallway. The coiled knot of power surrendered to an avalanche of relief, and for a second she was holding *him* up.

He gathered his wits together yet again, for they had no time to revel. "We need to try to reach the hangar bay and steal a ship. According to the panels, it's three levels down on the main wing. If we take the far transit tube maybe we can avoid security most of the way." He shifted them to face the direction of their first goal. "Are you ready?"

She nodded gamely, but tension hardened her expression when she began trying to walk. He supported her weight so she could concentrate on moving her legs.

Their progress was slow. Too slow. Frustration roiled off Alex in waves, and he doubted anyone in the universe wanted to run so much as she did at this moment...

TickTockTickTock

...but they weren't going to make it. Even if they were running, even if they'd never stopped running, too few seconds remained before security engulfed them.

He kept moving anyway, because not escaping wasn't an option he was prepared to accept.

Three meters from the transit tube, Alex pulled up hard.

"What's wrong?"

"I think I...." Her brow furrowed, and she twisted around to look behind them.

He did the same in time to see a whirl of lights, and suddenly Eren asi-Idoni stood there while a Kat dispersed into the hall.

"Did someone need a ride?"

Alex laughed wildly. "It is damn good to see you—alive, but more importantly, here. Glad you could drop by."

"No offense, but I'm not. Though I am glad you two are alive."

Caleb grunted; Alex had the full right of it, but they needed to stay on track. "We can celebrate once we're on the *Siyane*. What's the plan? You are here with the *Siyane*, aren't you?"

Eren held up a small, unmarked canister. "Yes. The facility is shielded by a solid wall of *diati*, which is why Mesme here didn't swirl in and swoop you away before now. This little toy is a gift from the anarch powers-that-be. It contains the tiniest iota of *diati*, enough to pass small objects—in this case, Mesme and I—through the barrier."

He gazed askance at Caleb. "It's only strong enough to ferry one Anaden-sized body and Mesme at a time, so we'll have to make several trips out of here...unless you can get yourself back to the ship?"

Caleb shook his head tersely. Mesme insisted he should be capable of teleporting himself to a known location, but damned if he could figure out how to accomplish it. Regardless, in his current state he didn't trust himself to teleport his shoe.

Eren shrugged. "Understood. We'll go one at a time—"

"Alex, you're first." Her mouth opened, but Caleb cut her off. "You're injured. No arguing." He took the canister from Eren, wrapped Alex's hand around it and gently nudged her toward Mesme. "Go."

Mesme didn't hesitate, surrounding her in light as she struggled to stay on her feet unaided. They vanished.

It got easier to breathe then. She would be safe.

Alarms erupted to peal through the hallway. He grabbed Eren by the arm and yanked him flush against the wall. "When Mesme gets back, you go next. I can hold them off."

The Anaden frowned. "No, I can—"

"Do what? Scowl them to death?"

He patted his belt. "I brought a parting gift for your captors."

A Watchman sprinted around the corner nearest them. Caleb spun, arm outstretched. The guard's neck had snapped before he finished the motion, and a rush of *diati* leapt across the open space like a spear blasting directly into his head.

He blinked, dizzy again. And worse. The modest dose was the drop to send the dam brimming over. *Too much too much.*

Eren gaped at him, vivid golden eyes wide. "Well, that explains that."

Caleb leaned on the wall and pressed his fingertips to his temples in an attempt to regain equilibrium.

Breathe in. Out. "Does it?"

"No. Not at all. By Hades, Caleb!"

A series of pounding, quick *thuds* approaching garnered their full attention. The next second a heavy mech rounded the corner.

Four arms consisting entirely of plasma cannons aimed at them and launched their barrage.

Caleb flung both arms forward. His skin ignited, and he became the fire.

The energy from the cannons slammed into a solid barrier of *diati*. As the mech continued its barrage, the barrier advanced until it enveloped the walking weapon. The deadly arms crumpled. The hulking torso crumpled, too, followed by the multi-jointed metal legs.

Cracks materialized in the walls to splinter down the hall as plaster fragments rained from the ceiling and the jagged, twisted remains of the heavy mech toppled to the floor.

Caleb stumbled as the *diati* rushed back into him. His hand found a brace, and he stared at an equally stunned and now dust-coated Eren.

Mesme reappeared before either of them spoke, essence empty save for the small canister spinning at the center.

Eren grabbed the canister and thrust it against Caleb's chest. "Whatever this black magic you've got going on is, you're a bloody wreck right now, and if you try to hold off what's coming, you'll destroy the station and yourself with it. Get out of here, and leave the station destroying to me. I will see you again."

Before Caleb could protest, Eren sprinted down the hall and disappeared around the corner.

We must make haste. Mesme surrounded him, and he was too rattled to move or protest or do anything other than allow himself to be carried away. The hall and cells of the facility faded in a shimmering haze of light.

An instant later they were replaced by the cabin of the *Siyane*. Home.

Alex had gotten herself to the cockpit and into her chair. He rushed to join her, then knelt and hugged her close, belatedly hoping he didn't burn her.

She gave him a wan but unsinged grimace and tapped her temple, an indication Valkyrie was giving her an earful.

He chuckled unevenly, trying to find the headspace where they were free and safe and he could be at peace.

She checked over his shoulder. "Mesme, why are you still here? Go get Eren!"

Caleb sighed. "He's not coming."

"What? Why—"

The viewport lit up as an explosion rocked the facility. The left wing of the facility ruptured and broke off to tumble into the void as cascading blasts tore through the heart of the structure.

"Oh. But…he'll be all right."

"I assume so." He offered her a weak smile. His body was crashing, though the rampant buzzing in his head suggested the *diati* wasn't of the same inclination.

'We should take advantage of the diversion and escape.'

Alex nodded. "Go, Valkyrie. Anywhere."

Mesme churned in perversely increasing distress about the cabin as they accelerated away.

It had already been such an absurd day, and Caleb's mind was reeling so outrageously, it really wasn't that much of a surprise when a shadow cast by nothing drew up beside Mesme and spoke.

"It is good you have escaped intact. But I am afraid you now have a far larger problem."

54

SIYANE

MILKY WAY SECTOR 7

"*E banatyi pidaraz!*" Alex squirmed in agitation, complicating Caleb's efforts to administer even the most minimal of first aid and clean the dried blood off her face, never mind determine if she'd suffered any internal injuries. "Valkyrie, get to a portal, *now!*"

'We are already in transit.'

Do you not want to traverse the primary Provision Network Gateway? It is the destination of the Machim fleet.

"Exactly—and thus the one place we don't want to be right now. We need to sneak into the Mosaic. Valkyrie, let's ready a message to broadcast the instant we're through. 'Red alert. Anaden military forces en route to portal network in order to destroy it and everything in it. This means you, so get your *zadnitza* here with every ship you have. Time's up.'"

He chuckled. Her mental faculties appeared to have bounced back just fine. "I'm guessing this message will be sent to your mother?"

"And whoever else is listening." She winced as he tightened the medwrap around her wrist and secured it. "But yes, she's the intended audience. Who else can mobilize tens of thousands of ships in a matter of hours?"

"Good point." He gave up on the first aid for now and leaned against the data table beside her. Concentrating on tending to her had helped quiet the buzzing in his ears, but now it returned in spades.

He glanced down at his hand. The trembling was almost imperceptible, but he felt as if he'd overdosed on synthetic adrenaline, and there was no nanobot mixture to counteract this overdose.

He needed to focus on something else. Conveniently, an apocalyptic crisis loomed a few short hours away. It would do.

Mesme's 'acquaintance,' the ominous shadow creature who claimed to go by the name 'Miaon,' had departed, but only after a hushed conference with Mesme. So Caleb figured Mesme knew more than it had shared. "How did they find out about the Mosaic?"

There has been the confluence of a number of factors, but the critical information was provided by a Katasketousya subjected to torture and threatened with death.

Alex frowned. "One of your own sold you out? Shouldn't it have taken one for the team?"

How many times must I impart to you the concept that we are not fighters? Subterfuge and science are our ways, and we are not brave.

She dropped her head back to contemplate the ceiling, then grimaced and brought her hand to her neck. "That's not true. You're brave, Mesme."

No.

"Yes, you are. You've risked everything you value—first to defy the Idryma and help us defeat their AI armada, then to protect us from the other Kats who continued to fear us. You did it again to sneak us into Amaranthe, teach us what we needed to know and get us the tools to act. You exposed yourself to help us retrieve the Machim data, and again to rescue us today. You're one of the bravest beings I've ever met."

Mesme quivered in the face of her words. She winked at Caleb, but he had heard the sincerity in her voice. She could never have forced herself to say it if she didn't believe it. Still, it was an act of supreme kindness on her part, and he loved her all the more for it.

I...thank you, Alexis Solovy. I have only acted in furtherance of what I believed to be right. I do not feel brave, merely driven and desperate. But I will accept your reckoning on the matter.

Caleb laughed. "As we all do before the end, Mesme." He started checking her over anew, in part because it calmed him to do so.

Other than her wrist, no bones were broken, though several tendons and ligaments were stressed. She'd suffered moderate nerve damage, which was why she'd had trouble walking, but her eVi was busily shepherding therapeutic measures to address the damage. Her neck had a sprain, but he'd sneaked in a muscle relaxer injection while she was talking to Mesme.

She'd be sore and weak for a couple of days, but she was heal- ing remarkably fast. Between her top-shelf cybernetics, boosted as they were by recent ware upgrades, Valkyrie's integration into her nervous system and the regenerative traces of Akeso left behind from when it healed her infection, she would probably never stay injured for any appreciable length of time.

In fact, he had to wonder whether, if something didn't kill her quickly, anything *could* kill her.

He hoped they'd never have to find out. Satisfied he'd patched up all the visible injuries, he kissed her forehead and stepped back. "Mesme, what do you know about the Machim's plan? It's time for details."

Being aware of one hidden entrance to the Mosaic—the one in the Fylliot stellar system—the Directorate correctly assumes there are additional hidden entrances. Since they do not possess a way to locate them, however, their intent is for the fleet to traverse the Provision Network Gateway and destroy all spaces they find, save the Provi- sion Enisles themselves.

"Really? Why not simply drop a massive bomb inside the Mo- saic and call it a day?"

Several reasons. First, they perceive—again, correctly—that this course of action would risk leaving some unrevealed malfeasance to survive, and they strive to be thorough in their Eradications.

Second, they need the Provision Enisles' production output. The service we provide is both unique and necessary, and for all its butchery, the Directorate can be pragmatic when pressured. Thus they will attempt to wrest oversight control of the Provision Enisles from us and enslave the Katasketousya required to continue the operation.

"Will they? Your colleagues—will they agree to run the Provision Enisles under the Directorate's thumb?"

I believe so.

Right. Not brave. "What if they don't? Can the Directorate keep the resources flowing?"

For a time, with diminished efficiency. Outside of collection and transport, the systems are largely self-sustaining. However, absent tending, eventually they will begin to fail. Admittedly, 'eventually' is measured in centuries if not millennia, so it is in the Directorate's interest to preserve the Enisles for the present.

Alex started to pace around the cabin, but it soon morphed into limping, and she paused to brace against the couch wearing an annoyed scowl.

Caleb went over to her and grasped her gently by the shoulders. "Sit. Rest."

"We don't have time to rest."

"You have time to rest your body. Sit while we plan. Give yourself what chance you can to recover."

Her nose scrunched up in displeasure, but she limped around to perch on the edge of the couch cushion, then reached up and urged him down beside her. "What about you? You've been taking care of me, but you got dosed pretty heavily in there, didn't you? Are you handling it okay?"

"Well...am I still glowing?"

"A little bit."

"Right." He squeezed his eyes shut and pinched the bridge of his nose. "The Inquisitor who interrogated me wielded more power than the one I killed on Seneca. A lot more—and I took it all. Later, I ran into a couple of Watchmen, and what *diati* they had leapt to me without effort."

When he opened his eyes, he found her gazing at him in concern and reassurance, but not fear. Never fear. So he didn't hide his own fear from her. "I feel like I'm in danger of bursting from the inside...like I can't possibly contain all the power, much less control it. But I will. It's already better than it was, so all I need is some time to adapt."

She touched his cheek and smiled softly. "I believe you will. Let me know what I can do."

He placed a kiss on her palm and nodded, and she nudged him away. "Now up with you. I'll sit if I have to, but you strategize better when you pace."

"Then I'll pace for both us." But he'd hardly made it around the couch when she dove in to the strategizing. It seemed she'd been *thinking* for both of them.

"All right. I'd assumed they were going to blow the Gateway. But if that's not their plan...I think we can use this. Mesme, can you change the wave configuration to activate the portals?"

No. The TLF wave system is built into their structure.

"Shit. You can move them, though, can't you? Not the main portal, but the ones that are hidden—you can move the location where they open into Amaranthe. The Mosaic, while absurdly complex, is also strictly ordered and symmetrical, but the portals don't open at evenly spaced locations here. They open where they're needed, or into empty sectors. So you can move them."

It is feasible to do so, yes.

"How feasible?"

Perhaps if you shared your idea.

She made to stand, then presumably remembered she was supposed to be sitting and sank back down. But she was on a roll, and he was frankly grateful she insisted on taking the lead. As soon as he'd stopped touching her, the buzzing in his ears and trembling in his hands had reappeared, and he could not make them stop.

"Our first and highest goal is to keep the Machim fleet—or any Anaden vessel for that matter—out of the Mosaic."

Given the size of the military force and the scope of the Machim—

"I know. We'll get to that problem in a minute, but for now let's assume we can stop them at the Provision Network Gateway today. We—or you, or other Kats—need to be able to get enough provision convoys through so people in Amaranthe don't start starving. Also, people and ships from Aurora may need to be able to move back and forth."

Caleb stopped his ineffectual pacing to stare at her, impressed. "You want to route ships through the other hidden portals, then move the portals after they're used so the enemy won't be able to track them down."

She shrugged. "Well, Mesme? Will it work? Is this a remotely viable plan?"

Such actions will require a great deal of planning and careful effort, but within reason, yes. Do you imagine the Directorate will turn a blind eye to Provision vessels docking and delivering their loads while under an Eradication order?

"It's not like Kats are piloting the vessels—they're operated by shackled AIs. Plus, you said it yourself. They need the provisions. Anyway, we can worry about the finer points later. For the moment we just need to try to maintain the ability to do it. Priorities.

"Oh, and you'd better contact Lakhes, because somebody needs to move the Fylliot portal straightaway."

She ran her hand through her hair, tugging it out of the haphazard knot she'd wound it into as she talked. "Now, about the cataclysm speeding headlong for the Mosaic, and how we can give my mother and AEGIS a fighting chance to defeat it."

55

CENTAURI E

MILKY WAY SECTOR 22

Casmir watched from the hangar overlook as the Igni missiles were loaded onto his Imperium and select battlecruisers. It was taking time, and his orders were to make haste. At this rate, it seemed the haste would have to be found elsewhere in the schedule.

The missiles consisted of two matter/antimatter cores surrounded by a shell of gas that, when subjected to an electromagnetic field, became highly ionized plasma. In order to guarantee the cores remained separated and the shell dormant until called into service, the procedure for loading and securing the missiles was rather more involved than simply rolling them into the ships' weapons bays.

An unsettling tickle danced along his skin to forewarn him the promised Inquisitor approached. A second later a man in a midnight blue cloak over dark gunmetal tactical gear appeared beside him at the viewport.

Casmir gave him an aloof once-over. "You're late."

"I had to make a detour. Ziton elasson-Praesidis. Now, turn around, as we're about to have an audience."

"What—?" He pivoted just as representations of his Primor and the Praesidis Primor materialized in the room with them. He instinctively squared his posture. "Sirs. This is—"

"There's no time for formalities, Casmir. Your mission is being modified slightly. You will be carrying one additional weapon into the Provision Network, to be used on one specific portal realm within."

Praesidis jumped in then. "Ziton possesses the information needed to locate the correct portal."

Casmir didn't care for being the odd man out here, but Machims were not ones to throw petulant fits. "Are there special precautions I should institute with respect to this weapon?"

"So long as it remains safeguarded in the casing you will receive it in, the weapon will pose no threat to your fleet. A scientist, Dr. Fisik elasson-Erevna, will also accompany you to ensure its proper activation and delivery."

He bristled at the thought of having two *elassons* on board his ship to 'oversee' matters, but he was more concerned about the increasingly bizarre turn the mission was taking. "Sir—sirs—what sort of weapon is this?"

R

There had been many names for this manner of weapon throughout history. Armageddon Machine. Ragnarok. The Final Solution. Doomsday Device.

The Directorate had elected to call this one the Tartarus Trigger.

It looked peaceful enough encased in a thirty-meter-long chrome cylinder, though the cage and braces surrounding the cylinder were a touch ominous.

"And this…device, what's inside all this casing…creates a black hole?"

Fisik wore the perpetually condescending scowl of all elite scientists. "Not an ordinary black hole, Navarchos. The Tartarus creates a black hole that is not only self-sustaining but inflationary. If left unattended—if not countered—it will continue to grow in size."

"For how long?"

"Forever. Or until it runs out of fuel, whichever comes first."

Casmir was not a scientist, so it took him a few seconds to piece together the fact that the fuel was space and to run out meant….

If Fisik were a Machim, or anything less than an *elasson*, Casmir would wipe the smirk off his face in a most unpleasant manner—slowly, so the man suffered at some length before being allowed to die and be reborn.

But he did not indulge the desire. He had important orders from his Primor to execute on, and the timetable left no room for vengeful torture. "Dangerous weapon. I assume we do have a method for shutting it down?"

"We do. It is not an immaculate process, and there is, shall we say, slag. But, yes, we can halt the black hole's growth."

"Well, that's a relief. How many of them have you made?"

"Only the one."

"I see. Will you excuse me a moment?" Casmir looked around for the Inquisitor and urged him toward a secluded corner. "What is so special about this little petri dish the Katasketousya are experimenting in? What is so nefarious the Directorate is willing to deploy..." he glanced over his shoulder "...*that* to destroy it?"

Ziton stared at him coldly, but an Inquisitor's stare was always cold. "I will tell you, because I've been authorized to do so, but first a word of caution. If we weren't needed to carry out this mission, no one outside the Primors themselves would ever learn this information."

"We both deal in secrets, Inquisitor. I know the rules."

"You've been briefed on the reasons for the larger mission, correct? You know what the Katasketousya are doing in these secret portal spaces?"

"Of course."

"In the portal the Tartarus Trigger is destined for, they recreated us."

"I don't—"

"They bred primitive Anadens and allowed them to evolve. They groomed them for war. Unable and unwilling to do the fighting themselves, they intend to use a bastardized knock-off of our ancestors as their weapons in a traitorous ploy to destroy the Directorate, the Primors and all of us."

Casmir almost choked on the revulsion. Of all the vile, reprehensible tactics! If it were up to him, he'd fire the Tartarus into the Provision Network Gateway and bury the whole construct in darkness.

But this was why he was not Primor; the Directorate proved wiser and shrewder than he. The citizens required the food, goods and materials the Provision Network provided, and they should not be punished for the Katasketousya's betrayal.

"You understand now, yes? The Igni missiles will sever the realms attached to the other portals from Amaranthe for eternity, but this abomination cannot be allowed to continue to exist. In any form. In any universe."

Casmir nodded solemnly. "I understand. Let us see to it the device is loaded posthaste. I believe we should be on our way."

56

ANARCH POST SATUS

LOCATION UNKNOWN

Eren awoke with far more sluggishness than usual. The transition was definitely getting worse. His consciousness had hardly had the chance to accept and settle into the last body properly before he was shoving it into a new one.

He was using regenesis too frequently; this much was becoming painfully obvious. The process had been designed to compensate for freak accidents and other untimely deaths, not three null outs in hardly a month.

Honestly, he was surprised to find he *had* a new body to inhabit so soon after the last one had been called into service—or had his essence been frozen in limbo until a new one was ready? How long? What had he missed?

Then he remembered he had a cybernetic clock, checked it, and dialed down the panic on seeing the gap was measured in hours, not years.

Regardless, he couldn't worry about the ramifications of too many body swaps right now. It was necessary, dammit. And now he needed to shake off the lethargy and crawl out of this capsule and get to work. He believed his friends had escaped the Helix Retention facility, but in doing so they had surely set off a cosmic furor of epic proportions, one which stood a decent chance of shaking Amaranthe to its very core.

No way was he missing the show.

So he worked to force his eyes open, struggling against the compelling desire to sink back into restful sleep. The capsule felt softer than usual. And roomier. He started to attribute it to his addled state...but thanks to his frequent capsule visits he knew what they felt like, and this one felt different.

He wasn't in the recovery ward at Post Alpha. He'd been returned to life somewhere else. Somewhere new.

That realization got his eyes to pop open quite spryly.

Instead of the usual Curative unit, he found a man hovering above the capsule. Dressed in a modest but well-appointed jacket over a silken shirt, the man's irises were a raven black that hinted at indigo and even a brighter sapphire in the shifting light. His features were hard, guarded, yet somehow kind.

The cover retracted, and the man smiled at him. "Hello, Eren. I am Sator Danilo Nisi. You must tell me everything."

57

KATOIKIA

Triangulum Galaxy
LGG Region VI

The Machim formation eclipsed Katoikia's sun to cast a shadow across the world.

The warships wasted no time engaging in the formalities of warnings or pronouncements. They simply opened fire.

There would be no Cultivation Unit to follow behind and scavenge for resources—Katoikia was to serve both as an example and an as implicit threat—and the weapons cut through the land like rampaging tempests.

Hours earlier, the pronouncement had resounded across the cosmos for all to hear: the Katasketousya's status as an Accepted Species was hereby revoked. And since there were only three categories, Accepted, Slave and Eradicated, it didn't need to be stated what happened next—but the Directorate had stated it nonetheless. Members of the species were 'kill on sight' by anyone, anywhere, free of repercussions.

The reality that the sole way to kill a Katasketousya was to disable their stasis chamber meant the decree had little practical impact, but the psychological one was tragic in its significance.

Now the footage of this desecration of their homeworld would be blared across every feed, projection and marquee as a demonstration of the Directorate's power and authority. A reminder to all to never cross it.

The disruptions in the crust from the powerful weapons soon generated earthquakes. The land split apart in ragged fissures; the towers crumbled and fell into the fissures to be swallowed up by the earth. Volcanoes erupted as magma surged upward from the planet's mantle to bathe the land in lava. The oceans boiled and tsunamis crashed forth to drown the lava.

In an hour Katoikia had been ravaged from pole to pole. Not a particle of soil remained undisturbed. Not a structure remained intact.

In time, its orbit would falter and it would either fall into its sun, drift away or break apart entirely. For now it hung brutally in the sky, beaten and broken.

Lakhes watched on from above, safely hidden inside a ship and behind shields and barriers, having left Mnemosyne to fulfill its own urgent mission.

It seemed as if aeons had slipped by, second by meticulous second—then abruptly time and events rushed headlong forward so rapidly everything appeared to happen at once. The hurricane could not be tamed, yet someone must attempt to do so.

Lakhes accepted its role as that individual. But first, a moment to linger here. As a witness, and a chronicler.

Had the Katasketousya once shed tears, when they were tied to their bodies and to the ground? Lakhes had lived longer than most, but it could not say. The soulful ache the scene evoked felt as if it were too much to bear without some release, some physical assertion of the sorrow.

Yet there was great relief to be found in the scene as well, for the towers had been empty. If lives had been lost, they numbered in the dozens, or possibly hundreds. But not millions.

Lakhes' attention followed the warships as they withdrew from orbit and vanished. They had not stopped to check and confirm the towers were occupied before wreaking their destruction. Perhaps their arrogance led them to assume the Katasketousya were both helpless and uninformed, or to believe the notion of attempting to flee the Directorate's wrath a ludicrous one.

Even so, given this was supposed to be an Eradication, they probably should have thought to do that.

MOSAIC

IDRYMA

Hyperion brooded through the halls of an ancillary wing of the Idryma. This had been Hyperion's primary activity since being banned from Amaranthe, which was why Lakhes had no difficulty finding the Analystae.

Hyperion whipped into an elaborate horned owl avatar on Lakhes' arrival. Vanity was not one of its better qualities.

"Praetor, how gracious of you to pay me a visit. Come to ensure I have not been troublesome?"

"Hyperion, I ask you to put aside ill sentiments and remember you have served the Idryma for epochs. I suspect you have served it because you believe profoundly in its purpose. If this is not so, say it and I will leave you to your lamentations."

"And if it is so, Praetor?"

"I will ask you to serve it once more."

"You offer to lift my exile from Amaranthe?"

Lakhes did not answer the question asked. "You directed an armada of warships in a campaign against the Humans. We are not fighters, but you have traveled closer to the reality of warring than the rest of us."

"An act for which I will not express remorse, so if your intent is to shame me I regret to disappoint."

Lakhes had spent cosmic ages manipulating the various personalities of the Conclave in such ways as to maintain harmony, cooperation and furtherance of all of their goals. Its skill in this endeavor was a primary reason why it was Praetor and the only reason why it did not so much as flinch at the provocation.

"You did so to cow them or, failing that, eliminate them, but the result was instead to unite them and urge them forward to greater accomplishments. For this, I am most grateful. Now you must listen, because our remaining time to act is no longer measured in centuries, but hours."

Hyperion stilled. "Speak, then."

"A new armada has been constructed and is awakened. Lead it—not against the Humans but alongside them. Add our forces to theirs in a gambit to destroy the Machim invaders who seek to destroy us both."

Lakhes sensed Hyperion's anxiety in the tremoring of the waves beneath its form, and waited.

"You realize we may merely be trading one master for another, and there is no guarantee the Humans will be the better option? I have seen their capacity for cruelty."

"As have I, but I have also seen their capacity for kindness. Yes, it is a risk, but it is one I will gladly bear. Regardless, it matters not, for the die has been cast. Katoikia is gone. We are declared for Eradication and hunted throughout Amaranthe. A fleet of warships approaches to shatter the Mosaic and all it holds. We stand up now or perish for eternity."

'Eternity' was not a word the Katasketousya used lightly, for they appreciated the magnitude of its meaning more than most, and Hyperion drew into itself. "I have devoted the entirety of my existence to ensuring our survival. I will stand."

"Then come, and let us wage our war at last."

AURORA

58

ROMANE

They'd moved Emily from the chamber in the ICU wing into a normal bed in a normal room by the time Devon got back to the hospital. He'd showered—for the second time today no less—donned fresh clothes and even eaten a meal while on the transport, all so he could appear the perfect picture of normalcy to her when she woke up.

Because she wasn't awake yet. Dr. Johansson said he expected her to wake up. Mia said she was going to wake up. Soon.

He tried not to dwell on how frail she still looked as he moved the guest chair over beside the bed and sat down to wait.

ℛ

Devon sensed her in his mind before his hand felt the movement of her fingers in its grasp.

Instantly he was leaning over her, one hand squeezing hers while the other gently stroked her hair. "Hey, babe. Can you hear me?" *Hey, babe, can you hear me?*

I.... "Devon?" Her eyes fluttered open.

He smiled broadly. "I'm right here."

She started to return the smile, then frowned and licked her lips; he retrieved the canister of water and offered it to her. Her brow knotted up as she sipped on it. "What happened? We were...leaving the amphitheater and...I don't remember."

"We were attacked by some thugs, and you got hurt. But you're going to be just fine."

She blinked several times. "Am I in a hospital? My eVi's all messed up."

"The doctors had to flush your cybernetics. But the good news is, this means we can write you the snazziest custom ware anybody's ever seen. It'll be better than before. Does that sound okay to you?"

She nodded. "Yeah. That sounds like fun. What did the attackers want?"

"They wanted to hurt me. But I took care of it, so they won't threaten us anymore. I'll never let them hurt you again."

The alert from Alex blasted into his mind, but he ignored it. Instead, he pulled a crystal out of his pocket and put it on the bedside table.

With a touch, colorful holo flowers burst to life and began rotating above the crystal.

Emily's face lit up in delight, and he thought he might die from happiness.

Devon, about the—

I don't care, Annie. They can fight this battle without me.

Mia studied Malcolm in growing suspicion as they settled onto the couch after dinner—the first proper, appetizing meal she'd successfully consumed since the night of the celebration. "You're unusually edgy tonight."

Granted, she knew what his reply would be before he said it; her thought was getting it out in the open may help him move past it. The edginess, as it were.

He huffed a breath, looking blatantly chagrined, and she rescued him by lounging her back against his chest and snuggling in close.

"After everything that's happened—after it tried to hurt you, hurt Morgan and that girl—I kind of wanted to invade New Babel with an army and smash the murderous Artificial to pieces with my bare hands. I'm glad we were able to destroy it without bloodshed on our side, but...I'm a little disappointed I didn't get a fight. Sorry."

"Don't be. It's understandable."

He hugged her closer. "Maybe, but you deserve to relax, and I should be helping with that—so no more edginess from me."

Mia trailed her fingertips lazily up his forearm. She felt simultaneously bone-tired weary and energized from sheer relief that the nightmare was over, but mostly she was happy to be here, now, in a position where she could afford to find his oh-so-honorable bloodlust cute.

"You know, you're not as different from him as you think."

"Who?"

"Caleb." She held up a hand when she caught his the expression flaring on his face. "I know, you don't approve of his career or many of the life choices he's made along the way. And believe me, you have a far, *far* greater respect for authority than he's ever shown. No question. I'm simply saying you two share a fierce sense of right and wrong, and a determination to defend not merely the people close to you but all innocents from harm. Your response to these attacks has made that quite clear."

Malcolm was silent for a moment, staring not at her but at the floor. "You care a lot about him, don't you?"

"Yes. He extended a hand and lifted me out of the gutter, and he's been there for me ever since." This wasn't a secret or a surprise, was it?

His eyes shot up to her, and the shift in his posture had the effect of nudging her away. "He wasn't there for you when you were left lying in a coma, or when you had to flee for your life from Earth."

The acerbity of his tone gave her pause. She'd picked up on the fact he didn't like Caleb, but this was another level of animus, or something else.

"He was and is doing important work to help protect *all* of us. I don't expect him to come running to my rescue every time life gets hard." She smiled and placed a hand on his knee. The last thing she'd meant to do was start an argument with her idle rambling. "Besides, you're here, and doing an excellent job of protecting me when I need it."

Instead of accepting the compliment, Malcolm lowered his chin and slid farther away, eyes hooded. His Adam's Apple bobbed several times. "Mmm."

He winced, studied the floor for several more seconds, then stood as she regarded him in growing confusion. "Okay. I'm going to go now."

She hurriedly stood as well. "All right. I bet you have a lot of work to do back at the Presidio, which you've been neglecting to be here with me. Once I'm confident Emily and Morgan are improving, I can come by and visit. If not tomorrow, definitely—"

"No."

The quiet but firm delivery sent her stomach churning. "No?"

"I don't mean—of course if you have business with AEGIS or…or anyone else you can come to the Presidio. But…" his jaw trembled, but his eyes refused to meet hers "…not to see me."

"I'm not sure I understand…and I think I missed something rather important."

He sighed and finally allowed his gaze to settle on her, but a soldier's mask hid any emotion. Impenetrable. "I know I'm so very far from perfect—I know I'm a small cog in a large machine—but I do have some pride. Enough pride to refuse to be the one you get when you can't have the one you want.

"Mia, you are a wonderful, amazing, *extraordinary* woman, and I will always be grateful to have been able to spend this time with you. But I will not be what you settle for." He turned on a heel and strode toward the door.

"What? No! Malcolm, that's not—"

"Stop. I don't want justifications or excuses. All I want is to leave with the smallest shred of dignity intact."

"Meno, lock the door."

He spun to her, eyes wide in enough shock to break through the mask, and it occurred to her she'd never seen him genuinely angry before. Well.

"For two minutes. After two minutes, Meno, unlock it."

'I will do so.'

"If you still want to leave when the two minutes are up, you can go on your way and I won't try to stop you. But please, listen to me first."

He squared his shoulders, clasped his hands behind him in a parade rest stance and locked a stony glare upon a spot on the wall somewhere over her left shoulder. The move had cost her, but hopefully not as much as letting him walk out would.

She began pacing frenetically, though her movement couldn't keep up with her racing mind. Clearly she'd acted out of panic; she damn well better make good use of the time she had. Her thoughtless mistake was blindingly obvious *now*, but fixing it was another matter.

"First off, I think you misunderstand the history and nature of my relationship with Caleb. We were never 'together.' There were a few years where we were more than friends, but it was just...the point is, *I* ended that part of our relationship years ago, and I haven't regretted it."

Her chin dropped to her chest. "No. You deserve an explanation, not a brush-off. Caleb *is* honorable and good-hearted, but...chaos is always either running from him or chasing after him. He gets near you, and suddenly you're in the center of the vortex, too.

"I worked too hard to escape that world to let myself get dragged back into it, even by my dearest friend. Which he is, and probably always will be. I'm not ashamed of it. But I don't want that kind of life—if you know me at all, surely you see the truth of this—and I don't want him. I want..."

...'you' would come off as both lame and pandering, and the least likely of all possible options to convince him of her veracity. If he would only *look* at her! She veered. "I've been on my own since I was eleven years old. I'm not asking for pity—I'm glad for what happened. It worked out, eventually. It's important now for this reason: friends and lovers have come and gone, but I've kept them all at arm's length. Given them a façade layered over the real me.

"It's a defense mechanism, and I recognize it is, but it's also often been the right choice. And now I have a flood of voices and people and Artificials floating in and out of my head...and I've never felt so alone. Except when I'm with you."

His focus darted to her. He quickly jerked it back to the spot on the wall, but the mask was visibly cracking.

Progress she dared not let slip away. "You are the kindest, most considerate, most generous man I have ever met. I think you may be the first person who, when I'm with you, I can simply...*be*. No façades, no veneers, no performances. You disarmed me, the first time I met you and every time since, with your unabashed forthrightness and damnable sincerity.

"I realize you're strong and tough and dangerous to the rest of the world, but to me, you feel like home." She smiled, trying to convey the truth of it. Brutal, terrifying, naked truth.

'Door unlocked.'

Malcolm's caramel eyes now fell fully on her, softening from fear through caution to something akin to hope. The parade rest stance vanished as a hand came up to work at his jaw. He didn't say anything, but he also didn't move toward the door.

"I'm sorry I haven't said any of this to you before now. I'm good at many things, but this doesn't appear to be one of them. I didn't want to frighten you away."

She inhaled deeply and took a step toward him. "So, to recap...and summarize...you're the only person I want here with me. Please don't go."

"I'm only good at a *few* things, and any fool could see this also isn't one of them." He considered the ceiling for a long breath before closing the remaining distance to her. "Forgive me. I was being stupid and petty."

"You were protecting yourself, which I understand intimately." She tentatively drew him close, shocked at the power and comfort of the sensations that accompanied his arms wrapping around her. Solace, perhaps contentment. "But I'm not protecting myself from you."

"God, I'm sorry. I'm an idiot who should have had a little faith in you. This wasn't even really about Marano—I hope he is what you say. I truly do. It was more...people I care for always seem to want something from me I can't give them. I've come to expect it, and now I'm jumping at shadows."

She didn't know nearly enough details of his past to pretend to comprehend the full scope of what he meant. But she didn't need to, because she knew him. Though he was far more than he believed himself to be—far more than a cog in a machine for certain—she'd told the truth about his forthrightness. Outside of the battlefield, he was utterly without guile or pretense. Sadly, it didn't surprise her that others had taken advantage.

Her fingertips traced his temple, down his cheek. "I'll try to be sure I don't make those sorts of demands."

"I know you won't, because you are entirely too wonderful to be real."

She placed the first kiss on his lips, along with a teasing whisper. "Yes, I have bad news: the last two months have been a dream."

"I suspected as much." He renewed the kiss with enough fervor to foreclose any further conversation. She surrendered to his embrace—

—The alert pealed through her consciousness to drown the suffusing joy in a tidal wave of dread, leaving in its wake a solemn acceptance. Perhaps it really had all been a dream.

She didn't flinch. She just held him close, cherishing the tender intensity of his embrace and memorizing the feel of his mouth pressed to hers. The final seconds were ticking down, and it might be a while before she felt it again.

Abruptly he pulled back from her, and the darkening of his expression told her the call from AEGIS had gone out. Leave it to Miriam Solovy to be scrupulously attentive and instantly prepped to move.

He dropped his forehead to hers, and his hands rose to cup her face. "I am so, *so* sorry, but it's time. I have to go."

59

ROMANE

'Kennedy, do you have a moment? I wish to discuss a matter with you.'

"It isn't anything to do with Machim warships, is it, Vii? I've been eating, sleeping and dreaming Machim warships for days now. I close my eyes and I see negatives of Machim warship schematics on the back of my lids."

She'd hardly gotten the optimizer switch-out handled and the assembly line running smoothly when the data dump from Valkyrie had come in. This resulted both in her returning to the Presidio from Earth and staying longer than she'd intended as her sleep-to-wakefulness ratio dove to perilous levels.

She yawned to emphasize the point.

'It is not, though I suspect we'll need to discuss them before too long. No, this is a more personal matter. When Valkyrie and Alex departed for Amaranthe, they left something in my care. A side project, one might call it. I haven't allowed it to distract from our work for AEGIS, but when time and cycles have permitted I have been working on it.

'My progress has reached a stage where I'm no longer comfortable keeping the project's existence from you. I was not hiding it as such, so perhaps it would be better to say I wish to affirmatively share it with you now.'

If Valkyrie *and* Alex were involved, it was guaranteed to be audacious, likely to be dangerous and possibly to be exciting. She groaned dramatically. "This ought to be good. Fill me in."

'Thank you. When—'

The door opened and Noah walked in carrying a package. Her heart did a spirited somersault in her chest. She'd sent him a message to let him know she was home, but she hadn't talked to him in two days and had been afraid to think about where he was.

She gave him a broad smile, trying to appear as welcoming as possible. "Hi."

"Hey." He'd hesitated in the doorway at first, as if he needed to be invited in, but now he continued on inside until he reached the front of her desk.

'Kennedy—'

"Can we talk about your project later, Vii? Thanks."

Vii responded, but she'd tuned the Artificial out. She was so relieved to see him—so busy perusing his eyes and stubbled jaw-line and the messy fall of his hair—that for a minute she forgot he was carrying a fairly hefty package.

She straightened up and cleared her throat. "What's in the box?"

He glanced down at the floor then back at her. Dammit, but she couldn't get a vibe from him. "I made you something."

"Really? Noah, I don't—"

"Please. Before you say anything, let me give you this."

She'd thought she was ready for this meeting; she'd been wrong. God, she hated feeling nervous. Frightened, even. Exposed. But she stood and nodded bravely. "All right."

He exhaled in evident relief. "Thanks. So—" he frowned "—I guess I should've put a streamer on the box, or a wrapper, but I was too—"

She placed her hands under his and the package. "Noah."

"Sorry. So, open it."

She took it from him, surprised at how light it was. Still, she propped it on the corner of the desk while she removed the top. She started to lean over the open box when an object flew up and out to hover in the air in front of her.

It was a scale model of the AEGIS cruiser she'd designed. Mostly virtual, an adiamene lattice outlined the strong lines of the hull and lent it tangibility. She peered inside the frame, but no matter how closely she scrutinized it the fidelity continued—

—except there was an oddity in the captain's cabin. She tilted her head and focused on…

…reclining on the bed was a holographic reproduction of Noah. Naked. Scrawled on his chest was a tattoo that said…she started giggling. It said 'Property of Kennedy Rossi.'

The reproduction grinned and waved at her.

"Noah, what—"

"It's not limited to the cruiser. Drop a crystal disk in this one slot in the back, beneath the engines, and it'll load the schematic that's on the crystal. So long as there's a captain's bedroom, you'll find me just so on the bed. If there's not a bed, I'll be on the couch. If there's not a couch…I'm not sure. I'll probably be lounging on a floor somewhere. Now, if you decide to use it for business presentations you *can* toggle me off, but otherwise, Junior's pretty happy in there."

He grasped her hands in his, dragging her attention from the holo ship and the miniature waving naked version of himself.

"Kennedy, I'm yours. You've made my life infinitely better in ways I never deserved, and I'm yours whatever it means. I don't give a shit about official institutions, but if they matter to you, okay. I never had a mother—I was raised by nannies and instructors and bots—so I don't have any kind of reference, good or bad, for what a marriage is supposed to look like. Then again, I don't have a reference for what any kind of stable, long-term relationship is supposed to look like. I've been making it up as I go this whole time.

"Anyway, I figure I'll keep doing that. If you want to get married, okay. I'm in. If you instead want to bail on civic responsibility and run off to Requi before the Anadens get here, okay. If you want to move back to Houston to be closer to your family…" he gazed at the ceiling "…okay. What matters is you. Me with you. Because…." He gestured at the tiny, still-naked him occupying the holo ship. And his tattoo.

She brought a hand to her mouth to cover a gasp, which if she wasn't careful was going to be followed by a sob. She breathed in; she needed to hold herself together for another minute.

"Before I say…things about that, I got you something, too. It's not nearly so shiny or sexy or spectacular, but…." She reached into her pocket and retrieved the disk, then handed it to him.

He stared down at it.

"You don't need to read it right now or—it's an irrevocable bequeath of all rights and ownership of Connova to you on my death or incapacitation. The company, its patents, designs, contracts, everything. None of it will go to my family. It all goes to you. This is the legacy I care about, and you're the only person I trust with it. So now it's yours, no matter what happens."

His throat worked. "Kennedy, I—first off, you're not going to die, so stop being morbid." He spun away from her. "You seriously trust me with this? Above everyone else?" His voice sounded shaky.

"You're the *only* person I trust with it. And this isn't the sole copy. The document's on file and recorded and everything. It's legally airtight." She walked around to face him.

She'd seen this look etched on his features once before—in Seattle, at the end of the Metigen war, in a hotel room. Stark, raw honesty.

"I don't deserve it."

"You do."

"Well, you're a lot smarter than me, so I guess I'll have to defer to your judgment." He smiled, and one or the other of them rushed into the other's arms. His lips devoured hers, and he was so very good at devouring.

When he came up for air, he was wearing a funny expression. He started to say something, then scrunched his nose up instead.

She did the same. "What?"

"I'm, um…so do you want to get married, or not? I know I said it doesn't matter, and I meant it. But I sort of feel as if we should go one way or the other, you know? So we can get on with this 'rest of our lives' stuff."

She dropped her hands from him to turn away, genuinely flummoxed by the question. *Did* she? Fantasy dreams competed with wild but real dreams in her mind, and finally she chuckled to herself as she turned back around.

"Can we...not, and take a honeymoon like we did?"

His eyes widened briefly in advance of his playful smirk. "Oh, yes, we can. Is that what you truthfully want? Because god help me, but what I want is for you to be happy. Also vacations, certainly. I am a fan of vacations and happiness."

She cackled and pulled him to her. "It is. I don't want to be my parents any more than you want to be your dad. Let's keep blazing our own path—which includes a beach, lots of fruity drinks and nudity. Life-sized nudity, though Junior can come, too."

"Oh, you are so the woman for me."

"Damn straight I am."

Vii interrupted them. 'I do apologize—this reunion is beautiful, truly—but unfortunately I believe your not-a-honeymoon will need to be postponed.'

ℛ

Even before she reached true awareness, Morgan knew she wasn't alone in her mind.

She awakened to a sense of *otherness* enveloping her. Of watchfulness. But it felt kind, bordering on gentle. And intensely familiar.

Stanley? How are you here? I thought you were...gone.

I have always been here, Morgan. You simply weren't ready to see me.

That doesn't make any sense.

Of course it does. The mind is a complicated yet highly nuanced organism.

Huh. And by your way of thinking, now I am ready to see you?

Now you needed to see me.

Well, that's rather selfish of me, isn't it?

I don't mind. You are who you are, and I accept a few selfish tendencies as part of the whole person. However, I would prefer it if you didn't try to 'kill' me this time. I will hide again if I must, but I found it dreary.

Ah, there's the dry humor. Yep, this is definitely you. But...how do I not kill you again? I mean, I didn't intend to the first time. It just sort of happened, so I'm not sure what to do differently.

I think we will be fine. I will endeavor to be more assertive when I feel pressured into submission, but I suspect it will not often be necessary. Brooklyn has softened you—softened your heart, which is as important to your consciousness as your mind. Symbolically speaking.

I want to argue with you in righteous indignation, but you're right. Evil woman.

And there is your humor. I fancy her quite a lot, by the way, so don't run her off.

So do I. If I can keep you around, maybe I can manage to keep her, too.

She blinked—in her mind, which was when she became aware of the fact her eyes were not open. She'd forgotten about the outside world. *There was a...not an accident. I was attacked. I'm guessing I was hurt.*

You were. But you're better, and you will be better still soon. Now, time is running short. So let's rejoin the living, shall we?

She forced her real eyes open in the real world. Thank god the room was only dimly lit, as the light there was promptly stabbed into her brain like icicles wielded by a gleeful madman.

After a few seconds she remembered how to squint; she gazed around to see Harper sitting beside the bed, her hands folded in her lap and her chin lowered. Deep in thought, or deep in brooding.

Morgan worked moisture into her mouth. "Hey."

Harper jumped halfway out of the chair, but quickly recovered to lean forward and clasp her hand. Blue eyes always so guarded and wary shone openly as she smiled. "You...you're awake? I mean, you're awake!"

"Yep...." Morgan grimaced and tried to adjust her position in the bed. "Ow. Well, this already sucks."

"Do you want me to get a medic?"

"God, no." She glanced down and was surprised to see both of her legs encased in medwraps, one substantially more bulky than the other. On the one hand, this should mean she hadn't been gone for months or years—on the other hand, what was wrong with her legs? "Um, am I all right? Because I look like a reanimated mummy."

Harper chuckled. "You will be all right. You mostly are now. Your head was the hardest part to set straight."

"I understand you went to some extreme measures to make certain it got fixed."

Harper stared at her askance. "How could you possibly know that? You've been awake for ten seconds."

"It appears I once again have a smartass Artificial in my head whispering all the secrets to me."

"It really did work, then?"

"Looks like." She studied Harper, suddenly nervous. "I don't think he's going away this time. Are you comfortable with that?"

"Seeing as I'm the one who put him there." Harper stood and leaned in to bring her lips to Morgan's ear. "He brought you back to me. I adore him."

So that felt warmer and more wonderful than pretty much anything in the world...

...and an alert from Alex crashed the party, banging around all loud and rude in her head. She winced. "Can I walk?"

Harper stepped away, adopting a suspicious countenance. "If you take it slow and cautious and accept a bit of help, I think so. Why?"

She pushed herself to a sitting position and dragged her legs over the edge of the bed. "You and I have a war to go fight."

PART VIII:

KAIROS

"Fairy tales are more than true; not because they tell us that dragons exist, but because they tell us that dragons can be beaten."

— Neil Gaiman

AMARANTHE

60

MOSAIC

Alex would have run to embrace her mother, if she could run. Instead, she threw the untapped energy into the fervency of the hug when her mother reached her. "One hell of a fleet you've got here."

The ships from Aurora had traversed the Metis portal to gather in strength inside the Mosaic, and the *Siyane* joined them while they waited for the last formations to arrive. The combined Alliance, Federation and AEGIS vessels took up the entire lobby space, and in damn impressive fashion.

"You're alive, again. I fear I'm starting to sound like a looped recording."

"I am. I guess dumping the Machim data on you without so much as a 'hi' to go with it might have caused some concern."

"A little." Her mother drew back, and her expression immediately darkened. "And I suspect with good reason. You look awful. What happened?"

"It's a long story—one that includes the reason for the lack of a 'hi'—but it doesn't matter now. I'll be fine."

Miriam arched an eyebrow, and Alex folded under the weight of it. She supposed she did share traumatic experiences with her mother these days.

"Okay, the short version: Caleb and I were captured stealing the Machim data, taken to a Praesidis interrogation facility and tortured for information. Valkyrie, Mesme and Eren rescued us."

"Dear lord, Alex. Is that all?"

We could tell her about the crippling anxiety and despair I experienced while I was cut off from you, unable to help you or even find out if you were alive or dead.

Or we could not. And it wasn't crippling—you acted superbly.

Yes, but it was hard.

"Also, who's Eren?"

"Mom, there is so much I want to tell you, and I promise I will. But enemy warships speeding toward us?"

"Right. Of course." She frowned over Alex's shoulder. "Does Caleb know he's got a sort of red aura surrounding him?"

She cringed and glanced at Caleb as well. He was hanging back, keeping his distance from other people and trying to be inconspicuous, though the preoccupied look on his face suggested he was silently talking to multiple people nonetheless.

"Yeah, he knows. He got dosed by another Inquisitor—a powerful one, apparently. Hopefully the effect will settle down after a while, but we're not certain what the higher concentration of *diati* means for him."

"I'm sorry."

"No, don't be. We never would've been able to escape from that captivity I don't have time to tell you more about if he hadn't trounced the Inquisitor. It's complicated, but the power's a good thing."

Miriam nodded in seeming acceptance. "All right. I trust your judgment"

Alex started to bask in the compliment, then remembered her mother probably *shouldn't* trust it. "Listen, I heard about the Rifter problem. In retrospect, I obviously didn't run the equations out far enough. I didn't imagine there would be ramifications so far out." She cringed. "In my defense, time was short and I wasn't at my best? Still, I feel terrible about it."

"Your less-than-best saved my life, and it's going to save a lot of lives today. Besides, we got it sorted." She squeezed Alex's shoulder warmly. "So, no time. What's the situation?"

"The Machim fleet should reach the Provision Network Gateway in about an hour and twenty minutes. We have a lot to do between now and then."

"You have a plan, and it involves something more devious than simply continuing on through the enormous blue portal my scouts tell me is up ahead a bit."

"I do, and it does. What's the range on your negative energy missiles?"

"Twelve and a half megameters."

Valkyrie did the math, and Alex prevaricated. "If we hightail it as soon as they launch, we'll be able to clear the blast radius. I need to borrow five of your Eidolons, each one loaded up with those missiles. Also, I need two missiles for the *Siyane*."

"Done. See Commander Lekkas for details on the Eidolons. What about the other forty-eight thousand ships I went to all the trouble of bringing?"

Alex smiled.

She found Morgan in aft Logistics, lying in a reclined seat and surrounded by a revolving sphere of holos. One leg was encased in a thick gel casing; the other leg and an arm were wrapped in less-cumbersome flex medwraps.

Alex made a face as she reached the periphery of the sphere. "What happened to you?"

Morgan scowled at her in return. "What happened to *you?*"

"Got tortured by an Anaden prison drone for eighteen hours."

"Nice. Montegreu's rogue AI tried to kill me by crashing my skycar into the side of a high-rise. Stanley had to bring me out of a coma."

"Stanley? But I thought...."

Morgan rolled her eyes. "Turns out rumors of his demise had been greatly exaggerated."

Alex decided to just go with it for now. "Interesting. I'm here about some Eidolons."

"I heard." Morgan spread the fingers on her right hand and the holos flared out into a line in front of her. "Meet ESC Flight One-Alpha, -Bravo, -Charlie, -Delta and -Epsilon. ESC One, meet Alex Solovy and Valkyrie."

Alex: Those aren't exactly inventive names.

Morgan: They're young and not overly sentimental. But they're real, so respect them.

Valkyrie: Wait—these Artificials are ships?

Morgan: Yes, they are. And your doppelganger helped to create them.

Valkyrie: Vii gave life to Artificials in the form of ships? That's...magnificent.

Alex: Stop squealing, Valkyrie. We have work to do.

Valkyrie: I don't squeal.

Alex: Uh-huh.

"Hello, everyone. My mother—Commandant Solovy—has authorized the five of you to help me execute a crucial opening move against the approaching Machim fleet. Are you game?"

They didn't have vocal transmission capability, but the affirmations rang through in her head. She smiled, sensing their enthusiasm and Valkyrie's in turn.

"Excellent. Meet me at the coordinates Valkyrie is providing to you in twenty-five minutes. Full stealth and noetic communications only."

She waved at Morgan. "See you on the other side."

"What are the odds?"

Alex gazed around the logistics center. Outside of Morgan's holo bubble, military officers worked purposefully at banks upon banks of screens and virtual modules.

She thought about how the bridge had buzzed with activity and vigor, and about the tens of thousands of warships gathering around the *Stalwart II*. Many boasted hyper-advanced designs, the end result of her mother, Kennedy and countless others having innovated around adiamene, quantum spaces, Artificials and Prevos in ways she never could have fathomed.

"I'd say the odds are pretty damn good."

61

PROVISION NETWORK GATEWAY

MILKY WAY SECTOR 41

"All vessels to full alert. Shields to maximum." It was overkill in the extreme, but so was loading his ships up with a hundred Igni missiles. The Katasketousya fielded no military; they had no internalized concept of violence and no way to commit it upon others.

But a lack of preparation was an unforced error waiting to happen, and Casmir did not take chances. No Machim did.

Something else he did not do was question his Primor, which rendered the internal dialogue moot in any event.

They approached the Provision Network Gateway and found the region surrounding it empty. The colossal portal hung quietly in space. During the time it had been within sensor range, no vessels had traversed it, which could be a sign something was amiss.

He checked Ziton, who stood stoically off to the side of the bridge overlook, but received no indication the Inquisitor desired any particular course of action.

"Tactical, launch a probe through the portal. Before we traverse it, I want to know if there are any traps awaiting us."

"Yes, sir."

The probe pierced the Gateway silently. Its presence failed to set off any attacks or explosions. It returned ten seconds later and transmitted nominal readings: empty, normal and unpopulated space beyond the barrier.

"Squads MW R14-20 and 21, proceed through the Gateway to a distance of 0.5 megameters and assume a defensive formation. Squads 22 and 23, prepare to proceed after them. Same directive."

Forty ships neared the portal in precise rows configured to stretch ninety percent of its width. The noses of the vessels comprising the first row began to disappear through the plasma—

—space warped in on itself.

Multiple vortexes formed within the plasma, devouring the bright white-blue energy until the portal grew blacker than the space surrounding it.

The Gateway wrenched apart as its frame buckled and fell into the whirling chasms of negative energy. The ships closest to the Gateway followed, row after row annihilated in the blink of an eye.

Waves of energy surged outward as the very fabric of space-time was dragged in multiple directions, falling into hidden dimensions only to be hurled back out into their own.

Farther from the nucleus of the turbulence, ships began to fall prey to the tremendous forces unleashed like dominoes set in motion, and the viewport lit up in the fire of engine core explosions.

Casmir should not have hesitated to act; military commanders must never hesitate. But the attack—if that's what it was—did not seem possible. Ambushes such as this did not happen.

He blinked. "All back full, all formations!"

He felt the propulsion strain against the weakening but still tenacious waves. His Imperium was positioned near the rear of his forces, and many of the vessels ahead proved unable to elude the chaos. He could only watch on as they succumbed to a kind of slow-motion dismemberment.

Fifteen megameters reversed, they finally pulled free of the perturbations. "Regiment captains, report in."

Dismay overtook him as the damage reports rolled in. He'd just lost over a third of his forces, with another quarter hobbled. The Provision Network Gateway was gone, rendering his mission a failure before it had begun.

And he had no idea who or what had struck at them.

"Sir, I've got multiple readings centered S 90° 21′ z E, four megameters distance and closing."

The bridge shuddered. Had they been *fired on*? "All Regiments, battle stations!" He expanded the radar in front of him and was greeted with a multitude of contacts.

The helmsman cleared his throat. "Navarchos, is that...an armada of warships?"

Casmir's mind threatened to reel from the successive shocks. It had been two centuries since he'd faced an ambush, and for his memory never one of this fashion. But he was an elasson-rank Machim, bred and molded to be the most formidable and stalwart of combatants.

His jaw locked into resilience. "We must assume it is."

"But...whose?"

62

AFS STALWART II

MILKY WAY SECTOR 41

The remains of the Machim fleet, vaunted for its structure and order as much as for its size, lay strewn haphazardly across six megameters of space in front of Miriam.

The Provision Network Gateway, a marvel of construction millennia beyond anything humans could create hung in shambles behind said fleet, ripped apart at a particle level by twenty-two 5,000-kilotonne equivalent negative energy bombs.

She allowed herself a small, private smile of satisfaction, then swiftly banished any glee-like sentiments and imposed combat decorum on herself once more. The element of surprise and the confusion it sowed only worked if they capitalized on it.

Commandant Solovy: "All Class A weapons free. Class B and C weapons are to be used solely within their safety parameters. Take out as many enemy vessels as possible before they recover and reform ranks. Go on the offensive and thin the herd."

She switched to the command channel. *"Marshal Bastian, sensors indicate the spatial disruptions from the negative energy bombs have dissipated. Stealth and swing your forces around behind the enemy vessels."*

Field Marshal Bastian (SFS Medici): "Solid copy."

Stealth on a dreadnought. Add it to the list of concepts thought impossible a short year ago. It burned too much power to use during weaponized combat, but in short spurts, especially to conceal tactical movements, it represented a potent tool that stood to redefine the role of dreadnoughts in warfare.

Commandant Solovy: "Admiral Rychen, give the enemy a set of big targets to shoot at so they don't notice the Field Marshal's flanking maneuver."

She wasn't throwing Rychen, his impressive new dread-nought, the *EAS Virginia,* and those under his command to the wolves. Alliance warships were and had always been the sturdiest vessels built. Now more than ever, they should be able to weather the assault.

Admiral Rychen (EAS Virginia): *"Eager to do so."*

Back to the all-forces channel.

Commandant Solovy: *"AEGIS 1ˢᵗ and 2ⁿᵈ Assault Brigades, swarm at will. 3rd Assault Brigade, glue yourselves to the Imperium currently located at the marked coordinates. Sabres, let the fighters shield you while you fire from a distance. Remaining formations, assign yourselves enemy battlecruisers and destroyers and go to work."*

If all those moves progressed smoothly, the Machim contingent may never successfully reform into proper lines, but she didn't dare hope for it to be so easy. "Thomas, what are we looking at? Talk numbers to me."

'Nearly three thousand battlecruisers, nine thousand destroyers, thirty-five hundred specialized vessels and approximately eighty thousand fighter-type craft.'

Based on Alex's figures, this meant the enemy was down thirty-five to forty percent of its ships. Scanning the scene out the wraparound viewport, she shuddered to think how the entire contingent would have looked. As it was, the Machim ships were a horde clogging the void.

She tracked a number of early AEGIS victories in the opening salvos while the enemy struggled to reorganize and properly engage their attackers. Another twelve percent of the enemy formations went down in the first minute, primarily due to the ability of the Sabres to unleash their considerable firepower unopposed.

At eight hundred meters in length and only sixty meters width, the vessels were glorified flying plasma railguns, staffed by less than a dozen personnel and an Artificial. The flipside to the armament-heavy design was a dearth of defensive shielding, and

criminally thin sheets of adiamene represented the Sabres' primary protection.

A massive explosion cascaded in the region designated Quadrant Five, off her starboard. She glanced at her XO. "Report."

"One of the Machim cruisers fired what was likely an Igni
missile. One hundred sixty-four Federation vessels and ninety-
eight AEGIS vessels are unaccounted for."

She exhaled. That was a lot of ships taken out in one hit. So
the Machim commander was going to use the missiles intended
for the portals against them instead.

Well, the news couldn't all be good, could it?

Commandant Solovy: *"All ships. Artificials need to monitor
nearby battlecruisers for Igni missile launches—the launch profile is
being distributed now. When such a launch is detected, immediately
disengage from your targets and evade at maximum velocity until
you're outside the range of the projected blast radius. Once the Igni
missile has detonated, reengage. Vessels operating on the active
perimeter, spread out. Extend the battlefield, and let's buy everyone
some space."*

There was nothing she could do for a ship targeted by one of
the missiles—no shield or adiamene hull was capable of surviving
a point-blank antimatter explosion—but she could save many
ships that would otherwise be caught in the blasts.

Mnemosyne's intel, as relayed by Alex earlier, suggested the
Machim forces carried one hundred of the forbidding missiles in
their arsenal. Perhaps some had been destroyed in the Gateway
explosion, but she couldn't afford to count on it.

Her orders should lessen the collateral damage, but the use by
the enemy of anything close to a hundred of the missiles stood to
wipe out her armada. And she had no way to know which of the
three thousand odd battlecruisers carried them.

...Or did she? "Reconnaissance, launch an additional set of
probes to the periphery of the combat zone. Have them focus on
the movements and energy signatures of the Machim battlecruisers. Feed all the data into the Connexus."

The Connexus was a micro-Noesis of sorts, a mindspace shared by the Artificials and Prevos serving in AEGIS. They had formed it on their own initiative and, since the Prevos involved were military first, instituted their own strict security measures to keep it private and protected.

'Very clever, Commandant.'

She appreciated that she didn't need to explain her idea to Thomas. "Do you think the Connexus will be able to identify enough of a variation?"

'Given the significant size and weight of the missiles, I estimate a 43% probability, in 52% to 68% of the targets, which is—'

"Better than nothing." She cringed inwardly as another explosion flared on the far side of the engagement zone. The small perceived size due to its distance belied the damage she knew it had caused. "Unfortunately, they need to hurry."

Admiral Rychen (Virginia): *"That left a mark. Not to give them ideas, but why don't they simply fire all the Igni missiles and be done with us?"*

Commandant Solovy: *"Cascading explosions of such magnitude will take out most of their vessels in addition to ours. It's a suicidal tactic."*

Alexis Solovy: *"The Machim Navarchos will sacrifice his entire fleet in a heartbeat if it means victory. They view their ships and crew as disposable, because, well, they kind of are. No, it's something else."*

Miriam smiled. She might chide Thomas later for giving Valkyrie access to the command channel, but...probably not.

Commandant Solovy: *"Hello, Alex. Brilliant job at the Gateway."*

Alexis Solovy: *"Hi, Mom. Thanks for the firepower."*

Commandant Solovy: *"Okay, so it's something else. If we knew what, we may be able to use their reluctance against them."*

Thomas (Transcendentally Hallowed Overlord of the Milky Way, AEGIS Sector): *'They expect to be surprised again.'*

She rolled her eyes and quickly deleted the call sign moniker from the system. She was definitely going to chide him for that, however.

Commandant Solovy: "What do you mean?"

Thomas: 'You have caught them unawares twice in a row. They are accounting for the non-negligible possibility you will do so a third time. In such a scenario they will want to have their remaining missiles on hand in case the weapons are needed to counter the new threat, the nature of which is, by definition, unknown.'

Admiral Rychen (Virginia): "Good. It means we've already earned their respect."

'The Connexus has identified the fifty-four Machim battle-cruisers likeliest to be carrying Igni missiles based on anomalies in their movements and engine output.'

"Excellent work." They weren't all accounted for, but each missile disabled in a contained manner was a win.

Now she switched to the *Stalwart II's* internal comm channel and contacted Logistics on Deck 5. "Commander Lekkas, has ESC Flight One returned intact and unharmed from its mission?"

"It has indeed."

"Good to hear. See that they're resupplied, then have them join up with Flights Two and Three to drop targeted negative energy bombs on top of the battlecruisers marked by the Connexus. We need to take those craft out before they decide to fire their Igni missiles."

"Fun. We are on it."

Admiral Rychen (Virginia): "It's starting to resemble a stalemate out here. Other than the Sabres, our weapons aren't causing enough damage to do more than whittle down their still ridiculous numbers. Any chance we do have a third surprise?"

Alexis Solovy: "Oh, yes."

Commandant Solovy: "Alex...."

Alexis Solovy: "Don't freak out, Commandant Solovy, but you might want to look to your...right."

Miriam's gaze darted to her right automatically, assuming Alex meant on the bridge. Her daughter was a ship junkie; if Alex had meant to the right of the ship, she would've said 'starboard.'

She didn't freak out at the sight of the Metigen swirling into solidity beside her, because 'freaking out' was not something she did. Ever. In fact, she even waved down the two MPs who had leapt to attention.

"Mnemosyne?"

I am known as Lakhes, Commandant Solovy.

She'd learned quite a bit about the Katasketousya in the last couple of months. "You're the leader."

An imprecise characterization, but it suffices. I recognize you have no time for idle consultation, so I am here only to convey this message to you: our vessels are at your disposal.

"Your—"

"Commandant, we're picking up multiple new energy signatures eight megameters distant past Quadrant Four."

"I need a visual."

A new feed materialized in front of her to zoom past the chaos of the ongoing conflict. Out of the darkness a host of ships emerged from her nightmares—from most humans' nightmares.

Column after column of superdreadnoughts entered the engagement zone as hundreds of thousands of swarmers detached and sped straight into the melee.

She spun to Lakhes. "What is this?"

They fight for you, and with you. On this you have my word.

A little warning would have been nice, and might have prevented a few heart attacks which were likely just suffered out among the crews.

Miriam drew in a breath and activated the all-forces channel once more.

Commandant Solovy: "All ships and all personnel. The superdreadnoughts and their swarmers are allies. Do not fire upon them. I say again: do not fire upon the Metigen vessels. They are here to...help us."

She turned back to her unexpected guest, and found that a second Metigen had joined Lakhes on the bridge.

Hyperion commands our vessels and will see to any tactical requests you have for them to perform. I wish you victory, Commandant. For all our sakes.

Lakhes faded away, leaving Miriam standing facing the Metigen who had orchestrated the slaughter of over fifty million people a short year ago.

There were limits to even deals with the devil, lines which should never be crossed...but she was beginning to wonder when she might find one.

She swallowed past the acrimony in her throat. "Follow the lead of our cruisers in choosing your targets. Fomenting disarray in the enemy ranks is one of our primary goals, and your swarmers are well suited to this task."

Hyperion's form coalesced into an ethereal representation of a giant horned owl. *I understand. Do you have any further guidance you wish to impart?*

"Yes. Betray us, and no corner of this or any other universe will be safe for you."

63

ECS FLIGHT TWO-CHARLIE

MILKY WAY SECTOR 41

Tricky task, placing a negative energy bomb with high precision and slipping away before it detonated and took you out along with the target.

The target in question was invariably moving, of course, so proper placement required analyzing its trajectory and historical movements and predicting where it would be in another five seconds. Except this was a space battle—a tremendous, unprecedented and chaotic space battle, to be more accurate—so the targets rarely moved in a *straight line.*

Seeing as she had hitched a mental ride and wasn't actually doing any of that difficult work, Morgan took the opportunity to soak in the ambiance of the clashes going on around her.

The amount of debris littering the field surprised her; the fact the vast majority of it originated from the enemy cheered her. The Machim ships were tough and robustly shielded, but with enough firepower applied, they were destructible, and by conventional means.

On the other hand, thanks in part to some creative hit-and-run combat tactics employed by a bunch of not merely unshackled but fucking *unleashed* Prevos, only the nasty Igni missiles had managed to take out more than the odd, unlucky AEGIS vessel. Missiles she and her little cadre of Artificial ships were here to remove from the field of play. Go adiamene.

Do you wish you were piloting for real? Your adrenaline level is well below its typical level during hostile engagements, and I seem to recall you enjoying the rush.

Sure I do, Stanley. But supervising isn't so bad—and being able to relax and soak in the view isn't terrible, either. Besides, yesterday I was in a coma, and I suspect you, Harper, the doctors and half the Connexus would kill me if I tried to get in a cockpit today.

We would probably opt for tranquilization rather than murder, but for certain.

The Eidolon she vicariously inhabited—ECS Flight Two-Charlie by name—glided unseen beneath the hull of a mammoth battlecruiser. The vessel cut an imposing profile, but mostly it was ugly. The Anadens, or at a minimum their Machim branch, clearly had no sense of style or panache. Not when it came to starships, anyway. She'd reserve judgment on their style in other venues, but she didn't harbor high expectations.

HarperRF: How are you doing?

Commander Lekkas: Flying around leaving surprise gifts for a few select Machim battlecruisers—virtually, so don't freak out. My weak and kitteny body is still safe in its lounge chair on the Stalwart II.

HarperRF: Kitteny? Really, Lekkas?

Commander Lekkas: I'm simply trying to entice you. How are you doing?

HarperRF: Hunting for something to land on while Malcolm shoots at all the ships. Do you think you could convince Solovy to let us infiltrate the Imperium?

Commander Lekkas: Not today, I'm afraid. Do what I'm doing and appreciate the show.

HarperRF: But I want to stab one of these assholes with my fancy new blade. Or twenty of them.

Commander Lekkas: You do realize they just come back to life in a lab somewhere, right?

HarperRF: Then I'll find them there and stab them again.

Commander Lekkas: That's my girl.

The hull shuddered as the force from the detonation of the negative energy bomb they had placed earlier washed over it. But it was hardly a tickle as she, Stanley and Charlie wove through the acrobatic symphony of combat in its highest form on the way to their next target.

SIYANE

MILKY WAY SECTOR 41

"There. Thirty or so degrees starboard. One of their strike fighters looks as if it's trying to sneak up the ass of one of our…did they call them Sabres?"

"I see it." Alex let Valkyrie handle the flying while she readied a delicate power-balancing routine that put an extra *oomph* into the *Siyane's* lasers then pivoted on demand and raised shield strength to maximum. "I desperately want to use the Rifter."

Caleb chuckled. "I know. But we're fighting close. You don't want to accidentally take out one of our own."

He'd been surprised to hear of the unanticipated side effect of the Rifter's energy diversion, but Alex had been shocked…for roughly ten seconds. She'd spent the next thirty minutes muttering on and off about how obvious it was. Easy to say, but many things were obvious in retrospect.

Like the fact the *diati* was without question an intelligent, sentient life form, and as much without question was tied inextricably to the Praesidis bloodline. *His* bloodline. A cold, hard truth he had better find a way to accept, and soon.

After the battle was won sounded like soon enough, though.

He checked his hands and was relieved to find them neither glowing nor trembling. It had taken hours, but he could now feel his body absorbing and incorporating the new *diati's* essence with its brethren, and the process didn't feel as odd, or alien, as it rightly should. The buzzing in his head had also quieted, which meant he could concentrate on other matters, so he filed away the puzzler as something else for soon but later.

He peered out the viewport as they flew deftly through the bedlam, a tiny spec in a sea of starships waging war on one another.

The degree to which their efforts were making an impact on the tide of battle was debatable, but it was important that they help. They'd brought everyone here, after all; by their actions they'd been leading everyone here for more than a year. When the pivotal moment finally arrived, it wasn't like they weren't going to join the fight.

The Machim strike fighter had just opened fire on the Sabre when Valkyrie glued them to the tail of the enemy craft, stealthed, and Alex let loose on it.

The data they'd stolen from Machimis had, among so many other things, enabled them to pinpoint a number of small weaknesses in every Machim vessel's design, and she targeted the small conduit running from the power core to the engine to space. The limited shielding covering the engine's exhaust nozzles and the conduit were two of those weaknesses, and the ship blew apart in seconds.

Alex boosted the *Siyane's* shields—less to protect against return fire, although the Machim weapons were soberingly powerful, and more to protect against the high-velocity debris which resulted. Chunks of metal and multiple dagger-shaped shards bounced off the strengthened shield as they sped away.

She rolled her shoulders gamely. "Next?"

He began scouring the area for another suitable target. "What about—"

A rush of blue-white lights flooded the dark cabin with light, and they both spun around. Unusually for a Kat, the entry appeared more fevered than dramatic, and the lights continued to dart around in agitation following their arrival.

Alex frowned at the vague outline of their visitor. "Who are you?"

She would've checked, and if she didn't recognize its base avatar…. Caleb tensed, instantly on guard. At least one Kat had already turned traitor, and several they knew could not be considered allies.

It is Paratyr. I come to you bearing a dire warning—late, far later than I should. I did not understand.

The identity of the Kat would not have led Caleb to relax in any event, as after the stunt the Sentinel had pulled in the Mirad Vigilate, he didn't trust or particularly care for Paratyr. But the Kat's words removed relaxation as an option.

Alex remained equally perturbed. "How did you find us? You've never been here and we're stealthed—not as if that's stopped half of Amaranthe from randomly showing up in our cabin whenever they feel like it."

Mnemosyne instructed me on how to locate your vessel, but it is not important. You must know this information, and you must know it now.

She nodded. "Okay. Talk."

The Imperium vessel situated at the rear of the Machim fleet carries inside it a weapon which, if detonated, will annihilate every ship, life form and molecule for many parsecs. If not countered, it will then destroy the galaxy, followed by the universe.

64

AFS SARATOGA

Chaos. Mayhem. Pandemonium. Any number of colorful descriptives sprang to Malcolm's mind, yet none did justice to the scene surrounding his ship.

Thrust into the heart of the conflict on Commandant Solovy's command alongside the bulk of the AEGIS fleet, he might even be responsible for a portion of the chaos himself.

The *AFS Saratoga's* primary function was to serve as a troop carrier, and it was presently filled with Marines going stir-crazy on account of having nothing to shoot at. But as a custom-designed AEGIS vessel, it wasn't only a carrier.

The added motive power from the engines of the four modular, detachable transports which made up the bulk of its frame meant that when it was whole, it could *move*. While hardly Sabre-level, the lightweight but precise firepower the modules wielded brought its aggregate weaponry up to respectable status.

Not unlike the ship, Malcolm's primary function was to serve as the AEGIS Marines Director, but it turned out it wasn't his sole function. His time on the *Orion* had earned him a reputation as a fair ship captain, and here, outnumbered and possibly outgunned, they needed every able-bodied ship in the fight.

So here he was, flying through the center of the maelstrom where order had long since departed—because that's where he'd taken the *Saratoga*.

Their current target blew apart from the inside out, and immediately a new one revealed itself through the wreckage. They were finding targeting the engines to be the most effective strategy, though it did tend to create something of a mess. "Frigate due ahead. When you lock on him, Ettore, let's play chicken."

"Yes, sir."

Ettore was a Major in the Earth Alliance, and he was also a Prevo. As of three weeks ago, his Artificial counterpart resided in the walls of the ship.

The arrangement was taking some getting used to, but not because he didn't trust Ettore or the Artificial. Events had taught him the greatest of respect for their capabilities, and while he hadn't worked with Ettore prior to his becoming a Prevo, the man's record was above reproach.

No, the arrangement was taking some getting used to because it upended the traditional roles of everyone on the bridge. There was a navigator in the pit, but the Artificial was really the navigator. Same with weapons and most other positions. The crew wasn't standing around with nothing to do—that honor was reserved for the Marines on the lower decks—but the evolving give-and-take was unfamiliar. New.

It seemed like Malcolm kept trying to settle into the familiar, and 'new' kept kicking down the door.

A shudder chilled his bones as two dozen Metigen swarmers latched onto one of the enemy frigates in their field of view. He accepted the reality that they were fighting on the same side, for their masters were the reason AEGIS existed in the first place. But he would never look kindly upon the monstrous vessels that had killed so many.

A Metigen death beam cut across the viewport to tear into a Machim battlecruiser, reminding him why.

The explosion when the battlecruiser ruptured gained an eerie corona from the detonation of a negative energy bomb beyond it. When the light faded, the Machim Imperium was framed perfectly in the span of the *Saratoga's* viewport.

He watched as it fired on one of the nearby Alliance cruisers. Its shockingly robust weapons ripped through the shielding until the adiamene was under full assault. *Jesus, use your Rifter already!*

A Federation cruiser crossed between them, taking the brunt of the fire for several precious seconds—then the chaos of the battle swallowed up his view of the engagement.

In the corner of his vision an entire regiment of Federation ships vanished under the blast of an Igni missile. The Eidolons were taking out the battlecruisers suspected of carrying the anti-matter weapons as fast as they could get to them. But, perhaps realizing what was happening, the missiles were being deployed with increasing frequency.

Intel suggested the Imperium carried at least ten of the Igni missiles, yet thus far it had used none of them. It was a hulking tank of a warship, and no AEGIS weapons were touching it, including Sabres. A negative energy bomb couldn't touch it—though twenty-two such bombs surely would, as the obliteration of the Provision Network Gateway had demonstrated. But they couldn't get close enough.

The source of the problem and the cause of all these failures was an impregnable physical force field encasing the Imperium. It stopped any missile, energy or vessel cold a hundred meters out from the hull, yet allowed the ship's own weapons to pass through unhindered.

His hand came to his jaw as a certifiably crazy idea popped into his head. What if....

"Major Ettore, how would you like to take a whack at the impossible?"

"No such thing any longer, sir."

Wasn't that the truth. "Let's try to prove it. See the Imperium out there? Tell me where we need to be situated so that, when it fires on us, our Dimensional Rifter will send its fire back out through an exit rift which will open about five centimeters off its lower stern hull. Right where the schematics we have say the weapons bay is located."

Ettore whistled. "Captain Casales, you have full weapons control for a minute. We're going to be a bit busy."

"Copy, Major."

It took almost twenty seconds—an eternity for a Prevo—but a set of coordinates appeared on Malcolm's primary screen. Ettore stood and came up beside him. "As the Imperium moves, these are going to change slightly. We can adjust on the fly, but I need to have navigational control during the attack."

"Understood." Malcolm paused. They'd explicitly been given free rein to act as they saw fit, but…. He activated one of the many comm channels operating during the campaign.

Brigadier Jenner: "Commandant, I have an idea for a way to take out the Imperium. Major Ettore, the Saratoga's *Prevo, thinks we can pull it off."*

Commandant Solovy (Stalwart II): "Will you be sacrificing yourself in the process, Brigadier?"

He needed to survive and get back home, as he had a date, an apology and a slate of soul-baring confessionals to finish—but if he wanted to survive to do those things, he didn't dare dwell on them now. He'd forced thoughts of Mia from his mind when the first shot was fired, and they had to stay there until the last one landed.

Brigadier Jenner: "Not part of the plan, ma'am."

Commandant Solovy (Stalwart II): "Excellent. Then I won't delay you asking for details. See what you can do—"

Alexis Solovy: "Wait! You can't blow up the Imperium!"

Malcolm's brow creased in surprise. *"Alex?"*

SIYANE

MILKY WAY SECTOR 41

Commandant Solovy (Stalwart II): "Alex, what do you know?"

She eyed the Kat currently gracing her cabin. *"There's some kind of black hole generator weapon onboard the Imperium."*

The silence before her mother responded lasted less than a second. *"Hold on."*

Then, still on the command channel: *"Admiral Rychen, you have fleet command. I'll update you momentarily. Brigadier Jenner, back off of the Imperium. I will loop you into a holocomm in ten seconds."*

It only took eight, during which time Alex played observer to Valkyrie prioritizing and cross-referencing two universes' worth of knowledge on black holes, their creation, destruction and weaponization while Caleb flew them out of the fray, to the extent such a place of safety existed.

The holocomm request came in, and they moved to the data table.

Miriam looked to be in the office situated off the *Stalwart II's* bridge, but she hadn't taken the time to sit. "Can I assume a 'black hole generator' is more or less what it sounds like?"

"Yes, but it's worse than that."

"Alex, how could it *possibly* be worse than the enemy opening up a black hole in the middle of the battlefield?"

She laughed; it had been a hellacious two days, and she just couldn't help it. "Apparently, this weapon doesn't merely create a black hole—it then fuels the black hole so it grows larger and larger, enabling it to draw the surrounding space into an ever-expanding vortex."

"Oh. I see. That is worse. Is there no way to shut it down?"

"No way we have for damn sure. But allegedly the Anadens do have a way to halt its growth, which is why we need to consider the possibility that they will use it should they decide the battle is unwinnable."

Malcolm had been conferring with an officer but now returned his attention to the conference. "All the more reason to destroy the Imperium before they have a chance to make that decision."

Miriam shook her head. "They're already losing. Once the command ship starts to take damage, they may go ahead and activate the device."

"No, our idea would in theory destroy it quickly enough the captain won't have time to react."

Caleb leaned into the table. "Alex got the download from your Prevo. It's a brilliant tactical move, Colonel—sorry, Brigadier. We've been gone. But you can't risk the attack while this weapon is on board."

Malcolm stared at Caleb in something akin to surprise for a second, but shook it off. "You're afraid the device will activate, detonate, explode, whatever it's designed to do, when the ship does. But if they've been flying around with it in the hold all this time, it has to be reasonably stable, doesn't it?"

More blue-white lights marked Mesme's arrival; it was beginning to resemble a damn circus in the *Siyane's* cabin. She lifted her hands in question. "Where have you been?"

Occupied. The Anadens include among their number many skilled and knowledgeable scientists. However, my colleagues in the Idryma know more about manipulating cosmic forces than any Anaden who has ever lived. They apprehend several ways to deliberately bring about the creation of a black hole. None are free of risk and most are highly volatile. However safe the Anadens believe their device to be, they are incorrect.

It was a forceful speech, but in typical fashion Mesme had circled around the crux of the issue. "So if the ship blows, the device will blow?"

Without knowing what method they have devised to power this Tartarus Trigger, we calculate at 36.21% the likelihood of this occurring.

Malcolm ran a hand through his hair. "And if the ship blows because the Igni missiles detonate?"

Their antimatter weapons? The likelihood approaches one hundred percent.

"Yeah, that's what I thought you were going to say."

Miriam drummed her fingers on the edge of her desk. "So if we ignore the Imperium and eliminate enough of their vessels to be considered victors, they may use the device, presumably ordering someone else to get here and shut the black hole down before it consumes the rest of the galaxy. Alex, as you pointed out earlier, they consider themselves expendable.

"If we destroy the Imperium, we probably set off the device and it destroys all of us at a minimum and possibly everyone. And we aren't so expendable." She sighed. "I'd like to hear Rychen's opinion, but someone's got to fight the damn battle underway out there. Brigadier, don't say Field Marshal Bastian—I've never seen him in action before, and I don't trust him enough. Not yet."

Malcolm looked as if he was trying not to smile. "Yes, ma'am."

Miriam surveyed those present. "Ideas?"

Valkyrie?

All my potential ideas thus far end in widespread destruction when a simulation is run.

Awesome.

Caleb was pacing with notable fervency, popping in and out of their holo projection. "Jenner, do you have *any* viable plan to get a team onto the Imperium? Even a stealth team of three or four people?"

Malcolm chuckled wryly. "Harper would dearly love to try it—but no. The force field is both physically and energetically impenetrable. Opening a rift inside the field is the only means of entry I can see and...well, I don't think we've figured out how to send people along for the ride quite yet."

"True." Caleb rubbed at his jaw. "Okay, what about—"

I will do it.

Everyone turned to Mesme, but Alex asked the obvious question. "Do what?"

The vessel's shield is indomitable here in physical space, but it is not pandimensional. I will access the vessel, locate the device and transport it away from the conflict.

Miriam frowned. "You can move so large an object? I mean, I assume it's fairly large."

Caleb nodded. "Mesme carried the *Siyane* through two Mosaic lobbies, a portal and a planetary atmosphere when...it was disabled." He stepped back, out of the holocam's range, and winked at her.

Alex was utterly gobsmacked. She had never imagined he would forgive her so completely. She hoped the kilometer-wide smile she flashed him said all she couldn't right now—then she hurriedly tried to look grave for the others. "Mesme, where will you take it?"

Away. The location is not important for now.

Given the nature of Mesme's existence and physicality, it should be a safe endeavor for the Kat. It didn't feel safe. "Are you certain?"

The violence all around us clashes and tears and threatens to shatter the world. It is abhorrent to me, and I ache to flee even now. But you called me brave. I do not know if you are correct, but if I do not step forward and do this, I will surely prove you wrong. Yes, I am certain.

65

IMPERIUM

A lex scouted ahead for Mesme via sidespace; it seemed the least she could do. Besides, a bunch of shining lights flickering to and fro would set off alarms followed by a cascade of calamitous events, so someone needed to find this evil little world-ending device before Mesme moved in.

She didn't have a visual of it to go by, but Paratyr had seen the Tartarus Trigger on one of the Mirad Vigilate's sidespace windows and had described it in detail. Thirty meters long, twelve meters wide. Shiny chrome. Suspended in a rack. Got it.

In a perfect world, she'd scrupulously observe the inner workings of this crucial enemy vessel, then pass the intel on for use in future battles. Instead, she sped through hallways and careened around corners with her mind, forcing her focus to dash ahead in leaps on the hunt for a single visual frame.

She found the suspension rack in the weapons bay, empty. Well, that wasn't good.

It only took her another few seconds to find the device from there—in a damn torpedo launch tube. They were actually considering using the *yebanaya* thing.

Bully on her for insightful analysis in predicting their behavior, but my god their adversary was fucking unhinged.

Valkyrie, mark our spot on the schematic and get it to Mesme. Mesme?

I have the location.

It looks rather tight in this tube. Can you manage to fit around the cylinder?

I can manage much.

She was pretty sure her eyes rolled in the *Siyane's* cockpit chair. *I assume that's a yes. The good news is, you shouldn't be seen, as there are no passages for people or drones down here. Whenever you're ready.*

The dark tube began lighting up almost immediately, but the points of light quavered and cavorted as Mesme struggled to fully envelop its contents. Only a few centimeters of space existed between the cylinder and the walls of the tube...this was going to be close.

Everything vanished. The lights were gone—and so was the device.

Mesme?

She didn't get a response. But the proof lay in the empty tube.

She opened her eyes and hit the comm. "Malcolm, you're clear to go. Good luck."

ᴙ

AFS SARATOGA

MILKY WAY SECTOR 41

"Copy that, and thanks." Malcolm raced through the checklist in his mind. They'd tried to stay roughly in the orbit of the Imperium while the Metigen worked its vanishing trick, but it had proved difficult what with all the warfare.

"All right, everyone, we are a go. Step One: we need to get the Imperium to shoot at us." *And withstand the storm for long enough to take it out.* "Navigation, close to 0.4 megameters distance from the Imperium then turn full control over to Major Ettore. Weapons, open fire on the target like we have nothing to lose. Once it takes the bait, we will pretend to flee and make for the designated coordinates."

The Imperium quickly grew large in the viewport, and he got his first proper view of the vessel. It didn't stretch as long as a

Metigen superdreadnought, but it was both wider and taller, forming a menacing octagon of destructive power.

He exhaled. "Engage."

The *Saratoga's* weapons fire splashed harmlessly off the force field, and several cycles of continuous fire were required for the Imperium to even notice them. But eventually it trained four of its ten powerful beams on them.

The floor began shaking as the defensive shield held off the fire—then the whole ship lurched as the beams broke through to impact the hull.

Major Ettore's voice was strained but steady. "Reversing course. Imperium is tracking, adjusting calculations."

Brigadier Jenner: "All ships. On my mark, get as far away as your engines will carry you from the Imperium. I repeat, prepare to vacate the vicinity of the Imperium at maximum speed."

They lurched again, harder.

"Hull breach on Deck 6! Sealing off Zones 6-C and 6-D."

Two modules met at the junction of 6-C and D; gaps and seams continued to be adiamene's one weakness, though it wasn't a weakness in the metal so much as a necessary weakness of design. And the *Saratoga's* highly modular layout meant it had more seams than most vessels.

"Arriving at coordinates in 3...2...1...full stop."

They lurched in the opposite direction from their momentum, which hurt. Malcolm gave in and grabbed the railing.

Ettore remained seated, eyes closed. "Activate the Dimensional Rifter."

Brigadier Jenner: "All ships, mark!"

The *Saratoga* stilled as the Rifter devoured the onslaught for it. The light from the beams consumed the viewport, so Malcolm enlarged a live scanner image of the Imperium.

A flare of florid orange materialized out of empty space directly beneath the ship, inside the force field. The flare looked pitifully small against the hull of the massive vessel, but it represented 1,500 kilotonnes of concentrated energy leveled at a weak junction. Would it be enough?

Right about now the Machim Navarchos was receiving an avalanche of panicked alerts, which hopefully distracted him from noticing his enemies were vanishing from the area.

Did the Navarchos yet realize it was their own fire being used against them? Without prior knowledge of the Dimensional Rifters, the deductive leaps required for understanding the nature of the attack were great indeed.

And the Navarchos was not going to have the opportunity to make them. The time between when the laser fire bloom altered its shape to surge into a hull fissure and when the Igni missiles detonated was too short for a human mind to measure.

The equation parameters for getting the rift to open where it did were such that the *Saratoga* was already a good distance away from the Imperium. But as space roiled and bucked and the cascading explosions consumed everything in their reach, it didn't feel nearly far enough.

"Reverse thrusters full!"

They fled once more, for real this time. Malcolm didn't begin to relax until they were another eight megameters away from the crux of the blast. He indicated for them to slow and come around to survey the results.

In an almost perfect sphere stretching some four megameters in diameter, nothing remained. Nothing but the void.

66

AFS STALWART II

MILKY WAY SECTOR 41

"So, what now? We won the battle—does this mean we've begun a war?"

Miriam contemplated how to answer the Field Marshal's question, for though delivered in his typically abrupt fashion, it was a valid one.

The remains of the Machim forces had fled in the wake of the Imperium's destruction. Her own forces had then retreated to a secret location several hundred parsecs away to lick their wounds, regroup and determine a path forward.

When she responded, she focused on Alex rather than Bastian. Alex and Caleb had invited themselves to the meeting, and she hadn't argued. She'd take any opportunity to lay eyes on her daughter, safe and alive. If they also had relevant information that could help AEGIS—which they of course did—all the better.

"This was more than a simple victory in a single clash. We demonstrated we can match them—best them—on the field of battle in spite of their superior numbers. When the Machim Navarchos, whoever it is, wakes up in their new body in a medical capsule somewhere across the galaxy, they're going to wake up feeling something I daresay they never have before: humiliation."

Miriam smiled. "Given all that, it would be a travesty for us not to give them a proper war."

"We gained an advantage through trickery."

"And we can do so again."

Not surprisingly, she agreed with Rychen's rebuttal to Bastian's negativity. "Yes, we can. We came here with full recognition any war would not be won with numbers, so the fact it's true changes nothing. We will need to use all our capabilities in order to defeat the enemy, of which trickery is unashamedly one.

"Now, I don't mean to imply any of this will be in any manner easy. We're in an unfamiliar environment populated with technology we've never seen and aliens we've never met. We don't even know what the rules are yet.

"Most of all, we don't know what victory means. The Katasketousya's plea for us to 'defeat' the Anaden Directorate is vague to the point of meaninglessness. If we're fighting a war—which I believe we are—then we need to define its boundaries and its goals."

She clasped her hands on the table. "I realize it's a daunting task and we're all exhausted, so let's start with a few more practical matters. The portal we used to reach Amaranthe is being moved by the Katasketousya as we speak. It and two other portals will continue to be moved every time they are used, so traversals need to be limited and pre-approved. The new locations will be provided to a select group of flag officers on a need-to-know basis."

Brigadier Jenner frowned noticeably. He was a regular attendee of Advisory Board meetings due to his leadership position and would probably be here now even were it not for his brilliant maneuver that took out the Imperium and ended the encounter. Nonetheless, she'd already decided the feat had earned him a permanent seat at the table.

"Are you worried we'll have spies in the AEGIS fleet? Or traitors?"

She forced her gaze to remain locked on Jenner and not drift to Caleb. "I think they look like us, Brigadier. Given this reality, we must take every precaution. A single Anaden finds and traverses a single portal carrying a large enough bomb, and everyone back home dies."

He nodded and sank back in his chair. "Understood."

"Now, we lost over 8,400 ships today, so we need to replenish—"

'I apologize for the interruption, Commandant, but Valkyrie has forwarded a message to me I believe you will find pertinent to your discussion.'

She glanced at Alex, but her daughter only smiled mysteriously. "Go ahead, Thomas."

'The message reads as follows: Sator Danilo Nisi requests the presence of the high commander of the military forces victorious in the hostilities at the Provision Network Gateway, as well as Caleb Marano, Alexis Solovy and the Katasketousya Mnemosyne, at a private meeting to discuss matters of mutual interest. Proceed to MW Sector 33 at your earliest convenience, where additional coordinates will be provided.'

Miriam pursed her lips. Quite the terse 'request.' "And who exactly is Mr. Nisi, to make such demands?"

Alex kicked her chair back away from the table. "The leader of the anarch resistance here in Amaranthe. Looks like you got someone's attention today."

67

SOLUM

Nyx knew the *diati* had not returned to her the instant she awoke in the regenesis capsule following the destruction of Helix Retention. The *diati* hadn't merely deserted her body; it had deserted *her*.

But how? *Why?* She had only ever served it, and served it in exceptional fashion. Who or what was the prisoner that he could strip away both the *diati's* physical bond and its personal allegiance?

The cover slid back, and she forced confidence into her bearing as she sat up and smoothly exited the capsule. Her legs were fine. Her body was fine. The grueling pain her former shell had suffered was a fading memory, soon to vanish on the wind.

Yet she felt...small. Ordinary. The Curative unit didn't seem to notice any difference in her, but it was only a machine. Others would notice, and they would not look so kindly upon her.

Her bones chilled at the notion of her fellow Inquisitors *pitying* her. Her Primor.... No. This could not be her fate.

The Primor's voice whispered to her in her mind as if an answered call. He touched her thoughts with his own, calming her turmoil beneath a soothing caress so compelling it was almost a spiritual experience.

Come to me, Nyx, and do not despair.

⚮

A sensation which must be panic sent Nyx's chest pounding as she prepared to enter the Primor's suite at Praesidis Command. She'd never known panic until now, and she cared not for it.

The amelioration of his mental touch had faded by the time she arrived, leaving behind this atrocious passion of fear heightened by anxiety. He was certain to be so disappointed in her. He might find no worth in her continued existence at all.

Her hands shook—how dare they betray her so brazenly—as she stepped inside to meet her fate.

When his eyes fell upon her, she hung her head. Overtaken by shame, broken by the magnetism of his presence. "Primor. Father. I can't...one of the prisoners, a man, I don't understand...."

He moved without motion, in a breath simply standing before her. His arms wrapped around her and drew her into his embrace. "Shush, my dear. I know what happened, and everything is going to be well. I will restore you. Here, take a measure of mine. I give it freely, and I command it to serve you as it has served me."

Her skin flushed as *diati* surged into her body. Warmth filled her chest and her mind. It felt unfamiliar, not her own, but she welcomed it and it her. In time they would become one.

She blinked, and the world was reborn. Peace returned to her soul, and she gazed upon his face with unabashed devotion. "I will serve you forever, Primor. Ask anything of me."

His hand stroked her cheek, and the skin of his palm glowed against hers as the final traces of *diati* passed from him to her. "Tell me about this man."

Nyx drew her shoulders up to stand tall before him. "I will, father. I will tell you about him, and then I will find him and I will kill him."

68

SIYANE

MILKY WAY SECTOR 33

They took the *Siyane* to the meeting. Showing up in the *Stalwart II* felt like a cheap power play they didn't need to make—plus, there would be all the extra guests to explain away.

The trip was relatively quick, and it wasn't the first time her mother had been on the *Siyane*. They spent the time catching up on the necessities and trying to reorient to each other's worlds. It was easier to do than it used to be; after all, they'd had a lot of practice lately.

When they reached Sector 33 in the Milky Way, Valkyrie received specific coordinates from her anonymous contact, which led to an unsettled but marginally habitable planet.

Scans failed to detect any structures, power sources or other signs of life on the surface. The coordinates pointed to an expansive, barren stretch of land, so that was where they landed.

Mesme arrived out of nowhere with characteristic abruptness as they touched down, apparently having survived the transport of the black hole weapon to…. "Where's the Tartarus Trigger now?"

Away. This is all you need to concern yourselves with.

Miriam glanced over while checking her gear. "A weapon so dangerous as this Tartarus device needs to be guarded and kept out of the hands of the enemy."

It needs to be kept out of the hands of everyone, and guarding it is a task we can accomplish far better than you.

Alex gave her mother a weak shrug. "Mesme's probably correct on that point. The Kats are very, very good at hiding things."

"Fine, but I reserve the right to revisit the topic in the future."

Mesme's response was to flit off to the surface outside, evoking a snort from Caleb as he brought the breather masks to them. "Rather infuriating for an ally, isn't it?"

Miriam rolled her eyes and accepted the mask from Caleb. "Almost makes me miss the politicians back home. Almost."

Everyone wore tactical gear and carried breather masks and weapons despite the fact the air was breathable and the temperature adequate, because this was her mother and Caleb she was talking about.

They exited the *Siyane* onto a stone and gravel surface. Mountains of bare stone rose in the distance. There were no trees, or any plant life at all, and the sky was a cool, dim slate that gave the impression of being frozen at the cusp of nightfall.

Alex scanned the scene twice and threw her hands up in frustration. "There's nothing here."

Miriam's gaze retraced the path Alex's had taken. "Perhaps a building is stealthed, in which case I expect a door will open any time now."

Caleb chuckled. "You two have obviously never had to meet a skittish, paranoid informant before. We're being purposefully led around on a circuitous path so we won't be followed, and so we won't know where we're going—or possibly where we end up."

He both sounded and acted more relaxed than he'd been since their prison break. As before, he was internalizing and adjusting to the new influx of power. It just took a little time.

Admittedly relieved to see him in better spirits, she flashed him an exaggerated grimace. "Well, where we are right now is the middle of nowhere, so it seems to be working."

She trailed off as Mesme swept past them toward a light which had appeared in the distance. The source of the glow was small and indistinct, but it nevertheless stood out against the stark landscape.

They followed at a less excitable pace, and her mother fell in beside her. "This is what your normal, everyday life is like, isn't it?

Landing on exotic, forbidding alien worlds, taking a few readings then striking out into the unknown."

Alex grinned. "Not *every* day, but...kind of, yes."

Miriam shook her head with a pensive sigh. "So long as you're happy."

"I'll be 'happy' if this meeting goes swimmingly and we win this war and the people I care about aren't sacrificed in the process of winning it. Will 'fulfilled' do for now?"

"Quite well."

Your serotonin levels spiked noticeably there.

So she gave me the warm fuzzies. I'm allowed to get warm fuzzies from my mom.

The glow took shape as they neared to form an archway three meters tall and two wide, filled with molten metal, or a form of amorphous glass, or...something else. The material rippled as water in a pond, but it was both more opaque and shinier than water. If it stopped rippling and stilled, it could be mistaken for a mirror.

"It is a teleportation gate."

She jumped in surprise at the disembodied voice. Caleb and Miriam both tensed and began visually searching the area for approaching danger.

A shadow encroached on the archway until the object was nearly obscured. She shivered as a chill ran over her arms. "Miaon?"

"Yes." The solitary word warbled through the air like the note of a reed instrument.

Caleb relaxed a fraction, but her mother remained tense. "*What* is Miaon? The shadow?"

"Yes. It's a—"

"I am an ally. We can acquaint ourselves in due time, but at present you are expected before the Sator. Accompany me through the gate. Mnemosyne?"

It will be an uncomfortable passage, but I will accomplish it.

So, quantum teleportation? Neat. They checked one another for confirmation, and Caleb stepped forward and through the archway to disappear. She quickly followed—

ℛ

ANARCH POST SATUS

LOCATION UNKNOWN

—and stepped into an airy, sun-lit room.

On confirming Caleb had reached the same location, Alex spun in time to see her mother step through an exact copy of the archway here in the room and Mesme to materialize in front of it. The shadow Miaon was nowhere to be seen.

Valkyrie, I expect you to be able to tell me how teleportation works in the next...three days? Do you need four?

I will do it in two, and spend the other two determining how you accessed sidespace without me at the Mirad Vigilate.

A good use of your time on both fronts, I think.

The archway vanished, revealing an Anaden woman in a beige pantsuit standing behind it. Her modest attire, fair skin and blond hair styled into a practical twist ruled her out as Praesidis, Machim or Idoni. Yet another Dynasty, then. Antalla? Erevna?

The woman nodded perfunctorily at them. "I am Xanne ela-Kyvern. If you will accompany me, the Sator is expecting you."

Or that one.

She knew both Caleb and her mother were scanning the vicinity for potential threats. Confident she was well protected, she scanned it instead for aesthetics.

The decor was bright, sleek and smooth, but displayed enough character to not come off as sterile. This felt like a place where people not only worked, but lived. People who weren't sociopaths or automatons.

Speaking of...she increased her pace to catch up to Xanne. "Excuse me. One of your agents has been helping us, and we haven't heard from him since—"

"Since now?"

Alex spun to see Eren swagger through a door to the left, looking not a whit like he'd been atomized the day before.

He stopped a meter or so away, which thankfully avoided the awkward determination of whether they'd reached hugging status yet, and smirked. "So there *are* more of you."

She grinned. "A few. Thank you for the rescue back at Helix Retention, truly."

Eren gestured in the direction they were heading. "Much as I'd like to take all the credit, I can only take...eighty percent of it. The rest goes to the Sator." He smiled. "You look much better, by the way." His gaze drifted to Caleb. "I guess you do, too. Less like you're about to go supernova on us."

Caleb nodded with a touch of amusement. "Yes. You have my thanks as well."

Eren made a face, then closed the distance and clapped Caleb on the shoulder. "Told you I'd see you again."

"You did. Are you coming to the meeting with us?"

"Love to—not really—but I'm on my way out. Got to see to a thing. Have fun, though. Nisi's, um..." Eren arched an eyebrow "...unexpected." Then he tossed them a casual wave and jogged out the door.

Alex caught her mother's dubious expression and motioned toward the door. "Eren."

"So I see." Miriam huffed a laugh. "You have collected quite the assortment of allies."

Xanne made a *tutting* noise and ushered them on before she could respond. "We shouldn't keep the Sator waiting."

They began traversing a sky bridge, and Alex finally got a glimpse of what lay outside. A lush forest stretched to the horizon beneath a clear capri sky. They were on a planet. Outside the bridge, two large birds soared and dipped above the trees.

She zoomed her vision in closer. Yep, they were Volucri. Though their colors and markings were different from the ones Felzeor had displayed, she nudged Caleb and pointed them out. It was oddly comforting to see them here and flying freely.

Ahead, a central structure acted as a hub for multiple bridges similar to the one they crossed. Beneath the hub, a brilliant, golden ball of energy spun rapidly in the air.

Unfortunately, it vanished beneath the growing profile of the hub before she could study it further, and a minute later they reached a door.

Xanne gestured to the door. There were no visible security routines blocking entry, but then again, they'd presumably passed through half a dozen silent scans. "I will return to retrieve you when your meeting has concluded."

Miriam took the lead in stepping through the entry, and they followed.

The door opened into an...office was the closest approximation, though it seemed to serve multiple purposes. Decorated in warm amber and russet, it felt even more welcoming than the rest of the facility. Several chaise lounges were arranged off to the left, near a wet bar and an Anaden-style kitchen unit. In the center was a large circular table, and a type of workspace framed it. On the far wall behind the workspace were two doors, both closed.

A man stood at the transparent wall to their right, gazing out at the jungle below. His back was to them, but he pivoted as soon as they entered.

Alex didn't need to be told this was the anarch leader, for authority radiated off the man in spades. He wore a simple cream-and-tan tunic and slacks that complimented olive skin and strangely abyssal raven eyes. Or were they indigo? They changed with the shifting of the light.

The door shut behind them, and her mother took several steps forward. She spoke slowly and carefully; she'd only received the translation files a few hours earlier, and her eVi was still assimilating the Communis language. "Sator Nisi? I'm Commandant Miriam Solovy, leader of the AEGIS fleet."

Nisi brought his hands together in front of his chest in a prayer stance and bowed slightly. "Commandant, welcome. I am not your Sator, so please, call me Danilo."

"As you wish. This is my daughter, Alex, and her husband, Caleb. You may have some knowledge of their presence here of late. The Katasketousya is Mnemosyne."

"Yes. Eren had much to say about all of you. Mnemosyne, our mutual acquaintance Miaon has recently seen fit to share some fascinating tales about you as well as your kin. We will speak further later—about a great deal, I suspect." He dipped his chin in greeting to Alex and turned to Caleb.

Caleb was staring at the man, a most peculiar look on his face, and now he hastened forward in greeting. "Sir—"

A tendril of crimson sparks drifted up and away from the exposed skin of the man's forearm; it was so faint it might not be noticeable if Alex hadn't gotten used to searching for such traces.

Nisi's eyes flared for a single blink, and he held up a hand in a firm warning. "You, do not touch me. Do not approach me."

The statement was delivered as an order, and a resolute one. Her mother started, taken aback. "Is there a problem?"

Caleb smiled enigmatically and retreated a deliberate step backward. "It's all right. Apologies, sir. For a moment you..." his brow furrowed "...reminded me of someone, and I neglected to consider what might happen."

Nisi's physical stance softened. "The mistake was mine. Please, do not interpret as hostility what is merely self-preservation."

Miriam cleared her throat. "Is there something we should know?"

Alex tilted her head in Nisi's direction. "He controls *diati*."

"Only a small measure of it, but what I possess I intend to keep."

"You're Praesidis?" Now that she thought about it, he did favor them, after a fashion. Lacked the cold malevolence that was the Praesidis stock-in-trade, though.

"Yes, and no."

Alex bit back a groan. "What does that mean? I'm not trying to be rude, but we've learned it's sort of important."

"Indeed." He clasped his hands in front of him. "I am no Dynasty, and all Dynasties. My genes are those of all Anadens, with no preordained destiny written upon them. I am and have long been free to follow any path I choose."

"So you started a rebellion."

Nisi arched an eyebrow at her; did she amuse him? "There was already a rebellion, tiny and desperate though it was, when I came to it. Sadly, the brave souls who began it are all gone, leaving me to honor their legacy by growing the resistance into something more."

"Gone?" She frowned. "What about regenesis?"

"Back then the resistance had but a single lab, and a rickety and spartan one at that. It was destroyed in a Machim attack, as was everyone at the base."

"I'm sorry."

"It was more millennia ago than I care to dwell on, though part of me continues to mourn the friends I lost. On bad days more than good ones, as is the way of such things. Now, I have naturally invited the four of you here for a reason, but first let me apologize for the inconvenient trip. Secrecy is our most paramount and constant concern. It tempers every action we take."

Alex wandered over to the window and peered down. "Where are we?"

"You can never know the location, I'm afraid. As I said, secrecy."

"Can I ask what the energy generation beneath us is? I've never seen anything like it."

"Actually, I believe you *have* seen something like it, albeit on a much smaller scale. It's a Zero Drive."

The drive on Felzeor's capsule had only been a few centimeters in size. This apparatus was *immense.*

Nisi's expression bordered on smugness. "I'm sorry, did all of you believe this was a building? On the contrary. It is a starship."

Her jaw dropped. "*Chush' sobach'ya.* Where can I get one?"

Caleb laughed behind her.

I know, I know. He's a terrorist, and we're in the opening hours of a war for the survival of humanity and liberation of pretty much everyone else. I still want one.

We win this thing, and we'll get us one, baby.

It's a plan. What was that about earlier, with Nisi?

I'm honestly not quite sure.

"Perhaps another time." Nisi's lips drew in tight. He'd opened the meeting with congeniality, but it could be her irreverence had begun to irk him. "To business, shall we? Your victory at the Provision Network Gateway will provoke a war, and my people will have no choice but to play a role in it."

Miriam squared her shoulders and lifted her chin. "Our war is with the Machim leaders who set out to annihilate our universe, and by extension with the Directorate that ordered their actions. I have concerns regarding the tactics you use, but the circumstances are such that I would welcome your assistance— but I am not demanding it or pleading for it. Your role will be what you make it."

"The circumstances being that you know nothing about our society, political structure, customs, varied alien species or technology."

The muscles in Miriam's jaw flexed. Barely. "I wouldn't say nothing, but far less than I'd like, yes. There is no denying we are newcomers to this place, while you have lived—" another twitch "—some thousands of years in it."

Ugh, enough with the alpha wolf dominance games. Alex grumbled loudly and stepped up to Nisi even as her mother took a quiet step back. "I'm sorry, Danilo, but don't you *want* the Directorate taken out? Isn't it the entirety of your purpose?"

"The entirety of my purpose is freedom, Ms. Solovy." His eyes ran across them in turn, and he exhaled ponderously, as if coming to an unpleasant decision.

"I cannot say this to the other anarchs, but I have never believed we could succeed in unseating the Directorate. The institution and its Primor members are vastly too powerful, enjoying unlimited resources at their disposal, and we are infinitely too few and too weak.

"My purpose these last millennia has been two-fold: firstly, to give a home to those who felt freedom's call, a place where they could live as they wished and conduct a life of meaning.

"Secondly, I have worked to build a universe-spanning network of spies, operatives, information caches and other resources. A network designed and crafted so as to be of maximum strategic value when the pivotal moment arrives at last and the fulcrum upon which the cosmos will turn emerges."

Alex regarded Nisi curiously. "And you believe our fleet is that fulcrum?"

Nisi smiled. The effect was surprisingly impactful—charismatic, thoughtful, a touch mysterious. "After the dramatic battle at the Gateway, it has without question proved its worth. I have no doubt it will be necessary, even indispensable for victory in the coming war.

"But, no, Ms. Solovy. Your fleet, formidable though it may be, is not the fulcrum I have prepared for and long sought."

The anarch leader settled his piercing gaze on Caleb. "He is."

TO BE CONTINUED IN

AURORA RESONANT BOOK TWO

RUBICON

COMING IN 2017

***

SUBSCRIBE TO

GSJENNSEN.COM

Receive updates on AURORA RESONANT, new book announcements, free short stories and more

Author's Note

I published *Starshine* in March of 2014. In the back of the book I put a short note asking readers to consider leaving a review or talking about the book with their friends. Since that time I've had the unmitigated pleasure of watching my readers do exactly that, and there has never been a more wonderful and humbling experience in my life. There's no way to properly thank you for that support, but know you changed my life and made my dreams a reality.

I'll make the same request now. If you loved *RELATIVITY*, tell someone. If you bought the book on Amazon, consider leaving a review. If you downloaded the book off a website with Russian text in the margins and pictures of cartoon video game characters in the sidebar, consider recommending it to others.

As I've said before, reviews are the lifeblood of a book's success, and there is no single thing that will sell a book better than word-of-mouth. My part of this deal is to write a book worth talking about—your part of the deal is to do the talking. If you all keep doing your bit, I get to write a lot more books for you.

This time I'm also going to make a second request. *Abysm* was an independently published novel, written by one person and worked on by a small team of colleagues. Right now there are thousands of writers out there chasing this same dream.

Go to Amazon and surf until you find an author you like the sound of. Take a small chance with a few dollars and a few hours of your time. In doing so, you may be changing those authors' lives by giving visibility to people who until recently were shut out of publishing, but who have something they need to say. It's a revolution, and it's waiting on you.

Lastly, I love hearing from my readers. Seriously. Just like I don't have a publisher or an agent, I don't have "fans." I have **readers** who buy and read my books, and **friends** who do that then reach out to me through email or social media. If you loved the book—or if you didn't—let me know. The beauty of independent publishing is its simplicity: there's the writer and the readers. Without any overhead, I can find out what I'm doing right and wrong directly from you, which is invaluable in making the next book better than this one. And the one after that. And the twenty after that.

Website: www.gsjennsen.com
Email: gs@gsjennsen.com
Twitter: @GSJennsen
Facebook: facebook.com/gsjennsen.author
Goodreads: goodreads.com/gs_jennsen
Google+: plus.google.com/+GSJennsen
Instagram: instagram.com/gsjennsen

Find all my books on Amazon:
http://amazon.com/author/gsjennsen

About The Author

G. S. Jennsen lives in Colorado with her husband and two dogs. *Relativity* is her seventh novel, all published by her imprint, Hypernova Publishing. She has become an internationally bestselling author since her first novel, *Starshine*, was published in March 2014. She has chosen to continue writing under an independent publishing model to ensure the integrity of the *Aurora Rhapsody* series and her ability to execute on the vision she's had for it since its genesis.

While she has been a lawyer, a software engineer and an editor, she's found the life of a full-time author preferable by several orders of magnitude, which means you can expect the next book in the *Aurora Rhapsody* series in just a few months.

When she isn't writing, she's gaming or working out or getting lost in the Colorado mountains that loom large outside the windows in her home. Or she's dealing with a flooded basement, or standing in a line at Walmart reading the tabloid headlines and wondering who all of those people are. Or sitting on her back porch with a glass of wine, looking up at the stars, trying to figure out what could be up there.

Made in the USA
Charleston, SC
23 December 2016